Reviews by Readers

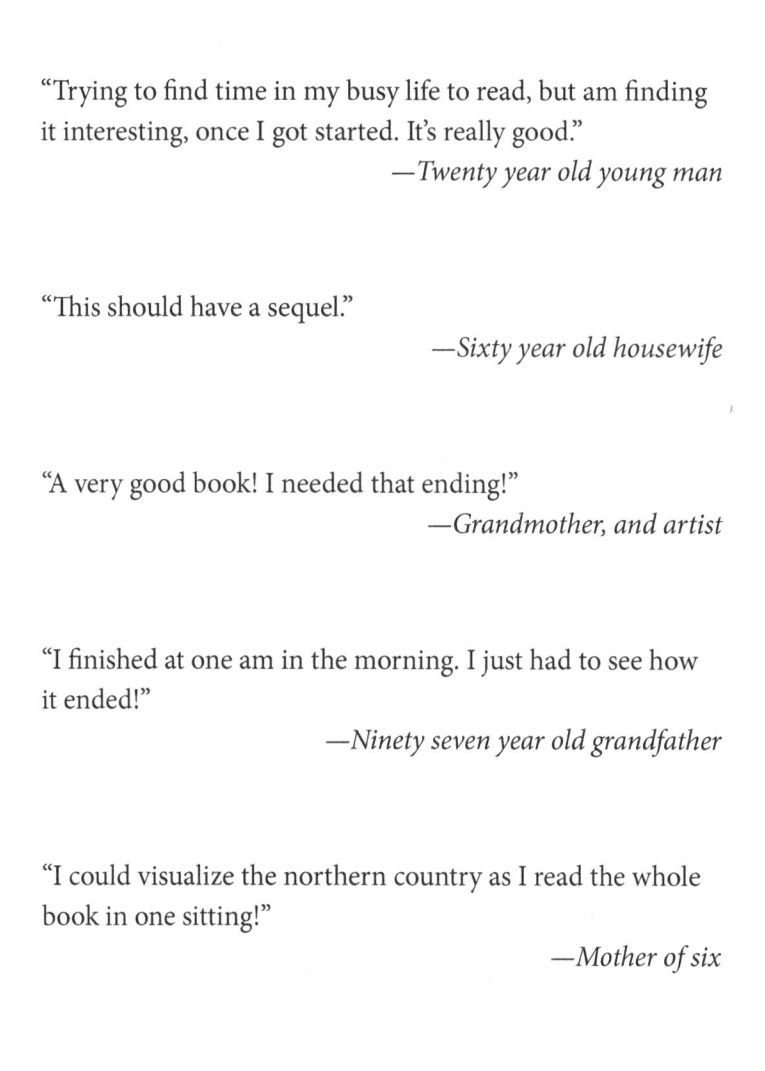

"Trying to find time in my busy life to read, but am finding it interesting, once I got started. It's really good."
—*Twenty year old young man*

"This should have a sequel."
—*Sixty year old housewife*

"A very good book! I needed that ending!"
—*Grandmother, and artist*

"I finished at one am in the morning. I just had to see how it ended!"
—*Ninety seven year old grandfather*

"I could visualize the northern country as I read the whole book in one sitting!"
—*Mother of six*

◆ FriesenPress

Suite 300 - 990 Fort St
Victoria, BC, V8V 3K2
Canada

www.friesenpress.com

Copyright © 2021 by John Zylstra
First Edition — 2021

This book is fiction. Any resemblance to real people is strictly coincidental. Operational details of the seismic industry or of the laws around international drug trafficking or gun registration may or may not be entirely accurate. Names, characters, places, and incidents are used fictitiously, as a product of the author's imagination.

All rights reserved.

No part of this publication may be reproduced in any form, or by any means, electronic or mechanical, including photocopying, recording, or any information browsing, storage, or retrieval system, without permission in writing from FriesenPress.

ISBN
978-1-03-910514-0 (Hardcover)
978-1-03-910513-3 (Paperback)
978-1-03-910515-7 (eBook)

1. FICTION, ACTION & ADVENTURE

Distributed to the trade by The Ingram Book Company

SEISMIC TRAIL

JOHN ZYLSTRA

SEISMIC TRAIL

Introduction

THIS STORY WAS A long time in the making. It began sixteen years ago, at a different time, when I was employed in two different jobs, one as a soil and water conservationist with the government, and one as a part-time farmer, with about forty head of cattle on 460 acres of land. I had a five year old daughter in the house at the time, as well as several grandchildren of some of our older children. It was the instigation of my wife for me to write a novel, but after a strong beginning, I discovered that I had no idea where the story was going.

   Life became very busy, and the story laid on the shelf, or hid in the computer until this year. My wife never really gave up, and I finally responded this spring with the rest of the story. It is a winter story, completely fictional, embedded in a less familiar part of the oil industry in the trees of northern Alberta, the exploration and discovery phase. The better parts of family life, the rugged outdoors, and the seedier elements of working in the oil patch are included in this story, with a great struggle of dealing with drug crime across borders. And then, the love story, between husband and wife. And faith. Hope you enjoy it.

Proverbs 17:15
"Acquitting the guilty and condemning the innocent; the Lord condemns them both."

Chapter One

THEY WOULD PROBABLY SURVIVE.

The bitter cold meant they had to eat more than usual to keep up their energy requirements. Being outdoors constantly meant they were used to freezing temperatures, but they still needed the proper balance of protein, carbohydrates, and minerals to keep from losing too much weight, and to keep from freezing to death. Even though they didn't travel much, and they took shelter from the wind under the trees, their energy requirements were higher than usual.

Jack Sandstrom pulled his hat down a bit, with his parka hood over his head, and then rubbed his heavily gloved hands together, trying to warm them up. Looking at his red-brown beef cows in the snow-covered pasture through the foggy breath he puffed out heavily from the exertion of climbing back on his tractor, he wondered if they would make him any money this year. He put the twine he had just cut off the big round bales, into the box on the side of his tractor. With the rising cost of fuel and fertilizer, and the reduced revenue from his cows due to closed markets, he began to think he was feeding them just for exercise. Perhaps he should have hedged some cattle prices about a year ago, but it just wasn't his style. In some perverse way, he thrived on the uncertainty, the hope, and the anticipation of the market. He loved the challenge of meeting the challenge, of overcoming adversity, of surviving.

His herd of 80 cows would not provide him with a living. They were just stock cows, a tool to help him manage his land, and in good times they could provide him about $40,000 to 50,000 per year gross. After fuel, mortgage, vehicle and machinery expenses, and feed costs, about $15,000 was left as income. In poor years, when prices of cattle were down, and cost of hay was up, nothing was left. This might be one of those years.

But his cows were a sideline for Jack. His main business was in the oil patch. He carried on several types of business there, including cutting line and drilling for seismic, as well as hauling water, and moving equipment. He kept his options open as well, sometimes putting trucks on the log haul, or pulling chip trailers, but that was less lucrative. With between twenty and fifty men working for him at a time, he required a payroll clerk/bookkeeper, and a contract accountant. The payroll work was done by Christy, a serious young female, who raised 150 cows with her husband Bob Froese. Her husband was the accountant. Jack trusted them both.

o o o

At the moment he had 20 men working for him on seismic operations. Seven small drilling rigs were mounted on tracked vehicles which travelled at a top speed of six miles per hour. Two rigs were mounted on rubber-tired vehicles, which had a top speed of 50 miles per hour, but they could not go through the rough terrain suited to the tracked vehicles. Three tracked vehicles carried a water tank only.

The men that operated these vehicles and the trucks that moved them to the job sites were generally good workers, young men mostly. More than half of them were not married, and for many this was their first real job. He paid them well, but expected them to perform. Careless men, and poor attitudes, did not last long. Men had lost fingers, or toes, either from frost bite, or from equipment. A drill had once gone through the foot of one of his workers several years ago, and the foot had been amputated. It was a dangerous working environment, handling dynamite, hydraulic equipment, travelling over rough terrain in very cold weather, and careless and incompetent men could not be tolerated.

As he drove his tractor back into the yard, Jack was wondering whether he had made a mistake in hiring one man, a six-foot tall, 200 pound, twenty-two year old with two years of college unrelated to oil-patch work, and some work experience with fast food outlets and pumping gas. He did not have some of the basic mechanical skills or welding skills that many of the other men had, but he seemed to be a good driver. Some of the other younger men were more capable all around. Kole Dearborn was strong enough and smart enough to do the job, but seemed to have an erratic personality. There were times when he worked smoothly, and there were times when he seemed to lose his temper for no reason. Such a man could be dangerous, but so far nothing bad had resulted.

His biggest job sometimes seemed to be to keep his crew free from drugs, and to keep alcohol to a minimum. Over the years he had fired several men due to drugs, and one serious accident related to alcohol had made him ever wary of that particular hazard. He had a feeling, with no real evidence, that drugs were being used by one or more of his men, but he couldn't determine what type it was, nor how many men might be involved, or whether he was just being paranoid. He certainly hoped that Kole was not involved. It was difficult to find dependable drivers who would work long hours for long periods away from home and civilization. The demand for workers was high, and that is why high wages were the order of the day in his business. And high wages meant that his men had money to burn.

He had bid on several jobs recently. He was successful on one, but still waiting for word on the other three jobs. His hope was that he would receive two or three out of the four bid. If he got two of the jobs, he could keep his crew busy, and pay his bills. If he got three jobs, he would have to hire more men, and work longer hours. If he got the fourth job, he would be in trouble, because he really didn't have enough equipment for that much work. He would have to see if he could hire another outfit to do the job, but it might cost him more money than what he bid, eating into profits from the other three jobs.

Fortunately, his foreman, Bill Mikela, understood what was involved on the business end, as well as the technical aspect of the job. Bill took his work seriously, which was why Jack had kept him on from the beginning, twelve years ago now. When times were slow and there was no income, Bill understood, and did his best to make the rest of the crew understand as well. Jack kept on as many as he could doing odd jobs, repairing, maintaining, building, cleaning, in order to maintain a core crew with experience, which really helped when times were busy again. When times were busy, Bill made the crew understand that their performance meant the success of future bids. Bonuses for the employees then would be very good.

Watching and feeding cows was a good time to ponder the state of his business, but Jack had given the friendly animals all the feed they needed for the next two days and so began putting the tractor back in the shed. He drove through the doors, stopped it, turned off the key, and then shut off the throttle to shut down the machine. Without a cab, it was cold in winter, but Jack dressed warmly, and liked the contact with the weather.

Getting off the tractor, Jack thought he could hear the phone ring in the heated shop next to the shed, and sure enough he soon heard a yell from the shop for him to get the phone. It was a good call; his bid on a second job had been successful. It had warmed up from –30 to –20 C, which seemed almost balmy in comparison, especially since there was no significant wind, although it had snowed four inches overnight. Four inches was about ten centimeters, an automatic mental conversion that he made everyday for things like this. Jack could remember days when it was only minus 10C, and yet seemed colder than now, just because the wind would whistle through his clothes. On those days his cows would seek the shelter of the trees. Today was not one of those days.

A few hours later, he had a problem. Not only had the third bid been accepted that morning, but now he was told on the phone, that the fourth bid was also successful.

Chapter Two

A WEEK BEFORE, HE had been wondering whether he would have enough work for the winter. Today, he was worried whether he didn't have enough equipment, nor enough men to do all four jobs in the timelines required. It was November, and these jobs were expected to be completed by the end of March. On three of the jobs, he had to cut a lot of lines through trees, and with the environmental guidelines, the objective was to cut as thin a line as possible. To reduce disturbance by dozers, much of it had to be done by hand, with chainsaw. A year ago, he had also purchased two brushers, which chewed up the smaller brush with a 200cm wide mower. In cold weather, it was always a bit slower picking up water for the drilling as well, since holes had to be cut in ice, and traction up and down creek banks was sometimes poor. Suddenly, his optimism regained its proper place. He grinned with the anticipation of the challenge. He would find a way.

One of the jobs would not start for another two months. Could he build another rig by that time? He decided to have a talk with Jacob, his handyman in the shop. Jacob Mitelski, usually called Jake, was a welder, mechanic, and all-round fixer. Jake had started working for him two years after he started his business, and so was well familiar with Jack's habits. As

Jack walked into the shop, Jake looked up briefly from his work with the press-drill, looked back down again, and then asked, "Overtime coming up?" Jack replied, "maybe."

Jack looked at Jake's work, and admired the steady precise measurements, and the methodical procedure that Jake used to drill holes in exactly the right spot in the bumper he was building for the rig they were building. There was a lot of work left to do on this rig, as Jake was just getting started. It was a rubber-tired rig, and still needed a back deck, a reinforced grill, a tower with cables and hydraulics, a water tank, toolbox, winch, and many other accessories to make it suitable as a drill truck. They would probably put dual tires all around on it as well, so it would handle soft ground better.

"How long you think it'll take to get this built, Jake?"

"You asked me that yesterday. Answer's still the same. About four months. Unless you hire someone to help me more than your own haphazard help," Jake replied. Jack liked to monkey around with the fabricating as well. It gave him a sense of accomplishment to build something out of nothing. But often he only helped Jake sporadically, since so many other things needed his attention.

They had gone over it yesterday, but now the fourth job had added urgency to his need for another rig. He had begun building his own rigs, because it kept his men employed, and it cost him about $40,000 per rig less that way. But it took time, especially since there was lots of trial and error in the process, with no blueprint to follow for most of the steel fabricating. And Jake still had other things to fix and repair in the meantime as well. If the rig was finished in three months, would it be soon enough?

Jack knew that he did not have any other men who were very good in the shop. Some of them could do some rudimentary welding, but they needed to be told what to do. They were capable of building drill stem, or repairing obvious breaks in metal, but did not have the experience or initiative required to design and build equipment. In the shop, they would be worth about one-third of what Jake was capable of.

"Tom can weld a bit. How about if I put him in the shop with you for awhile?"

"Could give him a try, I guess," said Jake. "He doesn't seem real bright, but maybe he can handle it."

So Jack phoned up Tom, and told him he could start the season a bit early, if he wanted to work in the shop with Jake. Tom, a thirty-year old with lots of experience in servicing rigs, operating them, and slashing in the bush, was also a truck driver, but truck drivers were plentiful, and Tom was sitting at home, collecting unemployment insurance, and hoping that Jack would call him up for his regular winter stint. He told Jack he could be there the next day.

○ ○ ○

An hour after starting work, Tom had already ruined two pieces of sheet metal by cutting them wrong. Jake was unhappy and grumpy. Tom was taking up more of his time than he was helping. By the time Jack came to the shop, he could see that this was not working. Jake was a better welder than a teacher. Without saying anything, Jake managed to convey to Jack that Tom might not be what he was looking for in the shop. Soon this became apparent to Jack as well, that Tom would require constant direction and instruction, repeated several times. Jack decided to leave them alone for the time being.

Jack went into his office at the back of the shop and looked at the timetable he had made the day before. He had one crew out with chain saws, cutting survey lines through patches of bush. A dozer was also working in the heavy bush, where the rigs would have to cross through. Dozers no longer cut straight lines, but rather, they would go around the larger trees, staying as close to the survey flags as possible, while doing the minimal amount of damage to standing trees. The lines were cut barely wide enough for the rigs to get through, and often branches from standing trees would later slap the front and sides of the rigs as they passed by. Which was why extra grills were required for the fronts, sides, and top of the cabs on the rigs. Even then, windows in the cab would still get smashed from time to time.

Another crew was preparing the rigs for battle. Hydraulic lines, cleats, oil changes, heating lines and pumps were checked. His rigs were worth between $100,000 and $150,000 each. Some of his competitors had rigs worth as much as $500,000. Some of his competitors' rigs could travel faster, but often they also seemed to require more expensive repairs more often. Jack counted his time in number of holes drilled in one day, and slow and steady seemed to do just as well for him.

Jack spent the next four hours playing with varying options, to see how he could get enough men and equipment together to finish all four jobs on time. If they worked long hours, and he put on some extra shifts by hiring a bigger crew, and if the equipment did not give him an unusual amount of trouble, and he brought back to life an old water truck he hadn't used for four years, he could do all four jobs. Except for one thing: he needed one more drilling rig. And another truck to haul equipment.

This was not so unusual for Jack. Since he had started his business with his first two rigs, he had purchased one or two pieces of additional equipment every year. This year he had already begun the process of building a new rig, which now wouldn't be ready until the season was half over, and he had replaced the cabs on two old rigs, put a new water tank on one truck, new tracks on two rigs, and a new engine in one. Plus he'd traded in two pickup trucks for four new red ones. There was no doubt that he would need all four pickups now.

Now he had to make another change. Usually he had time to plan this, but now he realized he would have to make a move quickly. Another rig, even used, could cost maybe $200,000. And a used lowboy truck maybe another $200,000. That was more than he wanted to spend.

He decided to check his email on the computer in front of him. A message from one of his daughters flashed on the screen. His oldest daughter Erin had a code name, "happygirl", and she had left a short message with fairly simple but amusing language, as she tried to impress him with her worldly knowledge and literary skills. "How are you today, daddy dear? Are you making lots of money? I suppose all your hired men are doing what you tell them, the way they should? Except for Jake, of course, he does what he wants. Mommy is feeding the dogs now. She says she will start the snowblower to clear the walk, and her parking spot, since you are too important to do such kind things for her. Bye for now."

Sure enough, Jack heard the muffled roar of the walk-behind snowblower, and by standing up and looking out the window, could see that his wife was bundled up and blowing snow away from the house, and over one of his pickups. He checked the computer to see when the message by 'happygirl' was sent; it was 45 minutes ago. At breakfast, he had promised and forgotten his promise, to clean her walk. He suspected she didn't actually mind going outside for awhile, even in the cold, but he knew she would deny that, and hold him to be irresponsible anyway. Well, she would survive, and he hoped he would too. He would have to get someone to plow the yard again too. Or do it himself. And he would have to find the right words, something nice to say to his wife. He did not relish sleeping in the shop office instead of beside his wife.

The next email was an advertisement from an auction company. He subscribed to several of these auction companies' email newsletters. Well, he didn't really have time right now to attend an auction in Venezuela, and was going to delete, when he noticed that it was an on-line auction for tomorrow. Somewhat idly, and as a break from his calculations, he began reading the items for sale.

Pictures were available for most of the items, which made scanning fairly quick. Numerous dozer tractors, lowboy trucks, backhoes, cranes, ditchers, pipeline haulers, water trucks, sump trucks, service rigs, and other equipment were advertised. His eyes lit up. Several seismic drills were shown as well. They looked pretty beat up. A couple had hoses missing, one had a track missing, another had no front winch. The details were itemized; it was a reputable auction house with offices around the globe. Several items indicated engines missing or inoperable, transmissions or drive gears destroyed, etc.

Here was a good one! At least so it seemed. Looked okay in the picture, which only showed the left side from the rear. Not too much paint missing, and even all the glass still in the windows. Description said that everything was in good working order, but the cleats and grousers were somewhat worn out. It was similar to the type he already had. It would likely need to be winterized, with antifreeze, lighter hydraulic oil, etc., but that was a minor detail. Should he put a bid on it? Venezuela?

He left the site and began to read some more email. Then he checked an industry site which advertised equipment around North America. Sort of a colored email classified section, with pictures. He checked for seismic drills, but was suddenly distracted by a picture of a truck tractor and lowboy for sale in New Mexico. It was a rough looking Kenworth, dark green in color, with a custom-built front bumper, including a winch. There were no shiny chrome rims, nor a shiny chrome gas tank. Description included a 525 horsepower Cummins diesel engine, rebuilt rear-end, and 450,000 miles on it. The trailer was a fifty-footer triple-axle with beavertail ramps. "Okay, what's he asking? Doesn't say? Phone number, yeah, well, okay, let's try it." Jack muttered to himself, and then dialed the number. It rang once, and Jack thought of hanging up. "New Mexico?" Even if the price was right, that was too far away.

A voice on the other end said, "McMann here."

Jack first thought he had said, "man here" and for a second hesitated. Then his business mind took over, and Jack replied, "This is Jack. I'm looking at an ad for a Kenworth that has your number on it. What can you tell me about it?"

After the voice had given him the same details that were already in the ad and stressed that the truck was in fairly good shape, mechanically, Jack asked the price. " sixty-five," replied the voice.

"Okay," said Jack. "I'll think about it." Which meant he had no intention of buying it for sixty-five thousand, if at all. Sixty-five American was about eighty-five Canadian, plus duty, plus getting it up here.

○ ○ ○

Back in the shop, Tom had finally cut a piece of sheet metal correctly. Now he had to bend it at the right angle. Jake drew the line on the metal, and Tom brought it to the bender. When he brought it back, Jacob was pleased that he had gotten it done so quickly, but suddenly he let loose with some uncomplimentary language. "What the ___!! Backwards? You're supposed to bend it to the line, not away from the line!" A pause. "At this rate, this rig will cost more than brand-new price!"

Just then, Jack walked back into the shop and heard the tail end of the conversation. Obviously, he was going to have to change something here soon. At this rate the new rig would take five months instead of four to complete. And in five months most of this season would be over. He motioned for Jake to come to the office.

The radio was blaring. A news item. Mexico border issues. And a story about twelve farmers, men, women, and two children, who had been murdered by some drug lords in Mexico. Two decapitated. The rest hanging from a bridge. Jack shook his head. He was glad that Mexico was far away.

"Have a look at this ad, here, Jake. What do you think?"

"Well, it looks just like one of our rigs. A cable mast drill. Can't see the front of it. Tracks look a bit worn. It says, if you can believe it, that its okay mechanically. How much they want for it?"

"Its an auction. What's it worth, you think?"

"Would have to see it first. But maybe $60,000, if its as good as they say."

"If its as good as they say, its worth $80,000. But its in Venezuela. That's a long ways from here."

"What about this other one here? Only one track, and no winch, and a cracked tower, but we could fix that."

"But we're running out of time, and Tom doesn't seem to be much of a help to you, is he." It was more of a statement than a question.

"Well, it's your money, Jack. Likely you know what you're doing. Even though it doesn't look like it to anybody with any sense."

"If I had a decent mechanic, or a decent welder in the shop, instead of you, Jake, I might look like I knew what I was doing." Jack shot back. Jake grinned a wide grin. Bantering back and forth once in awhile kept things interesting. It relieved the pressure. By this time, Jack had made up his mind. He would bid on that rig when it came up, and then see what happened.

He went back to his computer and sent an email to the auction house, asking to be registered as a bidder. They asked him to send a fax with his ID. Then they returned a fax with his ID and password. They knew who he was from their database, since he had attended and purchased at local auctions. They required him to send a $10,000 deposit via bank transfer, which they would refund if he purchased nothing. He sent it via his electronic banking, immediately. Then he went to the house for a cup of tea.

o o o

The auction started at nine am, and Jack was on the computer. He had no one else in the room with him. Once he started bidding, he didn't want any distractions, and no second guesses. He had his strategy figured out, and he would stick to it. He had no idea who the other bidders were, but their bids would be identified by number. He himself was number 357 in this auction. Some bidders would bid on many of the items. Some, like himself, were only looking at one particular item. Since he had just registered yesterday, he guessed that there would be between 400 hundred and 450 bidders who had each put down $10,000 to qualify. A deposit of $10,000 was not a lot, but it was enough to weed out mischievous bidders, for the most part. This auction was divided into three sections. One was for tractor trailer units. One was for dozers and backhoes. The third was for all the rest, which would include what Jack was looking at.

In all, there were 287 pieces of equipment for sale at this auction, which were all in South America, mostly in Venezuela, but also 53 pieces from Northern Brazil. Bidding was in USA dollars.

Silent bidding was different than listening to a noisy auctioneer talk it up. To make up for this, someone from the auction company would add interesting details about the equipment and several pictures from various angles. Jack wondered whether maybe a Dutch auction would be simpler. However, this was not a Dutch Auction system. In a sale like this one, someone made a bid on an item, and then the bidding would become competitive, raising the price until everyone except for one person would have dropped out. At that price, it would be sold to the highest bidder.

On the computer, it was merely required to point and click to indicate acceptance of the bid. The bidders were divided into the three groups, and they had a schedule of when certain types of items would be sold, which meant that some of them would only be on-line for an hour or less, while others intended to be on all day. Some sales had both live and on-line bidding, but this one did not.

The drill Jack was interested in was due to come up in the first hour, according to the schedule. Most items sold in about five minutes, unless there were a lot of bidders. The attitude was, if you snooze, you lose. This did not mean that most items sold below value, although a few might, especially at the beginning of the day.

Jack watched several eight wheeled ATVs sell at reasonable prices, and then an old Bobcat at what seemed about 20% overprice. A water truck sold rather high, and then one of the seismic drilling rigs came up. It was not the one he wanted, and although it went for $40,000, much lower than what he intended to bid, it was in much poorer shape and would require tens of thousands of dollars to bring it to working condition.

Next was the machine Jack was interested in. The initial online bid was $50,000. Jack upped the bid to $55,000. Only one other bidder, number 234, was playing, and he upped it to $57,000. Jack bid $60,000, was countered at $62,000, and upped to $65,000. The other bidder did not counter. The auctioneer/computer waited a full two minutes before announcing that Jack had won the bid, and the machine, and then faxed Jack a number to call regarding further details. The next machine was up for sale.

Jack wondered if he should continue to check the other machines, but decided he'd accomplished his purpose, and better figure out how he would get his machine home.

Chapter Three

JILLIAN HAD FORGIVEN HIM for not clearing her walk. She was used to forgiving him for things like that. It wasn't that she couldn't do it herself as much as thinking that he simply found his work more important than anything she might need or want. He was often late for lunch or supper, when he was home, and seemed to pay attention to her most when he was feeling amorous. She liked the attention when she got it, but it was irritating at the same time, to appear to be competing with his machines, "toys", she sometimes called them. Or she felt she was competing with the crew he hired, or the jobs he was on. She knew they depended on his work to make them a living, but he threw himself into it so completely that she wondered whether making a living was really what he was concerned about, or whether the challenge and interest in the "toys" and the work, was Jack's real motivator.

Jack sensed her feelings, but didn't really understand them, nor did he feel they were justified. Didn't he work hard to make a living, after all? Didn't she have the freedom to do whatever she wanted? These days she had nice dependable vehicles to drive as well, not like the old repairmobiles they used to own when he first started the business. She didn't even have to do the bookeeping like she did when they first started. As far as he was concerned, she didn't really appreciate enough what he was doing for her every day. Still, he had made sure to have one of the boys plow the yard neatly after the recent snow fall, and last night, he had read a story to the kids before bed time. He had even poured Jillian a cup of coffee and brought it to her while she was checking email on the computer. She liked that sort of thing and responded with a smile. By the time they had gone to bed together, later, she had been quite friendly.

This morning, Jack checked the cows before going to the shop. It was bitterly cold out, - 35, with a very slight breeze. In the morning twilight, he could see the coat of frost on his animals, and the frosty breath leaving their nostrils, as they lay on their straw beds, chewing their cud. He wondered in amazement, as he often did, how they could keep themselves warm in such weather, not even losing ears nor tails, with nothing more than skin and hair to protect them. Of course, he was reasonably warm too, with insulated hooded coveralls, insulated boots, and good gloves. But sleeping outside all night even in his warm clothes, would probably leave him half-frozen by morning.

He wondered how his slashing crew was doing in this weather. As if answering his question, his cell phone rang and Bill Mikela, his foreman with the crew gave him the news.

"Bad news, Jack. The Peterbilt hit the ditch and rolled."

Jack groaned. "How'd that happen?!"

"Not sure, really. Think probably the brakes froze up, and a slippery patch created the problem in a bend in the road. Jared was driving, and he's not a rookie. Too bad, though."

"Yeah, too bad," said Jack. "Good thing it's the older truck, and not the newer one. Trouble is, we needed that one too, especially with these other jobs now. How much damage is there?"

"The engine is likely okay, but the frame is bent, and a good part of the cab is destroyed. The trailer I'm not sure about, other than the ramps being twisted, and two flat tires on one side."

"It'll be a bit of fixing, for sure."

"Yep. At least nothing was on the trailer. We'd just unloaded. I don't know if we can pull it back over ourselves or have to get some winch trucks to help. Might be able to pull it back; its just on its side, although the trailer is upside down. The dozer is about four miles away."

The dozer was a D7 Caterpillar. About an hour away. It worked with the slashing crew and had a winch on it. Would one winch be enough? Maybe. "Give it a try", said Jack. "If you get it up, then let it sit for awhile, till I figure out what to do. If oil got into the cylinders, it will be tough to start, especially in this weather. We may have to work the other hauler extra hours on shifts, to make up lost time. Just keep on with the slashing job for now."

Jack went to the shop and started the chore tractor. While bringing several round bales to the cows, he pondered the dilemma he was in. Sometimes he felt he made a step backwards for every step forward. He was stretching himself thin with his recent purchases, and with the crew wages he was paying and would have to pay before these jobs were finished. The common practice in his industry was to work first, then send in the invoices to the oil company that had hired him, and then sit and wait for them to pay him, never knowing for sure when that might be. Usually one would have to wait for at least two months and often three months or more. A few years back, he had waited as long as six months before he finally got paid, and he had heard of a crew waiting eight months for payment once.

He put the tractor back in the shop about an hour later, after putting out enough bales to last about five days. With the sun now fully up, blue skies made the frost on the trees look pretty. He suspected the breeze would pick up enough by eleven am to knock most of the frost off the trees, but for the moment, it was beautiful! He loved the freedom he had to enjoy it, to be out there in the cold, calm air, glittering white frost on every tree in sight, brilliant white on the powerlines, fence posts, and on the tall grass that was taller than the fallen snow.

And quiet too. He loved the roar of machinery, and all the things that machinery could do, but he also enjoyed the quiet at times like this, when the tractor was shut off, and the dogs were not barking, and he wasn't in a city listening to traffic, tires whining down the roads, engines coughing, or horns honking.

The silence of the outdoors was broken by the sound of the press drill in the shop whirring and squealing as it began its job of drilling more holes in some metal pipe, and another piece of pipe clanging partially on the cement floor, and partially on other metal already lying there. Jack's brain kicked back into work mode, and he suddenly remembered the truck he had been looking at in the internet ads the day before. Perhaps, since he had to bring the drill rig up from Venezuela, this truck might not be too far away after all. He went back to the office in the shop to use that phone to make some calls.

Now where had he put that phone number? Oh, there it was. McMann was the guy's name. Okay. As he dialed he made a decision about how he would buy this truck. Calculating the duty that would be required on it, and the exchange between Canadian and American dollars, he decided that he should consider what he might save by hauling home the seismic rig on this truck. A secret part of him wanted to do a bit of travelling to the warm south, too. Even if for only a couple days.

"McMann, here"

"You still have that Kenworth and trailer for sale?"

"Yup"

"You taking offers?"

" Uh, yup"

"I'm offering $56,000."

" I'll take $60,000."

Jack hesitated. In Canadian money that meant $80,000. And he still had to pay import duty on it. And drive it back.

"Okay. Done. I'll be down in less than two days to pick it up."

After getting the registration number, and a faxed bill of sale, he sent a deposit of $5,000 via bank transfer. Then he got on the phone to book airline tickets. His air miles would take care of that. He decided to take Kole with him as an extra driver.

He called the auction house in Venezuela and made arrangements for the seismic rig to be delivered by ship to Texas. From Corpus Christi, it would be a 3000 mile trip back home.

Chapter Four

JILL HAD NOT BEEN too pleased about his quick departure. "Sure, going off on your fun trips again, are you? And leaving me home alone in the cold weather. Well, go then."

They had flown from Peace River, Alberta to Edmonton, then to Calgary and were now over the skies above Montana on the way to New Mexico. He had been fortunate to find connections and airlines quickly, so they had left that afternoon, and it was now evening. They expected to be in Albuquerque by midnight.

It meant he would miss a parent-teacher meeting at the school. Erin, "Happygirl" would not mind if he missed this one; she took everything in stride. Carla did not yet attend school and was usually busy in her own little world. But Jill resented his absences, and especially the unexpected ones. She had this feeling of being abandoned. Her common sense told her that Jack needed to do what he did, but her bitterness often came to the surface. Sometimes she was glad Jack left, because it simplified things for her. If she knew he was gone, then she wouldn't count on him to be there, and it was difficult to be disappointed if your expectations were low.

Jack decided he would call her later that night. Then he sat back and decided to get to know Kole better. Kole had slept most of the way so far but had woken up for supper. Supper had been eaten in silence; it wasn't great, but it was food.

"So Kole, you have a girlfriend?"

"Nope. Had one a year ago, but we broke up. Not really interested in a girlfriend right now. Want to make some big money first."

"Well, maybe you're lucky. Don't have to worry about keeping a woman happy. Not like me."

"There might be some girls in Houston, right?"

"No time for that Kole. We have to pick up this equipment as fast as possible. We have a lot of work this winter, and no time to waste."

"I guess."

"What made you quit college after two years?"

"Well, I finished my program. Cooking. I enjoyed it, but not enough money in it, and I didn't enjoy it as much at the end, as I did at the beginning."

"We'll have to get you to cook the crew a meal sometime when we get back, Kole. Two years of that and you should be pretty good."

"Ever get hooked into the drug scene, Kole?"

"Nope. Tried a little, but quit. And yeah, maybe I could cook a meal sometime."

Jack wondered how much "a little" was, with Kole. They made some more small talk, and then watched the movie that came on.

At midnight, they landed in Albuquerque.

○ ○ ○

By the time they got off the plane and rented a vehicle, a 2004 Ford Explorer SUV, it was almost 1am. Jack decided to drive by the address of the truck owner before going to a motel. He hadn't booked a room and would find one close by. A half hour later they found the McMann's address. His yard was on the outskirts of the city, large enough for several trucks. The house was dark, but a street light illuminated the Kenworth, and Jack and Kole got out to have a quick look around the truck before looking for a motel. The barking of two large dogs made them realize their mistake, as the lights in the house came on.

A voice from the house bellered, "Who's out there?! What you doing around that truck?" Jack could imagine the muzzle of a rifle edging around the frame of the front door as it opened. The dogs kept barking, but the rattle of chains indicated they were tied up.

Jack and Kole walked to the house. Too late now, they thought. Might as well meet the guy. The man was a big fellow, with a mustache, and a white tea shirt that didn't quite cover his big trucker's belly. His pants hastily thrown on, with belt undone, he peered at the two as they came to his door. As it turned out, he did not have a rifle in his hands, but no doubt there was one just around the corner. They identified themselves, and he scowled at them for being there at that time of night, but then recovered himself. After all, like many truckers, he often drove through the night himself.

He gave them a large flashlight, and some keys to the truck. He flicked a switch in the house and the yard light came on, illuminating the truck more completely. They went out to have a better look at the truck while he went to dress himself more completely. The truck had a sleeper in the back, not a large fancy one with TV and microwave and all the acoutrements, but it was a bed with a curtain. They started the engine easily in the warm temperature in New Mexico, but they wondered how it would start in −35C temperatures back home. They did their walk around, crawling underneath to check hoses, linkages, tire condition. The truck was in as good a shape as McMann had said, with a smooth-running engine, good exhaust color, and all around clean and solid.

"Do you ever use a block heater?" they asked McMann when he came out to them.

"Not unless I go up north to Idaho" he replied. "You saw the grill shutters? They're on thermostat." Grill shutters closed off the air coming in through the grill when the weather was cold, to keep the diesel engine warmer. Diesel engines that ran too cold in winter, had a much shorter life, and created little heat to warm the cab.

Satisfied, Jack and Kole and McMann went into the house to finalize the deal. The smell of fresh coffee greeted them as they walked in. McMann had set out some large cookies as well. There were some signs that a female lived there too, but Jack's guess was that she had not got out of bed.

They completed the bill of sale and Jack left a signed cheque for the balance owing, $55,000. McMann did not ask if the cheque was good, but said, "You might as well take the rig now, since its running anyway. Which way you headed?"

"Going to Corpus Christi, Texas, to pick up a drill rig, and then back up to Canada."

"A drill rig? You won't fit a drill rig on that trailer!"

"Not a big rig. A seismic drill," replied Jack. "It'll fit no problem."

"Oh. Yeah, I guess that will."

Kole got into the truck and followed Jack and the SUV back to the rental agency at the airport. They parked the vehicle, and locked the doors putting the keys in the drop box.

As Jack and Kole left the airport, Kole made a suggestion. "Why not go to Houston right now? We can skip the hotel and take turns in the sleeper."

"We should put on the new plates first. …but I guess we can do that in the morning in daylight." Jack had gotten new plates in Peace River on the basis of the bill of sale, and a phone call to his insurance company while on the plane had confirmed coverage for this new-to-him truck. They headed east on the interstate, and Jack crawled into the sleeper.

Chapter Five

BY FIRST DAYLIGHT, JACK was awake, but Kole was still driving. They pulled off the road at a restaurant where several other trucks were parked, and Jack went in to order for both while Kole changed plates on the Kenworth and the trailer. One of the truckers inside was trying to start a conversation, but none of the others was interested. By the time breakfast came to Jack's table, Kole had joined him, and they ate in silence.

They had travelled about five hours, and would have another ten hours to go, before getting to Corpus Christi.

When they got back on the highway again, Jack drove while Kole napped in the sleeper. Jack felt fortunate that the timing had worked out better than expected so far. He also was enjoying the ride in this truck. It had air ride suspension on the cab, air-conditioning, leather seats, power windows and door locks. The reasonably quiet cab, for a truck, made listening to the radio easier, and it was a comfortable ride. With no load on the trailer, he was making good time.

If they kept travelling at the same rate, they would be in Corpus Christi before the drilling rig was due to arrive the next morning at 7 am by ship. From there, it would be 3000 miles to home, about 50 hours of good driving, maybe more if the weather turned bad. At this time of year, icy roads, blizzards, and heavy snowfalls were possible, anywhere north of Dallas or the Grand Canyon.

Jack took a sip of the coffee he had taken with him from the restaurant, and he settled down for the ride.

Chapter Six

FIVE AM, AND JACK woke up Kole. They had taken a hotel room in Corpus Christi, so they could shower and sleep better, but Jack didn't sleep well in hotels. Kole had disappeared the night before for awhile; Jack didn't know where and didn't want to ask. If it was women, he didn't want to know. If it was drugs, he didn't want to know, at least not yet. If it was just sight seeing, then Kole would tell him, if he wanted him to know.

Jack decided they would meet the ship at the dock so they could leave as soon as possible. In a half hour, they were at a café on the dock, sipping coffee and waiting for breakfast. It was still dark, but lights were moving on the water, and they wondered which lights belonged to the ship that was carrying their track drill. They thought of it as "the drill". That was the main purpose of its existence, and that was the job it would do for them.

They often devised shortened, simplified names for some of their equipment. In some cases, they would call these things, "rigs", or "the rig", but that title was not as specific and could also be used for the larger trucks, or for the water carriers, which along with some of the drill carriers, were also called "Bombi's", because of the fact that the machines were actually made by Bombardier, or similar to such tracked machines. In this case, they began to think of the new machine specifically as "the drill".

They knew which dock it would unload at, and so they watched that one from time to time, even though it was not due until 7 am. Suddenly, Kole grunted and motioned at the dock. A ship was gliding up to it.

They hurried through their eggs, bacon, and pancakes, then got up and walked across the road to the dock. By the time they got there, various cargo was being unloaded down a ramp. The boat was relatively small for a cargo hauler, but a small dark man who appeared to be in charge, was running back and forth between three or four men, organizing the unloading primarily of boxes of what appeared to be fruit. The crew's industriousness was a bit unusual for that time of the morning, especially given the rather long trip they had just made across the Gulf of Mexico from Venezuela. Since putting in long hours was not unusual for Jack, he didn't think too much about it.

In a couple of minutes, Jack made contact with the person "in charge" and asked if the drill was on that boat.

"Are you from Venezuela?", he asked.

"Yeah. I am so," was the reply. "Why you want to know?"

"Do you have a drill on board?"

"A drill? What you mean?"

"A machine on wheel tracks? With a tower on the back?"

"Oh, yeass. I have so. Is for you? You have papers?"

"Yeah, I got the papers right here. How fast can you unload it?"

"Hmmnn, les see. Yeass, papers good. I unload right away, quick."

Sure enough, Jack heard the sound of an engine on board, and soon the machine was making its way off the deck and down the short ramp onto the dock. In the dark, he couldn't see the exhaust very well yet, but the engine sounded smooth, and the drill seemed to move smoothly, although slowly, with its top speed of six miles per hour. Kole had gone back to the café where the Kenworth was parked and was now bringing the truck closer to the dock.

The crewman who had driven the drill off the ship got out of the machine as soon as it was at the bottom of the ramp, and Jack took over. The controls were familiar to him, as it was very similar to some of the rigs he already owned, and soon he had the machine parked on the trailer of his new-to-him truck. The lowboy trailer had permanent beavertail ramps which made loading and unloading of tracked machines quick and easy. Two drills could fit on this trailer if need be, which would make hauling to job sites a quicker and easier task in the future.

Kole began to chain down the drill, while Jack signed some papers provided by the ship's captain, or "charge d'affairs", or whatever he was. He wondered about customs, but he assumed that customs had been dealt with by the auction company, and so he didn't worry about that point. In very short order, they left the dock with their new acquisition.

They stopped by the café to pick up some coffee, and some bag lunches for the trip, and then they were off.

Chapter Seven

A BLACK SUV WITH its hood up, was parked at the side of the road ahead of them, and a man stood in the middle of the road, waving at them. The vehicle looked like one that had passed them about ten minutes earlier, although Jack wasn't sure about that. Kole was driving, and before Jack could suggest that they just pass them by, Kole had already begun to brake. Jack decided to let him be, partly because he himself actually preferred people to be considerate enough to help each other on the road. They had made good time in the last hour, in fact in the last two days, and so they could afford to be charitable. Maybe they would just have to use their cell phone to call a tow truck, or perhaps a wrench for some small repair, which they didn't have because of their recent trip and purchase.

By the time Kole stopped, they were a hundred yards past the black SUV, and the man was running up to them. Kole and Jack got out of the cab, stretched, and ambled to the man, and to the vehicle. The man was a skinny individual with brown eyes and black hair. Jack classified him as a light skinned black man. He was too lean, almost a skeletal face, to be good looking. He gave a somewhat tortured smile, and Jack felt that somehow he was not the person in charge.

"Can you talk to my boss?" the fellow asked.

"What's wrong with your car?" replied Jack.

"Don't know. Can you talk to my boss?"

"Okay, does he know what's wrong? You guys have a cell phone?"

The man did not reply and began walking back to his vehicle.

As Jack and Kole followed him, they wondered what could be wrong with the engine of a vehicle that was so new. They walked with heightened senses, and wary eyes. As they neared the vehicle they saw the other man, the "boss", getting out of the vehicle. Other than a greater level of intelligence evident in his eyes, and being slightly taller, with a slightly lighter complexion, he did not look much different than his partner. Hispanic perhaps. With feigned friendliness, Jack smiled and shook his head in commiseration, "Vehicles", he said. "they just don't make 'em like they used to, eh?"

"The car is okay. I just wanted to talk to you. You got that machine off a ship this morning?"

Jack hesitated. A rather strange question. And a strange reason to stop a truck on a highway. Had they picked up the wrong machine? No…he had checked the serial number and all the papers matched. Customs? "Well, yes, we picked it up this morning at Corpus Christi. Why the question?"

"You got there early. They didn't think you would be there till tomorrow."

"Yeah, everything went smoother than I thought it would."

"Well, could I rent it for a day? I will pay a good rent, and you will have it back tonight. Okay?"

This was very strange. Rent a machine off a truck? For a day only? Here? At such short notice? Why this machine? "Well, no, its not for rent. We're in a hurry to get back. Lots of jobs waiting, and we don't have a day to spare, actually. There must be more machines around to rent or contract." Jack began to think that the man had intended to use the machine for a day without letting him, the owner know. Perhaps he had intended to steal it? Both Jack and Kole became increasingly uncomfortable with the direction of the conversation, and the setting.

The traffic whizzing by almost made it difficult to engage in conversation at times. The man repeated his complaint that they had picked up the machine earlier than expected. He became more insistent about getting hold of the machine for a day, and then he said that perhaps a couple hours would be sufficient. By this time, Jack would not have rented him the drill at any price, since he no longer trusted the man, whose name he still did not know. There was something going on here that was probably not legitimate, perhaps illegal. In the back of his mind, he wondered if guns or drugs was involved. Was that ship part of a drug running scheme?

Could these men have used the machine to import drugs or guns from Venezuela? They had not inspected the drill very thoroughly, and Jack knew it would not be impossible to hide something on the machine, although a very thorough search should be able to find it. Or were these guys just half crazy?

Jack had had enough. He said, "Sorry, its not for rent or sale. And we gotta go. Maybe you'll find another drill somewhere." He did not add anything about his irritation at being stopped for such a spurious and intrusive reason, although he was on edge, and close to giving them a piece of his mind on that subject. He didn't mind helping people in trouble, even though he often felt he was too busy to do so. But something like this was stupid. It was non-productive, and irritating, and the hairs on the back of his neck would be up for several miles down the road, if not for the rest of the day. He turned, and started to head back to the truck.

The man growled at him, "I asked you for a favor. Just a couple hours. Don't turn your back on me!"

Jack didn't look back, but out of the corner of his eye he saw Kole put one hand in his jacket pocket, and sidle away from the men. When Jack reached the truck, then Kole turned and quickly, but without hurry, came to the truck as well. They were back on the highway, and nothing was said until highway speeds had been reached. Then Kole asked Jack, "You know he was carrying a gun?"

"Serious?" countered Jack. "How do you know that? I didn't see anything."

"I saw it in his belt. That's why I put my hand in my pocket. The guy wasn't sure if I really had a gun or not, but it made him think. It gave you enough time to get to the truck. I don't think the other guy had a gun. But, maybe he did."

"They seemed to be trying something they hadn't planned on, I think," Jack speculated. "I don't like the looks of this at all." He wondered whether

Kole was pulling his leg, or just making himself out to be more useful and more alert than he ought to be, but then reconsidered, and decided that Kole was likely telling the truth. Given the unusual situation, it made sense. He looked in the rearview mirror and saw that the black SUV was following the truck.

○ ○ ○

They were traveling west, mostly, and Jack's brain began to consider the options. They had been travelling for about two hours from Corpus Christi now, and had about 35 hours to get to the Canada/USA border. If these guys were actually going to follow them, then they had to be most cautious at meal stops and fuel stops. They had filled up in Corpus Christi, and the tanks were large enough to contain fuel for twelve hours, depending on the terrain. A lot of hills could reduce the fuel efficiency substantially.

Jack doubted whether the SUV, a Ford Escape, had enough fuel for more than six or seven hours. However, it could be filled up more quickly than a Kenworth's large tanks. If he could find a fuel station with the extra large nozzles then the Kenworth could also be filled rather quickly. The Kenworth had lots of horsepower, and with the half load on, likely could travel at 130 or 140 km, which here in the USA was almost 90 miles per hour. In many places, in most of the states they would be passing through, the speed limit was 80 mph. He would not be able to outrun the Ford if it came to an actual race. A race would possibly lead to dire consequences if the police happened to have radar along the way, and there was no certainty that he could prove any evil intentions by the men in the black Ford.

If the men in the SUV continued to pester them, should they involve the police? That type of delay was not something that Jack relished. The truck and the drill were needed to meet the contract deadlines, and the sooner they got back, the better it would be. Maybe these two guys would soon give up. In the meantime, Jack's truck was bigger than the SUV, they had their lunches with them, extra coffee, a bed in the back, and they would travel, and see what transpired.

Chapter Eight

WITH THE TRUCK ON cruise control, driving was not a difficult task. So far the road was fairly level, and a minimum of shifting gears was necessary to keep up the engine rpms. After driving for five hours since Corpus Christi, Jack decided that it was time for Kole to take over. Kole had been listening to radio, changing stations as they changed towns. He liked country and western stations, while Jack liked the various talk shows. Jack let Kole choose the stations, and once in awhile they would join in the song if they knew it well enough. Conversation was not as free as it might have been, because the black Ford was still behind them in the distance.

From time to time it was far enough back that Jack wasn't sure if it was still there, but then eventually, it would creep up closer to them, and Jack had no doubt that the two men were still following. He was now certain that these two men had taken all the fun out of this trip, and that they were plotting and scheming. It was a beautiful sunny day, but Jack was not getting the joy out of it that he had anticipated.

Originally when contemplating this trip in the haste of all the business he was transacting, he had envisioned the occasional stop with a short walk along side the road, investigating the native plants, whatever they might be. He had anticipated feeling the various soils and rocks in his hand on these brief stops, getting a small sense of the contrast with his own soil, his own climate, and his own vegetation back home. They had stopped twice for such a walk between Albuquerque and Corpus Christi. But now, that would not be happening anymore. He felt like a prisoner and a hunted man. But he had done nothing wrong. Jack's blood was coming to a slow boil.

"Hey Kole, ready to drive?"

"Sure. Where do you want to stop?"

"Change on the go. Here, I'll just get out of the seat, and you get in."

"Okay. No problem."

Jack slipped out of the seat, while Kole held on to the steering wheel, and slipped into his place. Jack grabbed his lunch bag and began to eat. Normally, eating was a bad habit while driving, done just to pass the time away. It was the reason why so many truck drivers had bellies that were larger than their belts. That, and beer of course, which would not be touched by any professional driver while on the road but was a favorite pastime after hours. Jack, however, was not very hungry.

He wondered whether he was afraid. He admitted to himself that to some extent he was afraid. The situation was an unknown, and fear of the unknown was always the greatest fear. But his fear was combined with anger, as well as frustration. His own sense of decency frustrated him somewhat, as well as his fear of the law. He wanted to use his truck to run the Ford off the road. It was quite possible to damage the Ford beyond repair, while barely putting a scrape on the big Kenworth's front bumper. Or the trailer could do the job. He had once seen a car totally demolished by the trailer of another semi, engine and front end scattered across the road, the driver senseless, while only very close examination would reveal any involvement at all by the larger truck, which had half driven completely over the front of the car. But Jack was not yet ready for such a violent answer to the nuisance of two men following them.

After another two hours, they could not see the Ford Escape in their mirrors. Kole ventured, "I think I saw them pull off a little while back, but they were pretty far away, and I'm not sure about it. Maybe they gave up."

"Well, they probably needed fuel. We'll change routes to throw them off. Take the next road left at the lights, and we'll head west. It's not as good as the interstate, but the highway looks good."

The next road left came after a slight bend in the road in the town they were travelling through. The secondary was a nuisance too, because it was no longer a freeway, and they were occasionally required to stop for red lights. Soon they pulled out of town though, and were back up to speed, although they were now exceeding the speed limit which was 5 mph lower on the secondary.

After another hour, and no Escape in sight, Kole pulled to the side of the road. They needed a pit stop. "Going to water some trees." he said as he walked through the ditch.

"A stretch will be good. And its nice out here." Jack finally had his opportunity to enjoy again the sights and smells of a foreign place and a warm climate. The desert was a mixture of red, yellow and black sand and rock, of seguarros, choquatillas, and other cacti. It was still the dry season, and the cacti were not blooming. The uniqueness and strangeness of the different vegetation, and the still strong warmth of the descending sun warmed Jack's heart. His optimism returned, and Kole too could sense that a burden had been lifted with the disappearance of the two strange men.

"Look at that! On that rock." A lizard of some type was enjoying the sun too, motionless for a moment on a rocky platform, then ambled rapidly off behind some pear cacti and crumbling rocks. Jack did not smoke, but if he did, now would be the time to pull out a pack and light one. Kole was enjoying one right now. This was his first smoke since breakfast. Kole was a light smoker, which was good, because Jack did not want cigarette smoke in the cab of this truck while he was in it.

Kole shut down the engine to check the oil level. It needed no additions. Jack in the meantime did a more thorough check of the Drill. He looked at all the compartments, the rollers inside the tracks, the toolboxes, which were empty, and inside the cab, but could find nothing suspicious. While the drill was on the truck there were some compartments he could not check, such as the transfer case, the transmission case, and the hydraulic pump compartment. The machine had to be split to do that: an easy job in his shop, but impossible on the back of the Kenworth.

Soon they were back on the road again, and by Jack's estimate they would need a fuel fill in about five hours. Early evening would be a good time to fill up so that they could drive through the night. It would have to be at a larger town, since the smaller centers sometimes did not have the larger filler hoses for the big trucks.

Two hours later they were on another highway heading north again, making good time. Jack was sleeping in the back.

Chapter Nine

WHEN JACK WOKE UP, it was dark. Moving to the seat, he felt his stomach growl, and asked Kole if he was hungry. Kole indicated he could likely eat an entire cow, and Jack agreed and began looking for a place to have some supper. They entered a town a half hour later, but it had no visible restaurant. Another half hour and a sign for a Chinese restaurant gave them some hope. Sure enough, the café was along the road, and it appeared to be a popular place. A cattle liner, a car hauler, and two freight vans were parked nearby. Across the road was a fuel dealer.

After filling the truck as well as their bellies, Jack took over the driving. Kole was not ready for a nap, and they began to make conversation. Jack had phoned Jillian when they had stopped. She had informed him that Bill was keeping the crews busy, and they were making good progress on the first line of holes.

Jack knew that the holes were being drilled and prepared for the seismic crew from a geotechnics firm, which would follow several days later. The drillers would drill the holes and lay down the dynamite and caps or detonators, with wires leading to the surface. They would usually do this in pairs, two men per drill. A few days later, the seismologists and their crew would follow, detonating the charges which were underground at a certain uniform depth as decided by the seismologist, and reading the sonogram feedback by means of a receiver, and a computer. Geologists would later take the information and interpret it to decide where the underground formations were. If they looked promising then the real well drillers would be told to do some drilling for oil or gas in those areas, and which depth to expect a possible oil or gas find.

Jill had not been very friendly on the phone. It had snowed again, and the yard needed plowing. Jack had told her to get one of the boys in the shop to clear the driveway. She then brought up the fact of his absence from home when she could use him to help with the kids once in awhile so she could go to her art class in town. Not to mention his missing the parent teacher conference, which she also tossed in. She was missing more art classes than she liked, and she needed some recreational time for herself. She also didn't like to ask the boys in the shop to clear her driveway, since it seemed like it might be a husband's job to look after his own yard instead of wandering all over the continent just to buy another stupid truck. And couldn't he ask the boys to do it himself? Why did Jack have to make her feel like she was interrupting their work just for her driveway? So never mind, she wouldn't ask them. She would just drive through the deep snow, and hope she wouldn't get stuck, or get her boots full of snow.

Jack had rolled his eyes, which fortunately, she couldn't see on the other end of the phone, although he almost expected her to tell him to stop rolling his eyes anyway. He commiserated with her, consoled her and then parted company on the phone. Immediately he phoned his shop and instructed Tom to clear the driveway with the tractor. He had debated getting Tom to put out some more bales for his cows, but then decided to leave it for awhile. There should be enough feed out until he got home, if they got home in two days.

As they drove, Jack asked Kole, "Why did that woman leave you last year?"

Kole replied, "She left me when she realized I was going back to the oilpatch this winter. I guess she didn't like the idea of spending so much time alone. She'd been with another oilpatch guy before, and it was the long separations that drove them apart. She didn't want that again."

"Yeah, some of this business can get to be bad that way. Or good, if you need an excuse to get away sometimes…"

"I'll have to look for a woman somewhere else, I guess. I mean not in a bar. And maybe I'll have to find different work eventually. But for now I'm not going to worry about women. I'll take the chance to have a laugh at your woman problems instead." , chuckled Kole.

"Well, it's not all bad," replied Jack. "She gets a bit owly when I'm gone sometimes, but usually after a bit of an uproar when I get back, she mellows out. She does have a good heart; does a great job with the girls."

"Was she your first?"

"Yep," replied Jack. "I don't know why really. Maybe just lucky; blessed some would say. She was the right girl for me. And most of the time I have no doubt about that. Once in awhile she gets on my nerves. She wants me to do all these things for her, and she can do them pretty good herself. She does if she has to, but then complains about it to me. She doesn't always complain, but she does when I'm not expecting it. So she always keeps me off balance. I kind of hate it, but kind of like it too. I would never want to be bored by her. On the other hand, it might be peaceful and relaxing to be a bit bored once in awhile. Maybe not yet, though." Jack realized he was babbling. Talking out of both sides of his mouth. Well. Too bad.

"She's not ditzy, at least", said Kole. It was a high compliment from him. He detested ditzy girls. When he realized he was going out with a girl who was "ditzy", he began immediately to look for ways to unload her. What Jack could not understand was why Kole went out with these "ditzy" girls in the first place. He supposed it was their looks, their femininity, their sex appeal. There was a certain attraction to the "ooohing and aaahhing" that these girls would lavish on their men. But it often wore thin when the men realized that it was a shallow appreciation, coupled with a highly motivated sense of self-centered expectations.

"It's a good thing anyway." said Kole.

"What's good?"

"That she left me. She had a drug habit she could not shake."

"Serious?"

"Yeah. Serious. It hadn't ruined her yet, but she was on a downhill slide. If I wasn't around, she was into it."

"Tough."

To change the subject, Jack asked Kole what kind of things he had studied at college.

"Well, I took cooking mostly. But also took a class in Spanish. And a few other classes, like mathematics, and chemistry. I think they wanted us to be a bit more well-rounded or something. That's where I took a truck driving course too. And first aid."

"Yeah, that's right, I knew you'd had that truck driving course. It's about the only way to get any experience these days, I guess. How much Spanish do you know?"

"Just a bit. When you don't practice, you lose it pretty fast."

"Could you understand those guys on the ship?"

"Not much."

The conversation ended there, and Jack realized that they were approaching a weigh station. The flashing lights indicated it was in service. Both in Canada and in the USA large trucks were required to stop and be inspected for overweight loads and other various infractions. Jack knew they were not overweight, but he wondered if any other problems would be found with their rig. From their own inspection, and based on the word of McMann, the truck should be okay, but Jack had been surprised before, and irritated, by these roadside highway boys in uniform.

As they pulled into the turnout where the little office was, and then waited for the four trucks ahead of them to clear the scales, Jack noticed an SUV leaving the area to go back onto the highway, rapidly accelerating out of sight. It resembled the Escape that had been following them previously, which reminded Jack of the two men in it. He still didn't know why they had acted so strange. Why had they been so determined to get hold of his "new" rig? He suspected drugs, but he had nothing concrete on which to base his suspicions.

When they drove onto the scales, two officers began checking the tires, and the clearance lights. They asked Jack to touch his brakes, and his signal lights. All the lights except one clearance light were working, and Kole quickly replaced it with one from the spares in the cab. One of the officers checked the clearances on the airbrakes, and the other stood by the cab to relay instructions. When the brakes had been checked and found satisfactory, the officer suddenly turned to Jack.

"There were a couple of men here about twenty minutes ago, looking for a truck just like yours. Are you expecting to meet anyone?"

"No." replied Jack. "What did they look like?"

"Short guys. A black man and a white man, maybe Mexican. Drove an Escape. They waited here for about 45 minutes before they left."

"No idea who they are." replied Jack. "Must have been looking for someone else."

As they pulled away from the station, Kole raised his eyebrows. "No idea?"

"Well, ignorance is bliss," said Jack, "and I like bliss. I like blissful times and blissful thoughts. I don't like those guys. Actually I really don't have any idea who they are, or what they really want. If they come back here, then I don't want these cops to remember any connections. Maybe they won't mention us. And their ignorance would be even more blissful to me."

"What are we going to do now?"

"Keep on trucking. I wonder if they were in the SUV I saw leaving this lot when we pulled in. If it was them, it's surprising they didn't see us. I suppose they must have hooked up to this highway after they realized we had turned off, and then waited for us at the scales. They must think we moved to a different highway, or we're ahead of them. I guess we didn't totally lose them after all. They haven't given up yet. I'm getting mad all over again. …But they don't know we're here. We'll just keep on trucking."

Frustrated, Jack pulled onto the highway again, shifting through the eighteen gears until he reached the speed limit. He stayed at the speed limit, not wanting to catch up to those two guys in the Escape, until he had developed a plan to deal with them, if he should meet up with them again.

Chapter Ten

THEY WERE HEADING NORTH now, and Kole was driving.

The sun was shedding enough light for them to get a sense of the huge canyon. Colors played out on the west side, while shadows claimed the eastern slopes. As they climbed out of the Grand Canyon they travelled on a relatively narrow, winding highway, and the vegetation changed from rocky bare with sparse grasses, to junipers, and other assorted larger desert plants finding footholds in the rocks and ledges. Here and there a few cottonwoods survived along permanent creeks and waterholes.

They had not seen the Escape again. The roads were in good condition, but as they were now north of the Grand Canyon, snow was on the ground. Driving through the canyon would add several hours to the trip, but it was scenic, and Jack figured he would like to see something he had not seen before. Besides, it would be less likely that those two men would expect them to follow this route.

Conversation had been slight. Both Jack and Kole had tried to ignore the black cloud of the two men in the SUV, which seemed to preoccupy them much of the time. Jack developed several alternative plans in his mind, should they meet those two again. A couple of those plans he had shared with Kole, but there was no way of knowing if such plans would be successful, or if there would even be an opportunity to use them.

They would find a place to stop soon and fill up with diesel, breakfast, and coffee, and perhaps the cheerful conversation of a friendly waitress. The cab was warm, and the rumble of the engine was soothing. Jack dozed off again.

Chapter Eleven

AFTER THE PHONE CALL from Jack, Jill rolled over in bed, and wondered if it was time to get up. Checking the clock-radio on the night table, she saw that yes, it was time to get up and get up Erin for school. Carla was already up, she suspected, since she was an early riser. Thankfully, she knew how to keep quiet when she got up so early. Erin was a different story, and took a few calls, door-knockings or tugs to wake up in the morning. The school bus came early, before light, and it was always a rush to get the sleepy-eyed girl into warm coat, mitts and hat and down the driveway in the cold crisp air to meet the bus at the road.

As she hurried about the kitchen in her housecoat, making breakfast for the girls and packing a lunch for Erin, she realized how fortunate she was. Here she had a husband who had just called her, just to keep in touch and let her know where he was. She knew he didn't forget her when he was gone. Two beautiful young daughters who loved her and made her life full and fulfilling. A beautiful place in the country, in the same yard where her husband worked, when he was home of course, which he often wasn't, because he was too busy and gone so often especially in the winter when she needed him most in the cold weather and heavy snows.... here she was, going off again, from feeling blessed one moment, to being negative about her situation in the next moment. Why did she do that!? "Stop it Jill!"

After Erin had left for the bus, Carla climbed on her lap for awhile, and they read a story together in the comfort of the cozy big chair, with Carla snuggled in her arm and asking questions about the story. It was their together time, and sometimes Carla would snooze for a few minutes in the comfort of her mother's arms, before she woke again and found her usual energy to resume her playing.

Jill looked outside. The sun had come up, and yes, the chickadees on the bird-feeder outside, hanging from the snow covered spruce branch on the tree near the house were a delightful sight. Even the bluejays that sometimes invaded the feeder and sending the smaller birds scattering, had their own beauty. The sun glinting off the snow crystals on the snow-covered lawn outside, and the clear blue sky in every direction was marvelous, with a quiet winter beauty that calmed the soul.

Chapter Twelve

JACK WOKE UP TO a snow-covered highway, with flakes coming down heavily on the windshield. As he crawled out of the bunk at the back, he could see that Kole was tense as he handled the truck on the slippery black-top.

"Where are we at?" asked Jack.

"Somewhere in southern Utah."

"Oh, yeah. I guess you can feel the Mormons already..." he replied, chuckling. "It's interesting how the people can change the feel of a state from one part of the country to another. Somehow it feels that Utah is completely different from Arizona... partly its the weather, but its also the people and how they live... what their priorities are. And then Nevada, completely different again. I kind of like Arizona weather though. ... We must be on the I-15 now."

"Yeah"

"Want me to drive now?"

"Yeah, that'd be good."

After switching places, Jack automatically checked his rear-view mirror, and saw a couple vehicles in the distance through the heavy snowflakes. He wondered about the black Ford Escape that had followed them earlier.

Where was it? Had they given up? Or were they far behind? Or far ahead? What in the world did those two men want? Jack was certain that something illegal was involved, such as an equipment racket, large scale theft, or drugs. If it was drugs, why were these two men so incompetent? Why did they just let Jack and Kole leave so easily, and why rent such a small vehicle?

Jack shook his head, and then shrugged his shoulders.

Kole had not gone to sleep, but was riding in the passenger seat, looking at the road, almost as tense as when he was driving. He had driven in bad conditions before, but this heavy wet snow was no joke. He and Jack preferred the light dry snow of the north, which often blew off the roads, or at least was crunchy and stiff, giving good traction in the fields and roads.

To divert from the weather, Kole asked Jack about his family. "How does your wife like it when you're gone so long?"

"Not much. But my stomach is rumbling, and we are way past breakfast, we need to stop right away."

As they pulled next to a cafe at the next truck stop, they took note of the vehicles parked there. Two semi trucks, a police car, three SUVs, two small cars, and no black Ford Escape. Strange now how that SUV was on their mind almost all the time.

Inside, they sat down and ordered bacon and eggs, pancakes, juice and coffee... for breakfast they both seemed to like the same thing. It was almost eleven o'clock and could as well have been lunch time.

The problem with their truck was that it was distinctive with that drill on the back. Easy to spot; easy to remember.

When they'd finished eating, they got up to pay the waitress at the till, and then left the cafe. Hopping into the truck they took off down the winding road, which was at a relatively high elevation and still covered with snow. Although snowflakes had slowed down a bit, the snowstorm showed no signs of ending. Kole was driving. About five miles down the road, Kole noticed a vehicle behind them and didn't think too much of it at first, but then noticed it was somewhat familiar. It was black. Smallish. An SUV... Ford... he was sure of that.

Chapter Thirteen

"THAT VEHICLE BEHIND US looks familiar" said Kole.

Jack stretched to look in his side mirror on the passenger side. "Yeah, it does. Probably not the same one. It'll pass us soon."

Kole just grunted and concentrated on his driving. After another three miles, the vehicle was almost beside them on the passing lane. The snow was picking up again a bit, and both vehicles were traveling under the speed limit because of road conditions. The truck was blowing up some snow as it traveled.

As the black SUV drew up beside them, Kole took a quick look. Sure enough, the same two guys were in it. And they were looking closely at him, and at the truck. They had the "gotcha" look for sure. Kole ignored them, and slowed down a bit. They did too.

"It's those guys again. The S.O.B.s!"

"Crap!" muttered Jack.

Then the taller skinny one in the passenger seat motioned to Kole to pull over. Kole ignored him and maintained his speed, increasing it slightly. Jack asked him what he could see. "What are those guys doing?"

"They're telling me to pull over."

"Just ignore them." said Jack.

SEISMIC TRAIL

"That's what I'm doing. The boss guy is in the passenger seat. Wait! Now he's pointing something at me... yeah, its a gun, a pistol of some kind. Crap! Crap! Crap! I don't need this." Kole leaned his head back, and pushed on the pedal, kicking the 525 horses into full power. Tires began to spin on the truck, and they were immediately ahead of the little Escape. But the Escape scrambled to catch up, tires also spinning. It seemed to have good traction since it was not far behind.

"This is crazy! What do those guys want? Guns? A thousand miles just to follow us?! It is really getting me down!" said Kole. As the two men behind them crept closer, Kole pulled his truck in front of them. They tried to pass on the other lane, but Kole pulled back into that lane in front of them. He heard the ping of a bullet on something behind him, either the drill, or the headache rack on the truck, or some other part of the truck.

"Keep going! Don't slow down! And don't worry about bullets." said Jack.

Kole clenched his jaw and shook his head from side to side in frustration, as if to clear his head. But instead his innate anger was increasing. If those two pipsqueaks had confronted him in a bar, he would simply have banged their heads together and left them lying on the floor. To dare to chase him down! With their little wanna-be truck! He would force them to stay behind him. Without saying a word, Jack seemed to agree.

"If we were back home, and they tried that...." Kole left the thought unfinished.

"We'd probably have a rifle in the truck." finished Jack. "They would be singing a different tune."

As the vehicle switched from side to side, so did Kole. With the power under the hood and the relatively light load, Kole had no problem maneuvering. He figured he could do this all day. Few vehicles were on the highway, maybe a few more on the two lanes headed south, separated from them by a metal divider as the highway made its winding curves in the steeper narrower parts of the valley they were in.

"Oh crap! Did you see that?" asked Kole.

"What happened?"

"They hit the trailer."

"Still following?"

"Yeah, they seem to be okay. But now coming up fast again."

"Don't let em pass!"

More swerving and lane changing for the next four miles. The highway was winding more, and the southbound lanes across the divide could not be seen. The trailer sometimes drifted to the outside of the curves due to the slippery surface and too high speeds for the conditions. The little vehicle following them also swerved sideways on the snow, which was now falling more heavily, and obscuring what was behind.

The truck was in the left lane, and the SUV was trying to pass on the right. Kole suddenly noticed their attempt and swerved to the right. If Kole and Jack had been in the tailing vehicle, they would have heard a bang, and felt a sideways motion. They would have felt or heard a crunch of their vehicle against the rail on the side of the road. They would have noticed that the rail ended just about then as the road straightened out. They would have realized that they were not going to be able to stay on the road. They would have felt themselves and their vehicle rolling over and over in the deep ditch until it was stopped by a huge tree about forty feet down the embankment. But Kole and Jack didn't notice any of these things. It was the other guys who felt all these things.

Kole was looking in his left-hand mirror, and by the time he looked in his right-hand mirror, he could no longer see the vehicle due to its depth and the cloud of snow left by the truck, and the huge snowflakes coming down from the sky. The noise and size of the truck prevented them from hearing or seeing the smaller vehicle as it rolled into the road ditch.

But Kole wondered. It didn't take long to realize the smaller vehicle was no longer trying to pass them. And Kole knew that he had waited a bit longer to swerve, to scare those mongrels by cutting across close to them. Maybe too close.

Chapter Fourteen

JILL LEANED THE SHOVEL against the house, puffing slightly as she recovered from the invigorating exercise of shovelling snow from the sidewalks near the house. Erin was walking down the driveway from the road where she had descended from the bus, hopping and skipping in the vehicle tracks, and then tripping as she stumbled into the deeper snow between the vehicle tracks. She picked herself up, picked up her backpack and then walked more sedately for a few steps, but soon was hopping and skipping again. As she got closer, Jill could hear her singing a little song while she skipped along. Wouldn't it be nice, Jill thought, if we could all be so innocent, so carefree, so quickly recovered from our stumbles. How long does this stage of life last for her little girls? Jill didn't know whether to smile, or to let the underlying sadness take over. She smiled.

As she stepped into the house, she saw Carla playing with her dolls on the kitchen floor. She had a huge dollhouse, although most of Carla's dolls were too big to fit in the dollhouse. But she would put her smaller dolls in the chairs at the kitchen table or in the beds in the dollhouse, making up stories about them as she did so. On a plastic stove, she had her fake cookies and pies, which she fed studiously to her dolls in the way of the practiced routines of life that she had already learned in her four years of watching what was going on around her.

Jill listened to the news on the television as she prepared a plate of cookies for Carla and Erin. The weather was clearing up, and it looked like there would be no snow for the next five days. Temperatures were also promising to warm up to only ten degrees below freezing. That would be easier on Jack's equipment out in the bush.

Bang. The door slammed as Erin stepped into the house and dropped her backpack on the floor. She kicked off her boots and before taking off her coat and hat and mitts and snow pants, she reached for a cookie.

"Could I have some tea, Mom?"

"Here it is, Erin, all ready for you. Did you have a good day at school?"

"Yes." She said automatically. "But Joey threw snowballs at me at noon hour." She giggled. "But he missed. And I threw some back and hit him once. And Nancy threw snowballs at him too. Then we found pieces of snow and built a wall we could hide behind, but we didn't finish because the bell rang, and we had to go back in, and Joey pushed the wall down, and put some snow in my face just before we went inside. So that made me mad. But I didn't do anything back because he doesn't know better to not be mean, right Mommy? Can I go back outside again for awhile to play?"

Jill had to smile again. Her daughter had lifted her heart and made it light. "Right Erin. Sure you can go outside again, but it will be dark very soon... so you can go outside for fifteen minutes, and then come back in." Erin dashed back to the porch, slipped her boots on, and was soon running outside beside the dog, Moll, who loved to fetch anything Erin or anyone else would throw for her. Erin splashed her face in the snow as she tripped over some unseen obstacle in the snow, but quickly picked herself up again, brushed herself off, and took off running. She had no time to whine or complain because she would lose her time outside if she didn't make the most of it.

The dog was a black lab, female, who loved everyone as far as Jill knew. She would run for hours, following the tractor in the yard, or Jill on horseback. Moll would never stop fetching a stick as long as someone was willing to throw it.

Jill wondered about dogs... how could Moll jump into freezing water, chasing a stick over and over again, and not somehow catch some illness, or pneumonia, or even just get too cold to move?

To think that dogs were related to wolves, wild predators who kept their distance and preyed on the very same livestock that some dogs would protect or herd or guide in order to serve their human masters. Jill wondered about the very contrast. She knew that the contrast could be as great with people, some of whom would kill others for their own gain, or out of hate, and some who would die willingly for others.

Jill wondered about Jack, missing his presence, and hoping his trip was progressing smoothly. Her last information from Jack was that he was ahead of schedule, but the weather was poor. Well, this was not the first time that weather impacted Jack's work.

Chapter Fifteen

"MY GUESS IS THEY are in the ditch", said Kole. "I don't see them anymore, and I think they hit the back of the truck, or I bumped them off the road. Doesn't really hurt my feelings."

"Wonder if we should check on the damage?" pondered Jack out loud. They were already a mile past the likely collision. "They might be seriously hurt, going into that ravine," but at the same time he had no desire to rescue people who pointed a gun at him and threatened him and followed him for a thousand miles under those conditions for most likely illegal and dangerous reasons. Most likely those guys would just point a gun at them again, if they were conscious or able.

Under the assumption that the threat was specifically towards themselves, Jack surmised that anyone else who stopped to help them would not be threatened in the same way, although you never know. Those guys might try to hijack another vehicle, if theirs was seriously stuck or damaged. Jack shrugged his shoulders somewhat uncomfortably. He looked at Kole, whose face was grim.

Kole said nothing but kept driving. He was angry. Angry at those men for threatening his life. Angry at them for disturbing his peace. Angry at their brazen disregard for others. Angry that he had to swerve the truck so often in this weather to prevent them passing. Angry that he had bumped them with the trailer. Angry that he even had to think or debate about whether to leave them or help them now. Knowing he would just keep on driving, leaving them to their fate. Hoping they would hurt no one else.

In the meantime, the snow kept on coming, although the temperature was going down, and so it was a little less slippery. The cooler lighter snow brought a blinding snow cloud caused by large trucks as they barreled down the highway.

"Just keep going." Jack ordered. Jack knew he had to take ultimate responsibility as the boss and owner. Besides, he was just as ticked off as Kole about these intruders. He was reminded of the news reports he heard of drug dealers murdering civilians and police. They also kidnapped people, abused girls, abused missionaries, threatened governments and police, getting young girls and others addicted to various drugs. He didn't know for sure whether these two men were associated with the drug trade, but everything smelled like it.

Jack had several employees who were using drugs of various kinds. One of them was a 19 year old named Jim. Jim had quit school in grade ten and begun working on a seismic crew. He was a big boy in good shape and easily did the work of walking all day in the snow behind a drill truck, attaching dynamite to the lead wires and inserting the dynamite into the holes drilled by the driller. He did a good job, and Jack liked to keep him on. But in the off-season, Jack had to lay off most of his employees since he had no work for them.

Some of his employees had families and farms or other summer work, using the high winter wages wisely. But some of the younger ones like Jim were just waiting for Jack to call them again and had nothing to do but go to the bar everyday, gamble their pay-cheques, and try out new drugs and new women. When Jack did call them in the fall, they were dead broke, and sometimes had their brand new truck repossessed. The brand-new 4x4 pickup was often the only thing they really owned.... well, maybe they would also own a five-foot wide flat screen TV and huge sound system, and maybe a fancy 4x4 quad or sled (snow mobile). To say they owned it would be overstating it, as most of the time the bank really owned it, or the finance company or the dealership to whom they were still making payments. Jim fit into that category.

Three weeks ago, when Jack had called Jim to come to work, Jim had been hesitant.

"I wanna come, but I got a court appointment next week" he had said.

"What's the problem?" asked Jack.

"Gotta ticket I didn't pay."

"For what?"

"Speeding and reckless driving" replied Jim.

"I'll give you that day off".

"Yeah, but I got no way to get there if I come to work." Jim lived two hours away from Jack's business, and potentially even farther away if he was out in the field on the job.

"No vehicle? Truck broken down?"

"Lost the truck."

"Lost it?! How could you do that... oh you mean the bank took it?"

"Yeah." Jack didn't remind him that this was the second time this had happened. He told Jim he would bring him or get another employee to take him to court. This was not the first time he had done this for an employee. He believed in looking after his employees. He needed them to make his business work.

"Well, the bank was going to take it, so I was moving around, you know? But it was actually impounded by the cops."

"DUI?" asked Jack.

"Yeah."

This was not good. It meant that Jim would probably not be able to drive any vehicle on the public roads. He could still work, but it reduced the flexibility as he would always have to go with someone who still had his license. On the other hand, it would prevent Jim from driving while using drugs or alcohol...

Jack would prefer not to hire anyone who was involved with drugs, but realistically these guys needed work too, and it was hard to get only the most careful employees in the present labor market. And Jack himself could remember his own younger days, so he had a special place in his heart for these lost and searching young men.

"Okay, well, we'll work it out. Can you get here on Tuesday?" he had asked. Jim had shown up on time.

Jack was not far removed from the drug trade. He had fired at least three employees over the years who were obviously under the influence when they showed up at work, or in one case after the lunch break.

Kole too had been involved in the drugs as a user for awhile. He had narrowly escaped prison for assault, although he had been on probation when Jack had hired him. His temper was often visible, and he had a restless spirit that demanded something to occupy his time. Driving worked well, but any kind of hard work also seemed to fulfill a need, and it tamed his wildness for a time. He was both unpredictable and reliable, which suited Jack just fine.

While neither one of them would have left helpless innocent people in trouble or in a ditch if they could help it, in this case, these two Venezuelans from Texas, as they had begun thinking of them, deserved their trouble. They were not really Venezuelans, likely since they were a black man and a white man, who was potentially Mexican, or even an indigenous from the southern USA. The more trouble they got, the better. Jack and Kole were ultimately happy to leave them in their condition.

Chapter Sixteen

"GET OUT OF HERE!" yelled Jake at Tom. "Find something useful to do! You messed up another piece that I spent two hours getting ready for you. Why can't you keep your head on straight? Just go!"

Jacob was obviously getting more fed up with Tom's lack of common sense and his lack of care and precision. Maybe it was just a bad day, and Jake didn't have the patience he needed. But what a fiasco! Doing nothing but fixing Tom's mistakes, it seemed like. Sure Tom got some things right, but it seemed more things wrong. Jake could not sense drugs or alcohol on Tom, but he might as well have, based on Tom's work. Anyway, Jake needed a break from Tom. "Go get the tractor and clean the snow in the yard." he said to Tom.

Just then the phone rang. Bill the crew chief was out in the field. "We got the truck flipped back up yesterday with the D7 but the frame on it is twisted. And we need help getting it started. Must have got oil in the cylinders. Trailer seems to be okay."

"Probably should put the truck on another trailer and bring it back to the shop." replied Jake. "Or we can send out another truck and hook the trailer to it. Will that work?"

"Yeah, I think the trailer is okay. It's up on its jacks now, but two tires need repairs. Wires and hoses seem to be okay and no cracks anywhere that I can see. Ramps are twisted, but still useable. So yeah just send another truck and we'll hook it up and winch this one on to the trailer. We'll call the tire repair nearby to fix the two flats."

Jacob opened the shop door and looked for Tom, who was just backing the loader tractor out of the heated storage shed. Well, just getting started, and he would have to change his plan... "Tom!" he yelled. But Tom did not hear him over the noise of the tractor. Jake stood in his line of sight and waved him down. Tom stopped and stepped out of the cab and waited for Jake to speak.

"Change of plans. You have to hook on to the Mack and take it to Bill so he can hook on the flipped trailer. Then you'll have to winch on the Peterbilt and bring it back here. Can you handle that? Remember the chains and boomers and double check them after a mile or two down the road. Bill's location is on the desk in the office, and remember to take his phone number, and use the GPS to get to Bill."

"Okay." Tom started to get back in the cab of the tractor to put it back in the shed, but Jake then told him to spend fifteen minutes moving some snow away from the doors of the sheds, and especially near the garage that held Jill's vehicle. Then he could get going to Bill.

Tom liked driving. It was what he was good at and hauling almost anything was not a problem for him. Chains, boomers, ramps, slippery decks, big engines were his comfort zone. The comfortable leather seats in most of the big trucks, the radio sound systems, heating systems and the view, made his "driving office" nicer, he thought, than a lot of offices even of some well-to-do businessmen. Much nicer than Jack's office, and a whole lot nicer than Jake's shop and his incessant complaining about how Tom would cut this piece of metal or bend that one or grind that one. With a smile on his face, Tom gave his attention to his snow plowing, anticipating the preparations and two-hour trip to Bill's crew at the truck rescue site.

After about twenty minutes, most of the immediate yard site was clear of snow. The loader tractor was fast with its hydra-shift, and it had a huge bucket in the wintertime for moving snow. It was used for many things, including farming activities such as moving bales. It took about five minutes to change the bucket for a bale fork with quick connects.

Tom put the tractor back in the shed, and then started up the Mack truck, which had been plugged into a block heater which kept the engine warm. He let the truck run for awhile, while he checked the tires, the number of chains hanging on the rack behind the cab, and the boomers he would need for the job. He brought another two chains from the shop to the truck and noted the cable on the winch. Then he brought the truck to the fuel tank in the yard and topped up the tanks. Quickly he walked to the shop and retrieved his coffee cup, filling it up with coffee and fixings from the counter in the lunchroom beside the office. Putting the cup in the cup holder beside his seat, he adjusted the seat for his own physique, and made himself comfortable. He engaged the transmission and eased down the drive to the road. He was off. On his own. By himself. The way he liked it. Just him and the radio. Ah, this was the life!

Oops! He'd forgotten the GPS and the location he needed. Not good. The men would laugh at him when he came back to get them. He got to the road, turned around, came back and got the location piece of paper, and the GPS, all without looking at any of the grinning staring men in the shop. They didn't exist; they were nothing. He had it now, and he was off. Ah, this time, this was the life!

Chapter Seventeen

JILL WATCHED TOM LEAVE with the truck, come back and leave again. She smiled. Tom was a good driver, but sometimes a bit absent minded, or addle brained, or just in his own world.

She did enjoy the snow-plowed yard, as she walked to the garage to get her pick up truck. She thought she better check on the cows, since Jack was not home. Winters normally were not a problem as he could set out bales of feed ahead of time, and the cows simply licked snow for water. No shortage of fresh snow either right now. But it's always a good idea to check cows. Always when you think everything is fine and you take things for granted is when you have problems.

She drove the vehicle to the house and then went inside to get Carla. Carla still needed to get her boots on, but otherwise had dressed herself. They walked together, hand in hand down the short walk to the truck, and Jill boosted her into the back seat. "Tie my belt, Mommy!" said Carla, as Jill was about to walk away. Since they were only going a half mile down the road to check on the cows, Jill didn't normally worry about seatbelts, but of course Carla had her routine figured out, and depended on the consistency of fastening her seat belt on her booster seat. Other wise things were just not right! Jill turned around and fastened the seat straps, and Carla was happy.

Closing the rear door and opening the driver's door, Jill stepped on the running board to get herself into her truck, which was a bit higher off the ground than most pickups. Jill was not tall. Not real short, but certainly not tall. She grabbed onto the steering wheel to pull herself in and started the truck. As they coasted down the drive, she noted the blue skies and the sparkling snow on the wire fences. With no wind the frosty snow would sparkle-whiten the fences and power lines for some time, unless the temperature became warm enough to melt it.

On the shoulder of the road, she could see by the hoofprints that the neighbor down the road had been going for a morning horseback ride. Sometimes she would ride with her neighbor girlfriend, but sometimes they would just like to ride alone. It was true of many people in the country, and especially in this part of the country, that they liked being alone sometimes in the great outdoors, just enjoying the blue skies, white snow, frost, and winter birds. Or in summer, the rustling of the trembling aspen, the swimming of ducks and Canada geese on the beaver dam pond, the swarms of dragonflies, the circling and screech of the red-tailed hawk, with the chance of a sighting of some white-tailed deer, or a coyote or red fox, or even a black bear or a moose.

As they neared the field where the cows were feeding, she noticed two cows on the road. What?! Why would two cows be on the road? The fences were good, and even had electric shock power on one strand, and the cows had lots of feed. She was feeling somewhat irritated, and as she got closer, she realized that they were not cows, but bulls. And one bull was not theirs. It was a long-horn bull, and it had put up a challenge so that one of their bulls had jumped/crashed through the fence to meet it out on the road. They were turning and churning and pushing and shoving, turning up chunks of snow and gravel as they went.

Now what? Should she wait till they got tired? Or open the gate and hope they went in without any of her cows going out? Another pair of hands would be nice. But Jack was gone, and she hated to interrupt the work of the employees. She waited a bit, but the bulls showed no signs of tiring or giving up, so she honked on the horn and crawled closer with the truck. Some of the herd was standing by the fence, watching the entertainment, so she got out of the truck, walked to the gate which was where the bull must have jumped the fence, and chased the herd away from the gate. Then she opened the gate and hoped for the best.

As she walked back to the other side, one of the cows came back to the gate and bawled at the two contestants. Her bull took a step or two towards the cow, and the other bull kept pushing and shoving. Amazingly, eventually their pushing and shoving got them both into the pasture, where they continued their games. Jill was able to go back to the gate and shut it, leaving both bulls in the pasture. She would contact the neighbor two miles down the road, who likely owned the strange bull.

They had four bulls for their cows, but it was the dominant bull that had taken on the Longhorn. The other bulls kept their heads down, although with one eye open to take advantage of a cow in heat if the main guy was too busy defending against the intruder. This cow likely was bred before, perhaps several times, but simply did not become pregnant.

As she sat in the truck watching the bulls in the field, she was thankful that the problem was so easily solved, and thankful that she had decided to check in the first place. A strange bull in the herd at this time of year was not a big problem, since all the cows, well all but one, had already been bred, so the different breed of bull would not impact their calf crop next year.

"They were really fighting!" Carla exclaimed, as they drove back to the house.

"Yes, it was exciting, wasn't it Carla?" replied Jill.

"Did they get hurt, Mommy?"

"Not too much, Carla. They are pretty strong, but our bull is bigger than the one with horns, and it seems like neither one really was getting hurt." They had stopped fighting perhaps because now the other three bulls were also chasing the stranger, and he was simply running around the field. Soon one of the three stopped chasing, and then another, and eventually they all spaced themselves in the field, and began eating the baled hay.

She looked closely at the fence and realized the bull had not jumped out at the gate, but just beside it. Two staples had been popped out and the barbed wire was sagging. She got out of the truck again and reached into the back, where fencing supplies were usually kept. She found a hammer and a couple of staples, walked to the fence through the knee-deep snow, and hammered them in. As she turned to go back to the truck, she felt a pain in her ankle. "Ouch!!" and realized she twisted her foot on a rock or lump of dirt under the snow. She limped back to the truck and grouched at herself. If Jack was home...

Suddenly she heard her cellphone in her pocket... well, she felt it too, because she had it on vibrate. Taking off her glove, she grabbed the phone and saw that it was Jack's cell phone calling. "Hello" she said somewhat non-committally.

"We're at Salt Lake City, going through it. We are doing okay. The snow has stopped falling, and the traffic here is not too bad. We should be seeing you tomorrow sometime, hopefully. How's the girls doing?"

"We had a neighbor's bull visit and they were fighting on the road, but I just got them back in. I mean the longhorn was fighting with Domino, but they're okay, both in the pasture now and eating hay. I'll get hold of Buren's as soon as I get home, but there's probably no hurry to get their bull back."

"Fun."

"Carla's with me in the truck. Erin's still not home from school yet. Tom cleared the snow in the yard and is off somewhere with the Mack truck."

"Yeah, he's going to get the Peterbilt. Jake told me about it a little while ago." Well wouldn't you know he'd talk to Jake before calling her.

"How's Kole doing?"

"Kole is okay. We're just switching and sleeping on the road. Hopefully home late tomorrow. Or maybe afternoon. About twenty hours of driving still. But the roads have improved."

"Okay. Drive carefully."

"Will do. I've gotta go now, but just want to tell you I love you."

"Sure I love you too. Don't mind Kole hearing you?"

"He's sleeping in the back."

"What? You're driving? with distraction?"

"Yeah, well you're always distracting me now aren't you?! But I'm using the blue-tooth in this truck. It's a pretty nice truck. Not much missing from it. And the rig is staying on the deck of the trailer pretty tight. Anyway, I'd better let you go, since I know how busy you are with bulls, and fences, and snow blowing and all. I'll call you later this evening."

"Okay, see you later."

Jill was comforted by the phone call. Jack sounded like himself, and everything seemed to be going smoothly. She complained to herself a lot when he was gone, and sometimes to him, but in reality she was used to him being away, since that was the type of work he was in. She also knew that Jack was a rambling man, and that even without the excuse of work, he would sometimes be gone for a few days, or even a couple of weeks. Sometimes it would be for hunting, or maybe for horse racing, or auctions in other cities, even when he didn't really need anything. But he always came back. As far as she knew, he'd been faithful to her and to his daughters, but there is no doubt that he had the wanderlust. Whenever she could, she would go along, but it didn't happen so often now that they had the girls to look after.

Chapter Eighteen

AS JACK CLOSED THE phone call, he knew he had left out an important detail in the conversation. He had not mentioned the two guys following them. In fact he had said nothing about it right from the beginning. He didn't want to worry her. He had said nothing about it to Jake either, nor Bill, when he talked to them earlier today. He and Kole seemed to have an unspoken agreement, that they wouldn't mention it. But he better confirm that with Kole. Make sure he wasn't guessing about Kole's intentions.

No one else needs to know, especially since they may have left two injured people in the ditch, without even calling 911 or anything. Who knew what trouble that might bring. At the next overpass, Jack pulled off, and into a truck stop. Instead of using his cell phone, he used a pay phone at the store. There were fewer of them around now that everyone had cell phones, but here was one. The call couldn't be traced back to him with a pay phone. He called 911.

A few minutes later he was back on the highway, after explaining to a groggy Kole what he had done. Kole went back to sleep. Jack had told them very little, other than seeing part of a vehicle on the north-bound highway ditch, and gave them an approximate location, which was a ten mile stretch of road in the mountains. He told them he had no cell phone, so couldn't call earlier, and also didn't think of calling since he wasn't sure that someone hadn't already called or been there. But then he began to worry, he said, maybe they were missed, so he called. Had they already been picked up, he asked? The lady on 911 didn't know, because the location was out of her district, so she would have to relay the message to the other district. "Okay", he said, and he had hung up.

Well, hopefully they survived. He was surprised at this thought, since these two men had threatened them with their lives and had even taken shots at them. Had it been the other way around, these two men would have just driven right over them, no questions asked. He was sure about that.

But why did he want them to survive? I mean, why care about that, he thought. Who cares? Yet, somehow he didn't want to be responsible for their death. A few injuries, sure, it would serve them right. A bit of frostbite maybe, a little hypothermia, a concussion, and maybe a broken leg. That would be good. Maybe it would make them think about doing something like this again.

Jack put the truck at 80mph, which was the Utah freeway speed limit, and equated to 130 kmh. He had to laugh at that. The freeway in Alberta between cities was 110 kmh. And here in Salt Lake City, there was no slowing down for the city on a ten-lane highway (five lanes each way). Like that would happen in Alberta, where it seemed merely the sight of a building would reduce the highway speed by ten or twenty kmh. Yeah right. Oh well, he still wouldn't want to live in Utah, even though the scenery was nice and speed limits high. He loved his country living in northern Alberta, where towns and cities were smaller, he knew the country roads, and it was home.

He looked forward to seeing Jill again too. Even though he loved traveling and being on the road in different places, cherishing the independence and the potential for the unexpected, still after three days he began to miss Jill and his girls and the comforts of home. He missed the smiles of his girls, and their innocent enthusiasm. He missed the contact with his wife, both verbal and physical.

He was glad to have a competent crew foreman that he could leave in charge of the drilling crews when they were on the job out in the field. That was something he didn't have to worry about.

Having talked to Bill before talking to Jill, he learned that the truck was now upright again and the flipped trailer still useable, although the truck would need some repairs. So it was doubly good that they had bought this new/used truck. It was a Kenworth, but eight years newer than the Peterbilt, and with a few more options, and a bigger motor. With the air-ride on it, it was fairly smooth riding compared to the old Peterbilt, and the sleeper on it was an added feature that the Peterbilt did not have. His Mack truck also had a sleeper on it, and Jack felt good that his equipment was improving.

The used equipment market was a big benefit to Jack. There was no way he could justify or even afford all his machinery if he had to buy it brand-new.

Another man in the same line of work also bought a lot of new equipment, and even bought fancy toys for his personal use, but in the last slow-down, had been forced to sell all his equipment and his main shop building in town. Jack had bought that building at fire-sale prices and was now renting it out to another businessman.

When Jack bought his "toys" he paid cash for them, whether it was a boat, or an antique Corvette, or a new Harley. His personal pickups were also debt free.

Jack liked his equipment and machinery, whether it was his loader tractor, or the snow-blower, or his bombi drills, or the trucks and flat bed trailers. And the tools in the shop were part of his personality too, not just necessary things for work. It made him feel good to design a new piece of equipment, or to build his own drills rather than just buy them. Even though he usually had men in the shop to do the routine work of fabricating, cutting and welding and painting, it gave him a sense of satisfaction to sometimes do some of the handwork himself. He had welded steel and aluminum since he was a teenager, and his drill press, air compressor, lathe, shop lift, and all his other tools made him feel competent and whole.

As they continued north, they soon were travelling through Idaho, which would take a few hours. Roads were good, skies were clear, although it was nearing evening and getting a bit dark.

On these trips, drivers had a lot of time to think. Or listen to the radio. Sometimes they would pick up hitchhikers to relieve the boredom and have someone to talk to. But Kole would have to do, and he seemed to be waking up. Yup, there he was, crawling out of the bunk into the passenger seat. "Gettin' hungry. Need a pit stop." plain basic rudimentary words that got the message across. Jack started looking for a truck stop, or any kind of a place to eat. Looking at the fuel gauge, he decided to fuel up too. No use taking chances on running out in the night. Not knowing where the next truck stops might be, he took the cautious approach and filled up when one of his two tanks was empty.

There... there was a truck stop. Two fuel dealers near each other and you could use a credit or debit card at most pumps now. However, you needed a USA zip code to access them. Jack travelled enough that he had a credit card on a USA bank, with an appropriate Zip Code with it.

While Kole went inside, Jack fueled up, and then went inside to have a sit-down feed. One meal a day, usually supper, they took a break for an hour to eat and smile at the waitresses and maybe talk to another trucker or two. The food was great and they were not so eager to go back to the truck after such a filling meal, which started to make both of them drowsy. So they prolonged the break for another twenty minutes, but then Jack said, "Let's get going. I feel a great need for a snooze, and might as well do it laying down as sitting in a chair. Are you okay to drive?"

"Yeah. I'll try it. I'm a bit dozy, but let's go. If I need a nap, I'll stop and take one for ten minutes. That's usually enough to rest the eyelids."

○ ○ ○

Jack couldn't sleep. He was half asleep, lying behind the curtain on the bunk, but his thoughts kept him awake. He had thought he was more sleepy, but okay, he would get up for awhile and talk maybe. It was still early evening, maybe that's why he couldn't conk out.

Crawling into the front seat he asked Kole if he liked what he had on the radio.

"I like Country and Western. But I like other music too, if its good. Sometimes classical if I'm in the mood. Some light rock sometimes. I used to like the hard rock, but since I quit the drugs I also don't care for the music as much."

"About the same as me." said Jack. "but I like the talk shows too. They keep me awake and get me thinking. Sometimes they get me mad, but at least my brain is working."

Kole said, "Well switch it then. You're the boss."

Jack grinned. "Yeah I am. But seriously, I can listen to this station too."

"No, No. Go ahead, I'm ready for something different. Just as long as the talk program is not about females and their relationships..."

"Okay. Hey listen to this. It's a money management program. What's the deal? Oh, it seems they like debt free management. Good deal. I'm with them on that. Now what's this? Telling this woman to sell her house? That's no good. Oh, its a second house and she's got lots of debt. Okay... but it could still make money for her. These guys should consider the benefits of borrowing in order to invest."

They listened to three more callers, and then with the fourth caller, the host of the show was advising them to give their tithe to the Lord. "A Christian program?? That's quite the money management. Giving it away?" said Kole.

"We give a bit to the church, not a tenth, but some. A tenth of what I make would be too much, and besides it would be hard to figure what a tenth would be. Is it like ten percent of gross or net? Is it ten percent of the business income or just for the salary that the business pays me? The business doesn't go to church, just people go to church. But we do give some. Usually my wife writes the cheque."

"Why do you give money to a church," asked Kole. "What's the point?"

"It's good to support your community. And the church does a lot of good stuff, for the kids, for older people, for sick people. I haven't really needed it, but I go once in awhile when I'm home; Jill likes it. She goes almost all the time, and I'm okay with that. She believes in giving to the church because God gives to us first. I agree with that too, but well I think the church sometimes wastes the money. And some churches have really abused people."

Kole did not respond at first. But then he had an impulse to say something.

"Yeah, they just suck money out of you and try to control you. Lots of those preachers are just hypocrites... what about the ones who abused kids, or stole from their church, or the ones who committed adultery just like everyone else? So what's the big deal? They're not so perfect. But they pretend they are."

"My wife's church... the preacher is okay. He has a family, and he's never cheated or anything like that. He admits he's not perfect, no more than anyone else, but he sure is concerned about the kids. He seems to be a straight-up man. Sometimes he's a bit confusing. But to me he seems sincere and honest. Time will tell. But the kids like him."

"I guess some preachers are okay."

"Jill claims its not just about the preacher anyway. It's really about God. I guess she's right. But a poor preacher really messes it up. And God is not just in church. He's everywhere."

"Even here in this truck?" Kole asked skeptically.

"Yeah, probably here too."

"Wonder what he thinks of those two guys we left in the ditch. If he even concerns himself with stuff like that."

"Never thought of that." Jack replied pensively. He was starting to get uncomfortable. Probably time to change the subject. "Those guys got their own trouble. They asked for it. They got no one to blame but themselves."

"Yeah, for sure," agreed Kole. "Wonder what happened though. If they got out without too much damage, I wonder if they would still follow us, or give up and go back."

"Hard to say. Depends on how much money is involved. Or depends on how stubborn they are... or the size of their egos. Or fear of their bosses if they have any."

For awhile they were both silent, considering the possibilities, involuntarily checking the rear-view mirrors again. Then as if by mutual agreement, they began listening to the radio again. Another talk show, this time on sports. Football, mostly. Vikings and Seahawks seemed to dominate.

"Did you ever play football, Kole?"

"Just in high school. Linebacker."

"Not me. I was more interested in hockey. Played forward, center. I figured if you were going to play in the cold, might as well play on ice..."

Jack chuckled. "At least then you would be indoors, out of the wind. And more action. Even if you did have to wait on the bench for your turn to play. I liked scoring goals too."

"I liked the heavy hitting in football. Just smacking into someone to send him flying. That was great. Once in awhile someone would nail me, but I usually got him back later on in the game. Sacking the quarterback was my favorite. Felt sorry for some of them when they had a poor offensive line, but nailed them anyway. Put one guy in the hospital when he didn't see me coming. He was back out two days later, but he didn't play for the rest of that season."

"In hockey we were always checking the other guys, but no one really got hurt that I can recall. Or at least not much; a couple guys did have to go to the dressing room to get some repairs. They would stitch them right up in the dressing room, if it wasn't too bad, or just use one of those bandages to hold the skin together. One guy got a concussion when nailed from behind, but I got a penalty for that one. He should have kept his head up."

"I got a concussion once when I sacked a quarterback," said Kole. "nailed him, and sent him flying, and he lost the ball. In the scramble to get the ball, one of their guys landed right on top of me and banged my head to the ground. After the play was called down, I still had the ball, but I had no idea which way was north or south, and all the faces were a blur. Took me twenty minutes to get back to normal, and I missed the rest of the game."

"I still have a scar from when a puck hit me right in the face, in the cheek. Don't know what I was thinking… I should have got my glove up in time to catch it, but I didn't. Was trying to stop the shot from going to the goal. Can't see the scar much, but I was seeing stars for sure. Was back on for the next turn for our line though and scored a goal. Would like to play again, but this winter work doesn't let me. Just gone from home too much."

They continued to trade stories of their old sports days, revelling in the egos and testosterone, the glory of wounds and bruises, of victories and defeats.

Eventually, Jack felt sleep come on, and he crawled into the back, into the bunk to sleep.

Kole listened to his country and western music, using the earbuds so that Jack would not be kept awake by the music.

Chapter Nineteen

BY THE TIME JACK awoke, they were in Montana. The sign said 105 miles to Butte. Kole was ready to turn the wheel over to Jack, and Jack was ready to take it. It was dark, still the middle of the night, but getting closer to morning.

Kole was not interested in talking, nor was there much to see in the dark, so he went into the bunk at the back, not to sleep but to listen to his portable radio with his earbuds. Jack was fine with that. He was reminded of the last time he had been in this area, which was last summer with his family.

They had taken a vacation to Yellowstone Park about 150 miles to the east. It was the first time he had seen it, and August was polluted with sight-seers. The park was amazing, with many geysers, springs, falls, pools... 10,000 features they said. He hoped to go back again sometime as there were parts of it that they had missed. He had always heard that Old Faithful was regular as a clock, and indeed it popped up right on schedule.

The buffalo and elk in the park were also nice to see, although Jack was very familiar with buffalo and elk near his home. Some of his neighbors raised bison on their farm, and others further away raised a herd of elk.

At Yellowstone the elk were a nuisance, especially in the town of Mammoth Hot Springs. They grazed on the lawns, walked across and down the roads. Sometimes one of the elk bulls would attack a vehicle with its big rack of horns, especially during the mating season. But people in the town seemed to enjoy the elk in the summer, sitting on the decks of their cabins in their deck chairs while sipping on a latte or a beer. Interesting though that most of them would have a chain across their steps to deter the elk, who had been known to climb right up on their front porches.

The road was still clear, as Jack put his eyes on it, although there were some icy patches. The temperature had dropped, as it usually did at night, but in this area the snow that had fallen already more closely resembled the snow that Jack was accustomed to, a lighter drier snow, less sticky.

Just then, Jack was slowly passing another truck, a B-train with two trailers. He had not quite caught up with it, when they began to enter a curve. Jack was on the passing lane of the divided highway, and then noticed an icy patch on the curve. He took his foot off the gas pedal, and sure enough noticed then the other truck suddenly whip-tailing on the ice as it went through the curve. Heart in his throat, he hoped the truck would recover, and soon it did, the trucker expertly bringing the truck back into a straight line again as it entered the straight on the highway. The big trucks had a lot of rubber on the road, but ice could still cause major problems for them. Fortunately this was only a close call.

Jack's mind knew his wife and girls would be sound asleep, safe and secure in their beds right now. Once he and Kole had entered Arizona, this trip was in the same time-zone.

His mind wandered to the two Venezuelans, as he thought of them, though he knew they probably weren't from Venezuela. Who knows where they were from... Texas? California? Chicago? Who knows? Were they in the hospital? Driving on the highway? Driving north? Driving south? On a plane somewhere? Or in the morgue?

He decided to leave that train of thought alone. He couldn't do anything about it anyway. He smiled at himself grimly as he thought he had to leave it in God's hands. He was not used to being helpless, and he didn't like it. He was a "fix it" kind of guy, enjoying solving problems, finding solutions, making things work. Giving it up to God went against his nature. He was not that passive. Not that weak. That was more for wimps and for the apathetic, in his opinion. But he knew this was a loose end, that he would not do anything about, at least for now.

Jack felt the beginning of a different vibration in the truck. It became worse, and then kind of levelled off. He went through a mental checklist: engine? No, the engine sounded good. Drive train and axles? No... that didn't quite seem right. He checked his rearview mirrors as he slowed down. He noticed then that on the passenger side, one of the tires on the trailer was throwing rubber off. Better check it out.

When he stopped the truck, Kole poked his head out of the curtains dividing the bunk from the main cab. "What's up?"

"Tire trouble. I'm gonna check it out."

Kole decided to get out as well, and together they checked the tires. Jack went immediately to the right-rear, while Kole checked the rest. "Lost some retread here," said Kole on the left side of the trailer.

"There too? Here on this side some retread is coming off too. Tires are still holding air though. Well, we'll have to get them replaced at the next town. But its only five-thirty. Might have to wait a couple hours before anything opens up."

They continued on to Great Falls at a slower pace, holding their breath that the tires would hold out. Once all the tread had come off the two culprit tires, the vibration was reduced but not eliminated. It was not an ideal way to travel, but it should get them to a repair shop, hopefully.

"Wonder if the tire was damaged when we bumped those guys off the highway" said Kole.

"Thought you weren't sure you actually hit them." replied Jack.

"Well, thinking it over, I'm pretty sure now."

"Okay then. But these tires don't really look scratched or scraped. I think it's just a faulty retread."

At Great Falls, it was still dark at 6am. Businesses were closed, but they noticed a restaurant at a hotel that seemed to be open. Since they had to wait for a tire shop, they decided to have some breakfast.

Coffee first. It felt good to get out of the truck for awhile, and to talk to someone else besides themselves, even if the waitress seemed to still be waking up to the day. The breakfast buffet included bacon and eggs, toast, oatmeal, juice, cantaloupe and melons, with yogurt if they wanted it. Also milk and bananas. They ate till they were stuffed, and then sat back and read a local newspaper. A local byelection was highlighted, some news on the high-school football teams, and a statement by the local senator on the Free-trade agreement.

Jack wondered how much trouble he would have at the border, for the vehicles he was bringing across, one from Venezuela, and one from New Mexico. He anticipated paying GST for both, but sometimes additional taxes and fees would be dropped from the sky, so to speak, on things that shouldn't be taxed at all. He snorted at the "Free-trade" talk. The hype was always bigger than the reality. The barriers and obstacles were a nuisance, unproductive and costly. He jumped through the hoops. What else could he do. As long as the costs were not too high he would probably continue to buy cross-border. He shook his head. The politicians would continue to find a way to siphon money out of the taxpayer somehow.

Kole was dozing off right on his padded bench on the other side of the table. He banged his head against the window beside him, and then opened his eyes briefly, but soon closed them and dozed off again.

Jack was an ambitious guy, and he sometimes wondered how his men could often be so passive and bare bones in terms of their approach to life. As long as they had a pay cheque they would be happy. Tomorrow could look after itself, and they just wanted a place to sleep, a full stomach, and a wide-screen TV. Jack was glad these men were available for his business. He knew he was oversimplifying a bit, and some of these men did have homes and families that were important to them. In the meantime, he gave them work, provided them a living, while they made money for him. It was just the way it worked, and it suited Jack just fine.

Chapter Twenty

SEVERAL HOURS LATER, THEY were at the border.

They had gotten the tires replaced with new retreads. Many truckers used retreads on their trailers, although not on their driving wheels. The costs were significantly lower. When the retreads came loose however, as they often did, they could create hazards for other vehicles, at least for cars and small trucks.

Now, today after leaving the tire shop, they had continued their journey in blue skies and on dry roads. At the border they found themselves in a short line up. This location was never as busy as the border crossings in Ontario at Sarnia, Windsor or Fort Erie, but it did often have a few vehicles ahead in line. Vans and bulk haulers could often be held up for some time as they were inspected. Jack figured that he would be held up a bit too, since he was importing both the truck and the drill rig.

However, since Jack had Canadian plates for the truck, the paperwork was reduced. He had to pay the GST as well as a vehicle inspection fee. This was so that the truck could be shown to meet the Canadian transportation safety requirements.

The drill rig was another matter. The customs agents could not decide whether it was a vehicle or not under the highway traffic act. He made phone calls and asked questions. Since it was a tracked machine and had no lights on it and no plates and no registration, and a top speed of ten miles per hour, it was merely assessed a GST fee on the price on the Bill of Sale. But this was after another half an hour of waiting and uncertainty.

Finally they were back on the road. It felt like home because they had crossed the border into Alberta. It didn't feel entirely like home for Jack, because of the scenery, because the land was bare and flat, no trees, and just a skiff of snow. In this part of Alberta, there were frequent chinooks which melted the snow that might be there in the winter. So far this winter southern Alberta had not received much snow, not as much as Salt Lake City or Idaho Falls.

They passed Milk River. A strange name for a river which was more of a creek than a river. Jack was used to the Peace River and the Smoky River. Big rivers. Not something you could wade across, and usually too cold to swim across. A few years before, Jack had been here at the Milk River with his family, camping in their holiday trailer at Writing-on-Stone park. Erosion over the years had created some very interesting formations in the sandstone, which were called hoodoos. Although not as spectacular as Dinosaur Provincial Park and the Badlands of Alberta near Drumheller, they were still unique. The river itself was shallow, but here it broadened out and was almost waist deep in some quiet bends, where you could do some splashing and swimming.

Jack chuckled. It was hard to believe that the water in the Milk River actually ended up in the Gulf of Mexico via the Missouri and the Mississippi Rivers. In central Alberta, the rivers ended up in the Hudson's Bay, but in northern Alberta, the Peace River near his home contained more water than all the other rivers in Alberta combined. This water flowed north into the Artic Ocean.

Jack preferred the trees in the north to the wide-open spaces of Montana and southern Alberta. He liked being able to get in the shelter from the winds which were so cold in winter, and his cows also got shelter from the trees. There were two kind of people, those who like the open distant views, and those who like the trees and the shelter from the wind. Jack was one of the second group.

He did like southern open views sometimes, such as looking at the Rocky Mountains from a distance, or across the foothills, or large river valleys. But where you live is where your heart is, and the protection of trees, the new buds greening in summer or the contrast of green spruce in the white winter, and the falling of yellow leaves in fall were a part of his blood, his identity. Visiting other different exotic desert places made him realize his attraction for things back home. He was eager to see the next twelve hours of driving pass by.

Now that they were in Canada, Jack felt better in regard to the two guys who had been following them earlier. If those two guys had survived, and if they were still in action, it would be harder for them to follow them now without revealing who they were or what they were doing, due to the records kept by the custom agents at the border crossing.

Of course, nothing was guaranteed, and Jack knew they were still vulnerable to a persistent couple of guys with bad intentions. But at least he felt he was in home territory, familiar territory, where he had a few aces up his sleeve. He had a heightened sense of confidence, and his anxiety level dropped several degrees.

○ ○ ○

Jill slammed the door shut as she ran to her truck. It was cold and she needed to start it quickly to warm it up a bit. But she was in a hurry. She had to go to the hospital, to the emergency. Erin had been helping with breakfast and had decided to cut some tomatoes to put on toast. Now two of her fingers were bleeding profusely, and a simple bandage would not be enough to fix it. At first she had just looked at the damage in shock, but now she was screaming without stopping. Twenty miles to town of screaming was not something Jill was looking forward to, and she still had to dress Carla as well.

She did not think to call Jack about this incident. It just did not seem significant enough, and anyway, what could he do about it. She would have to handle it on her own.

Wrapping Erin's hand in a towel and telling her to hold on tight, she carried her to the truck and put her in the front seat. Then she brought Carla to her car seat in the back and strapped them both in. Putting the truck into gear, she stepped on the gas as fast as the truck could go without spinning on the snow. After a mile of gravel, soon she was doing 130kmh on the clear pavement towards town.

Erin was still sobbing and crying, while Carla had fallen asleep on the drive to town, as they entered the driveway to the hospital. Jill parked in the emergency lane, taking the keys out before walking to the other side to help Erin out of the vehicle. She would leave Carla in the vehicle briefly, of course realizing that leaving a young child in a vehicle was not normally a wise thing to do. But she would just bring Erin in and leave her with the nurses for a moment until she could come back to get Carla. At least that's what she thought.

After bringing in Erin, the nurse told her to sit down, and then asked her for her Medicare card, name and postal code. Just a minute, Jill told herself. After answering questions about Erin, and about her healthcare plan, she suddenly realized that she had left Carla outside in the vehicle for more than fifteen minutes. Frantic, she jumped up and ran to the vehicle.

There was Carla, still sound asleep in the vehicle, warmly dressed. Had she locked the vehicle... she couldn't remember. When she checked, she realized that she had locked it. And the keys were in the pocket of her coat, which was in the waiting room where she had become warm and automatically taken it off. Shivering and taking another quick peek at her darling Carla, she ran back to the hospital emergency to check on Erin, thinking about how vulnerable they both were, and praying for their protection.

Erin was talking to a strange man in the chair next to her. She was holding her left hand with her right, keeping the loose bandages and the towel in place while she waited for the nurses to give her some attention. She seemed quite animated as she talked to the stranger, and Jill heard her saying that her daddy was gone far away, to Texas. The man commiserated with her and asked when he was coming back.

"Pretty soon." explained Erin with the remnants of tears in her eyes. "I think he will be back home tomorrow, and Mommy will be happy again."

Jill rolled her eyes. Surely? But yes, she would be happy to see him again, home, safe and sound. But who was this stranger, and why was Erin talking to a stranger when she knew she shouldn't?

SEISMIC TRAIL

As the man turned to look at her, she realized it was a neighbor about two miles down the road. "Hello Jill. Erin is sure a talkative little girl. She has no fear, does she?"

"No... she certainly can communicate. What was she bothering you with? "

"Nothing serious. She did explain her father was away, and how she cut her fingers, and that Carla was sleeping in the truck." he smiled, happy to have someone to talk to. He was an older partly retired man who had become a widow about four years earlier, after his wife had been in a long-term care facility for about two years. The nurse called his name, and he got up, walking not too swiftly towards the nurses station, where they began to ask him some questions.

Suddenly Jill remembered Carla again, and looked for her coat. There it was, and she checked for the keys. Sure enough they were there in the right-front pocket. She wondered if she should leave Carla for a bit, but the social pressure of not leaving a young child alone in a vehicle convinced her to get up. On the other hand, did she want to leave Erin alone again? Who would she be talking to next. While she knew a lot of people in this small town, she did not know everyone. Who knows who might be coming along ... and there always seemed to be news reports of abducted children, abused children, or molested children. She was torn, deciding to take a quick look at the truck from her window. The truck seemed to be okay, no one was around. Okay, another five minutes. Maybe by then the nurses would have called Erin in.

Sure enough, in a short while, Erin's name was called and they went to the nurses station again. This time they took her past the curtain to one of the treatment rooms. Jill went along for a bit, soon asking if she could just go back to her truck to see her other little girl. The nurses smiled, saying they could handle Erin, who seemed quite content to go with them, although tears were coming again as she felt the pain in her fingers.

Jill ran as quickly as she could back to her truck. When she could not see a small head in the car-seat, she became alarmed. Where was she? How could someone take her? Who would take her? Why would they take her? Was the door unlocked somehow? Drawing nearer to the truck, she grabbed hold of the door handle and stepped on to the running board. It was then that she noticed Carla leaning completely over to one side, still fast asleep. Heart beating loudly against her chest, she let out a deep breath, tears of relief suddenly threatening her cheeks. How much she loved her little girl. How much she loved both of her little girls. She would never let anything happen to them, if she could help it.

Chapter Twenty-One

A HUNDRED AND TEN miles north-east of Jill, the tires were spinning on the snow as Tom tried to hook on to the trailer, which was still partly in the ditch. The trailer was leaning to one side, and his truck was sliding sideways as it backed under the trailer. So it missed the pin on the trailer, and Tom had to drive it back on the road, and try again. But the slight upgrade with no weight on the driver tires meant that he was spinning. Hoping he wouldn't have to put on the chains, Tom carefully tried to get enough traction, but no way it would work.

Tom had enjoyed his drive in the Mack for the last few hours and had had no difficulty finding the location of the flipped truck, by using his GPS. He had been listening to the radio, watching for deer and moose so he wouldn't run into them on the road. A herd of elk had been in one field, about a half mile from the highway, and two deer had been grazing in a ditch, but none had run across the road in front of him. The Mack had a moose bumper in front, which was a huge grill made of two inch pipe that could withstand a collision with a moose. Tom did not want to hit an animal anyway, as it made a mess of the truck, and in fact, Tom did not like destroying animals.

Tom had once hit a deer with his pickup truck. It had destroyed his bumper, his grill, his hood, radiator, and fender. Thousands of dollars later, the truck was fixed, but Tom was fortunate he had not been hurt. If he had hit a moose, which was not uncommon in this part of the world, he could have ended up in the hospital.

As Tom was about to climb out of the cab of the Mack, he saw the dozer come to the front of his truck. Bill pulled on a cable on the winch and hooked it to the truck. Then Sam on the dozer moved slowly forward and pulled the truck out of the ditch. Tom tried to line up the truck again, this time allowing for some sideways slippage, and managed to put the trailer pin exactly right into the hitch on his Mack.

After hooking up the cables, the air hoses for the brakes, and the electrical wires, he climbed back into the cab. He gingerly engaged the transmission again, wondering if the extra weight of the trailer would give him the traction he needed, or whether it would keep him from moving forward. Nope, the empty trailer was not enough weight, especially since there was still snow in front of the trailer tires. The cable was hooked on once again, and the dozer pulled the truck out of the ditch.

Now things were cooking. Tom parked the trailer on the road, and they began the second step of the operation. Two tires on the trailer had to be repaired, and the service truck which had just arrived, began to change these two tires. In relatively short order, these two tires, both outside tires on the duals, were replaced, and the old tires and rims thrown on the trailer and tied down.

Now they had to get the other truck, the Peterbilt, on to the trailer. The trailer did have some fold down ramps, but they usually were used for the drilling rigs, which were a bit narrower and lighter than a truck like the Peterbilt. The Mack had a winch on the back which would pull up the Peterbilt, which was facing the same direction as Tom's Mack. Two tow-hooks were on the front of the Peterbilt, so that made it easier.

Tom backed the trailer to the Peterbilt, and they flipped the ramps down to the ground. Then they hooked the cable to the truck, and Tom engaged the winch, and slowly brought the truck onto the ramps. The ramps began to bend under the weight. Tom pulled some more, and the front wheels were soon past the midway point on the ramps. The ramps held. The rest

SEISMIC TRAIL

of the pull was uneventful as the winch pulled up the truck while Sam was steering it.

After tying down the truck with chains and boomers, Tom was ready to head back towards the shop at headquarters. However, while Tom would enjoy the drive, he wondered about coming back to the demanding Jake in the shop. Tom was not a mechanic, nor a welder. He was a driver. He decided to stop for a coffee on the way home.

○ ○ ○

Jake was just as happy that Tom was not in his shop. He had made considerable progress on the new drill since Tom had left. He had experience in building other drills out of new and old parts in the past, so it wasn't his first time. He had a pretty good idea of how long it would take to make a new drill, and he knew when things were going smoothly, and when they were not. Right now, they were going smoothly. The frame for the drill tower was being built, and the water tank on the drill was ready to be installed.

But still, it would take several months to get it finished. Hoses, connections, mounts for the hydraulic motors and pumps needed to be installed; new engine was waiting in its crate. Jake loved the work, although he did not put on a happy face very often.

Chapter Twenty-Two

SIX HUNDRED MILES SOUTH, well actually now that he was in Canada, it was about a thousand kilometers south, Kole turned off the highway onto Stoney Trail to bypass most of Calgary. Stoney Trail was also a divided highway, a freeway that kept a lot of vehicles off the old Deerfoot Trail which was an old winding highway that curved itself through the valley in the middle of Calgary from south to north.

These trails were a subset of highway 2, which had been renamed the Queen Elizabeth II highway by a popular premier, a fact that Jack found ridiculous. What did the queen have to do with this highway? Nothing. Why not name the highway after an Albertan? Why name it after someone who spent ninety-nine percent of their life and days in Britain, and who was only nominally Canadian? Sure, Jack knew she was theoretically the monarch of Canada, but in reality, although she was probably a nice person, she was basically irrelevant to Jack. Jack bet to himself that she had less actual power than the mayor of Calgary.

Jack was sitting in the passenger seat, but noticed that the fuel gauges were getting low, and suggested to Kole that they stop in Airdrie to fuel up at a cardlock station. The road was clear and dry, with a skiff of snow in the fields nearby. The truck was running well, the tires humming, and life was good. He relaxed.

"You know, I'm getting sick of this," said Kole.

"What? What do you mean?"

"I'm getting sick and tired of this."

"Sick of what?"

"I'm still checking out vehicles to see if those guys are on the highway."

"You mean those Venezuelans?" asked Jack, sitting up straight, even while knowing already that was exactly what Kole was meaning.

"Yeah, those guys. Every black Ford Escape and everything like it makes me look to see if its them. Makes me sick."

"Forget about them. They didn't come this far. We lost them."

"I wish we knew for sure. It's the strangest thing and I don't trust it. They came a long way just to give up and go back." he thumped the edge of the seat beneath him.

"They are probably in the hospital. Or dead. Forget about them." Jack nonchalantly looked out the passenger window.

"Hah. I don't trust them. They'd probably follow us even if they were hurting. I hope you're right, but I don't trust it."

Jack mused to himself whether he was as sure as he was trying to make himself believe. He had to admit that he would not be totally surprised if he did see them somewhere. But he remained optimistic that they were out of the picture.

When they arrived in Airdrie, Jack decided to call Jill. At first there was no answer, which surprised him because she tended to carry the cell phone wherever she went. After four rings, she finally answered the phone a bit breathless.

"I'm in the hospital right now." she said.

"What happened to you? Are you okay?" Jack asked, a bit anxious.

"Oh. It's not me... its Erin. She cut her hand while cutting tomatoes. Well, she sliced two fingers and they are stitching her up."

"She cut off two fingers?? How did she manage to do that? Can they sew them back on?"

"No, no, not that. Just cut them too deep for only bandages. They are just about finished stitching. I was just coming back from the truck with

Carla who was sleeping in the truck but just woke up. I tried to wait to answer the phone until I was back in the reception room with her."

Jack was a bit speechless for a moment. Then he responded with his characteristic simple optimism, "She'll have a story to tell at school now. How is Erin taking it?"

"She screamed all the way to the hospital, but with the painkillers, she is okay now. A lot quieter. I think she is learning a lot from this experience, about how hospitals work, about doctors, about painkillers. Hopefully she is more careful next time."

"Yeah, if she wants to touch a knife again." Jack paused. "We are in Airdrie now, fueling up. Roads are good here. How about there?"

"Yeah roads are okay up here too. At least the highways are clear. I was speeding pretty good to get Erin to the hospital."

"Okay, we should be home in about nine hours if all goes well."

"Okay, I'll put the coffee on."

"Coffee sounds good, but some meat and potatoes might be even better!"

"We'll see." blandly replied Jill, knowing full well that she would have a good meal ready for her husband when he came home provided he called a couple hours before arrival. Giving the impression that he was not too important to her, was an old habit she could not break, but Jack knew her well. It was very rare that she didn't have a meal ready for him if he needed it.

And he appreciated it.

As they neared Leduc, Jack's phone rang. Kole was still driving and the roads were still clear. It was now light again, and 9:30 am, traffic a little lighter than the earlier rush hour. They would take the bypass west around Edmonton, and then head north-west towards home. Jack answered his phone, noting that the number was his office number.

"Jack here"

"Hi Jack. This is Christy, your busy bookkeeper. I just got a call from the bank saying that your account is over drawn. Should I send out the paycheques anyway, or wait? They didn't tell me what the overdraft amount was." This was not the first time such a situation had occured and Christy was not in a panic. Not yet anyway.

"Really? Overdrawn again? Okay, just wait for now... I should be home tonight. I will give the bank a call."

"Thanks Jack. I'm counting on my own paycheque too. Maybe I will just not wait on that one."

"Hah. For that one you will need my signature."

"You do remember that your wife also can sign, don't you? And she likes me more than you do."

"What a person does in his weaknesses… never give your wife signing authority!"

"Too late. And remember Bob gets real upset when we don't get paid. He's been pumping weights a lot lately and doesn't even look like an accountant anymore. Anyway, we'll see you soon?" Bob was her husband, a mild-mannered guy who pumped weights once or twice a year just so he could say he did. He did use his rowing machine four days a week. He had never been seen upset about anything, which made him an ideal contract employee for Jack's business, which could easily make less flexible people very upset from time to time.

"Yeah, in about six hours we should be home."

Jack ended the call and then punched in the bank number. "Hello Lisa"

"Hi Jack. What can I do for you?"

"I'm informed that the chequing account is over drawn."

"Let me check. … yes, it is over drawn by $37,600. What would you like to do about it?"

"Can you increase the line of credit?"

"Yes, we could. Your line of credit is not as large as last year, yet. How's your business doing?"

"Well things have been moving fast, so I didn't have time to stop in. But I have one more contract than I was expecting, and that means I had to increase my equipment as well as hire more people. We haven't increased the payroll just yet, but in two weeks that will change. And I've just bought another drill and another big truck."

"Well, that sounds normal for you, Jack. How much more will you need?"

"Just transfer $200,000 from the savings account to the chequing account, and then increase the line of credit by $300,000."

"Sounds good Jack. Will do, and I'll send you a confirmation by email when it is done."

"Great, Lisa. I appreciate your work and your bank. Have a great day!"

Chapter Twenty-Three

JAKE LOOKED OUT THE window of the shop as he heard a motor growling up the driveway. There came Tom with the truck, with the trailer, and with the wrecked Peterbilt on the trailer. Great... more work. Well, why complain about work? It kept him employed and gave him something to do.

Jake liked working for Jack, who gave him lots of independence and freedom, and together they often had fun with the challenges of repairing, rebuilding, or renovating equipment. Working on older equipment was much more enjoyable than the repairs on new equipment, where mostly it was about electronics.

As the door opened and then slammed shut against the cold outdoors, Tom asked Jake, "Where do you want the thing parked?"

"Just put it beside the big shed for now." answered Jake. "Take the Peterbilt off the trailer and put it beside the shed, but leave the trailer hooked up for now. Does it need repairs? Nevermind, I will go check for myself after you take off the Peterbilt."

"The trailer pulled okay, but one of the ramps got bent."

"I'll check the alignment on the trailer later. It's hard to tell without the laser and on a flat surface."

"Okay. I'll just get a coffee and then unload."

"Gotta satisfy that caffeine addiction, eh?" by now Jake was less upset with Tom, since he didn't have to put up with him for the last five hours. In fact, Tom was a rather unflappable fellow, a mellow kind of guy, and when just spending time together was fairly pleasant. But when trying to get him to make something or fix something, wow he could be obtuse…grrr…. thought Jake, and then realized he was working himself up over nothing at the moment. He realized that though he wouldn't admit it, he had some affection for Tom, as he did for many of the workers. Huh.

The phone rang and Jake grabbed it. "Jake." he said.

"This is Bill. Can you send Tom back here? We need a Bombi picked up, cause the engine cratered. It's one of the drills. Do you have any working spares there?"

"Just the one we just finished changing engines on. Haven't completely checked it over for anything else, but the engine is good."

"Could you send it down? Everything else on it was working okay before we sent it to you."

"I'll get right on it, Bill. Will get Tom to unload the truck and load up the Bombi. He should be able to drive it right down. Besides, it keeps him out of my shop." It'll be a couple-three hours before he gets there."

"Yeah. We'll get this one ready to load."

"Talk to ya later."

Chapter Twenty-Four

FOUR HUNDRED KILOMETERS SOUTH,
"Hi, how ya doin? "
"Good"
"How long you been standing there?"
"About an hour. I was walking before that."
"Where you going?"
"I'm headed for Fort Vermilion."
"Okay, hop in. I can't take you to Fort Vermilion, but I can drop you off near Peace River."

The dark-haired indigenous man climbed into the cab of the truck as Jack got ready to shift it back into gear. Jack had noticed the hitchhiker standing on the shoulder of the road with his small backpack a few miles past Mayerthorpe. These days one did not see so many hitchhikers anymore, compared to several decades ago. Occasionally they still appeared, mostly indigenous men going to a job or coming back home. Sometimes they went to Edmonton for medical appointments, or to some town to the employment office.

Kole was sleeping in the back, and Jack had taken over the wheel, and on impulse had decided to pick up the hitchhiker. Sometimes he could find another employee that way, and if not, at least it was someone different to talk to.

Soon they were back up to cruising speed, and Jack asked the man if he lived right in Fort Vermilion or nearby.

"I'm from Jean D'Or actually. But most people don't know where that is."

"I've been there," said Jack.

For some moments there was silence. Often an uneasy peace existed between the natives and the whites until they could figure out each other's attitudes. The continual struggles between native rights and white farmers and ranchers and oilmen meant that people became careful about what they said that might impact their rights, or what might impact the financial compensation awarded to the natives by the oil companies. "Traditional uses" was a favorite code phrase for putting a claim on government owned land, even though it was not a reserve or settlement area. They liked to be called "First Nations" to give them legitimacy in negotiating with federal government authorities. Presumably it put them on equal footing with provincial governments, although usually the provincial governments provided them with all kinds of services under provincial jurisdiction. Such as healthcare and education and most highways.

But in this case, the silent pause was merely a common human condition about wondering what to say next, if anything, when two total strangers knew they might spend the next four hours travelling together in an enclosed space, a vehicle front seat. How much is personal, or confidential, and how much might the other person be willing to share... How much do you want them to know about yourself... Is he a decent person, or a maniac psychopath?

"Do you still live there, or just going for a visit?"

"Going for a visit between jobs," replied the man. "Going to visit my brothers, and maybe visit my girl..."

"Well, my name is Jack. I hope you have a good visit up there."

"I'm Richard." He said the name with a french accent... reeesharde. "I haven't been there for almost a year." The man had shoulder length black hair, tied in a ponytail. He looked to be in his early thirties, a healthy strong man, with a pleasant smile. "Last time was for a pow-wow up there, summer a year ago. Got friendly with a girl but haven't seen her since. Don't even know if she's still interested in me, 'cause I don't write and haven't called."

"don't use facebook or email?" asked Jack.

"No. Never bothered with a cell-phone. Should get one, but just never have."

"Think she'll be waiting?"

"Maybe."

"Parents live there?"

"Mother is there. Father died when I was ten."

Conversation continued between them at this pace for the next twenty miles. Soon Reeshard knew about Jack and his business and a little about his family, his two girls. Jack learned that Richard had worked in logging and oilfield before, as well as in fire fighting forest fires, which was a common summer occupation for many aboriginals and Metis in the north. Richard's brothers had traplines, and also fished and hunted for additional food and income. One of his brothers was a guide for American hunters, and he had built a cabin as a type of low-cost hunting lodge and hunting headquarters.

"We'll stop for a meal at Whitecourt", said Jack. "and the meal is on me."

"Oh, I'm okay, I can pay for my own" said Richard.

"Yeah, sure, but I'm going to pay anyway" replied Jack. "It'll be on my expense account. Maybe you will work for me someday. Call it a recruiting expense. In fact, here's a business card with my phone number."

When they entered the full-service restaurant, Jack grabbed a news paper to look at while eating. After sitting down, he looked at the headlines. "Look at this, Kole. Those ISIS guys just captured another 80 young girls from a boarding school. And here in a different incident, four more guys hauled to a beach and beheaded." He shook his head. "Makes you wonder what makes those guys tick. I mean how do they justify their attacks on innocent people?"

"They're sick." Kole's brief, succinct comment.

"Could you call them insane?" wondered Jack aloud. "Does their religion really drive them to do this? Or do they just use their religion to justify their evil nature?"

"Maybe it is about territory, and testosterone." interjected Richard.

"Just having a purpose. A cause." Kole replied.

"Everyone wants a cause. But why not pick a good cause? Why pick an evil mean cause?"

"They think their cause is just. Or so they say."

"So they are not just defending themselves. They are attacking innocents, raping and murdering. They say it is part of a larger battle where everyone is a soldier." Jack was getting worked up. "Does that justify our defending ourselves from them by going to their country and bombing them? They will attack anyone, and would come here to attack us if they could."

Kole agreed. "Get them where they are, and don't let them spread. The USA has that right."

But Richard wondered… "How do we know we aren't doing the same thing as them, then? And giving them more reason for their beheadings and kidnappings."

"Somehow you just have to decide. Can you convince them to stop, or can you only force them to stop with greater firepower. We try to do things by persuasion, not by kidnapping young girls, beheading people just to terrorize and make a point. They use different methods, which is only terror and power at the end of a gun. No democracy in that, and no freedom. No life for children, orphans or widows. Just terror. They have to be stopped." That was Jack's summation, as the waitress walked up to their table with a coffee pot in her hand.

"How are you guys this morning? Have you decided what you want to eat?"

Jack ordered the bacon and eggs and pancakes, and Kole and Richard followed suit. Jack was paying after all. The waitress filled their cups with coffee, and then left to bring their order to the cook.

Richard tentatively offered this thought in his gravelly voice… "ISIS is a threat, right?"

"Yeah, they are."

"So should we beat them to it? If someone threatens your life, do you have the right to kill them first? Or do they have to actually look like they can carry it out?"

Both Jack and Kole were also considering the Venezuelans who had pursued them, but neither one mentioned those two men to Richard or to each other.

"Good question. How do you judge actual intentions. A lot of empty threats have been made. I hear kids telling other kids they are going to kill them for this insult or that, but everyone knows they are not literally serious. They are just expressing their feelings or displeasure, and sometimes it is even just a bit of a joke."

Kole put in his two-bits... "And then there's the odd kid who does bring a gun to school and shoot a bunch of classmates. Or at a university."

"It would be easier to deal with a threat to myself, than to my kids or to my wife." said Jack. "If someone threatened me, I might even think I deserved it, or at least would have to deal with it and give the guy every chance to change his mind, or to prove his real intentions. But if someone threatened my family, I would err on the side of protection. It's no joke. It would be a bad threat to make."

Silence took over as the three men pondered the various possibilities and consequences.

"But the law. What would the police do? And what would the courts think?"

"Too often the courts protect the bad guys. They use the excuse of innocent until proven guilty. They use the excuse of unreasonable search and seizure of evidence. They try to protect the innocent, but often end up protecting the guilty, and letting the innocent victims suffer."

"Police have to follow the law. But sometimes I think they would like to push the limits of the law to catch the bad guys."

"Sometimes the police make mistakes. Sometimes they are biased. Even racist." This from Richard.

"Yeah, sometimes they make mistakes. A few are racist. But I have to say it really riles me up when they find evidence and it gets thrown out just because they didn't get a warrant." Jack was firm on this.

"What about when they plant evidence? A friend of mine said they planted drugs on him so they would have some evidence of his drug using." Kole related this tidbit.

"Was your friend a user?"

"Yeah, he did use drugs. Even sold some. But the time he was arrested, he had none on him. He had made sure to ditch it when he saw them coming."

"So then...." Jack left the sentence unfinished.

Silence again paused the conversation. More possibilities. More consequences.

Jack decided this was enough. Time for some lighter topics. "Look who they have running for president in the USA now. Hillarious." and the conversation carried on awhile on that and other topics such as the weather, sports, and a serious vehicle accident between a semi with grain trailers and a pickup truck driven by a 22 year old in which the young driver had been killed. The pickup had crossed the median on the highway and ran head on into the semi, a loaded Freightliner with 40 tonnes of grain. The pickup had burst into a flaming inferno before anyone was able to rescue the driver.

Soon they were quiet, each one eating his breakfast which had been delivered to the table, along with a second cup of coffee. The waitress diligently looked after their needs, and they were content. The food was good, warm, and filling.

When nearly finished, Jack had decided that Richard was not a maniac psychopath, but just an ordinary guy who tried to make a living and find his way in life. "Have you got a job waiting for you up north?"

"Not at present. I have a possible job next spring and summer with the fire fighters, but nothing right now." replied Richard.

"I've got some work, if you're interested. Pays good, and you can start right away."

Richard hesitated.

Jack continued, "I guess your brothers are waiting for you. And that girl. She's sitting on the edge of her seat, looking through the window for you coming walking down the drive."

Richard grinned. "Yeah, she hasn't eaten in a whole year because she hasn't seen me. And my brothers are heart-broken."

"If they knew you were coming..."

"Which they don't"

"Since you don't have a cell-phone," interjected Kole.

"I was really set on going to Fort Vermilion..." mused Richard.

"$600 per day plus expenses," said Jack. "If you work out. And after two weeks, you can take a break and go to Fort Vermilion. I might even be able to find you a ride. Or at least I will pay your bus ticket."

"Sounds good," responded Richard. "I can wait two weeks for my visit."

"No drugs. No alcohol on the job site. No fighting. And show up on time."

"Sounds good," said Richard. "Don't touch alcohol anyway, since my Dad died from alcohol. Haven't done drugs for three years now."

"All right then, that's settled. We will be dropping you off near Peace River with the guys who are working there now."

Richard pondered the quick change in his plans and appreciated the promise of some considerable pay to improve his personal cash flow. A quick change in plans was not new for him, but always nice when the change in plans was due to a promise of better things rather than an accident or broken promise.

As Jack paid for the meal, Kole and Richard walked back to the truck. Kole asked if Richard would like the bunk in the back for a while, and Richard was agreeable to that.

Soon they were on the road again, now keeping wide eyes open for deer and moose crossing the highway. Although they were a bit behind schedule, due to picking up the hitchhiker and stopping for a full meal, it was still mid afternoon, and deer would be easier to see than at dusk, or just after dark, when both deer and moose tended to wander across highways from grazing areas to bedding down areas, and when they were particularly difficult to see.

For awhile, all was quiet in the cab as they pondered the things they had been talking about while eating. Soon a quiet snoring was heard in the bunk behind them.

○ ○ ○

Seventeen hours south, two slim men, one taller than the other, walked painfully out of a hospital in Salt Lake City. The taller man had a cast on his left arm, and a large bandage on his head. The other man was using a crutch and favoring his right leg, which had a cast on the foot. His right hand was also bandaged up, and he had some scrapes on his forehead and right cheek. The man with the arm cast managed to pull a cellphone from his right front pocket, hold the phone lightly with his left hand, and punch in some numbers. After a conversation with an acquaintance, he then dialed another number. After some time, a green GMC Denali pickup truck pulled up, the driver leaving the vehicle for another vehicle which had followed. The two men entered the Denali and the man with a cast on his arm sat behind the wheel. They pulled out of the hospital parking lot and followed the streets to the main highway. They headed north.

Chapter Twenty-Five

DARKNESS DESCENDED LIKE A fog now as they came down the hill into Peace River. Leaves had separated from the trees, except of course for the green spruce that spotted the north facing banks of the river. It was now dusky, and hard to pick out the spruce from the dark shadows. Two micro- climates existed in this river valley... north facing south banks were usually covered with spruce, especially when the 900 foot high river banks were steep. The north banks, which faced south, often tended to be dry, grass covered slopes, sometimes almost desert environments, even containing cactus and garter snakes. The valleys in the creeks that fed the river were also very deep, and if they travelled north or south, then most of their banks were covered with aspen, sometimes interspersed with grass or spruce.

As they came down the 6% grade into the town, which spread out on both banks of the river, they could see the lights ahead in the valley. Construction was happening on the overpasses and the bridge, but it was almost finished for the year, since it was getting too cold for this kind of work. The highways on the banks of the Peace River were always the first to be snow plowed and sanded, since they were so long and steep.

Jack's stomach was rumbling. "Hey guys, you hungry?"

Richard had been awake for an hour, and Kole was still in the front seat. "I'm game to eat if you are." Richard agreed with a simple, "Yuh."

Jack decided to cross the river, and then halfway up the hill on the other side, pulled off to a restaurant which he had eaten at numerous times before. It was not a fancy eating place, but the food was satisfactory and filling, and it usually arrived in a reasonable time.

As they waited for their meals, Jack prepped Richard on some of the work he would be doing with the seismic drillers. "I'll start you off as a driller's helper. You'll be packing the dynamite and leads and stuffing the holes the driller makes. He will show you how to do it, and then you will be hoofing it to keep up to him. He gets paid by the hole, and he will expect you to keep up."

Jack paused. "But first you will come to the shop, and see what goes on there, and help out around there for a day, until the crew is ready to start drilling at the new site. And fill out some paperwork. And take a quick safety course."

Richard nodded. Jack went on, "I assume you have your driver's license in good order?"

Richard nodded again. He wasn't saying much, but his eyes seemed to indicate understanding. "You have any questions?"

"Not really. Wondering when we start and quit."

"In the morning, we want to start drilling when it gets light. Days are short in winter, and we need the time. But usually we're done before dark, with the drilling, depending on the ground, how much rock, or sand, or clay. And depending on what the job calls for, depth of holes, and number of holes per mile. And then we have to drive back to town to the hotel, unless we have a camp we can stay at. Sometimes we only drill for about six hours, other days it will be two or three hours more."

Paused again. "Have to get up in time to eat, warm up the vehicle, and be on the road before daylight, so to be at the job site by daylight. Your driller will let you know."

"Safety regulations mean you have to fill out some safety sheets every morning. It's a nuisance, but just do it as fast as you can. Your driller will help you with that too."

Kole interjected, "Here comes the food. Smells good already!" They thanked the waitress, who was wife of the cook, and had already given them coffee. Then they pitched into the food and stopped talking.

○ ○ ○

"We are in Peace River, Jill. Eating. I found a new worker too. And I should be home in a couple hours." Jack held his phone to his ear.

"Well, that's nice to know. Erin and Carla will be glad to see you. I'll keep them up till you get home, so don't waste any time."

"Absolutely. Looking forward to seeing them again. And you too, of course. You too."

"Bye"

"Yeah, bye. See yah."

○ ○ ○

Two hours later, Jack, Kole and Richard entered Jack's yard in their new truck, with another "new" seismic drilling rig on it. Jack honked the horn three times. Loudly.

Erin came out on the doorstep and waved, as Carla stood behind her. Then Jill quickly shooed them inside, and also waved once, briefly, as Jack drove the truck past the house and into the work area, in front of the shop. He left it running, and then brought Richard into the workshop, and pointed up the stairs.

"Up there is a coffee/lunchroom. And a bunk room beside it. You can stay there tonight... It has four beds, but there's no one else in it right now, so you have your choice of bunks. There is coffee and tea. And some snacks in the cupboard, and in the fridge. Help yourself. See you at the house for breakfast at 7."

Jack didn't often invite employees into the house for meals, or breakfast, but in this case he would make an exception. At least one time. It would give his wife a chance to evaluate, and he valued her opinion. Kole would go home for the night as he lived nearby.

After being gone for three days, Jack was looking forward to spending some time with his family. Especially his wife. Just the two of them. Alone. He was a young man after all, and she was a pretty woman. And the girls would go to bed soon. Better read them a story first though. Or maybe just tell them a story about his trip. They would like that.

o o o

In the morning, Richard showed up at the door, promptly at 7am.

"Come on in Richard." said Jill as she opened the door for him. "You like coffee in the morning?"

"Yup. Sure do."

"Well just put your coat over here, and your boots can stay over there," she said, pointing to the coat rack, and then to a corner of the floor where other footwear was prevalent.

"Washroom is just down the hall, and then you can grab a chair at the table. Breakfast is almost ready, and the girls are hungry too."

He had already used the washroom at the shop but decided to wash his hands again anyway. Then Richard came to the kitchen, and found Jack already sitting there. But Jack was busy checking the news on his cellphone, and also smiling at his daughters.

"Sit down Richard. Jill poured you a cup of java. You can add whatever cream and sugar suits you."

Then he turned to the girls. "You ready for school, Erin? Got your lunch ready?"

"Yes daddy. I've still got twenty minutes before the school bus comes. Don't worry."

"I made a lunch too, Daddy." said Carla. She would be staying home, but liked to do what Erin did, so she made a lunch which she would remind mom about at noon. Then she would take it out of the fridge and she would pretend to be at school eating lunch with her friends, just as Erin had told her about.

Jack sometimes couldn't believe how blessed he was with the two girls. Sure, a boy would have been nice. I mean what dad doesn't want a boy. A boy who could follow him around. A boy who could learn to fix machines or drive them. Who could stand the severe cold weather, and work right through it. A boy who would play basketball and hockey like the boys of his foreman Bill. A boy who would drive a quad as fast as it could go.

But these two girls had wormed their way into his heart, from the time Jill was pregnant. And more so besides, with their antics, their ebullient natures, and their admiration for their dad. Besides, they were cute... as an unbiased father he had to admit the obvious. And maybe, who knows? They might like to play basketball or drive a quad. Erin already was driving her little 40cc minibike around the yard. Who knows where her interests would take her in the future.

Jill didn't sit down with them, as she was too busy bringing and fetching and making food. Well, sometimes she would sit briefly, but never for long, because something would need doing, like more coffee, or combing Erin's hair, or finding a sock, clearing a dirty dish or two. Jack ate somewhat absent-mindedly, part of his mind trying to organize the days activities, while the other half of his mind was just breathing in the loveliness and liveliness of his girls. So good to be home!

"Do you need a lunch today, Jack? Or will you be at home for lunch?"

"A lunch would be good. Yesterday I thought we would spend the day here, but I think we will be leaving before noon, after the paperwork is done, and general safety course is finished. Richard might as well join the crew in the field. It will give him half a day to see what is happening there, before he starts full speed tomorrow."

"Okay. I'll make you a few sandwiches to take along. You'll be home for supper tonight?"

Jack was busy looking at his cellphone and didn't answer right away.

"I said, will you be home for supper tonight?" Jack looked up with a bit of a distracted look. "You know, there's a news item just came up. It says a dozen people were found hanging from a bridge, yesterday."

"Really? That's terrible. Was that in the middle east somewhere?"

"No. It was in northern Mexico. Probably drug trafficking related. Gangs. It's not the first time. But for some reason it bothers me more today than usual. A dozen people. Hanged for everyone to see. And the Mexican government, what does it do? What can it do? Some of the Mexican police and government are involved in these gangs too. How do they get them out, or get them neutralized?"

"Sounds bad. But it's a long ways away. We are not planning any Mexican trips soon."

"Mexico is not that far. We were almost on the border, at Corpus Christi. And drugs flow across borders. Along with the violence, crime, shootings and gangs. They don't have any respect for any laws, except how to get around them. Or to use them for their own criminal benefit."

"Aren't you getting a bit more upset than you need to be on this? How do you know that the dozen hanged were not involved in drugs themselves? One gang taking out another."

"It says in here that those who were hanged were local farmers, not gang members. They included men, two women, and a child of ten years old. They are trying to intimidate the innocent, the farmers, landholders, into turning a blind eye, out of fear. Or to grow drugs for them."

Jack did not mention the two men who had followed them and tried to get hold of the drilling rig he had bought. He didn't want to worry Jill. But he himself was still worried about those men. He had a nagging suspicion that they had not given up, unless they were dead.

"Bye Mommy. Bye Daddy. Bye Mr. Richard." said Erin, as she opened the door to get to the road before the bus got there. It was dark outside, barely lightening in the east, as the door slammed and then her quick footsteps could be heard crunching on the hard packed snow, as she trotted down the driveway.

Jill looked out the window to the west, to the road, and saw the red lights of the school bus flashing as it waited for Erin to get on. It was too dark to see Erin, but soon the red lights quit flashing, and the bus started up the road again, to the next stop, about a half mile down the road. The lights of the bus were soon lost behind the trees, which hid the road from their house, and the sound of the bus engine also disappeared gradually into the quiet of the wintry morning.

Jack sipped on his coffee and pondered the fact that his young daughter started her day before he did. The hour-long bus ride was taken for granted, but it was nevertheless a long addition to the day at school. Erin would be gone from 7:30 in the morning to almost 4:30 in the afternoon. Kids were tough though, and when she came home, she would still often like to play for a half hour outside before supper.

They had a good bus driver this year, but sometimes the bus drivers were not up to par. They would let the kids do what they wanted, and that often led to the teasing and bullying that made life miserable on the bus for the younger ones. Erin neither enjoyed the bus ride nor hated it. She did have a friend who came on the bus to sit with her, but that was only the last fifteen minutes of the ride in the morning, and first fifteen minutes on the trip home.

"Let's go Richard. Lots of paperwork to fill out."

"I can show him what needs doing, if you want." said Jill.

"Thanks, but I'll do it this time. I want to show him around the shop anyway."

"Okay, but make sure you get his Alberta Healthcare number. We don't want to be looking all over for it in an emergency."

Jack and Richard put on coats and hats and gloves and boots, and then headed out the door, after Jack took the last sips out of his coffee cup.

As they walked into the warm shop, they took off their gloves and hats, and then walked to the office, which was just below the coffee room upstairs. Jack opened a filing cabinet, then removed forms and placed them on the table which had a few chairs around it. "You can fill these out right here. If you have any questions, just ask."

"And when you are done with those, I'll go through the safety discussion with you, and then you can fill out some more forms and sign them."

The phone rang and Jack answered it. "Jack here."

"Is the drill ready to go? We need it here." That was Bill.

"You serious?"

"Partly. The drill we got yesterday is running, but don't know how long it will last. It was sputtering yesterday. Jake said the engine was good, but it doesn't seem that good. Don't know why. And a bearing on the right-hand tracks is gone. Tracks still go, but its wearing stuff out."

"Okay." Jack was thinking now. "trouble is we haven't tried out this new drill yet. So we don't know if it has any problems or not. I drove it on the truck, and it sounded good. But haven't really tried the hydraulics, nor checked the bearings, nor serviced it yet. I'll check it out, and if its good to go, we'll get it there this afternoon. Alright?"

"Okay. We'll keep going. The other drills are working fine."

Just then, Kole walked in. "What ya got for me today, boss?"

"I want you to check out the new drill. If its all good, then you'll bring it to Bill and bring back the one he is using, which needs some fixing up. I'll help you check out the new drill after I get Richard all set up. He will go with you. Keep your eyes open for anything unusual."

"Like what?"

"I don't know. But those guys wanted this drill for something illegal. Who knows what it was, or where it might be on that machine."

Kole grabbed a form from the rack. A rack on the wall held a number of different forms which mostly related to fulfilling various safety requirements. This form was a daily pre-work safety form, indicating what safety factors needed to be considered before the job began. It contained a number of questions, such as "what kind of safety equipment does this job require? And what type of safety procedures should be performed?" Kole indicated, among other things, that this was medium hazard activity, where helmet and gloves were not required, but steel-toed boots would be advisable. He would start the machine, and then operate the hydraulic drill with all its options, and check for leaks, cracks, cracked hoses, missing bolts, seized bearings, etc.

"Oh, and Kole. Check the oil too. And change it if its dirty. And grease the bearings. Check the antifreeze. Transmission fluid, and brake fluid cylinders, too. And hydraulic fluid levels. "

"Will do, boss." Kole would have checked most of those things anyway, but he had not thought about checking the anti-freeze. He wondered if the antifreeze was at the right measure for cold weather. It should be at -35C, but they had not checked it before. It had not been exceptionally cold on the trip, but certainly had been below freezing. If the antifreeze was just water, it could freeze and crack the block. Although he knew that Jack would accept responsibility, he worried about not thinking about this before.

"Make sure the drive cogs are not worn off too much too, Kole. If they are not good enough, we will have trouble in the field in the snow and the cold."

Kole took a quick look at the drive cogs, and there was lots of wear left on them. But he noticed a few bolts missing in the tracks and put that in the back of his mind to replace the missing bolts later. First, before he missed it, he would check the anti-freeze. He grabbed a tester from the back of the shop, and then opened the radiator cap. He inserted the tester, grabbed some fluid, and looked at the gauge. It showed temperature good to -10C. This meant he would have to drain it and put new fluid in, to get it to -35C.

"How are you doing with those forms, Richard?" Jack had gone back to the office to see if Richard was having any problems.

"Don't have the information on what level to fill out for income tax deductions." replied Richard.

"That's all right. We'll put down a rough figure. How much did you work this year?"

Richard told him he had worked about five months that year, and what his average wage had been. Jack did some quick mental calculations, and wrote down a reasonable figure on the form.

"Taxes deducted won't be that high, cause you were not working full time. But we want to take enough off so you don't get stuck paying extra taxes next spring. Okay, you got the forms done. Let's have a quick safety discussion, then you can fill out a safety form for practice."

Jack proceeded to explain about the hazards of the job, from the equipment to the weather, to fatigue, to other workers. Then Richard filled out the daily startup form, and Jack had a look. "Looks good, Richard. I think you got it. We try to do these as quick as possible, because it cuts into our productivity. But on the other hand, we don't want people getting seriously hurt, either. Losing a fingernail, or the top of your ear to frost-bite is your decision. But we don't allow people to lose a foot or a leg, because it slows you down too much when you are following the drill truck." Jack grinned, and Richard acknowledged the humor with a grin of his own. "So watch yourself."

Chapter Twenty-Six

KOLE ROLLED OUT OF his bed in the back of the Kenworth truck and rubbed his eyes. It was light out, and his stomach was rumbling. He must have slept well, but much longer than he expected.

Yesterday, everything had taken longer than expected. Jake had inspected the new drill and didn't want to send out a big problem to Bill. They replaced four hydraulic lines, changed the oil, and noticed two rollers on the track drives needed to be replaced. By the time they made the changes, greased all the bearings, and loaded the drill on the truck it was five hours later. Jake was already clocking overtime, and now Kole had to bring the drill to the worksite. But it was dark.

Kole drove to Peace River and met up with the crew there. Then decided to wait until tomorrow to unload, and after some visiting, and a beer and pizza, Kole went into the truck for the night. In this weather, he had to keep the truck running because he had no way of plugging it in for the block heaters. This truck also had an auxilary interior heater since an idling diesel engine did not give off much heat. The rumbling of the engine had purred Kole to sleep. This morning, the rest of crew had not woken him. He guessed they were eating breakfast without him... or maybe gone already, since it was already light outside.

The restaurant at the truck stop was beckoning to Kole, or at least to Kole's stomach, and he needed a caffeine fix. His phone was buzzing.

"Where are you?" he heard the voice, and it took him a minute to realize that Bill was talking.

"I'm coming. Just at the truck-stop. Need some coffee and I'm on my way." he replied.

No point in telling them he wanted breakfast. Bill would just ask why he hadn't set his phone alarm. He would grab something to go, and then head out to the job site.

He walked to the store, filled his coffee cup, picked up a sandwich, then thought again, and picked up two more. He might not be back by lunch. Paid for everything and stepped out of the store. Looking toward his truck, he saw a young man, maybe an older teen, standing on the running board of the truck, looking in the cab with the door open. "Hey!! What you doing in that truck!!?" He began a half run towards the truck, trying not to spill coffee or drop his sandwiches.

The man dropped down, not bothering to close the door, and ran off to the back of the truck, towards a vehicle standing there with a driver inside. With free hands, he ran much more quickly than Kole, and the vehicle left the parking lot. It was a midsize car, about ten years old. Kole quickly checked the cab of the truck, mentally cursing himself for not locking the door. Had they taken anything? Done any damage? No, everything looked like it was still there, and he had taken his phone and wallet with him. The truck was still running. He decided that they were looking for something to steal, but he must have caught them before they could do anything.

However, Kole was now on edge. He double-checked all the chains and tires on the trailer, the fuel caps, boomers and tire chains, and decided no harm done. He decided to forget about it, jumped in the cab again, and took a sip of coffee. Then he pulled out and headed to the job site. Once he had shifted through all the gears, he took another sip of coffee, and opened the breakfast sandwich. Traffic on the highway was light. It would be an hour to the job.

Meanwhile, at the job site, Bill had his crew warming up machinery. Most of the machines started after about a half hour of warming, but the drill that was going to be exchanged was causing problems. The working machines began driving out to the lines to where they had stopped yesterday, and soon the two- man crews were drilling and planting dynamite again. It was minus 26C this morning and promised to warm up to a balmy minus 15C, which equated to +5F. Bill wanted to get the last machine running so it could be driven on the truck when Kole arrived. Then he would get the water bomby filled with water so he could resupply the drills with the water they used for lubricating the drill bits while drilling their holes. They would be drilling to 40 feet down on some of their holes in this job.

He grabbed a large tarp, actually it was part of an old used parachute purchased from army surplus, and he draped it over the machine. Then he put a propane heater under the tarp and soon it was getting warm underneath. After a half hour, he tried starting the machine again, but the batteries had lost too much power. He grabbed a booster pack and connected it, then turned the starter again. Finally, after a lengthy turning over there were a few puffs of smoke from the engine. Then, another minute of revolutions, the engine coughed and sputtered to life, a kind of uneven pulsing roar which would be enough to keep it going. Bill removed the tarp, folded it up and put it back in the box of his truck. Time for a sip of coffee.

Bill had been doing this kind of work for two decades already. Before that, he had worked for a couple of years as a rig hand, on the big drilling rigs. That was a bit more intense, sometimes drilling through the night, with huge lights showing the equipment, and the crews working in shifts. Drilling rigs were expensive, and when times were good, the more they worked, the more they made money for their owners. But the intensity also led to friction, to long hours, and to accidents. Bill had lost a buddy on a rig when a chain slipped and his buddy got hit on the head with some pipe. It was not long after, that he looked for a different type of work, and began to work on the seismic drilling.

These drills were much smaller, and they did not work often at night, since they were moving through fields and through bush. Occasionally they might work a bit for an hour or two if the moon was particularly bright, but only if they were behind schedule, or had unusual problems during the day, or had only a few holes left to do on a particular line.

After working on a seasonal basis for several different operators for several years, about twelve years ago, Bill had begun to work for Jack. Jack had made him foreman after one season, and found off season work for him as well, either in recruiting helpers, fixing equipment, or driving equipment to various locations, or back to base. Bill worked from six to ten months of the year for Jack, depending on the year. He had a wife and three teen-age boys, and they lived in Peace River.

Bill usually had the summers off, and could spend time camping with his family, or boating on the lake. Bill liked his toys, including the two quads, a side by side, and three dirt bikes, and a thirty-five foot fifth wheel holiday trailer. He did not live exactly in Peace River, but nearby, on a ten acre parcel which gave him plenty of room for all his stuff.

While sipping his coffee in his insulated cup, waiting for Kole to show up, Bill was thinking about his life, his family, his summers. Every year was different, but most years paid the bills quite well, and his mortgage was nearly paid off, while his toys were bought on a cash basis. Sometimes the work would be farther away, perhaps six hours, or ten hours away, making it difficult for him to attend all the basketball games of his 14 year old and 15 year old boys. A few times they had even been sent to jobs in eastern Canada, such as Quebec or New Brunswick.

He could hear the rumble of a truck coming. Sure enough, there was the Kenworth, with the new drill from Venezuela on the trailer. In a couple hours, if all went well, it should be out in the field drilling, and the old drill going back to the shop for repairs. Bill would operate this one himself, taking a man off the water bomby to be his helper.

o o o

Jack and Richard drove into the job site just after lunch time. They had picked up some pizza slices at the convenience store in Grimshaw, and now were sipping on some coffee from their insulated cups. No one was at the site, since everyone was out in the field working. They had passed Kole headed in the opposite direction, with the old drill on his trailer.

Richard and Jack had not left for the job site yesterday after all. They had spent time on the new drill with repairs. And then Jack had toured Richard around the yard, showing him the equipment that remained in the yard, including some brushing machines he had purchased last summer. Had Richard ever operated a machine like that? No, but he was willing to try.

Jack had put Richard to work in the shop for awhile, where he followed Jake's direction to put some things away, sweep up part of the floor, and help Jake with holding some parts for the new rubber-tired drill under construction in the shop. Afterwards, Jake had indicated that Richard was catching on fairly well. Maybe Richard could be an assistant in the shop later... Jack filed that away in his mind.

This morning, after breakfast, Jack, Richard and Tom had brought the bent ramp into the shop, and spent some time straightening it, and re-bracing it before putting it back on the trailer. Then they had headed out to the job site where Bill and the others were drilling holes. Meanwhile, Tom was working on the other beavertail ramp.

Jack called Bill on his cell. "Where you at? I've got a new guy here. Where can you use him?"

"I'm on a line two miles north of you. You could bring him here. Is he dressed and ready for work?"

"Yeah, he is all papered up, fed up, and dressed up. Ready to go. No experience so needs training."

"He can walk?"

"Yeah. He's been firefighting and logging."

"Okay. He can help me, and I'll get Freddy to load up the water-bomby."

"Sounds good. We'll be there in a bit." Turning to Richard, while he turned the truck around, he said, "Bill is a good guy. He will show you what's what. I'll drop you off with him and bring his helper, Freddy, back here to the water tanker. We call the drills and the water tankers, bombys. Hopefully they don't bomb out on us too often."

"Bombies?"

"That's short for bombardier, tracked machines. That's what most of them are, though we have a few other makes too. You will learn as you go."

"Appreciate the opportunity. I like learning new jobs and new equipment."

"Well, you'll get your chances after awhile. Today you learn to be a helper. It'll only be a half day, but the rest of the week you'll earn your keep."

"Sounds good."

"Hope your boots are good enough but get ready for blisters. If you need different boots, let me know. Try to keep your gloves on as much as possible. If your hands get too cold, you will start to have trouble handling the dynamite and wires. But the walking usually warms you up. You are lucky the snow is only ten inches deep... but you can walk in the track of the drill bomby most of the time."

Richard realized that although his new boss had a sense of humor, he took his work seriously. And he seemed to care about his workers. He hoped he could keep up to the demands of the job, but he was optimistic. He was in pretty good shape and loved the outdoors. Sun was shining today, and just a slight breeze. He was eager to get out there and see what he could do.

When they arrived at Bill's drill, the one from Venezuela, they both got out and walked to the machine. Jack wanted to have a good look at it in the daylight, while it was working. "How is it running?"

"Not bad. Engine hesitates once in awhile, but not serious. Generally reasonable. Could fix or upgrade a few things when we have time, but its okay for now. Hydraulics once seemed low on fluid, the way it was acting. But I checked, and fluid is okay. Haven't had any problems since."

Bill finished the hole he was working on, and then put the drill in position for moving to the next hole, about 100 yards away. They walked around the machine, and discussed its operation, and what might need some work in the off season. Freddy by now had caught up to them, with his bentonite and poles in hand, and introduced himself to Richard. Freddy was a younger fellow, not quite 20 years old, and curious about Richard's experience.

"You want to watch me do one hole before I leave?" asked Freddy.

"That would be good." Freddy grabbed a dynamite gel cartridge from the back of the track drill, and also a blasting cap with attached wires from the other side. He cut a hole into the dynamite cartridge and inserted the blasting cap. The attached wires had been cut to match the depth of the holes being drilled for this job. He attached a plastic cone to the downward side of the blasting gel, and then pushed the whole thing down the hole with special ten foot wooden poles with brass hook ends, which connected together and couldn't be separated until the poles were free from the hole.

The wire ends were left out of the hole so they could later be connected to power and ignite the blasting caps by the seismology crew which followed a few days later. He poured some bentonite into the hole to plug off the top of the hole and hold the wire ends at the surface.

Meanwhile, Bill left for the next spot, and began to drill the next hole. When Freddy was done, he picked up the four poles and the pail of bentonite, and then walked to the track drill where Bill was drilling. Then the whole sequence would be repeated.

The seismology crew would come later, perhaps a few days or week later, with their seismic recording truck. They would lay out the geophones and set up the connections to the wire ends which were sticking out of the ground. They would ignite the dynamite and would read and record the soundwave reflections coming back. From those readings they could later make a diagram of the density and shape of layers far below the surface, which would give them an indication of the potential for finding oil or gas below.

Richard watched Freddy carefully, asking questions along the way. "how about if I do the next hole, and you watch me to make sure I am doing it okay?" "Sure" replied Freddy. "No problem if Jack is okay with it."

"Go ahead. That's a good idea." was Jack's response. Jack was busy on his cell phone, talking to Jake back in the shop.

"You ever had dynamite go off accidentally?" asked Richard.

"No. The caps are attached later, so it can't go off on the truck. Once it is in the hole, power is needed to set off the blasting caps. Our biggest problem is hitting water under pressure, which then comes up the hole. We can't put the charges down in that case, and have to skip that spot. It doesn't happen too often, but in some places there are shallow aquifers, or underground springs. "

They trudged to the next spot, where Bill was still drilling, but almost done. Bill watched Richard duplicate what Freddy had done at the other hole.

"Good job. Make sure you don't stretch the wires too much because we don't want them broken, or they won't be able to blow the hole. A wasted hole costs money. And it doesn't do Jack's reputation any good. Our jobs depend on a good reputation for good work. Sometimes he doesn't even have to make a bid. They just hire him and pay what he bills them. ...Hop in." Richard hopped into the cab, which could handle two people, and they drove to the next location. Richard watched Bill drill the hole with the hydraulic drill as he added water to the hole to soften the material and lubricate the drill bit. When the hole was finished, Bill left for the next hole, while Richard finished up with the charges and wires.

Meanwhile, Jack had driven Freddy back to the water bomby, and left him there. Jack headed back to headquarters. Decisions had to be made about the new truck, the Kenworth, the damaged Peterbilt and the trailer. He had to make a timeline for the third and fourth contracts he now had. How many more drillers and helpers and drivers would he need. Where would he get them. Would he get back before the girls went to bed. Would Jill smile at him this evening.

Chapter Twenty-Seven

JACK WAS ABOUT HALFWAY back to home base, when his phone rang. He pushed a button on his steering wheel which connected the blue-tooth. "Yup. Jack here."

"Where do you want this drill parked?" It was Kole. He had made it back and wanted to unload.

"Put it beside the damaged trailer for now."

"I had an experience this morning."

"Really? Like what?"

"I was getting some coffee and breakfast sandwich, and a couple guys were checking out the truck."

"Well, that's no problem. That's not an experience."

"One guy was on the step, with the cab door open. Looking in."

"Oh. That's no good. What was his excuse?"

"He didn't stop to explain. When he saw me coming, he ran off, hopped into a car with another guy, and they peeled out of there. Don't trust them. But maybe I won't see them again. Guess I'll have to lock the doors next time."

"Yeah, I guess so. Shame. Maybe you just scared them off. You look pretty scary to just about everybody."

"Yeah. Sure boss. Sure." Kole chuckled. "Anyway, thought I'd better tell you. I didn't see anything missing. Nothing damaged. But its been on my mind."

"Sure enough, Kole. No problem. I'll be there in about an hour."

"See you later."

It made Jack remember the two guys he and Kole had encountered in the States on their trip up. It made him wonder again if they had died, or just been injured, and if injured, had they gone back south? What was their game? When he got a chance, he would have to go over that drill with a fine-tooth comb, and a magnifying glass. What was it about that drill that interested them so much?

○ ○ ○

A green GMC Denali pickup truck arrived at the border crossing. The Canadian Customs officials asked the two men inside, one dark brown, one white and tanned, where they had come from, and where they were going.

"From Tuscon. Going to Calgary." as they passed over their passports.

"How long are you staying?"

"Two weeks."

"Business or pleasure?"

"Business."

"Bringing in alcohol or tobacco?"

"No."

"Vehicle registration. …. This is from Great Falls?"

"Yeah. Had an accident. Slid off the road. Had to rent a vehicle."

"Okay. On your way. Careful driving. Have a good trip."

Chapter Twenty-Eight

CARLA COULD NOT REACH the handle of the door on the minivan. Jill had to open it and slide it backwards, so she could put Carla in her car seat. They were headed to town for groceries and a doctor's appointment for Jill.

The weather, though still cold, was calm and bright. The sun was still low in the sky, so it shone directly into Jill's eyes as they headed down the highway to town. She pulled down the visor, and squinted into the windshield, where she could just see the surface of the road in front of her. It was dry and clear, since traffic had blown off the bit of snow which the snowplows had left behind. Even the shoulders were fairly clear of snow and ice, and the traffic was light.

About ten miles later, Jill adjusted the radio station on the dashboard. She glanced at the station number and pushed the button again for another station. She wanted the Christian station this morning; it was the kind of music she liked most. And she was tired of all the bad news that news programs so often seemed to focus on. The Christian radio station also reported the news, but with a different attitude, and less focus on the sensational isolated cases of violent crime.

Suddenly she caught a glimpse of something in the corner of her eye, and she jammed on the brakes. The deer, a big buck, was about twenty yards ahead and had not slowed down to cross the road from the left. She let up on the brakes but then there was a second deer, a doe. This one barely missed the vehicle. She almost stopped completely and then a third deer ran out of the ditch onto the road. This deer stopped briefly, then turned around and ran back into the field. Jill noticed two more deer, likely this year's crop, also halting their trip across the road. As she continued slowly past the group, she was thankful she hadn't hit any deer this time around.

She had had several encounters with deer in the past, usually on the gravel roads. One she had hit had dented the hood of the van. Another had run right into her vehicle and bent the side mirror. The worst case had been a previous van, which had its hood and fender and grill totally destroyed, along with bending back the radiator, and destroying the front bumper. It had been a write-off.

It was always an edgy, traumatic experience to have these close calls. Especially with one or both of her girls in the van with her. Hitting a moose at high speed could be fatal, as they were much larger.

She remembered the year before, she had been driving down the road with the big dually pickup, which had surprised a couple moose in the middle of the country road. The larger male had jumped into the deep snow piled in the ditch by the road grader, had struggled through it and disappeared into the trees beyond. The smaller female looked for an easier spot to leave the road. Jill had simply followed it for a quarter mile and enjoyed watching it run in the middle of the road. Eventually however, the moose ran on the shoulder of the road, and Jill had edged slowly passed it. As she came up beside it, the moose suddenly panicked, and dived into the ditch, almost swimming in the deep piled drift and then ambled into the forest.

These memories flashed in her mind as she left the deer behind on the highway today. The beauty of the animals, the way they ran, or walked, or trotted, and the way they looked with ears straight up alert for danger from coyotes or hunters, was something Jill appreciated. Wild animals were part of the everyday environment that Jill experienced as part of nature, part of God's good creation. It brought her closer to God and calmed her spirit.

At the doctor's office, Jill took Carla in with her to the examining room. When the doctor came in, she looked at Carla, raised an eyebrow, but continued on with the questions and examination. She confirmed something that Jill had suspected for awhile, and Jill was glad she had a female doctor. Carla was entranced by the equipment in the room, and the charts on the wall, and was oblivious to the meaning of the conversation between doctor and patient.

Chapter Twenty-Nine

"SHUT THE DOOR" YELLED Jill. The open door let in a blast of cold air as Jack and Kole entered the house.

"What's for lunch?" asked Jack.

"You'll get what you get when you see it. Shut that door!"

"Want to know if we should drive to town for something good."

"Well, it won't be good if you don't shut that door."

"Shut the door, Daddy." echoed Carla. "Mommy's got some soup for you."

"Okay, Sounds good, Carly."

"It's real good, cause I had a taste!"

"Okay then, girly!"

"We have some visitors, Jack." Jill put in.

"Oh? Do I know them?"

"I don't think so. They just heard about you and are looking for work."

"Okay then." Jack had seen a strange vehicle parked in the yard, but he was not aware of anyone that was supposed to be there. He had not seen it drive up, nor anyone get out. He suspected someone must have gone to the house, probably less than five minutes before.

When he and Kole had removed their boots and gone into the kitchen, both were surprised. Shocked actually. They registered the shock for a brief second, before turning impassive faces towards Jill again. "Looking forward to the soup, Jill." said Jack.

"If you are looking for work, you'll have to wait until after lunch, and meet me in the shop." suggested Jack to the two men. "I'll be there in twenty minutes."

Both rather skinny men, one white, one black, they had a smirk on their face as they surveyed Jack's reaction. The tanned man, a bit taller than the other, a dark brown skinned man, had a cast on his arm. Kole turned red, and his shoulders tensed up, but he said nothing. Somehow the troublemakers from their southern road trip had found them and had replaced the black Ford escape with a green GM Denali pickup truck.

"Just looking for work." said the taller man, as he put his right hand in his coat pocket suggestively. "Been looking for awhile." After a brief hesitation, and glances at each other, they both got up and walked out of the house. Glancing through the window, Jack saw them head to their vehicle. He decided to have a bowl of soup, and with a glance at Kole to not say anything, they sat down to eat. He needed some time to think things through.

Somehow the two men had survived their accident and managed to follow them all the way home. That implied some organization behind them. They must have found out that he had purchased the machine, and located his address from his name, or bill of sale for the machine. Jack was more and more convinced drug running was the game behind all of their actions. But what would he do now?

Chapter Thirty

*"Like a muddied spring or a polluted well
are the righteous who give way to the wicked."*
Proverbs 25:26

KOLE WALKED TO THE shop. With his belly full of soup, he was feeling a bit sluggish, but the knowledge of the two men in the Denali kept him on high alert. Did they know he had been driving, when his truck had knocked them off the road? Yes, they must have known, because they had come up beside him just before that. Unless they couldn't see into the cab clearly at the time.

Anyway, did it really matter? They were after something. They were persistent. And having found Jack's family made everything more ominous.

Kole heard the truck door slam behind him, and he realized they had gotten out of the truck to follow him. He picked up his pace, and soon was inside the shop. Looking from side to side, he spotted a four foot length of steel pipe, which he grabbed as a possible weapon of self defense. But he knew they likely had a gun, like they did before, and a pipe would not be a very good defense against that.

Meanwhile, Jack had left the house just after the men had gotten out of the truck. He followed them to the shop, and saw Kole enter, then shortly after, the two men also entered the shop. Jack was there moments later, and the four of them stood in a circle, facing each other, and bracing for some type of action. Silence and tension filled the area for some time. Then, one of the two strangers spoke.

"We always find you. You never get away."

"You gonna pay for this." growled the taller man, pointing at his left arm. " No one messes with me like this. You gonna pay."

"How did you find us?" asked Jack. "I thought you had learned your lesson."

"You gonna pay. You gonna pay. We have friends at the dock. They found your address on shipping slip for the drill. Where is the drill?"

"Ah, friends. You are not making any friends here. You got no friends here. Better go back while the going is good." Jack was playing for time.

"This is my friend." the taller man said, pulling out the handgun from his pocket. "A really good friend. I want you to stop talking. Stop asking questions. I will do the talking now. No more mister nice guy. I know where your woman and your girl live. They can be hurt. In many different ways, they can be hurt. And we will have fun with them. Me and Manny here. We like hurting little girls. And big girls. So shut up and listen."

Kole became very red in the face again. "What the ...??!!" He held the pipe in both hands and took a step towards them. Manny's boss held up the gun in Kole's face, and Kole stopped on the edge of his toes.

Jack was not as cool as he pretended to be when he said to Kole, "Let's just listen, Kole. We can probably come to an agreement. Just cool down and hear what they have to say."

Turning towards the other two, and masking his true feelings, he gently asked them what they wanted. "So you are on a mission. And it is important, obviously. How about letting us know what it is."

"We need that drill." was Manny's interjection.

"Shut up Manny. I'll do the talking."

"Okay, Maurice. You do the talking."

"Shutup Manny. Now they know my name. Just shutup."

Turning to Jack, Maurice began to lay out his thoughts. "We wanted that drill only for an hour. We need to get something off of it. Now you made a one hour thing into a week long work. Maybe more. You will pay. We need something from that drill, and you will show us the machine right now, we will have it for an hour, and no one gets hurt. If you give any more trouble, we will get your little girl, we will make her, and maybe sell her. Or kill her. And we will kill your woman also. After we make her. She is young.... we will make her for a long time and you will not know her anymore. So no more trouble. Give us the machine. Now!"

"The machine is not here. It is almost three hours away." Jack tried not to show his anxiety, his fear, and his rage, while he forced his brain into more rational productive channels. "We can take you there right now. Kole will take you there and show you where it is." Jack did not want to leave his family alone, while these men were in the country. "Kole, you can take Richard with you. Show them the drill, give them time alone. Give them some tools if they need them. And let me know when they are done."

"Don't call police on us. If you do, we will get your woman. And the girl. Sometime, someplace, somehow. It will not be pretty. Don't think about calling police."

"Okay, I understand. No one calls the police."

Richard suddenly popped out from behind a wall. He pretended he had not been listening all along, and asked if Jack wanted him for anything? Kole grabbed his arm, and pulled him to the side, and muttered something to Richard. Kole had been thinking during his rage, while listening to the back and forth, and Richard nodded his head in agreement.

"We need to take along some tools for the drills in the field. We'll just throw them on the truck, and then they can follow us to the drill site." Richard went to the shop, picked up some tools and material, and then out to the yard where he picked up some cable and an auger, as well as a couple cases of engine oil and hydraulic fluid.

Kole and Richard hopped in the diesel dually pickup and began to leave the yard. The two strangers had also hopped into their own half ton truck and followed them out of the yard. It would be a few hours before they got to the job site. Kole and Richard had some snacks in the truck, and a cup of hot coffee in the cup holders. They would get to the job site after the other crews were already gone. It would be dark then. They had no idea if the other two guys had anything to eat or drink, and they didn't really care. They were making plans for when they arrived at the job site.

Chapter Thirty-One

AT GRIMSHAW, KOLE PULLED into the UFA (United Farmers of Alberta) cardlock fuel station. He needed to fuel up, or they would not make it back to town. The two drug runners (as he thought of them) pulled up beside him, and said they needed gas as well. He told them to go back to the Shell and get their gas there. He would wait for them to get back before they left. Surprisingly, they obligingly turned around and headed back to the Shell.

Soon, they returned, and by that time Kole was filled up and ready to go. They continued on down the highway for almost an hour, and then turned off on to gravel roads to the job site. By this time it was getting dark, although there was a quarter moon to give some light. The roads wound past some trees and fields, and more fields and more trees, with snow covering the ground everywhere. The moon was obscured by clouds about half the time, and it felt grey and cloudy, quiet and ominous.

Eventually they reached the jobsite. While Kole got out of the truck, Richard walked to the drill, and immediately got in it and started it up.

Manny and Maurice got out of their truck and walked to Kole. "Where is the drill? Which one is it?" Three drills were at the job site, plus one water-bomby.

"Follow me," said Kole. "But I need to take a couple things along." He grabbed a pipe, some cable, a pipewrench, and a few smaller items which he stuck in his pocket. They did not question why he needed them. They were completely focused on the three drills, one of which was running.

"Well, you are here now. You can tell me the truth. Would you really have hurt Jack's family if he didn't help you? I mean you were just kidding, right?"

Maurice turned back to Kole. "You have family? We will find out. We will hurt them too. We have killed many people."

"Nah. You are just playing, right? Just scaring people. Threatening them. Right?"

Maurice took a step back to Kole. "No joking around. We have hung two women, Manny and me. In Mexico. They taste good. And make much noise. And three kids. One man. But the man had no head." He laughed mirthlessly. "We kill two men in Texas. We will do it again. And we will find your family too." The black eyes were hard, edged, dark pits.

Kole hid his thoughts from them. "I have no family. Come on, lets go to the drill."

As they got closer to the drills, Kole could see that these guys had relaxed somewhat. They probably felt they had achieved their objective finally, and that Jack and Kole and Richard were properly scared of them and would let them do what they wanted to do. The threat of hurting Jack's family had done the trick. A threat like that would not be taken lightly, especially with the news items of families hung from bridges in Mexico as a reminder.

"It's the one running." said Kole.

"Shut it off. We don't need it running," growled Maurice. "Shut it down!"

"You tell him. You will have to get closer; he can't hear you from here."

"Manny, you tell him to shut it down. Now!" Maurice didn't want to be told by Kole, but delegating Manny was acceptable. Manny started trudging across the pack snow to the machine. As he arrived at the machine, Richard opened the door. At that exact moment, Kole hit Maurice on the back of his head with the pipewrench he held in his hand.

For some reason, perhaps the look in Richard's eyes to the scene playing out, Manny turned around, and saw Maurice go down to his knees. Suddenly alert, but not quick enough, Manny realized they were in trouble.

Reaching into his coat pocket for the knife he kept handy, he was too late, as Richard jumped on him from the cab of the machine and knocked him flat to the ground. Richard bopped him on the head with a flashlight he had grabbed from the cab, and then choked the groggy Manny with his right elbow, while searching his pockets with his left hand. He found the knife in one pocket and tossed it to the side of the drill.

Kole meanwhile had little resistance from Maurice, whose head was leaking blood, and whose arms and legs were limp. He was out cold, and Kole quickly found the pistol in one pocket and a switchblade knife in another pocket. He began searching the other pockets for identification and anything else interesting, and found a passport from Arizona, and a driver's license with a different name on it from Texas. And another driver's licence from Mexico. He left the man's face pressed against the cold snow, while he pulled out a piece of rope from his own pocket and began tying up his hands behind him. Then he wrapped up the feet with more rope and looped the hands to the feet.

Richard was about six inches taller and fifty pounds heavier than Manny. As a logger and fire fighter, and with the exercise of the last few days with Bill on the Bomby drill, he had no problem subduing Manny. After tying up Maurice, Kole came to Manny and began tying him up in a similar fashion, while Richard made sure that Manny did not surprise them with any threatening moves. Soon they were laying side by side in the snow, Maurice having regained consciousness, enraged and thrashing, but not so confident anymore.

Bluster had not ended though, since Maurice began threatening them both with all kinds of mayhem if they didn't let them go. But they had played their hand, and there was no way out now for any of them.

"When the police let us go, we are going to get you good. We will phone our friends down south, and you will not see your next birthday. You have made a big mistake."

"Police? That's what we thought. Police would just be a temporary setback to you. You wouldn't respect the law, would you." It was more of a statement than a question.

"The law will let us go. You have no evidence of anything. We have not killed anyone here. There is no evidence, no record of what is down south.

In Mexico or in Texas. So they will have to let us go. They are not like Mexican police. We know that much." Paused for breath. "And when they let us go, we will finish what we started."

Kole pulled out the phones he taken from their pockets. "What about these? No evidence? What will I find on here?"

"Nothing. Nothing. I am not stupid. I don't leave evidence."

Kole paused. He was quiet for a moment. Everyone knew the ball was in his court. His decision. What would he say? What was he thinking?

He suspected the phones would not provide enough evidence. It might be some corroborating evidence for some things, like perhaps drug running, but they had never mentioned drugs. Previous murders would likely never have been mentioned on the phone. The exact nature of personal threats would be obscured and indirect, meaning insufficient to convict. Perhaps they would be detained for trial, but chances were greater than 50% that they would have a plausible story, and would be set free either before or after a trial. Perhaps fined for importing an unlicensed gun, or for false ID, or maybe the passport was legitimate.

"You will not leave this place." intoned Kole. Definitively. "Today is your last day. You have made one threat too many. You have convicted yourselves on your murders. So this is it. You are done." He drew a deep breath.

Now that he had said it, he realized the enormity of what he had said. Richard and he had discussed this in the truck on the way here. They had decided to give these guys a chance to back track, to pull back their threats once they had their eyes on the drill. But they had dug their own hole, by confessing to prior murders. They preyed on the weak and helpless. In Mexico. In Texas. And they would do the same here.

Kole had a great deal of affection for Jack's family, especially as a single man without his own family. Richard did have some family, and so he understood how serious these threats were. He felt them as threats against his own family, even though he was sometimes away from his family for extended periods. And Richard really appreciated Jack's personal attention and attitude towards his employees, especially in the brief period of time he had known Jack. Jack had treated him right. As a human being, and as a worthwhile person.

Between them, Kole and Richard felt protective towards Jack, and especially towards the women in his family. For someone to threaten one of his daughters.... These guys would no doubt have no hesitation in doing a number on the older daughter either, if they knew of her. And Jack's wife was nothing more than a stray dog to them, a tool to devise evil on Jack, to gain his compliance. They would rather hurt Jack through his family, than hurt Jack directly, although they were not averse to that either.

Kole ground his teeth. He hated what he was planning to do, but he saw no way out of it. Richard became impassive, inured to the inevitability. His heart became hard. He took no pleasure in what they had talked about on the way here, and he realized that the results would be unpredictable. The future could be very bleak, uncertain, and always fraught with dangerous possibilities, but sometimes a course of action needed to be chosen.

Kole nodded at Richard, who walked to the truck with him, and together they grabbed the auger in the back of the truck. It was a larger auger, 14 inches in diameter, not used too often. It was about six feet long, and could attach directly to the drill, or to an extension on the drill. It had some serrated teeth on it and would be able to grind through the frozen soil.

Most of their drills could not handle an auger this size, because it would run into the side of the mast. This drill had a special fitting on it that allowed such a large auger to be attached. They attached it to the drill, which they drove a quarter mile towards a grove of trees on the seismic trail. They began to work it on the frozen ground.

Slowly it chewed up chunks of soil and began a definable hole. After about a foot, the ground was no longer frozen, since it was early in winter, and the snow insulated the soil from frost. After going down the length of the drill bit, they detached it and added an extension. Then they drilled down another six feet. They had to keep pulling back soil from the hole with shovels as the drill brought it up to the surface. The hole they had drilled was now twelve feet deep. They repeated the procedure at another hole about fifty feet away.

They drove back to the men, and tied them to the drill, then returned to the holes, dragging the men behind them. Manny and Maurice already had frozen hands and ears, which got even colder as the snow sprayed around them while being dragged along feet first. They yelled and shouted, then screamed loudly, then were silent, as they realized no one else was nearby to hear their useless cries.

Chapter Thirty-Two

KOLE AND RICHARD WERE quiet on the way back home. It would be after midnight when they returned. How would they explain it?

They had told the two men what they were going to do. They had been clear and explicit. Had told them to repent. Had given them time to repent. But even repentance would not prevent the consequence. After all, how could they trust them? The repentance, if there was any, had been between them and God. They didn't want to know if they had repented, because they did not want to soften their actions, nor change their intentions towards these two men. So it had ended. Two larger holes on the seismic trail.

They had driven the green pickup truck into a deep pond next to the road about twenty miles down the road. Kole had put the truck in gear, given it some fuel, and some momentum, and then jumped out before it hit the pond. The ice had supported the truck near shore but was still thin in the center and the truck had gone down quickly. The cold weather would soon form a new layer of ice over it. Clouds had now completely hidden the moon from sight, and snow was falling steadily, covering the tracks of the truck.

Back near the job site, snow was also covering tracks. Previously they had sweated heavily in their winter clothes as they shovelled the dirt back into the burial chambers. They had compacted the dirt down with the drill, so that hopefully it would not leave too much of a depression next spring when everything thawed and settled. The remainder they had spread out evenly, so no piles of soil were visible. Snow would hide everything now.

A propane torch had been used to burn identification and phones, and anything else that could provide identities. The ashes were then deposited in another smaller hole under a tree stump a mile away from where the truck was buried in the pond.

Now they needed to return the large auger to the shed next to the shop, without Jack noticing anything. They had cleaned it completely so no soil was sticking to it. It had not been used since last spring, and Kole wanted to remove any obvious evidence.

They had left the oil and hydraulic fluid at the job site as a presumed reason for being there in the first place. But Kole and Richard were careful otherwise to leave the site as it was when they got there. They had scrubbed the flashlight and the pipewrench with snow, not knowing if it was sufficient to hide all traces of blood or skin, but at least they looked clean.

When earlier they had discussed the option of drastic action, doing what they had done, they had wondered about whether to let the two strangers actually find what they were looking for, so that they would know what it was. But in the end, to reduce their own risk, they had taken the opportunity as it presented, and decided to ignore whatever it was about the machine that was so important to these drug runners. Maybe someday, when work was slack and the machine was back in the shop, they would seriously take it apart to find the hidden stuff. But it would affect the story they told Jack.

As they travelled back, many thoughts went through their minds. Although both had been in fights with other guys before, this was something different. Every fight had a potential for injury, and even for death, but this was not some drunken brawl or ego filled display of testosterone. This was something more. They knew the names of the two men but tried to forget them. They tried to purge from their minds the last agonizing pleas. It was easier to de-personalize them. As enemies. As dangerous felons, rather than as men who had stories and histories of their own. Who likely had families and relationships. Maybe even dreams and aspirations.

Obligations to people back at their homes. At their line of work. All ended now.

Finally, one of them spoke. "I would like a coffee," said Richard. Richard was driving now. Kole was trembling and nervous. Kole knew he had taken primary responsibility. He wondered if he had let his rage and anger and impetuosity get the better of him. He wondered if he was a violent man at heart. But the consequences of what they had done haunted him, now that it was done.

"Yeah, a coffee would be good."

"We have to be cool," advised Richard. "Pretend it never happened. All we did, was we let them look at the drill, we were sitting in the truck, talking and waiting, and next thing we knew, they had gotten in their truck and driven off. We have no idea what they were looking for, and they didn't even stop to say goodbye."

"Yeah. I know." They had discussed all this before. Although Kole had taken the leadership before, now it seemed like Richard was the strong man, stiffening them both to do what they had to do now, to maintain their story, to live ordinary lives, day to day.

"Is anything open? Let's try that Shell station. It looks open still."

"Nope. Closed. They close at 11 pm. Everybody uses cardlock now, so they don't need people here to sell their fuel." Richard drove by on the service road without entering the lot. Everything else was also closed, the restaurants, A+W, Subway. So they were forced to continue without coffee. Kole's stomach growled, but he put his head against the window, and tried to nap.

Chapter Thirty-Three

"HEY GUYS! I DIDN'T hear you come back last night. Must have been late." Jack was ebullient and cheerful as he encountered Kole and Richard in the yard on the way to the shop. He was optimistic that they would not hear from those two men or any associates again, now that they had what they wanted.

"Yeah, it was after midnight. Snow was falling. We didn't want to wake you." Kole's response was relaxed. He had time to think last night. What was done could not be undone. Whatever the consequences might be eventually, he had to accept all the possibilities, and would live or die with them. Might as well relax. He had actually slept reasonably well, after tossing and turning and churning his thoughts in the truck on the long way home.

"Did they find what they were looking for?"

"We think so. We waited in the truck while they were on the machine. We were about a hundred yards away. It took them awhile, but when they left, they never stopped to say goodbye. Just hopped in their truck and drove off. We took a quick look at the machine and didn't see anything wrong. Then we took off for home."

"Were they happy?"

"Have no idea," replied Richard. "They didn't seem upset. But we were not close enough to hear what they said to each other."

"Well, good then. They're gone. And we can get back to work."

Jack scratched his scalp with his fingers. He needed to get his mind back on track. Although he had slept soundly at times last night, it was a night broken up in a sweat with unpredictable awakenings, his brain automatically considering all the possibilities that those two criminals had evoked with their threats. The threats of violence had turned him into a violent man that night; he knew full well that if it came to it, he would defend his family with his life. But he was happy that it had ended as it had, peacefully, with everyone happy.

"What's on for today?" questioned Kole.

Jack wrenched his mind back to work. "Start off in the shop. Tom is helping Jake with the new machine, but I want you guys to go over the trailer that flipped in the ditch. See if the ramps are finished and fixed. The Perkins motor needs to be taken out of the old drill we brought back the other day. I haven't decided whether we rebuild it or replace it with a new Cummins engine. Tomorrow, Richard will go back to the job site, and help Bill again."

"Once the engine is out, then Kole can help Jake, while Tom brings the engine to a rebuild shop. Or picks up a new engine."

Jack's phone rang. He pulled it out of his pocket. "Jack here."

"Why did the drill get moved?" without waiting for an answer, Bill added, "We need fuel. We have enough till noon, but two of the drills will be out for sure by then. And the service tank is dry."

"Can you send someone to get fuel? Or order some delivered from UFA?"

"Yeah I called them already, but they lost one truck to a brake job. And the other truck is real busy, so they can't get here until tomorrow, or late this afternoon. So we will lose a half day, probably on three machines." That meant that six men would be idle, and no money for no holes drilled.

"How much snow did you get?"

"About three inches, with a bit of drifting, not much. It stopped snowing and skies are still grey, but not much wind."

"Sending Freddy for fuel means about a half day lost. Okay, I will send someone with fuel to last for the day."

Stepping into the shop, he turned back to Richard, who was just behind him. "Change of plans. You will be taking the truck with jockey tank of diesel right away. They are short of fuel, and we don't want them losing time on this job. Make sure it is topped up before you get there. You can help Bill, and Freddy can drive the water truck, unless Bill has different ideas. Kole and Tom will work in the shop with Jake."

Richard began his preparations for returning to the job site. He was beginning to get used to the long drives back and forth. He didn't mind the driving but getting outdoors in the weather was also good. With exercise in the raw cold and wind... it made him feel alive. Hopefully it would make him forget last night.

Kole went to see what Jake was doing. He was building hydraulic hoses, and fitting them to the new drill under construction. Jake was glad to see Kole. Even with little experience, Kole seemed to have a knack for a lot of things, though he liked driving best.

Right now, Kole preferred something to do with his hands that would also keep his mind busy. He didn't want to rethink last night anymore. So he was glad that Jake told him to cut some pieces of metal for him that he could use as brackets to hold the water tank on the drill. Every drill had a water tank on it to help with the drilling.

At noon, Jack decided to eat with his men. Jill had gone to town for some shopping and wouldn't be back until later. Soon, after eating his lunch, Jake went back to the shop area. Tom decided to go outdoors to check on the trailer that had flipped a few days before. Kole and Jack were alone in the lunch room.

"I got a question for you, Jack."

"Okay, shoot."

"You ever think about those guys got hung in Mexico? You know, on the news?"

"Yeah, what about it?"

"If you were a Mexican, and knew they were coming after your family, what would you do?" Kole needed Jack's thoughts on this.

"Yeah, I wonder if they knew ahead of time or not. Wonder if they were caught by surprise. Or maybe just so scared and intimidated they had no answers."

"They were probably just not gun packing gangsters. Probably didn't stand a chance. Would have been shot if they had run. But they got hung instead. And at least one man was beheaded." Kole was despondent.

"Some people are just plain mean and vicious. What a black life. An empty desperate hell hole of a life."

"Would you just let them do what they wanted?"

"Not if I could help it. Don't know exactly what I would do. I'm not in their situation. But if I knew for sure, then I would probably get one of my guns and protect my family. I would probably shoot them as quick as I could. But I would have to be sure. Not just guessing their intentions." Jack looked at Kole curiously as he responded.

"Not in revenge. But pro-active. Preventive."

"Yeah. Defense by being proactive. Like the USA carrying the battle to the middle east to prevent terrorism at home.....I'm reminded of a book I once read." continued Jack. "Well, a couple books, actually. One was about a man in the deep south, who shot a couple guys who had raped his eight year old daughter. They had caught the guys later. He shot them right in the court room. During their trial. Was arrested for it, but he didn't care. He knew the guys would get off. Or get some light sentences. For damaging his young daughter for the rest of her life. Just because she was black, and they were white. He couldn't handle that. He didn't want it all to come out in court and didn't want his girl to testify, hurting her even more. He didn't want them to get off, or get some light sentence. So he killed them. He needed to do what he did.

"The other story was a western, about a Texas Ranger who was chasing some train robbers. The Rangers were lawmen. They were supposed to capture the criminals and bring them to justice. To the courts. One of the gangs was led by a guy who liked to kill people. He especially liked to burn people alive. Or dogs. Children too. He had been captured a couple times, but always escaped before he could be hung. The last time, he threatened to burn the ranger's girlfriend and her two children. The texas ranger eventually caught up to him again and ambushed him from a high hill. Shot him at a distance. Dead. Shot five of his gang members at the same time, as they were all riding horses through a valley. One gang member got away.

"So the question is, was the Texas Ranger above the law? Was he the law? Was he right? Was it necessary? No trial. No court of law. No official hanging. Those are things I think about."

"But didn't God say, vengeance is mine, I will repay?" suggested Kole.

"Yeah, I thought about that too."

"But when you protect your family, or friends, are you thinking about God?"

Silence filled the moment. How could one just let these evil guys have their way. They thought they were so powerful. Power to hurt. Power to control, to dominate. Yet, they were little guys, not that big. Big men with a gun or a knife, but still not that big.

Mean like some bulls. Vicious like some dogs. And could be put down the same way. But they were people. What did it mean that they were people? What did it mean? Was the end of their life different than the end of a dog? The end of a mean bull? The end of a poisonous snake, or a fearless tiger?

Jack spoke aloud, "Self defense is allowed under the law. If you end up killing someone in self-defense, then the law will let you go free. But it can't be premeditated. The danger has to be imminent, it has to be right there in your face. And violence must be met with equal reasonable force, not with something excessive. That's how the law looks at it."

He continued, "It doesn't always apply it fairly though. Sometimes little technicalities catch up the defender, the protector. And often the perpetrator, the would-be murderer gets off. Or he gets prison, where he can sometimes still pull strings and get other people to do his dirty work. How does a man protect against that? It gets hard." Jack paused. "Sometimes though it is pretty clear what justice really is. That Ranger killed that crook because he was afraid of the threats for his girlfriend and her children. He wasn't even married to that woman but had only recently met her. But the threats were real. There was proof of that. And the crook and his gang had already killed several men, and viciously murdered several innocent families as well. So there was no question he deserved to die."

"But every circumstance is different. Every situation is different. I decided to let those two guys go, because if they got what they wanted, they would probably leave me and mine alone. I took a chance on that, but... What does bother me though, is that those guys likely have already killed other people, and will likely do it again when they get back to their home territory. And then I ask myself, what have I done to stop that? I just let them go back to their murdering malicious vicious ways???"

"I'm sure it was drugs, don't you think?"

"Yeah. I'd bet my life on it. What they don't murder with their guns and knives, they will destroy with the drugs they sell. They are poison, and they sell poison."

"Is there any possibility of change for them? You know, a kind of repentance, maybe? Or are they beyond hope?"

"Repentance. Well, I haven't attended church much. Not since Easter this year. Well there was the one wedding of some friends. But not much. Jill would have an answer.... I think Jill would say there is always a chance for repentance. Yes, she would say that. Always. She attends church pretty regular. And reads her bible too. Yeah, always a chance."

"Really? You are kidding right? Hitler could repent?" Kole was incredulous.

"Well, I'm trying to remember something she once told me.... oh yeah, she mentioned something about Paul, the apostle. Paul was murdering Christians, but then he had an encounter, some type of experience. And repented. Changed. I mean really changed. Because he became a christian. Just like the people he was murdering and chasing down before. The people he had been hunting down eventually forgave him and began to trust him. And he was in the bible. So if a guy like him could repent in the bible, I suppose anyone else could too. But a murderer should still get justice, even if he repents, I think."

"Then the thief on the cross. You heard about him? Hanging on the cross, but he confesses. Repents, I guess. And Jesus forgives him in his last day. Lets him come to paradise. Yeah. But he still gets punished here on earth. Dies on the cross beside Jesus."

"Everybody dies eventually. The just and the unjust. The big and the small."

"True. True. Wow! Time to get back to work! Interesting talk, Kole. Hard questions, but it looks like you and me were thinking about the same things lately. Anyway, better get back at it. Wonder if Richard made it back there by now. Hope they didn't run out of fuel. Bill won't be happy if they ran out."

Chapter Thirty-Four

RICHARD SAW THAT THE machines were all working, when he arrived at the job site. Taking a quick glance at the area he and Kole had been busy with last night, he saw that snow had covered everything, and he saw nothing to cause anyone to ask questions, or to even wonder what had happened.

He soon found Bill at his line two miles away, working with Freddy as helper.

"Fill it up, Rich. It's just about empty." Bill did not need to comment further. Richard pulled up with his truck beside the drill, grabbed the filler nozzle and turned on the electric pump.

"Who else needs some fuel?"

"Eldon needs some. And Skyler needs some. The others are okay."

"Yeah. I don't know where they are. How about I put sixty gallons in each?" The tank on the back of his truck only held 200 gallons, so he would have to share with each. Sixty gallons would last them the rest of the shift, but they would need more for tomorrow. Hopefully the delivery truck would come tonight, or early morning.

"Skyler is working a line just behind those trees. And Eldon is a mile north. You should see them when you get close. You probably will see tracks for Eldon, because he had parked at the fuel tank and drove there this morning after the snow stopped."

"Okay".

"Actually, why don't you let Freddy bring them fuel, and save a bit for the water bomby. Then he can bring them water too if they need it. And you can help me instead."

"That's okay too." Freddy had just finished the hole, one back, and was walking to the machine now. By the time the fuel was pumped, Freddy had arrived at the machine, so he and Richard exchanged places, and Richard was back to helper status.

After working for another couple hours, Bill decided to take a break. Everything was moving smoothly, and he was relaxed. A short break, a bit of cold coffee and conversation with Richard, and they would be back at it again. His gloves were getting muddy and stiff, his boots were slogging mud, and his pants also covered with frozen mud. Course he was used to it but exchanging for his last pair of fresh gloves today would be nice.

"Let's take a break", he yelled at Richard. Although Richard was a rookie, he was catching on quickly, and was managing to keep up to the driller. Soon he was with Bill, and he grabbed his own coffee out of the cab. It was not frozen, it was not warm, but it was wet and he had a few cookies left. Some guys ate all their lunch at about 11 am and then worked without a break till quitting time. Richard like to space out his breaks and his snacks throughout the day and had discovered that Bill liked the same.

They sat down on the front of the drill, which was the cleanest. The tracks were not too bad, since they drove on the snow, but the back of the drill was covered with splattered mud from the drill bringing up dirt, which came up mixed with water that had gone down the hole to lubricate the drill bit.

"How are your boots doing, Rich? Sore feet?"

"Not bad today. My feet are getting used to them. They were sore a couple days ago."

"If you need clean gloves, there's more in the cab. Hands staying warm?"

"Well, no. They're cold. But not frozen. I warm them up a bit sometimes."

The helpers had battery operated warmers along with them all the time so that they could warm up fingers before handling the dynamite and the wires. If hands got too cold, they would become clumsy, lose time, and maybe break something. So Jack supplied them with warmers. They charged the batteries at night at the hotel or the bunkhouse. Or in the vehicles.

"This is a miserable job, actually, don't you think?" Bill posed the question as an open question. "I mean, really, why would anyone want to do this? Frozen cold weather. Heavy clumsy clothes... boots.... frozen gloves. Mud all over. Knee deep snow to walk in. And later in winter, sometimes waist deep snow. Weather isn't bad today, but sometimes there is a wind driving right into your face, bringing grey dull skies that dump blinding snow across your path and over your work. And then tripping over logs or stumps or branches under the snow, which you can't see. Sometimes snow drifts you can barely drive the drill through. Other times branches from trees right in your face if you are the helper. Or branches trying to break the windshield of the bomby."

"For the money."

"What?"

"For the money. That's why we do it."

Bill laughed. "Yeah. Of course for the money. You're right. For the money. Where else could you make this kind of money. But you know what? I like being outside too. Sitting behind a desk all day would drive me nuts. Drive me to drink. Not that I don't like the odd drink anyway."

"Not me. I gave it up."

"Don't drink at all?"

"Nah. Used to. Too much. Ended up seriously hurting someone when I was drunk. Didn't know it till later. Drunk too often. The guy was in a wheelchair for a year. It was a friendly fight. It started out friendly. So, I quit. Within the week, I quit. Stuck to it, too."

"Yeah, hurting someone would do that. I never get drunk. Maybe slightly dizzy. So I guess for me its different. I know when to stop."

"Yeah, everyone is different. I worried though. Thought he might try to get even somehow."

"Did he?"

"No. He told me he was drunk too. I don't know if he quit. But he just took his lumps. But me, I didn't like it. Didn't really want to hurt someone like him. It was just a stupid argument over whose turn it was at the pool table. If he had been mean, or hurt someone, or been threatening my family, would've been different."

"What would you have done then?"

Richard jerked up his head, looking carefully at Bill. Then he took another sip of the lukewarm, or fairly cool coffee, which was almost gone now. "Well, I would protect my own. Especially my family. What would you do?"

With the question directed back at Bill, Richard relaxed a bit. He and Kole had wrestled with this question yesterday. It seemed that finding out what others thought about it, at least in theory, as a theoretical question, would help them to calm their own conscience, or maybe it would convict them, who knew? But it was a pressing question.

"Yeah, this business about calling the cops and letting them handle it, sometimes works and sometimes doesn't. Too many guys get off free, or with short sentences, and then get back out, doing the same thing again. Sometimes you just don't have time to call the cops, or it takes them too long to get there. You gotta protect yourself, or your family, or you are gonna be dead. Too late to decide then."

"How do you decide if a threat is real, or just big talk? That's what I can't figure out." Of course, Richard had figured it out recently, but he wasn't going to give that out to Bill.

"You get a feeling, I think. Long as you're not drunk. When you're drunk, you can't figure out feelings. And if the other guy is drunk, it is hard to figure out his feelings. Maybe he doesn't even know if he means what he says. But if he is sober, and if you are sober, you should be able to figure out if the threat is real."

"Yeah, I guess."

"And if its real, you got no choice. You can't sit on your hands. You gotta act. And do what is right. What works. Nail him before he nails you. And no way he is going to hurt your kids. You got any kids?"

"Not that I know of. One girl I was with a few years ago.... she was with too many guys, might have had a kid, but who knows. I guess DNA testing could find out, but she never came after me. Never said anything. I don't even know if she ever had a kid."

"Well, then you got nothing to worry about."

"If I had kids, and someone tried to hurt them, I would get mean. Real mean."

"Yeah, I suppose. Well I got kids, and I would get mean too. We better get back to work. It'll be dark soon."

Chapter Thirty-Five

"MORNING." MUTTERED JACK AS he came back into the house for breakfast. It had snowed again, and the driveway and parking area would need to be plowed clean. He had started the tractor and was warming it up. He wanted to have most of it done before his men started showing up for work at 8:30 am.

"Erin doesn't want to go to school today."

"Oh? Why is that?" Jack pulled his boots off.

"No temperature, but complaining of a stomach ache."

"Well, its probably just nerves or something. She having trouble with any kids at school?"

"Not that I've heard of. She complained yesterday about her teacher. Asking her to do something she didn't want to do."

"Oh? Asking what?" Jack mouthed between sips of coffee.

"To go outside for play time after lunch. She didn't want to go... wanted to stay inside."

"Well, its good for her to go outside."

"Yeah, you would think so. She likes to go outside at home. So she must have a reason." Jill put the eggs and bacon on the table as she responded.

"Well, better find out what it is."

"I'll find out later. I'll give her some time."

"But she'll miss her bus. Better do it now." Jack took a bite of his bacon.

"Quit ordering me around like you do your men. I'm not on your payroll. I'll do it when I'm ready."

"Getting your knickers in a knot. She shouldn't be staying home all day if she's not sick. And she'll miss her bus."

Jill stopped moving. One hand on her hip, one on the counter. "You don't care about her, do you? You need to give her time, not just shove your way through."

"What?" Jack was getting a bit irate. How did this happen? Why were his comments being so twisted?

"She's not a tractor. She's not some hired man in your shop. She's a little girl."

"I know that! She's my little girl. I don't want her growing up being a sissy, or looking for an easy way out of problems."

"She's only six. What's the matter with you?" Now Jill was becoming quite irritated. Even upset. "I don't know if you can handle another little kid. They will all just become projects. You will tell them all something, but you won't listen!"

"What?? another little kid? What you talking about? Erin?"

"I'm pregnant. But maybe three kids is too many.!"

"What? What? What? Pregnant? When did you find that out?"

"A couple days ago I got it confirmed at the doctor." Jill was not the kind of girl who burst into tears and helplessness. Her emotions more quickly played out into anger and action. But she was sobbing, trying to catch her breath. She wondered how Jack would handle it. They had not recently, during this very busy season, talked much about anything, and especially not about enlarging the family.

Jill knew he was busy and had lots on his mind. But she was not aware of the two criminals who had pursued them all the way from Texas. She was not aware of the stress that was causing Jack. Jack had not totally processed the extra stress himself, although it certainly affected him. His work was a challenge. The drug running criminals were a worry.

"Okay..." Jack paused. "Wow! You know, that's great! Really. ...Another kid. Wow! Wow! Wasn't really thinking about that. Hey hey!! How far along?"

"Ten weeks."

"Well. Took you awhile to tell me. Hey! Maybe it's a boy!"

"Maybe. Don't know." Jill's tears had stopped.

"Say, that'll only be number three. We can handle that."

"I don't know. You sure? It won't interfered with your lifestyle?"

"My lifestyle? What? Hey. Sorry about being hard on you about Erin. I want the best for my girls."

"Sure you do." Jill, a bit cynical, a bit hopeful.

"Hey, c'mon. We'll adjust. I love kids. I love my kids. I love you. You..." he sputtered, trying to change the mood. Wanting to call her some affectionate name, but not trusting himself, and not trusting how she would handle it. "Look, I'm glad you told me. Really glad. Honest. It'll make my breakfast taste better. And you made a fantastic breakfast. I really got to eat this bacon and eggs. Tractor is running, and I got to plow snow in the yard for my pregnant wife."

A slight quirk of her lips gave the lie to her next comment, "You're just plowing it for your men when they come in. You started the tractor before you knew I was pregnant."

"Yeah, just for the men. Love those men. I just don't want them walking through snow. My wife? Huh. Snow isn't a problem for her. My kids? What do I care? One kid more or less lost in the snow... not my worry."

"Here. Eat your pancake. And here, take your coffee along. Hurry up. I need to go to town, and don't want to drive through all your deep snow. I'm taking Carla to town, so she won't miss the bus because she won't be taking the bus. I need to go shopping today."

"Ah. So." Jack quickly scarfed up his breakfast, grabbed his cup, put on his boots, and trotted back to the tractor. Soon he was moving the snow off the driveway and the parking area. Another child. He was convinced it had to be a boy. He loved his girls of course. But, a boy! That would be interesting. A different kind of fun. What if it was another girl? Well, that would be okay too.

Would the house be big enough? Well, yeah, for now. When the kids were small. But in a couple years.... did they need more room? He could add on a piece easily enough. One didn't run out of room in the country... you could add on pretty well whatever side you wanted. His organizing mind examined the options. Maybe a bedroom? A bigger dining area? Bigger kitchen? What to do with the gas line coming in? Can't really go closer to the septic tank. In no time, he was examining options, dreaming of possibilities, redesigning.

But then he shut down that train of thought and put it on hold for later. Right now, he had to go check his cows. Would they need more feed? Some bedding with the extra snow from recent snow fall? He drove the tractor down the road a half mile, waving at Jake in his truck who was on the way to the shop. When he arrived at the field, he realized that he had decided to sell his steer calves this fall but had not yet gotten around to it.

He generally didn't keep his steers over winter, since he didn't want to get into feeding grain. He would sell some of his heifer calves as well, keeping about half of them this year for replacements for some of his older cows. Between the steers and heifers and a few old cows, he would have a truckload to go to market. He could get a few of the guys to help him round up the cows and separate the calves. He gave his cows eight round bales of hay and a bale of straw. He headed back to the yard.

Chapter Thirty-Six

AS JACK PULLED INTO the yard, his phone was ringing. He parked the tractor, then pulled his phone out of his pocket. "Yup. Jack here."

"Where are Manny and Maurice?"

"What you talking about?" Jack was stalling for time. Why would this unregistered number call him? Manny and Maurice should be halfway back to Mexico. Or Texas. Or Arizona or wherever they were going by now. Was this their boss? Or something?

"They came to see you?" posed as a question, it made it seem like this guy on the phone had not received word from them yet?

"Who are you?"

"None of your business. Manny works for me. I haven't heard from him in two days. I know he came to you. Where is he?"

"Yeah. They came. I sent him with two guys to see the drill a few hours away from here by truck. They saw the drill two nights ago. Spent about an hour on the drill while my guys watched from a distance. Then they got down, into their truck, and took off without saying goodbye to my guys. I have no idea where they are."

"Did they find the stuff? What they were looking for?"

"I have no idea. What stuff? My guys couldn't tell if they found anything or not. We assume they found the stuff. If it was there in the first place."

Silence on the other end of the phone. Obviously, Manny and Maurice had not made contact with their headquarters. This would seem to be unusual, odd.

"You think they just grabbed the stuff and skipped out? Kept it for themselves? What was it they were looking for?"

"Valuable stuff. Very valuable." some more words in spanish, which Jack assumed were cuss words. "They wouldn't dare skip out. It would cost them their life."

"What if it wasn't there to start with?"

"It was there." the voice sounded positive. "It was there."

"Did you put it there yourself? So you know?"

The voice was silent. Probably he did not put it there himself but was heading the operations. Jack imagined him playing out the scenarios, thinking about the guys he had delegated to plant the stuff. Would they double-cross him? Or not? Something was wrong, and he was going to find out. Maybe he would stop at nothing to find out.

"If you won't tell me what it is, at least can you tell me what's the stuff worth?"

More cuss words. "Millions. None of your business. You did this wrong thing, not stopping for my men in Texas. Somebody will die. Somebody." He hung up on Jack.

Jack climbed down from the tractor and met Kole entering the shop. "Doggone idiot calls me about those two drug lords," muttered Jack. "How am I supposed to know where they are. We gave them access to the machine. I thought we were done with them. Idiots. Stupid crooks. They better not send someone down here. I am getting completely ticked off."

Kole heard him, but had nothing to say. Nothing.

Chapter Thirty-Seven

"I WANT YOU TO give me a hand tomorrow," Jack ordered Tom and Kole, who were in the shop. I am going to sell some calves and a few old cows. I have a trucker coming in tomorrow about 11am. We need them sorted and ready to go by then."

Kole nodded. "What time you want to start sorting?"

"We'll first bring them in from the field, and then start sorting. We'll go at 8:30; should be light enough by then. We'll not use the horses, just shake the oat bucket, and they will probably just come, with you guys getting the stragglers behind."

"Sounds good," indicated Tom. Both Tom and Kole were familiar with cattle, and had helped Jack a few times before. Tom had even driven a cattle truck a few times a few years back. Jack had a special corral system with swinging gates and a long narrow chute. All cattle would go through the chute, which would divide into two large pens. A swinging gate would be moved by someone back and forth. Calves would be forced into one pen, and cows into another.

That would just be the beginning of the sorting, because a few of the old cows would also be sorted for slaughter, and because some of the heifer calves would not be going on the truck so they would have to be sorted out. Jack would handle the gate. That way he only had himself to blame if an animal got into the wrong pen.

o o o

Next morning, Kole and Tom arrived to see the tractor running. Jack motioned for them to follow him and he started driving to the corrals, a couple hundred yards away. He cleared the snow from the gates, and in front of the chute area, and cleaned some of the snow out of the big corral. The cows would tramp down the rest of the snow in the smaller corrals and in the chute area. Kole grabbed a scoop shovel and cleared snow from the swinging gate area, so it could be moved back and forth.

Soon, the cows were bawling and moving towards Jack, who was shaking a pail of oats in his hands. The cows remembered the oats from last spring, when Jack would feed them oats as a treat, and the calves followed the cows. Tom and Kole went round back of the herd to move a few stragglers, and soon they were all in the large corral.

After another hour of sorting, cows were in one corral, and calves in a third pen. Jack indicated three old cows, and between them, they managed to split them from the herd fairly easily. They moved the rest of the cows back out to the pasture. Then the calves were run through again, but this time Jack made decisions about which heifers to keep as future cows, while the rest of the calves were redirected back to the pen. Some guys weaned calves earlier and conditioned them for sale, but Jack weaned the day he sold. He suffered a little on the price, but it reduced his handling of the calves, and when the weaned calves were sold to market, then the mothers and calves could not hear each other bawling, so they became quiet much sooner.

By this time, the truck had arrived and backed up to the loading chute. In fifteen minutes, the steer calves, the three old cows, and the heifer calves that Jack did not want to keep, were on the truck. In the end, Jack kept two more heifers, because the truck was too full for any more. Jack signed the bill of lading, and the trucker, a familiar old neighbor from about ten miles away, left with the cattle for the market, which this year, would be a four hour drive south.

SEISMIC TRAIL

Now they had to listen to the remaining heifers bawling for their mothers. Tom and Kole brought oats for the calves to the feed bunks, and that helped some, but between mouthfuls of oats, the calves would turn to the cows and then bawl some more. Jack knew it would be a racket of noise for several days before it quietened down, but there was not much he could do about it. He turned on the electric fencer, so that the wire along the corral fence between cows and calves would keep the calves away from it. The cows were probably happy that they didn't have to feed the calves anymore, but there was a special attachment between cow and calf, which could last for several years, even though the cow would no longer feed the calf.

Jack brought the tractor back to the shed, and Tom and Kole headed for the shop. It was time for lunch, but afterwards, they would help Jake with his new machine.

o o o

Lunch in his belly, Jill in an acceptable mood, Carla playing in the recreation room downstairs, Jack drove down the highway to meet with his accountant at his home. He needed to make sure they were on the same page with budgets for the winter, with tax deductions and tax credits, and with payroll. It would not be a long discussion, about an hour, but Jack liked to do some of these face to face.

Two miles out on the highway, he noticed flashing blue and red lights behind him. He looked down at his speedometer, and thumped his hand on the wheel. Really??!! He hardly ever saw cops on this highway, but today one was there? And he hadn't noticed, when he turned on the road. The narrow light band on top of the white truck looked like the top of a headache rack that many company trucks had installed. Cops were often driving pickup trucks now, or SUVs that looked like trucks from a distance.

"Do you know how fast you were going?"

"Well, when I looked, I was going too fast. Yeah."

"Can I see your license and registration please."

Jack reached into his glove compartment and got the registration, and dug out his license from his wallet. He had one radar ticket last year, but no demerits from that. And a highway that barely had any traffic at this time of day. Except for a half-bored cop who needed something to justify his job. Why wasn't he hunting down druggies, molesters, or dealers? But Jack didn't say that out loud. No point to that.

"You were doing 125 km/h. You know the limit is 100 km/h."

"Yeah, yeah. I know. I just was thinking about something else. These darn trucks just seem to take off. Last week I came back from Texas, and every highway was 80 mph, that's 130 km/h. Even two lanes like this were usually 70 mph...115 km/h."

"This is not the USA. If you had been going about 10 km/h less, I would have let you off with a warning. But I have to give you a ticket. Slow down!"

Jack did not reply to that. He was frustrated and angry, but knew he had no real excuse. He deserved the ticket. While the officer wrote the ticket summons, Jack called his accountant, Bob, and told him he would be a bit late.

"Its okay, Jack. It gives me more time on my rowing machine. I've got everything ready for you when you get here."

"Hah. You get your exercise inside, I'll get mine outside."

"Yeah, you can freeze your buns off while I am nice and comfortable inside."

As he continued to the accountant's office, which was a home-based business, he put the ticket out of his mind, but he did drive slower. Only 5 km/h over the speed limit this time.

Chapter Thirty-Eight

"HEY! YOU'RE SLOW!!" BILL yelled down the field at Richard. Richard could hear him clearly in the cold crisp air. In fact, sometimes they could hear the next crew over a half mile away, as they talked to each other. Bill's comment was not appreciated by Richard, since he knew that sound carried a long way, and the other guys would be chuckling at Richard's expense if they heard it.

"What's keeping you? Move it man!" Richard was getting a bit irate. The snow was deep, his hands were cold, and it took time to warm them with the electric warmers in his gloves, between the various steps he needed to do.

"I'm coming!" he yelled back. He saw Bill sitting on the track of the machine, opening up his thermos of coffee. Waiting for him. Richard finished his hole, and then trudged to where Bill was. Instead of beginning work on the next hole, he too sat on the track, sipping on his coffee. "You got the easy job. Want to trade, and see if you keep up?"

Bill grinned. "Nah, that's all right. If we switched, I'd be waiting for you to drill the holes."

"Sure you would. Sure, you think you would."

"You never drilled before, right?"

"True, but watching you, it looks like you got the easy job."

"Except for the mud."

"Yeah, except for the mud." Changing the subject, Richard thought to ask Bill about his family. "You asked me the other day about my kids, which I don't have. But you got any?"

"Kids? Yeah, I got three kids. All boys. Teenagers. But from what I hear, boys are easier than girls. At that age, anyway."

"That right?"

"My sister has girls, and you wouldn't believe the stories I get from her husband about their girls. Emotional, wow! Unpredictable. Moody. Course they love their girls, but one of their girls is giving them a lot of problems. With boys. And homework. And helping around the house. The other two girls are much better."

Richard hesitated, "Yeah, I got some nieces and nephews. I heard stories. But you got boys, huh?"

"Yeah. They are fourteen, fifteen, and seventeen. Love to go dirt riding with me. They fix their own bikes, and the oldest saved up enough money to buy himself a quad, a used Honda. We live on an acreage, ten acres. Its a bit small for dirt riding, but we some crown land about a half mile away with lots of trails. It keeps the boys busy."

"I hope to have some kids someday. Have to find the right woman."

Bill looked at Richard, "I thought you had a woman?"

"Maybe. She might be the right woman."

"What is the right woman? What do you want her to be?"

"Don't want someone who drinks too much. I quit. I don't want a drinker. And someone who likes kids. Who is smart about kids."

Bill nodded, "Well, that sounds reasonable."

"Yeah. Not a drinker. And no drugs. And a one man woman."

"You think she is it?"

"Maybe. I'll find out when I get back."

"Yeah, my wife is something else," Bill replied. "I can't believe how patient she is. She works too, but has a job where she is always home when the boys get home from school. And when I'm gone, she doesn't complain. Always takes the boys to their hockey. Course now, my oldest boy can drive, so he does a lot of the driving, taking his brothers here and there."

'That's the kind of woman I want."

Bill grinned. "We never argue. But we do have our moments of intense fellowship, if you know what I mean."

Richard, confused, "Fellowship? ... oh, yeah, I get it. Intense fellowship. No arguments. Hah."

"One of these days you should come to my place for a visit. Then you could see my boys. You would like them."

"Hey. Maybe."

"We better get back to work. We got a bunch of holes to get done today, yet." Bill, got up and put his thermos in the cab. Richard put his big cup in the cab too, and noticed the rifle laying behind the seat.

"You ever have to use this gun when you're out on the line?"

"Once, but just a warning shot. The bear ran to the trees."

"Do all the guys pack a gun? The drillers I mean?"

"Most carry a rifle. Some of the helpers have hand guns, but the law about that is dicey. All kinds of rules about packing a loaded handgun, or unloaded. So most carry pepper spray. But some just take their chances. No one has been attacked by a bear so far. A couple guys have seen a cougar. Wolves stay out of sight in the daytime.... I guess the noise of the drill keeps them away."

Bill paused, and then added, "I'd say about three quarters of the guys are hunters. So they have a bunch of guns at home. I shot a moose the first day on the job this fall. Put in a long day... after drilling, hauled the moose home, and the boys helped me skin it and hang it up. Three days later we cut it up and wrapped the meat."

"Jack doesn't mind you hunting on the job?"

"Nah. As long as we have tags for the area and its in season. Jack hunts too, when he gets a chance."

"Well, I guess I fit in then. I hunt too sometimes." By now Bill was in the cab and beginning to move the machine. Richard grabbed his gel and blasting caps so that he could begin his work with this hole.

Chapter Thirty-Nine

"HEY, YOU SURE YOU don't know where those guys are? Maurice and Manny?"

"Why are you calling me again," asked Jack, irritated. "Didn't I already tell you? Look after your own people. If they haven't called you, they are likely leaving you. Took off somewhere on their own. Or got run over by a truck. Maybe eaten by a bear. Maybe in prison somewhere. Quit calling me. It's not my business. I don't know. And I don't care."

"Someone going to die. Maybe them. Maybe you. Maybe your family. Nobody does this to me. Nobody!"

"Don't threaten me. I don't know, and I don't care what happened to your men!"

"I send two more men. Better men. Nobody does this to me!"

"Don't threaten me. Don't even think about it. And don't call me again!"

Jack turned off the call. But he wondered. Would those guys really turn on their boss and keep the drugs for themselves? Would they take such a chance? He walked out of his office into the shop. "Kole, can you come here a minute. ... I am getting phone calls from someone who wants to know where those two guys are. Someone from Texas I think, or maybe

Mexico. Now he is talking about sending two more men. What was the last thing you saw after those guys got on that machine?"

"Well, they were checking out the cab, and under the cab, and the undercarriage. I wasn't watching real close, because we were talking, Richard and me. They got a few tools from their truck and loosened some bolts on the other side of the machine. Couldn't really see what they were doing... they seemed to find something, slapped each other on the back, and took their things back to their truck. Then they just took off. Didn't even wave goodbye."

"So what did you do?"

"We were a hundred yards away... we drove to the machine, made sure it was okay, keys were turned off. Then drove away and came home, here."

"Okay," Jack hesitated, then turned back to the office. Kole looked after him, and then returned to his work in the shop.

o o o

"Hello boss." Richard was surprised to get a call from Jack. Jack usually talked to Bill, not to Richard, out in the field.

"I want to ask you something about those two guys you brought to the drill. I've been getting phone calls from their boss, and he hasn't heard from them. What was the last you saw of them? What were they doing? What did you see them do to the machine?"

"Well, Kole and I were in the truck. Not too close to them. They were climbing around the machine. Checking fuel tanks and the water tank. Crawling around. Under and over. Then they found something on the far side of the machine it looked like. They took it, we couldn't see from where we were, a couple hundred yards away. They took it to their truck and took off. Didn't stop. We went to the machine, checked it out. Then we left for home."

"You were two hundred yards away?"

"Yeah, about that, I think. Didn't really measure it or step it off, but it seemed like 200 yards. About."

"Did they use tools? Did they get tools from their truck?"

"Uh, maybe. Can't say for sure. They might have had some tools with them."

A long pause on Jack's end. "Well. Okay. This guy is giving me grief, and I need to know everything. I don't want any problems, and he should be leaving me alone. ...okay, I'll let you get back to work."

o o o

That night, Jack couldn't sleep. He usually slept like a log, and seven hours were enough for him most nights. He churned some distressing thoughts in his mind. Why did he get the impression that Kole and Richard's stories didn't line up? Why did he have this uneasy feeling that they were hiding something from him?

Their stories made sense. It was the way it should have happened. The way he had ordered them to do. They didn't seem suspicious, and yet, yet there was something. A little thing, like had those guys gone back to their truck to get tools. A little thing, like were they one hundred or two hundred yards away. With some guys, not knowing the difference between one hundred and two hundred yards might not be unusual. Distance was nebulous, vague and pure guesswork. But for his men, who worked outside for hours, measuring distance between one drilled hole and the next was second nature. Richard had been doing that for several days now. And Kole was a hunter. Hunters knew the range of their rifles. They had to if they were going to sight-in their scopes, if they were going to make accurate shots, and make sure the deer were not out of range of their rifles. One hundred yards vs two hundred yards was a big difference.

So maybe they had not been paying attention. But Jack couldn't get the thought out of his mind. Something was not quite right. And he wasn't sure if he really wanted to know.

Chapter Forty

THE TWO MEN WORE sunglasses as they sat in their new black Escalade at the Mexican border, waiting to cross into the USA. They were dressed in crisp new clothes, wearing gold necklaces and watches, and had their passports and visas in order. They did not look like migrant workers desperate for some dollars to send back to their families. When they were asked for vehicle registration, they did not blink, but handed it over to the customs official.

Both men looked like Mexicans, well-to-do Mexicans. One was a medium height slim built man with a scar on his left hand, and a missing pinkie finger. The driver was a larger, heavier man with a trim black moustache and beefy fingers. Both had their hair neatly trimmed, and looked comfortable in the tan leather seats of the Escalade. When the customs official asked them to remove their sunglasses, they quickly obliged, putting them back on as soon as he had checked them against their passport pictures.

Traveling through, they said. Headed to Canada. Back in a month.

He made a notation in his ledger, and handed their documents back to them.

Ten miles down the highway, they turned off on a side road. They took off the Mexican license plates, and exchanged them for American ones which they had under the seat in the back. They exchanged the vehicle registration papers in the glove compartment, putting the Mexican ones in the compartment with tire changing equipment. Then they resumed their journey.

Chapter Forty-One

"WE NEED TO GET that old drill back in the field." Jack had walked in to Jake's work area that morning full of steam. Jake pulled off his goggles and laid down the welding torch.

"Okay, I guess. One of the other drills causing trouble?" Jake was slightly puzzled.

"I want that Venezuela drill back in the shop. We need to go over it with a fine-tooth comb. Have to find out what those two guys wanted with the drill." Jack had formulated a plan, and he wasted no time to carry it out.

"Those two guys.... you mean the guys that were here a couple days ago? The mexicans?"

"Yeah. They wanted something from that drill. I don't know what, but I think it was drugs. I don't know if they got it or not. So we are going to check that machine from top to bottom to make sure there is nothing there. We have to fix this older one here to bring it to the field so Bill and Richard can keep working."

"Alrighty then. I'll get right on it. The engine was rough. You want it rebuilt, or replaced?"

"Replaced with a new cummins. I will get Kole to run to town to pick it up from the dealer. They told me they had one on standby."

"D'you mind if Tom goes to get it? I'd rather have Kole helping me take out this other engine. And we need to check a few other things too."

"All right. That works too. If it all goes good, then we can bring this machine back to the job first thing tomorrow morning."

Jack went to the office and made a call to the Cummins dealer, about an hour away. "Hold that engine for me, will you? I've got someone coming to pick it up."

"Will do. Want to pay for it, or charge it?"

"Just bill me, okay?"

"Will do. Have a good day!"

Jack decided to go back to the house across the yard for a bit. Jill had not made breakfast for him that morning, and had gone back to bed after getting Erin on the school bus. He needed to talk to her.

"How you doing, girl?" he asked as he entered the bedroom. She rolled over and turned her back to him, hiding under the sheets.

"Not feeling well?"

"No." terse reply.

"Anything I can do? D'you need a couple advil?"

"Maybe."

Jack retrieved a couple advil and a glass of water and put them on her night table. Then he went to the kitchen and poured two cups of coffee, putting in cream and sugar. He had made the coffee that morning, and already had a cup, but was ready for a second, after his sleepless night. Bringing the other cup along to the bedroom, he wondered what was bothering Jill.

"Here's a coffee, Jill." He noticed she had taken the pills and finished the water. She had lain back down again but got up when she noticed the coffee.

"Thanks. Coffee smells good."

"You okay? Something bothering you?" He could do that, she thought, almost resentfully. Such a pain, so much time he spent at his work, ignoring her, or taking her for granted. But when she needed it, he paid attention. Must be why she married him. She didn't know whether to resent him, or appreciate him.

"Yes, I'm okay. Sorry I didn't make your breakfast."

"You know what? It's no problem. I'm going to make something right away. Did you have something to eat?"

"Yes, I had some cereal with Erin. Carla is still sleeping... usually she's up, but she went to bed late, watching a movie."

Jack toyed with the idea of crawling into bed with Jill. They had done this before, once in awhile, getting special joy out of being together while men were working in the shop. It was a special illegitimate treat, possible because he was his own boss, and he could set his own schedule. He grinned thinking about it. But he decided it wouldn't work. He was still too upset with thinking about the Mexicans, Venezuelan drill, and the threats to his family.

"How about we have some breakfast, and then go check the cows together?" he suggested to Jill.

After a pause, she slowly replied, "Okay. I think I would like that. I want to apologize to you, Jack."

"What for? Missing breakfast once? No big deal."

"Well yes, for that. But for being upset with you yesterday when I told you I was pregnant."

"Hey, no big deal. I was busy. You were busy. It got me by surprise, that's all. I had stuff on my mind. How about we talk it over while having breakfast? I'll make something while you get dressed." Jill nodded, and Jack left for the kitchen.

On the way, he checked his phone, but amazingly, there were no messages. Through the kitchen window, he saw Tom leaving in the pickup truck for town to pickup the new engine. He pulled out a frying pan, and some pancake flour. Why not some pancakes and eggs? It would be a nice change from oatmeal.

"Jack, you know what's funny? Here I am, apologizing for stuff, and instead of making your breakfast and coffee, I lay in bed, sulking to myself. Why did I do that?"

"Like I said Jill, it's okay. Everyday you get my breakfast, get the kids up, Erin ready for school, make my lunch, sometimes shovel snow. And now you're pregnant. Here, have some more coffee."

"I listened to this psychologist doctor on the radio yesterday. He was asked by the radio host if he believed in God. The psychologist said he didn't like the question. He said too many people said they believed in God, but it made no difference in their life. So, he said his answer was, that he tried to live like there was a God." now that she had started, Jill was on a roll. "I realized that I should look at my own life, how I live. I go to church most Sundays. I say I believe. But do I live like it?"

Jill continued, "And I realized that I don't always live like it. I get selfish, resentful, even mean sometimes. I always expect something in return for whatever good I think I do. I want to apologize."

Jack was quiet. He nodded. "Look. Nobody's perfect. Not even my perfect wife."

She grinned. A brief grin, and then serious again. "Well, I know that. But I think I was just making excuses for myself. Or thinking I was better than I am. And that made me worse than I actually want to be. Does that make sense?"

"Well, its a bit deep for me. So I just want you to eat these pancakes. How about that?"

She sighed in relief, and she smiled. "I keep asking you to come to church with me. But I am the one who needs it, not you. I remember now what I heard last Sunday at church. It was about Jesus meeting Zaccheus. I listened to the preacher, but it didn't sink in until this morning. He was a tax collector. Zaccheus invited Jesus to his house. And then he promised to repay anything he had taken that he shouldn't have, like if he collected too much tax. But not till now do I get it. It had an effect on his life. He didn't just listen to nice sayings, or watch things happen. His life changed."

"I think I wanted you to come to church, because I believe in God. Because its nice to go to church. To talk with other people. To be seen there. To feel like you know God, and like you will go to heaven, because well, you are doing the proper things. But Jesus expects a life change in our attitude. I'm not sure I really understood that. So, I want to apologize to you, Jack, for whenever I have grumped and complained. God has been so good to me, actually. And you have also been so good to me, a gift from God. I want you to know that."

"Wow. That's something! That's nice to hear! I almost wonder if I have a different woman here this morning. But you know, I always loved you. I think in your heart, you always were that way, even if you didn't always show it on the outside." Jack went to give her a hug from the back, as she sat in her chair. "Don't worry about me. I got your back. Always will."

She snuggled in his hug, and then spiked another piece of pancake. "This is a good pancake! And love those eggs. Done just right!"

"So, are you happy you are pregnant again?"

"I'm happier today than I was a couple days ago. I haven't had any sickness issues, so that's nice."

"Think we need to add on to the house? A room maybe?"

"Maybe. But no rush. A little baby doesn't take up that much room. By the way, what was keeping you up last night? You were tossing and turning and tossing and turning."

"Just work. Figuring out how to keep everything working." Jack had no desire to share his actual dilemma with Jill. Hoped he would never have to. No need for her to worry about things.

"You usually sleep so good. Lay your head down and gone to sleep in about ten seconds."

Jack wanted to change the subject, "Let's go check those cows. Getting outside for awhile will be good for both of us, especially you. I want to make sure the calves are staying separate from the mothers. And make sure there are no sick calves."

Jack pressed the remote start for the truck. For Jill, a bit warmer truck was good. Together they put on winter boots, parkas and mitts. As they got into the truck, Jack opened the door for Jill, not something he did everyday. But today was a bit special, one of those stolen moments in time, that hopefully they would remember as a good day.

Chapter Forty-Two

"LET'S GET AT THIS thing." Jack looked at Kole and Tom as they stood beside the Venezuela drill. Yesterday, they had changed engines in the older drill, and loaded it on the truck. Early this morning, at five am, Tom had driven it to the job, and had loaded up the newer Venezuela drill. He had made good time, and just after lunch was back in the yard. Tom went to get a bite to eat from the kitchen in the shop, while Jack came from his lunch in the house. Now they were looking at the machine, and Jack was formulating a plan of action.

"Kole, you follow the way those two guys were crawling over the machine. Check everything that makes sense, that they were possibly checking. Tom, ya, you don't know what we are doing exactly. Two Mexicans were real interested in this machine. We think maybe they had stashed drugs on it. Kole thinks they found it. But I'm not sure, because I got a strange call from someone who is likely their boss. I want to check this machine from top to bottom, to make sure something is not still on it. That way I can tell them there is nothing there."

Kole proceeded to start checking everything, starting by crawling on his back between the tracks.

"Hold it. We are going to bring it in the shop first, and we'll put it on the ramps so it is higher off the ground, and easier to get underneath." They drove it off the truck, into the shop and up some steel ramps which raised the entire machine about eighteen inches off the ground. As the doors shut, the heat from the shop started to melt the snow and frozen mud off the machine, making the floor wet in places.

Kole grabbed a mechanics creeper from the wall, and crawled under the machine, laying on his back. Tom and Jack started looking in the cab. They grabbed an electric drill and an impact and started to remove covers and panels which might hide something. After removing everything possible in the cab, they found nothing. The seats looked untouched, with rusty bolts holding on the imitation leather. Side panels on the doors were open and showed nothing.

"Okay, nothing in the cab. We might as well put all these covers back on." Which they did.

Kole came out from underneath, wiping some melted muddy snow off his face, and said he had seen nothing suspicious. "I can't see anything strange. I guess maybe there could be something in a water line or fuel line, or in a hydraulic hose, but it would plug up the line. And the machine has been working well."

"You know, Bill said it had hesitated a couple times, but then kept running. I wonder if something in the fuel tank might be closing off the fuel line once in awhile, and then bouncing free again?" Tom put in his wisdom.

Jack stood up, after peering beneath the machine. "I'm thinking if someone wanted to hide something, the fuel tank or hydraulic tank would be a good spot. The fuel would reduce the sensor's ability to pick up something. Would reduce odors too, so the border dogs couldn't pick up the smell. We should check the tank."

"You mean drain it and take it apart?"

"I don't think we can take the fuel tank apart. Maybe the hydraulic reservoir, but not the fuel tank. I have an idea." Jack went to the tool bench in the shop and picked a tool from the wall. It was a magnet attached to a semi stiff but flexible wire about four feet long. "How about if we stick this in, and see if anything comes out?"

"It would have to be metal to be magnetic." put forth Kole.

"Yes but lets try it. If we get nothing, maybe we can try a hook on it, or make something we can fish with." Putting the magnet through the filler tube, Jack tried to move it around the bottom of the tank. It stuck to the bottom of the metal tank, but when he twisted the wire, the magnet also twisted, and he was able to move it. He pulled it out several times, thinking he might have something, but nothing was attached to the magnet. Meanwhile, Kole was making a hook on another similar cable, to be used if the magnet didn't work. Giving it one last try, Jack inserted the magnet again, trying to head it to a different part of the tank. This time he felt extra weight on the line as he pulled it out of the tank.

Careful not to pull too fast, he gently eased the line out. Peering into the tube, he could see something attached. As he pulled, the object dropped off as it scraped the side of the filler tube. But now he knew it was there, so he reinserted the magnet, made contact with the object, and pulled it more carefully, making sure it didn't scrape the tube edge, and voila! Pulled it out!

It was a metal nut, ¾ inch, and it was attached to a non-metal line. He gently pulled on the line, which eventually tied to a metal line, which was attached to a narrow package. He kept pulling, and the package came out, but the metal line continued on the other end, and another package followed. Jack continued, until he had removed seven packages finally, all tied on the same line.

They just stared at the packages for a minute. Wondering what was in them, Jack put the packages on the work bench, and then said, "We have to try the hydraulic reservoir too." The hydraulic tank was fairly large, a forty gallon tank, because a lot of hydraulics were used to operate the drill.

Sure enough, by using the same process in the heavier thicker fluid, they found another ten packages in the hydraulic reservoir. "I think we found what we were looking for. And I guess they did not find it then." Jack rubbed his forehead, which was aching, and which turned it into a black smudge from his greasy hands.

The drill had a second fuel tank, which fueled a 300 cfm compressor motor. The air compressor was used to blow dirt and rock cuttings out of a hole in the ground as it was being drilled. Jack looked at the second fuel tank, wondering if it had more packages. But the filler tube for it was smaller, and he could see the packages would not fit through. He was confident they had not used that tank for more packages.

"Let's grab a coffee a minute and give this a think."

After a few quiet moments, sipping on coffee, and chewing a cookie, Jack said, "I think we got it. I doubt there is any more." They had fished a while with Kole's improvised hook and line, and they had found nothing more in either tank. "We'll load up the drill, and Tom can bring it back to the job site tomorrow morning. No rush, as long as all the other drills are working okay. You guys can load it up, and then help Bill until quitting time." Jack began washing the plastic packages with soapy water, wondering if they had stayed dry inside. He wondered how much stuff was here, maybe half a kilo per package? Nine kilos? Not a small amount.

So why did those two guys not find this stuff? It was quite an ingenious idea to hide it like that. Not easy to get back out either. Although the stuff was wrapped fairly well, a hook of some type could possibly puncture the packages, if it grabbed them the wrong way. But the cylindrical magnet would not puncture anything. The magnet could be wrapped with a thin plastic film and still work, although it would lose a bit of power. The fluids allowed it to slide on the bottom or sides of the tank better than on dry metal.

Each package was about a half pound, or 250 gms. Jack used the little bench scale to weigh them. He guessed it was heroin, for no other reason than a suspicion.

"What do you think it is, Kole?" Kole had some experience with drugs for a brief time in the past.

"My guess is heroin. Doesn't look like cocaine to me." The clear packaging allowed some idea of color and texture, but they did not open the packages. "But don't know how pure it is."

"What's it worth?"

"Well, it used to be sold for about $300 per gram. But I don't know what it is worth now. Be different on the street, compared to wholesale. Cocaine would be about half that." Kole scratched his memory. But back in those days, memories were erased, not made, and dollars became often meaningless.

"At $300 per gram, this stuff could be worth $75,000 per package. That's $1,2750,000 for seventeen packages. More than a million. Street value."

"Makes you wonder if this is the first time for this method, or if they have done this before. In equipment fuel tanks."

Kole and Tom were silent. They imagined what they could do with that money. But neither one was overly interested. Tom had quit drinking a few years before, because of the problems that the alcohol was causing him. He did not want to lose his license again. Kole had quit drugs for two reasons; money disappearing, and a lack of purpose overtaking him due to the drugs. He had only tried heroin once. Mostly it was cannabis, and the occasional foray into cocaine. For awhile he had some struggles with the addictions, but his determination had won out in the end.

"What you going to do with it?" asked Kole.

Jack contemplated the threats he had received from the two, Maurice and Manny, as well as their boss down south. He could possibly reduce the threat just by turning the drugs over to these guys and closing his eyes to the whole thing. But there was a streak of resentment that had built up since the time they first met these guys. The resentment was caused by Jack's spirit of independence, not wanting strangers telling him what to do on his own turf, or with his own equipment. The resentment had been magnified and multiplied by their overt threats to his family.

Jack had buried the resentment for awhile, thinking discretion was the better part of valor, but now it surfaced again. And he wondered if somehow the easy way out was not the path chosen for him. After all, here were the drugs he thought he had eliminated.

He had strict rules about drugs on the job. Even alcohol. And here was evidence of the whole underworld trying to ruin his workers and other workers like them. Here was the substance of the stuff that ruined many lives of teenagers, and innocent family members of addicts. Here was the evil poison itself, profits and power of the careless manipulators, drug lords and enforcers who supported them. What side of the battle was he on?

"I'm going to give this some thought. I'll take it into the house. I want you guys to promise me that you will not tell anyone else about this."

"I think you better include Jake in that. I think he knows what we found." indicated Tom, with a nod of his head to the man in question.

"What do you know, Jake?"

"I heard. I saw you weighing the stuff on the bench. I won't tell anyone else."

"Would it be okay for me to tell Richard when I see him?" asked Kole. "He and I were at the machine when those guys went over it, and I think he should know what we found."

"Okay, Richard then. But no one else. I have to decide how to handle this in a way that no one gets hurt. These are mean guys with huge egos, lots of money incentive to do the wrong things. I don't want you guys getting hurt. Nor my family either, or your families. So, do I go to the cops or not? What is the story? And which cops?"

"If you go to the cops, it'll be the RCMP. They will want to start an investigation. But it'll be international, because the drugs came across a couple of borders at least. And through the USA, so their FBI, drug enforcement, and maybe CIA could get involved. A million dollars is a lot, but still not much compared to some things." Kole was thinking out loud, and Jack and Tom were nodding in agreement.

"Question is how much effort will they put into it. Will they get to the criminals before the criminals get to carry out their threats?" Tom posed the question that made them the most uncomfortable. It was the question that worried Jack the most. His two daughters. And a pregnant wife. He felt like the top bull in the herd, and a mother bear all at the same time. A dog protecting its owner, a doctor protecting a patient, what were they, compared to a father protecting his daughter?

"I'm going to leave this here. I don't want Jill asking questions about it. I'll be back in a bit. Give Jake a hand for awhile till I get back."

Jack walked to the house, and noticed Jill hanging up laundry outside. "Isn't it a bit cold for outdoor laundry?" he asked Jill.

She looked at him for a moment. "I'm pregnant. I have a license to do silly things. I like the smell of sheets after the fresh air. I've already dried them in the drier."

"So now you'll have to put them in the drier again just to warm them up, before anyone will sleep in them." Jack grinned at her, hiding his anxiety, and trying to get her to relax.

"True, that. Are you coming in for some tea?"

"If you have some on. Or coffee would be okay too."

"I've got tea on. And some pie. Carla is downstairs, drawing some pictures. Erin will be home in a couple hours. No, about an hour and a half."

Jack settled on a chair and sipped his tea. "I'm going to be gone tonight. Have to go to Edmonton for some business. Look at some equipment and talk to one of the contracts."

"You're not forgetting what day it is?"

"Why? No, yes, I know it's Friday, isn't it? These guys are available tomorrow, so it'll be okay."

Jill forked a piece of pie. She liked the saskatoon pie, but as usual, had taken a piece about a third the size of Jack's. She put on the pounds too easily, if she wasn't careful. On the other hand, it seemed Jack could eat all day and it didn't make a difference.

"I guess if you want to be there in the morning, you'll have to leave tonight. I'm going to miss you." It was a six hour drive, maybe a bit less if the roads were good. It was not the first time Jack would leave in the evening. He could fly there, but it gave him less flexibility for arrival and departure. With the security at airports these days, and the aiport an hour and a half away, he didn't save much time by flying to Edmonton. In this case, he preferred to drive, because he intended to take the packages with him. Putting them on a plane was out of the question.

"Yeah, I'll miss you too. But this can't wait. I'll be back tomorrow night. We'll go out for supper."

They were comfortably quiet for awhile. Jack recalled Jill's professed change in attitude, and he had to admit that he could see it coming through. He hoped they wouldn't lose their friendly verbal tug of wars. He had often enjoyed those.

o o o

A half hour later, Jack was on the highway southbound. He had called his sister Marie in Spruce Grove, just west of Edmonton, and she had a spare bed available for him. He often stayed there, as he much preferred it to a hotel, and it gave him a chance to visit. It would take him about a half hour from there to the RCMP downtown.

Chapter Forty-Three

THE SKY WAS STILL dark, but starting to lighten up in the east, the direction Kole was headed with the Kenworth as he pulled the trailer loaded with the Venezuela drill back to the job site on Saturday morning. Pavement was clean, although the shoulders still had a skiff of snow on them. Traffic was light, no wind so far, and temperature was a decent minus 25, with a promise to warm up about ten degrees C, later this afternoon. The steady rumble of the engine, along with the faint humming of the tires relaxed him on this beautiful morning as he listened to his favorite music on the radio. It seemed no time at all before he arrived at the job site.

"Hey Kole." said Bill as he walked up to Kole, who was unloading the drill from his trailer. "You are here early enough."

"Yeah, thought I would start early so I can quit earlier too. I have some plans with some friends for tonight."

"The Venezuela drill again? You picking up the other one then?"

"Yup. Leaving Vinny and picking up Spinny."

"Hah. Yeah we should call it Vinny. Cool."

"How's life? I brought a few refinished drill stem too."

"We are doing good. No breakdowns yesterday, got lots of holes done. Richard is getting the hang of helping, and the water truck too." Tom went to the drill to start it up and just then Richard showed up as Kole was about to climb back into his Kenworth cab.

"How's it going?" asked Richard.

"Good, good." replied Kole, a bit hesitantly. "Good drive down. Clean roads."

"How's Jack doing?" Richard was asking more than his question implied.

"He's good." Kole decided Richard deserved more details. "We found some packages in the drill. In the fuel tank and hydraulic tank. Drugs."

"Hmm." Richard sounded noncommittal, but wasn't really.

"I think Jack is a bit suspicious about what happened to Manny and Maurice. But he didn't make any accusations. He is bringing the stuff to Edmonton."

"Oh?" raised eyebrow. Richard had made the fatal decision with Kole a few days before, but they both knew that future events could be critical.

"He had a call from down south somewhere, about those two guys. More threats. I think he worries about some more guys coming up from there. Anyway, he says don't tell anyone anything."

"Good idea. That's fine by me." Richard turned away. Then turned back, "Let me know anything going on, okay?"

"Will do." Kole climbed in, shut the door and eased the truck back onto the road. Everytime he came to this site, he looked around but did not see anything to cause suspicions.

As Bill waited for Richard to get back to him, he wondered about the snatches he had heard from Kole. Drugs? Edmonton? Threats? He thought that hauling the Venezuelan drill back and forth so quickly was very strange, and suspected it had to do with the mention of drugs. But didn't understand what Edmonton or threats had to do with it. Obviously, Jack was involved. But Jack wouldn't sell drugs, would he? He had strict policies about not using drugs on the job. As far as Bill knew, Jack never used drugs. Never had. Well, maybe smoked some weed once, but that was it.

With his twenty years in the oil business, Bill knew lots of guys who had been on the tail end of the drug chain, users, heavy users, occasional users, and even some dealers. But he himself had managed to stay away from it. He knew what weed smelled like, had even puffed a couple. But it did not turn him on. He'd much rather settle down with a bottle of beer or two. His enjoyment of fresh air was not enhanced by the smoke of the weed.

"Let's get this thing going." Bill said to Richard as he returned. "Let's see what Vinny will do."

Chapter Forty-Four

AS JACK PULLED UP to the RCMP Divisional headquarters on 111 Avenue in Edmonton, he wondered if his plan would work.

"Can I help you?" asked the clerk at the counter as he stepped through the door.

"I'd like to talk to the drug department."

"Okay. Can I get you to fill out this form please."

Jack looked at the form closely. This would not do. "I can't fill it out. I need to talk to someone in person, with no paper trail. And I need to give them some stuff. And find out what it is."

"Yes, but we need some information first. Please fill out the form, and then wait in the lobby."

"No. I don't think so. You fill out whatever form you want but get me someone who knows street drugs. I need anonymity and action. Not paperwork. And I need it quick, because I have to get back to work."

She paused, familiar with odd behavior, but having to go through the protocol. "I will see what I can do." She picked up the phone and had some conversation which Jack could not hear. He heard a few snatches of "drugs, leather jacket, medium height, brown hair, looks sincere". "Some one is coming. Just sit down in one of those chairs. He'll be here soon."

Jack sat down. Whoever was coming, did not come soon. At least not in Jack's opinion. But Jack was not a waiting type of guy. Not sitting waiting for things to happen. He got up, walked a circuit in the room and sat down again. Three times. Just as he was about to get up again, the door opened and a slightly balding man wearing a slightly wrinkled gray suit entered. "Are you Jack?"

"Yes."

"Last name?"

"Let's leave that alone. At least for now. What's your name?"

"Inspector Charles McMorton. Normally I'd send a sergeant, but as it happens, they are all occupied. Nancy seemed to think you were legitimate, and it might be worth our while. So here I am. Is it worth my while?"

"Depends. Are you on the drug squad?"

"I am in charge of drug detectives. What is your problem?"

"I need someone who can keep confidentiality. Anonymity. I have received threats to my family and I need to find a way to defuse those threats. But I also want to turn over some stuff. Don't know for sure what it is. But I don't want it coming back to me. Understand?"

"Can't promise that. If we want to prosecute, we need witnesses, we need evidence. We need an evidence trail. Without that, we can't do much."

"So if I have a million dollars in drugs, that's okay then?"

McMorton paused. "A million dollars?"

"Well, I don't know for sure. I'm not a dealer. Not a user. Just guessing. But I think it is a really good guess, given the circumstances."

"We could just arrest you, I suppose. Then we would have the evidence and the witness." Jack saw the glint in McMorton's eyes.

"Yeah, I thought about that. So I don't have the evidence on me. But if I get your promise to protect my anonymity, then I will get it." Jack's eyes were hard, unyielding. "This is really important to me. I could just burn it all, or bury it. But this is your business, catching these guys, getting stuff off the street. I am interested in hurting these guys, slowing them down, making life miserable for them. And this is international. If you protect me, I can give you the whole story."

Jack could see that McMorton was becoming interested. "A million dollars of junk?"

Jack said nothing. Mc Morton paced back and forth a couple times. Looking around at the people beginning to enter the lobby, he said, "Let's go to my office." He had thought this would be brief, he would push off this guy and get back to other work, but, maybe not. If it really was a million dollars worth, he would have a hard time explaining why he hadn't followed up. If it was that much, he wouldn't pawn it off on a subordinate.

Opening the door, he made way for Jack, then closed the door and sat down in his chair. Jack sat down without being asked, and waited. "I can't guarantee you might not be subpoenaed sometime. I can try to keep you out of it, but judges and prosecutors over- rule us all the time."

"I know. I can't guarantee I can help you either. I have this junk, but I don't know who put it there, how long it has been there, or even what it is for sure. I'm not interested in witness protection either. I know this has got to be part of some gang activity, some smuggling racket, but I know very little. You have to get the information. You have to investigate, and get cooperation from the USA and other countries, which I will tell you about later, on your promise. You can use my information, but you can't use me. You have to preserve my anonymity in this."

"Okay."

"Okay? Just okay? Just like that? Can I have that in writing? Something I can use for another detective, or for a prosecutor, or for your superiors?" Jack was pushing the envelope. He knew even a written promise would not necessarily guarantee immunity or anonymity, but he had to try.

Leaning back in his chair, McMorton smiled. "You got it figured out, don't you? I'll write something down for you. If this doesn't pan out, then you won't need the note. If it does pan out, who knows where it might end up. But it won't pan out if it doesn't get started. So I'll write you the note. I'm getting close to retirement anyway so I don't worry so much about if it goes backwards on me."

McMorton leaned forward and began typing a note on his computer. Printing it off, he signed it with a flourish, added the date, and gave it to Jack. On his own computer he saved the document, unsigned.

Jack took the note, read it and put it in his pocket. Then he got up and left the office. He walked back to his truck, reached under the seat in the back and grabbed a gray-brown backpack and walked back to the building.

Soon, he dumped the backpack on McMorton's desk. McMorton had made a phone call to the lab in the meantime and called a sergeant to accompany him. The sergeant waited outside the office while McMorton opened the backpack and looked at the packages.

"Where did you find them?"

"I found them hidden in a fuel tank, seven bags, and in a hydraulic reservoir, ten bags. Hard to get out of the tanks. Two guys wanted my machine, and I got suspicious so I went looking. I got the machine from Venezuela, and the guys wanted to get the packages out in Texas. I drove it to my home... well, I had bought a truck in New Mexico, and used it to haul the machine up north to my business."

McMorton looked quizzically at Jack. "How come those guys didn't get the stuff out?"

"They didn't tell me why they wanted my machine. I haven't got time to fool around. It was my machine, my time, my trouble. But they followed us all the way home, eventually." Jack left out the finer details of the trip back. He didn't need complications from the collision between his truck and their little SUV.

"I told my guys to let them have the machine for a bit, but keep an eye on them. I thought they had gotten the stuff. You see they threatened my family, and I was not interested in putting my wife and kids at risk."

"Uh, huh. Yes. But they didn't get it out?"

"I got a call later from someone, don't know his name, slight Mexican accent, who asked where those guys were. He must be their boss. I told him they got the stuff, and they must have gone awol. But I got suspicious, and I wanted to cover the bases. So I checked the machine from top to bottom, and then began fishing in the tanks. And found this." Jack left out the fact of the assistance from his employees. No point in getting them involved in this if he could avoid it.

"Anything else you can tell me?"

Jack thought a moment. Anything else? "They threatened my family. That's why I want anonymity. I don't want their safety compromised. I can put a bodyguard on them, but for how long? One of my girls goes to school. We live in the country. Open spaces. My wife will get real upset if she sees someone following her all the time, even to protect her. And these guys claimed to have killed people in Mexico and in Texas. I mean torturing them, hanging, beheading. They claimed a half dozen people altogether. So I am taking them seriously."

"But still you bring this here? Why not just hand it over to them?"

"I don't know where those guys are. Haven't seen them since they went over the drill. Maybe they got injured, or in a fight. Or frozen stiff in some farmer's field. I don't know why they didn't take the stuff. So my story is that they did take it, took it back down south to Edmonton, set up their own operation, and you guys found them, and managed to get their junk somehow. They escaped the sting, but you got the junk. You will have to finish the story."

"That's not bad. For starters. I think we will go with that. I'll let you know how it turns out."

"Great. If anything else comes up on my end, I'll keep you informed. You got a number I can use? And did I tell you, I've got some more threats against me, my family, and anyone else he could think of, from this boss guy down in Mexico? Well, maybe Mexico, maybe Texas, maybe Arizona…. he didn't say actually where he was calling from. So I'll be thinking about that and I want you to keep that in mind when you do your thing."

McMorton stood up. "I've got your number, and you've got mine. We'll stay in touch, but probably I won't call you until I need to. Thanks for what you are doing. I'll let you know what the lab says when they get everything analyzed."

Jack walked out of the office with his head turned, while the sergeant came in. McMorton and the sergeant together took the backpack to the Lab in the basement to see what this really was.

○ ○ ○

On his way back home, Jack stopped at his sister's place again.

"Hey. You got your business done already?" She poured him a coffee as he sat down at her kitchen table.

"Yes. It went a bit smoother than I expected." He grabbed a cookie from the bowl in the table center. "I have to stop on the way back at Whitecourt to get a part for one of my trucks. They normally close at noon, but he promised to have the part for me at the door. So I got to get going right away. But thanks for the coffee."

"Well let me make you a sandwich to take along. Too bad you can't visit with Rob for a bit before you go back. He had to take the boys to hockey this morning."

"Yeah, well we had a nice talk last night." As Jack's brother-in-law, Rob was a kindred spirit, liked to hunt, drive snowmobiles and quads. He was a rough and tumble kind of guy, but not in oil. Rob owned a small construction company with five employees. "Say hello to Rob for me again, and thanks for the coffee and sandwich." He gave Marie a hug, stepped out the door and soon was back on the road west-bound.

Thirty minutes later, he was headed north, and his phone rang. His blue-tooth took over, and he was talking to Jill. "Marie just phoned me and we talked a while. She said you had just left."

"Yeah I am on the road, hwy 43. You got plans for tonight?"

"No specific plans, no. So you're feeling guilty because you were not home last night?"

"Missed you. I think we should go out for supper tonight when I get home. Can you find a sitter?"

"I'll try. Maybe mom will come. Maybe mom and dad both." Jill's parents lived five miles away, to the west of her home, and had no kids at home anymore, since Jill's siblings had all left the nest. One of her brothers had taken up grain farming on 1200 acres, and her dad spent time there. Her parents loved spending time with their grandkids, and even though her dad had his own acreage, with a couple animals, a mule and two horses and a couple dogs, he loved visiting Jack's shop. It was a manly place to be, and exciting actually, to see all the things that Jack was building or repairing there.

"Great! Looking forward to it!"

Chapter Forty-Five

JILL LOOKED OVER THE shelves in her cold storage pantry in the basement. Food from the garden had been canned and placed on the many shelves earlier this fall, and during the winter they had carrots and beans and beets available for any meal. Some of the garden produce was frozen, sitting in the large upright freezer in the same room. A wooden bin in the corner was filled with potatoes. Onions were laying on a high shelf. Jill also canned crab apples she would pick from her own trees, and from neighbors and friends.

The canned and frozen vegetables on the shelves reminded her of the summer time and the longer bright sunny days. Garden work in the summer was a joy to Jill, especially when the girls helped plant, or weed the plots, or helped to harvest. The sun and breezes, the smell of fresh earth, the climbing beans and the peas, the way the potato plants covered the ground and the corn and sunflowers shot up higher than her head. And in her warm greenhouse, where she sometimes planted watermelon and tomatoes and peppers and basil and cucumbers. It brought her closer to God, knowing the amazing variety of plants created that people could use and enjoy in order to live.

This morning she was looking for peaches. She had canned a couple dozen jars of peaches last fall and wanted some for Sunday morning breakfast. She found them, and then decided she would take a jar of beans and some potatoes for supper as well. As she turned off the light in the cold storage room and headed back upstairs she thought about the date with her husband the night before.

Jack had arrived back home at 7pm, and her parents were already there, waiting. They had come for supper with Jill and were playing a game of dutch blitz with the girls. Erin was winning and her parents were laughing. Once in awhile they would make a sly move to help out Carla, to keep her in the game.

Jack had put on a clean shirt, and he and Jill had said goodbye to the girls and hopped into the truck. Jack knew the minivan made more sense, cheaper on fuel, and they didn't need the larger vehicle, but somehow the extravagance of the truck for a date with Jill made him feel better. Bigger maybe. The sense of unease with the recent events, including his trip to Edmonton, had made him feel more aggressive, more possessive, more protective. But he had tried not to let on to Jill.

"Had a good day?" he had asked as they pulled out of the driveway.

"Yes, it was okay. Nice to talk to Marie on the phone again. We should visit sometime. Or have them up for a weekend."

"We could do that. Although summer is nicer, when it is more relaxed around here and the weather is nicer with longer days."

"True enough." Jill had been quite content at the moment. Her desire to be pleasant to Jack also had made her appreciate his effort to spend some alone time with her.

As she recounted the meal at the restaurant, the choices of menu, the chit chat with Jack, she had noticed that once in awhile, Jack was not as relaxed as she might have expected. She had put it down to his work, his busy schedule, and thought no more about it. But this morning she wanted a good breakfast, something special. So, the peaches. With a bit of whipped cream on them. Some pancakes, fried eggs, sausage. And canned peaches with whipped cream. Coffee. And juice.

Last night, as they had arrived home, the girls were already in bed, and Jill's parents soon left. Jack and Jill sat on the couch for awhile together, holding hands. It was hard for Jack not to talk about his conversation with McMorton. Usually he talked with Jill about virtually everything. But not this. So he seduced his wife. Told her she was beautiful. Told her she produced the most beautiful girls. Her cooking was fantastic. She was hardworking. And she would look very beautiful pregnant. He meant every word. And she was friendly to him that night.

She smiled, remembering. He had promised to go to church with her this morning. That was something. In the busy season even. She smiled again. It didn't mean he had suddenly converted, or changed his thoughts about God, about Jesus. It didn't mean he would do this every week, like she did. But it was something. She was going to enjoy it as much as she possibly could. The whole family going to church together. Her heart was bursting.

"Jill!" he yelled down the hall. "What do you want me to wear?"

So he hadn't forgotten. No rash promise made in the heat of passion. A considered commitment. "Wear what you want. What you feel comfortable in."

"Want me to wear a tie? Those black pants?"

"If you want. If you are worried about what people will think, then don't worry. They will just be happy to see you. Really. About half the people wear a tie and dress up some. The other half don't; they wear casual pants and no ties, no fancy shirt. It's up to you."

Jack came to the kitchen, wearing a casual shirt and pants. Clean and neat. "I guess no point in putting on a show. I haven't gone much, and a suit and tie won't change that."

"Could you get the girls to come for breakfast, Jack? It's about ready and we don't want to be late for church. Did I tell you I really appreciate you coming with us this morning?"

"Yes. I'll get the girls."

When the girls saw Jack sitting at the table with them, it began to dawn on Carla that her father was actually pacing his breakfast with theirs. That he was not dressed in working clothes. "Daddy, are you going to go with us? To church? Could you? Please, please, please?"

Jack smiled. He chuckled. He stroked her hair. "Carly me girl. Sure and of course I can and I am. Sure and of course I will. Yer mither has enticed me with her wimenly wiles, and I have nither the will nir the way to resist her."

Carla laughed out loud. "You talk so funny, Daddy! I'm so glad you are coming! I love the singing, and you will sing too, right Daddy?"

Jack laughed. "Eat your pancakes, or I will eat your peaches too." His phone rang.

"You were right. It's high quality junk." said the voice on the other end. McMorton was apparently working on Sunday. "I wanted to know, so I got the lab to test it yesterday right away. Street value one and a half million."

"Thanks for letting me know. Appreciate that. I've got to go now. We are leaving for church. First time in quite a while, and I don't want to disappoint my family. Thanks for calling."

"Okay. I'm working on a plan to find these guys. I'll be contacting the FBI next week... I mean this coming week. Either tomorrow or Tuesday. We'll get them Jack. We'll get them."

As he hung up, Jack tried to refocus on the immediate task at hand. He said a quick prayer for his family's safety. And it made him wonder whether the prayer really meant anything. Would the prayer make a difference? Would God really care? He stepped out of the house, and saw the girls waiting for him in the van. Okay, let's do this.

○ ○ ○

"Home James!"

Carla laughed. "That's not James, mommy. That's daddy!"

"Yes, Carla. How was your sunday school class?"

"We drew pictures."

My pictures are nicer than Carla's." Erin had to interject.

"You should be nice to Carla, Erin. Don't make fun of her coloring."

"I am nice to Carla, mommy. But she colors outside the lines."

"How about you, Jack? What did you think?"

"It seemed like he was talking about some of the same things you were telling me about, Jill. Like forgiveness. Repentance."

"Yes, but what did you think about it?"

"Well, he barely mentioned Zaccheus, and then went on to talking about forgiving seventy seven times. I don't know if I could do that. It's like enabling someone. Like being part of the problem."

"Forgiveness is hard to understand. How God could forgive us. How Jesus could forgive us."

"Course, I would forgive my girls, Jill. I could do that. But its harder to forgive adults. Or criminals. Drug dealers. Or murderers."

"Or husbands, sometimes."

"Yah, yah. Sure, we husbands are hard to forgive." he chuckled and took a quick glance at her smirking face. "I will say I enjoyed getting together with the people there. I enjoyed their singing too. They were pretty enthusiastic and friendly."

"Would you go again? Next week maybe?"

"Maybe. We'll see what happens." Jack truly had enjoyed himself. But he also had another reason for spending more time with his family. As long as the threats to his family were not resolved, he was reluctant to let them go places by themselves. He knew he couldn't shadow them like a mother hen, but when the opportunity was there, he could keep an eye on them. He didn't know how serious the threats were now, he didn't know where Manny and Maurice were, and he didn't know if any more men would be sent up here from down south. He was uneasy. And protective.

"I think we'll have some soup for lunch. Then the girls can play outside in the sun for awhile." Jill was planning meals. The weather had warmed up to minus five Celsius, and with the sun shining, the girls could easily be outdoors.

"I'll get one of the quads running and pull them around the yard in a sled for awhile."

"Yay! Sledding!" Carla had overheard the comment. She loved sledding. Erin was just smiling. Spending time with daddy was one of her favorite things. Especially since he seemed to be so busy all the time, and often gone to work. Today was a good day.

Chapter Forty-Six

JACK ROLLED OUT OF bed and got dressed. In the kitchen, he turned on the coffee pot, and poured himself some cereal. It was about a half hour before the rest got up, and he wanted no conversation. No distractions. He had woken without an alarm clock. He usually didn't need an alarm to get him up, regardless of when he went to bed.

With a coffee in his hand, he walked across the yard to his shop. The coffee kept his hands warm but cooled off rapidly in the frigid weather. Still, this morning at minus 22C promised a nice day, calm, no snow. The crews should be able to get lots of work done today. Wind was their nemesis, although the crews working in the trees had shelter from the wind. The forecast for this evening was some light snow, and colder temperatures tomorrow.

The man on the phone... Jack thought of him as the Mexican boss. He had promised to send two more men down. But how long would that take? Was it just an empty threat? Probably real. A million dollars was not something to abandon quickly. Plus his reputation was at stake, Jack supposed.

But if his family was in danger, what should he do? Send Jill and the kids to her parents? How about her brother on the farm? That was an hour away, maybe harder to discover.

For today, he would let Erin go to school as usual. But tomorrow? The day after? Would he be forced to tell Jill everything after all?

Jill was not some wimpy helpless child, after all. She was tough enough, working hard in the summer outside. And she knew how to drive a tractor, could operate the snow blower. She had her own firearms license. In fact, two years ago, she had bagged her own deer, and helped skin it and cut and wrapped the meat. She was a good shot with her rifle. It might be good if she knew what was going on.

Jack was wary of her reaction, however. He did not really want to face her wrath for allowing her life to be disturbed, and her children to be in danger.

Jill was not a mother who was scared to let her children get hurt. The cut that Erin had gotten on her finger two weeks ago was only slightly upsetting to Jill. As long as Erin didn't lose a finger, she would be okay. Erin would soon go back to using a knife to help with the food preparation.

But real danger was a different matter. When lives were threatened, or real serious danger to life and limb appeared, Jill was a fighter, a mother bear. Jack was sure there would be no tears, no helplessness. There would be a complete fortress, an entire array of defenses quickly assembled to protect her daughters.

Maybe he should let her know. But not today.

○ ○ ○

"Tom, we need some more drill stem. Better hard surface another twelve pieces." Tom was greeted with these words by Jack as he entered the shop. Jake entered soon after and began working on the rubber-tired drill he was building. A minute later Kole entered, and seeing what Tom was doing, he began to help Jake, continuing where he had left off the week before.

Jack punched in Bill's number, "How are things going on your end, Bill?"

"Half the guys are here already, Jack. But Freddy phoned in and said he would be late. He is not feeling well but thought he could still work. He might have had too much to drink last night. Or maybe he has a bug of some kind. We'll see. We can do without him for awhile, but not too long."

"Richard still working out okay?"

"Yah he is here already. I think he will be a top worker. I think he could handle the drilling end, with some training."

"We'll keep that in mind. In another week this job should be done, and we'll move the crews and stuff down to Grande Cache for another job."

"Okay. Is it going to be in rock? Will we need the air hammers to make the holes?"

"No. But there will be gravel in some places. Likely need some bentonite to shape the holes. Well, might be some rock to hammer through, but they tell me mostly not."

"Anything else you want to know, Jack? The rest of the guys are here, and the sun is up. We should get at it."

"Sounds good, Bill. Have a good day. Talk to you later."

Jack decided to check his cows. He took the quad he had used the day before to pull the girls around the yard in a calf sled. The two girls fit into it quite nicely, with its high sides, and had laughed and shrieked as Jack pulled them around in wide swinging turns. Now he drove it to his cows.

Jack saw all the animals were where they were supposed to be. The bawling of calves and cows who couldn't get at each other, was slowing down and becoming less constant. Jack noticed one calf with a running nose, but it seemed to be frisky enough. He would keep an eye on it, and treat it if necessary with anti-biotics. But not today.

They were on their last bit of hay. He would have to give them some more round bales this afternoon. Afternoons were warmer in the winter, the sun would shine, and it was easier on the equipment than in the colder mornings. Easier for him to take the twine off the bales as well.

Back at the shop, Jack sat down with the shop crew with coffee in hand for a quick morning break. They started trading stories about different machines, and then about cows. Only Jack actually owned cows, but Jake and Kole had been raised on farms, and their parents still owned cows. So they knew about calving, and baling hay and straw. About fencing and corrals.

"Kole, maybe you had better tell Jake and Tom all you know about those men who came to look at the drill." Jack suddenly changed the topic. He wondered how Kole would proceed.

"Maybe you could do that?" suggested Kole to Jack. Kole needed time to gather his thoughts and was interested in Jack's take on the whole thing.

"No, you start. I'll fill in." Jack insisted. As an employee, Kole was obligated to comply.

"What do you guys know... well, you know we found some drugs last Friday. Maybe you don't know that two guys had come up to get them from the machine. Jack and I had picked it up in Texas, and a few miles down the road we stopped for a vehicle that looked like it was in trouble. These two guys had actually set us up and wanted us to let them look at the drill for an hour or so. Jack got ticked off by their attitude and said no. We took off. Eventually they followed us all the way here, and talked to Jack, and he said, okay, go to the field site and have a look. Richard and I showed them where it was, and watched them." here, Kole hesitated. "They spent almost an hour on the machine, then took off to their truck, and drove away."

Jack took over the story. "We assumed they must have found what they were looking for, but I got a phone call from someone, their boss I guess, and didn't know where they were. Hadn't heard from them. What you need to know, is that those two guys had threatened me and my family with really sick threats, if I didn't let them look at the drill. I decided to let them have what they were looking for. I don't want any harm on my family. But this guy from down south, a Mexican boss, I think, also made some really bad threats. Rape, torture, murder. I'm telling you this, because if he sends two more guys, like he said he would, I need you to be aware. If its too much for you, you should make yourself scarce until this is all over. I went to the cops in Edmonton with the drugs on Saturday, and they are making a plan to investigate, but it will probably take some time."

The men were silent, heads down. Jack noticed Kole clenching his hands. Jake had grabbed a ball-peen hammer and was smacking it softly in the palm of his other hand.

Tom spoke first. "I'm not leaving. Mexicans, Texans, whatever. Threats to women and children?" He interjected with some vile cusswords. "No way, Jack. No way. Drugs gave my sister a lot of trouble. Made a mess of her. And I'm not stepping back if you need my help."

Kole and Jake nodded in agreement. Jake said, "I got family too. What some of those guys have done in Mexico, hanging and beheading ordinary farmers. They think they can do that here? No. Not past me."

Kole remained silent but nodded.

"I went to church yesterday," Jack said. "I heard about repentance and forgiveness. And I think its important. But to me, we have to protect innocent people. Fight against wrong. Against evil. Maybe you've heard this from me before. But now its also personal. My wife, my girls. And so I'm doing some thinking, planning, about what to do. Haven't got it all figured out yet, but I just want to know who is on side. Thanks for your support. This is not what you are hired for."

Kole had some more thoughts on the matter, because he knew something Jack did not know. When Jack left the shop, he went to the washroom and punched in Richard's number.

"Yeh, its me, Richard speaking. Who is this?" He did not know Kole's number on his display.

"Richard, its me Kole. Jack wanted to know if we would stand up to the threats on him and his family. Jake and Tom and me are not backing down. Not running off. I know you won't either. I know you pretty good that way. But you should know that the boss man, the Mexican, also made threats on Jack. You should know that Jack took the drugs down to Edmonton on Saturday, and the RCMP are involved."

"I thought he might."

"How about you? Where do you stand?"

"Kole, I'm not running. You and me, we have less to lose anyway. And we are in it deep."

"I thought I would let you know."

"Thanks, Kole. You keep an eye on Jack. On his family. I have to move it here, I'm falling behind. Bill won't be happy."

"Talk later."

As Richard put his phone back in his pocket, he heard some yelling from Bill. The air was crisp, and what Bill was saying was not nice. Richard raised his hand in the air in a salute, and down the thin track line through the trees, could make out Bill getting back to his machine, taking out the sections of drill pipe. It looked like Bill had finished his hole ahead, while Richard still had to finish filling his hole here.

"Phone call?" asked Bill, as he sat on the track of his machine, sipping a coffee, waiting for Richard to meet him.

"Yah. Why did you wait for me?"

"I saw a bear crossing 200 yards behind you, and you didn't notice. Thought I would keep my rifle handy in case the bear got any ideas."

"Oh? I would have like to see that bear. Won't be long and they'll be going to winter sleep."

"You packing your pistol?"

"No, its just extra weight. I got my bear spray on my belt. Thanks for keeping an eye out."

"I'm just itching for an excuse to use my SKS. But would have to wait till he knocked you over first."

"Uh,huh. Thanks a lot. Let me get mauled first, then shoot?"

They both chuckled. Then Richard made an instant decision to fill in Bill about what Kole had called him.

"It was Kole on the phone. Jack has some issues because somebody packed drugs on the drill he bought from Venezuela. He has been getting threats to him and his family if he doesn't give those drugs back to the drug gang. He brought the drugs to the RCMP in Edmonton on Saturday. But he is worried about the threats. These drug lords sometimes hang people or behead them. And worse. You probably heard it in the news."

Bill listened calmly. Then he picked up his rifle from the seat of his Bomby. Sighted along the barrel. "What about the guys in the shop. What do they think?"

"They're not running. Not hiding."

"And you?"

"Same. Not hiding. Kole promised to keep an extra eye out for Jill and the girls."

Bill said nothing for a moment. Then he looked at his watch. "We're losing daylight. Better get back at it."

Chapter Forty-Seven

"HOW IS THE DRILL stem coming, Tom?" Jack sauntered to Tom's spot in the shop. "The crews in the field are going to be needing it right away. They are slowing down with the worn out drill stem they are working with."

"I've got one more to do. Got the rest done yesterday." Tom could work well, once he had an established procedure to follow. He had made good progress on resurfacing the drill stem.

Jack had fed his cows yesterday, and this morning was feeling optimistic. Work was progressing well, and he could begin his second contract next week. One down, three to go. He was making money this winter.

"Going to have this drill ready by January, Jake?"

"Not if you keep interrupting me. You're slowing me down. Why don't you find something useful to do?"

Jake's response would have astonished Tom last year, but now he was used to the way that Jake and Jack bantered back and forth.

"I am losing money on you, Jake. Tom here would have had this machine ready for the field by now."

"As long as you were not helping him, he might."

Jack went to his office. He had picked up the morning safety reports filled out by Jake, Kole, and Tom that morning. Paperwork, not his favorite activity, but it had to be done. Filing safety reports and environmental reports was another pain in the neck, but an inevitable part of the business if he wanted to keep operating.

"Some one is here," yelled Tom from the shop. Jack got up from his desk, his behind sore from two hours on the chair. Looking out the window, he saw a new black Escalade, dirty with salt and sand from the highways. Two men came out, one on each side. Black hair, one slim, the other bulky. They looked like they meant business. With sinking heart, Jack realized that the promise on the phone was not an empty threat, and these men were likely the ones sent from Mexico.

"Hey guys. Keep an eye out. These look like more drug bangers. I'll see what they want, but back me up."

The men looked to the house, as if they were headed there, so Jack opened the door of the shop and called to them. "Can I help you guys?"

"We are looking for man name Jack."

"That's me."

"We need to talk."

"Where you from?"

"Those two men that were here before, two skinny men, one black. Where are they?"

"How would I know where they are?"

"You saw them?" They watched Jack carefully for any hints of hesitation, gult, hidden knowledge.

Jack's response was swift. "Of course I saw them. Where are you from?"

"Mexico." The terse reply was given with a distinct Mexican accent. "Where is the machine? We need to see it."

"None of your business where it is. Its not your machine. You better go back to Mexico."

"So, tough guy? You want trouble? We can give trouble for you." Just then, they noticed Kole coming from behind the shop. He had taken the back door, and then circled around the side and was standing behind the Peterbuilt truck, half hidden, yet obvious. A window opened above, and Tom peered out from his position in the bunk room.

"You need any help, Jack? I've got the drill stem finished now." Tom kept his right hand below the window sill.

Jake peered out over Jack's shoulder. "What do these guys want, Jack? You need any help?"

The men withdrew their hands from their coat pockets. Jack was guessing they had pistols in their pockets, but with three more men scattered and half hidden, they were not so certain of their dominance. But they did not retreat.

"Just need a look at your machine." Heavy emphasis on "your". A little more respect now, but they were not thwarted in their objective. "Just a look. We won't hurt your machine. Then we go."

Jack relented. "Machine is almost three hours from here. In the bush. My men are working with it. You can have a quick look, but then you need to go. To be gone. Yes?"

"Si. Yes. Just a look. How do we find it?"

"I will draw you a map."

Jack invited them into his shop where he grabbed a notepad and began to draw the route as they watched. Tom made noise upstairs, while Kole came in the back door again and began to help Jake with his work. The two men took note of the rifle within easy reach just above the work bench. They didn't know it was not normally there but had been placed there by Jake just before he had appeared beside Jack at the door.

A shot suddenly rang out from above them, and the two men grabbed for their coat pockets. Jack calmly kept drawing the map, pretending he hadn't seen their reaction, and said, as an aside, "There he goes again, shooting at coyotes."

"Well, here it is. Just follow the map, and you will find it." He did not give them a legal location because he did not want them to find it on a GPS. They did not ask either.

As they left, Jack picked up the phone. "Bill? In about two and a half hours, two guys will show up, if they don't get lost. Two guys from Mexico. They want to have a look at the Venezuela drill."

"A look at Vinny?"

"Is that what you are calling it? Okay then. Vinny. Yes."

"I think I know why, boss. Richard told me some things yesterday. You want them to have a good look?"

"Yes, a good look. Give them some tools if they need them. Make sure they don't wreck anything."

"Okay boss. Will do."

After Jack hung up on him, Bill began calling the other crews. The closest was a quarter mile away, the farthest was three miles. They listened attentively to what he began to tell them.

o o o

Emile and Pedro, for that were their names, the two Mexicans who were now travelling to Bill's work site, had never been to Canada before. In Arizona, New Mexico and California, they were inconspicious, blending in with the numerous latinos who lived in that area, and with the migrant workers who came across to work at various seasonal jobs, mostly in the irrigated agriculture. Here the latinos were uncommon, and so they were obvious, although people would sometimes get them confused with the indigenous, or the Filipinos.

This far north, they were not used to the cold weather. These freezing temperatures, with seat covers completely stiff from frost in the morning, left them shivering for an hour after they started driving. It made them uncomfortable, even though now they were warm, in a warm vehicle, travelling first east, then north.

Most of the trip north from Mexico they had seen bare ground, with skiffs of snow beginning in Idaho, disappearing in Montana, and then reappearing in central Alberta. Here, it was cold. They had purchased some gloves and warmer coats in Calgary, but they were woefully underdressed for the minus 20C weather today.

The sun was shining off the snow, now at their back, but sunglasses removed some of the glare. Frost was still thick on the shady side of the trees, although a breeze was picking up and threatened to blow it off. As they turned off the highway onto the gravel road which led to the work site, they drove on hard packed snow. The road though cleared, was not heavily travelled, except by Jack's men, by Bill and Freddy and Richard and the rest.

Now they turned off the road, just past an old homestead, where a house without windows or doors, and an old wooden grain bin, not in use for ten years, stood as a marker. The trail they followed began on the edge of a hay field, and then entered the forest, where poplar dominated, and spruce were also present. The occasional clump of willow stood in a low spot. It was still broad daylight, but the sun was low on the horizon, signaling the end of another short winter day.

Suddenly they saw some signs of color ahead of them, some red paint. As they drew nearer, they saw two machines standing side by side. Pickup trucks also, seven of them. Scattered around the machines. Some men sitting on a log, sipping coffee from steel covered cups. More men in some of the trucks. Rifles in racks in the back of the truck cabs. A rifle in one of the machine cabs. One man, who appeared to be the leader, walking out of the trees towards the machines, carrying a rifle with a scope on it. A couple more men standing on the edge of the clearing. Two men on a tailgate of one of the trucks. To the Mexicans, it looked like there were about twenty men in the clearing.

They rolled down their window, letting in the cold air. They had not expected this.

"Jack told me you were coming. We were just having some lunch. The machine you want is the one on the right. That one." It was the one without the rifle in the cab. Bill had removed it and was carrying it thoughtfully and carefully as he talked to the men in the Escalade.

"Yes. We will look at it?" Although it was a question, out of politeness engendered by the large number of men and their apparent comfort and ease with their firearms, they expected only one answer. Bill nodded. And then he sat down on the tailgate of a truck with Freddy. He grabbed a sandwich out of his pocket, unwrapped it and began chewing on it. It was almost three o'clock, not really lunch time, but it was important to him to be casual, careless, coincidental.

His men made small bits of conversation, while they looked at the two men out of the corners of their eyes, as Emile and Pedro began walking to the drill in question. The breeze was picking up, and the sun was behind the trees. They began to shiver as they stood next to the drill. They had a tool with them. Two tools, similar to what Jack had used to fish out the packages. One had a magnet on it, the other a blunt hook. They began to insert them into the fuel tank. After a frustrating half hour, they could barely hold on to the wires, their hands were so cold. They found nothing.

"We will warm up," they said to Bill as they walked back to their Escalade. Bill nodded but said nothing as they entered their vehicle. The crews continued doing what they were doing, wandering slightly around the clearing, or sitting on a log, or in a truck cab. They showed no signs of getting back to work. This was noticed by Emile.

"These men, just sitting. Not working." He said to Pedro.

"Yes. Sitting outside. Not getting cold?"

"We will warm up. Then check the other tank. I think we find nothing."

"No? Nothing there you think?"

"No." Emile now saw Bill walking up to him, still carrying the rifle. Although reluctant to open the window, he had no choice. It was better than standing outside. He turned up the heater full blast.

"You find something?" asked Bill.

"No. Nothing."

"I guess you are looking for drugs?"

"Can't say. But we find nothing."

"Yes. You are looking for drugs. You will find no drugs. Your men have taken them, and they are gone." Bill turned his head towards a new sound. There was another of Jack's trucks coming down the trail towards them. Jack himself, with Kole, had arrived. Bill stepped back as Jack walked to the Escalade.

"You find anything?" he asked Emile, who was sitting behind the wheel.

"No." Emile was getting impatient, having to repeat himself.

"Those other men took the drugs. They took them and left. They are gone. They are hiding from you. Somewhere. You will not find drugs here."

"Maybe. Maybe not. But we have to look. Our boss said, look. Look careful. Check good."

"Maybe the drugs were never put in there in the first place. Did you think about that?"

Pedro was surprised. Obviously he hadn't thought about that. Emile sat for a moment. Thought it through. "Never happen. If they couldn't get them in, they would let my boss know. If they take off with drugs, they are dead men. They still have to get them across the border. But now they would be dead men. Not happening. ... so, we check."

Jack shrugged. "Your problem. But don't take much longer. Don't sit in the truck. We need to get back to work." He called Eldon and Skyler over to his truck. Kole opened the tailgate and began to pull out the drill stem that Tom had resurfaced. Jack pulled out some also. Then Kole ran, scampered to the truck cab, opened the door, and pulled out a rifle. He stood, carefully took aim, and shot into the trees. Then he did a fist pump, and Jack clapped him on the shoulder.

"Another coyote! A mangy one! Good shot, Kole."

Jack's truck was close to the Escalade, and none of this had escaped the view of Emile and Pedro, although they had not seen the coyote which was apparently off in the trees. They became rather pensive.

As Jack walked by, he thumped on their window. "Get going. Finish your job. Quit sitting around! I want you out of here."

Emile and Pedro decided to get out and check the machine some more. This time they were quick. A couple passes with the wire, and they shrugged. "Nothing here in hydraulic tank." Pedro pointed out. Emile agreed. They no longer expected to find anything and were going through the motions. Their bravado was gone. The cold weather, the guns, the number of men around them had done their work. And these men lived in the cold. They worked in the cold. They knew what they were doing. They had no fear. That was obvious.

"Let's go. You drive." Emile sat in the passenger seat as Pedro clambered behind the wheel. He did not smile. He did not wave goodbye. He pretended not to see Jack or his men, as they left the clearing.

Jack and Kole watched the vehicle leave. When it reached the road, they turned back to the rest of the men. "Thanks guys. You didn't have to do that. We could have managed."

"Boss, you could have managed. I could have managed. But those guys, those Mexicans need to know what they are up against, if they ever think of doing something stupid. Then, maybe they won't try something stupid." Bill put his rifle back in the drill cab.

"Jack, I think Bill had a good idea, getting everyone here. I wish I would have thought of it." Kole gave his support.

Jack nodded. "Did you really shoot a coyote? I didn't see one."

Kole chuckled, "No coyote there. If there was, I would have nailed it and drug it back here. I think those guys were convinced, though."

"Nice going. Good thinking." Jack shook his head, as if shaking off the memories. "Okay men. Get back to work! You got an hour left. I'm going to fire that dumb foreman of yours for letting you goof off so much. Get something done!"

The men grinned. It had ended well. Jack was happy. Bill was pleased. They would put in another hour or so with better drill bits, and then head for a warm vehicle, a warm drive, a warm meal and some TV, and a warm bed. Life was good.

Chapter Forty-Eight

MCMORTON ARRIVED AT HIS office at eight am the next morning. Stamping snow off his shoes from the parking lot, he hung up his coat, and turned on his computer. Still no news from Jack, and no news from his men on the issue of the fake heroin bust. He turned to another case, a cocaine sting they were setting up in a small community north east of Edmonton. It promised to be a good one, nailing several smaller dealers, along with their supplier. Some of the users and one of the dealers were actually businessmen in that community, but hey? The law did not distinguish the crime based on the clothes you wore, or what people thought of you.

His cell phone buzzed, and he grabbed it from his desk where he always placed it when he came into his office. He could see the number was from northern Alberta. "McMorton speaking."

"Its me Jack. We had two guys here yesterday checking out the drill. They found nothing."

"What did they look like?"

"Driving an Escalade. Mexicans, at least they looked like and sounded like Mexicans. One was a skinny guy, the other was taller and heavier, a tough guy. Heavyweight. Skinny guy had a scar on his face and missing a pinky finger."

"What happened? Don't leave anything out."

"They came first to my home. My shop. Threatened me again. Those guys. Always with the threats. But I had another three guys at the shop, and they toned down. I gave them a map to the drill they wanted. About three hours away, maybe two and a half hours. They found it, and they found my men there having lunch together in the bush. My foreman showed them the drill, and they started looking. Fishing in the tanks. But they got cold. Found nothing."

"How many men did you have there?"

"About twenty. Some of them have hunting tags, and rifles... Then I got there with some supplies. And I talked to them... they were still warming themselves in their truck. I told them the drugs had been taken by the first two men, or maybe it was never put in the tanks in the first place. Told them to hurry up and do their thing and then get out of there. I think they were still cold, but they did a bit of fishing in the hydraulic tank, and then left. Said they found nothing."

"So where did they go? Why didn't you call me last night?"

"It was getting late by the time I got back. I was just happy they left. And I didn't want you following them from here. If they saw you, it would have been too obvious. I don't want them knowing I'm connected to you."

"Did you get the license number?" Jack said yes and proceeded to give the number to McMorton. McMorton was a bit upset Jack had not called sooner. But he realized he needed to protect Jack if he wanted cooperation.

"They could be in Calgary by now. But maybe they got a hotel somewhere. I will put out a call for their vehicle. Just for observation, not for an arrest. See where it ends up. I have men waiting already to begin surveillance."

"I wanted you to know what happened. If I hear anything else, I will call you."

"I can't arrest them. Maybe for having a gun, which might be unregistered or restricted. But that would ruin the bigger picture. Ruin chances of getting at the drug supply and the trafficking chain. But I would sure like to see where they go."

McMorton had some other plans afoot which he did not mention to Jack. Not yet. He had sunk his teeth into this one, and he had several options available. In the meantime, let's see what a general call on the plates would bring in.

As Jack terminated his call, he began to think about moving the crew to Grande Cache for their next job. He dialed a seismic engineer, who was responsible for firing the dynamite, and drafting up the seismic responses with the geophones. He let them know they were nearly done on job one, and they could begin to come in with their equipment.

Then he called two of his men who were already at the Grande Cache jobsite. They were operating two brush mowers, and they supervised two chain saw operators. They had been making the lines ready and open for the drilling crews. In the old days, the lines were straight and obvious, opened with a dozer. All the trees on the line were cut down, and after the seismic crews had finished, these lines were good for the hunters who could see wildlife down the lines and use them for access for their quads.

These days however, the lines were opened barely wide enough for the tracked bomby, to minimize the environmental impact. Branches from trees on the side would often slap the front of the drill bomby as it passed by, which was why every windshield had a protective metal grill over it. With the use of GPS, and the grid maps provided, they could open the lines without needing the survey crews that Jack had used in times past. A couple of years later, it was usually hard to tell they had even been there.

The brushers and chain saw operators had been making good progress, having opened enough lines for the crews to begin their operations there next week. But they also expressed the need for a break. Usually they worked ten days on and two days off. They had already worked twelve days in a row, and they asked for the weekend off. Jack agreed. "How deep is the snow?" he asked.

"It's getting deep. Some of the lines we opened up earlier could probably use a snow clearing. We tramped down snow the last two days, but earlier lines are deep."

Jack put that bit of information in his mental filing cabinet. "I'll send the dozer down when we move there. Some time off sounds okay. I'll let you know."

Chapter Forty-Nine

BILL LOOKED AT THE grey cloudy sky. Looked like snow coming soon, but not yet. It was December now, and in this country there would be no chinooks to melt the snow. It was here to stay until end of March for sure, maybe even to the end of April. Six months of winter, a month of spring, three months of summer, and two months of fall. More or less. When he retired, he was going to spend some time traveling. Maybe become a snow bird. He was one of the oldest of Jack's crew, but he still had twenty years to go. Oh well, so be it. He would have to save some more money first anyway, or traveling would not be an option. Just now he had finished the line he and Richard were working on.

The other crews would be done their part of this project by the end of the day, most likely. So it was time to get in travel mode. He gave a call to Kole. "Tomorrow we move, Kole. Jack said we are going to Grande Cache."

"Yeah, he told me. You want me to bring the truck down there tomorrow?"

"Well, I'm done my line. You interested in coming this afternoon?"

"I'll ask Tom. See if he can go with the Mack. I'm busy with Jake now. But I can take the Kenworth tomorrow."

"Tom could pick up my rig, and probably Eldon's. He is got two more holes to do. It'll take Tom awhile to get here." Two rigs would fit on a trailer.

Barely. If Eldon was not ready, probably the water bomby could be hauled by Tom as well. "Is the Peterbuilt ready to go?"

"The Peterbuilt will run. The trailer ramps are straightened on the trailer. But the cab is cracked, and the passenger door has not yet been fixed. So I would have to check with Jack whether he wants us to use it or not."

"Okay then. It will take a few trips anyway. If Tom picks up this afternoon, he could just drive back to the shop tonight. I think we are all ready for a couple days off anyway."

"Yeah, it would be nice to have a weekend off for a change." Kole turned to Tom in the shop. "Could you pick up a drill this afternoon? Maybe two, with the Mack?"

Tom was only too happy to agree. He was happy to get out of the shop into the cab of a truck. Any truck would do, but the Mack was one of his favorite. He knew it would mean coming back in the dark, but that was okay. A bit of overtime was always welcome.

"I should take the Kenworth," he responded, knowing what Kole's response would be.

"I don't think so. That's my truck. You are on the Mack."

Tom chuckled. He was happy with the Mack. Kole grinned too. Kole, with just a bit of unofficial seniority over Tom, was going to stick with his choice, and Tom was okay with that too.

"Better ask Jack about taking the weekend off. The guy sometimes doesn't keep track of the days. He's a workaholic and never quits."

"Where is Jack, anyway?" He had not been in the shop nor in the office for about two hours.

"He's been feeding his cows." replied Kole, who was generally very aware of where everyone around him actually was. "I think I hear the tractor coming back though."

Tom put on his coat and went outside to start up the Mack. It had been plugged in for the block heater to warm the engine almost continually, since they never knew when an emergency call would come from the field site to bring a spare drill, or to haul away a broken down rig.

"Bill is finished his line. He wants to move." Kole greeted Jack as he entered the shop.

"I see Tom started up the Mack already. Going to pick up a load tonight?"

"Yeah, assuming its okay with you. I'll go with the Kenworth tomorrow. What about the Peterbuilt? Should we use it too?"

"It's ready to go. Needs a little work on the cab, but that can wait. It's been serviced after the roll-over and hasn't been used since." Jack contemplated who would drive it, since there were several options. He put that thought aside for the moment. "I guess the guys might like a couple days off. The brushing crew asked me for the weekend. Maybe everyone should have a break."

Kole was surprised he didn't have to ask Jack, but the brushing crew had beat him to it. Good. The young guys all had a lot of stamina, a lot of energy, and could work long hours and long days, but no breaks could lead to a type of dangerous routine, a doldrum of attitude, and a careless over-familiarity with the work that might lead to accidents. A weekend off would raise their spirits.

○ ○ ○

Jack had gone to visit his brushing crew last week. The machines were working fine. He had purchased the machines two years ago, adding them to his fleet, and hiring workers directly, instead of contracting out the brushing. It worked well because he could coordinate the activities better and move the crews around at different times. So he knew exactly where the field site would be. A little clearing ten miles off the highway in a flat area just off a side road, but hidden behind trees on a small hill, a small rise in the land, so that travelers on the road would not see it.

At night they had to leave the machines in the field or in the bush, and that always left them vulnerable to vandalism, or to fuel theft. It didn't happen very often, surprisingly, but Jack tried to put equipment where it was less likely. He had never yet had a drill rig stolen, maybe because they were not easy to start in the colder days of winter.

He gave some thought to the Peterbuilt truck and trailer. He could drive it himself, of course. Some other men also had a class A license, like Bill and Skyler, so they could drive too. Skyler's helper had lost his license entirely, due to drinking and driving this past summer, before hiring on with Jack again in the fall. So that had to be considered.

His phone rang. "Jack? Can I talk to you?"

"Yeah, I'm good for it." as Jack walked into his office, he left the door open. What McMorton was about to tell him was not entirely highly secret, since his men knew much of what was going on.

"We found the car in Calgary. Emile and Pedro are in a hotel there. Looks like they booked in for two nights, so they are not bee-lining for home. We might get some action."

"All right. Thanks for letting me know."

"Haven't actually seen them do anything suspicious yet. No grounds to arrest them. No evidence of anything. We have not seen them make contact with anyone."

"Uh, huh." Jack didn't really know what to say.

"I'll let you go now, but thought I'd tell you. If you hear anything on your end, let me know."

"Will do."

Jack wondered if these men had left his life for good. Or not.

Chapter Fifty

JILL WATCHED ERIN STAND on her mat, head turned sideways, waiting for the music. She turned, ran to the other corner, twirled, and then did a somersault on the mat. Getting up, she danced to the music, ran to the other corner, did a cartwheel, then a rolling somersault again, ran backwards to the middle, did a backwards roll, stood up, jumped, and stopped, arms outstretched in the grand finale. Jill laughed to herself, proud of the efforts of her daughter.

It was a mother-child day at school, where the kids entertained the parents, mostly mothers, in the last afternoon of the week. Art pictures hung around the gymnasium, music came from another room, and some short stories also hung from the walls, with the name of the student prominently displayed. The physical demonstrations of gymnastics were the big attraction, with two instructors from the community who came to volunteer for this activity once a week. This week however they had come to school three times, just to prepare for today.

Jill chatted with several other mothers. She also complimented the lone father on the artwork of his son. He was a single father, his wife having died in a car accident two years earlier. He managed to take care of his son with the help of his parents, with his wife's parents also pitching in sometimes.

But he had to juggle work with home care, and it wasn't always easy. Working as an insurance agent gave him flexibility in his schedule, which helped. He happened also to be the insurance agent for Jack's business.

Suddenly, Jill became aware that something was wrong. What? Where was Carla? How long had she been gone, not sitting beside her? She tried to think. Carla had been beside her while Erin was on the mat. But somewhere while she was talking with the other parents, Carla had no longer been in her chair. Had she gone to the restroom? To the music room?

Not overly concerned, yet automatically anxious, Jill started looking for her. The school tended to be a safe place, generally. Teachers and aids and parents were in every room. On the other hand, while many parents knew each other, there always seemed to be a few strangers, parents who came for the first time, or an uncle or aunt, maybe grandparents, who were not known to the others, at least not known to Jill. Theoretically it would be easy for a stranger to come in as if they belonged there.

Jill did not see her in the music room. The restroom had a couple eight year old girls in it. Not Carla. Could she have gone into the boys room? Jill ran to the single father and asked him to have a look. He checked the boys room. No Carla. Now what? Where could she be? Her anxiety level rising, Jill went to the entrance, and then looked outside the door. She did not see her little girl playing in the snow. Surely she couldn't have gone far?

Looking up and down the halls, checking rooms along the way, she was walking fast. She didn't notice anyone higher than waist high. What was she wearing? What? Oh yes, her blue pants and red shirt. Did she still have her coat on? It was a white coat, with a fringed hood. It was no longer on the back of her chair; she must have it on, or with her at least. Where is she! Where?? Where??

"Mommy, could you buy us some cotton candy?" a familiar voice spoke up behind her. Erin. All changed into her street clothes.

"Erin, you have to help me find Carla. I've looked everywhere. I can't find her. Have you seen her? Where is she??"

"I'm right here, Mommy!" Carla popped out from behind Erin, a huge smile on her face. "Didn't you see me? I'm right here!"

A huge sigh of relief from Jill. She almost slid down to the floor. Of course her girl was there. Where else would she be? It was such a safe town.

Nothing to worry about. Mothers worried though. "Carla, don't leave me without telling me where you are going. Don't just leave, okay?"

"She went with me to the change room, Mommy. She helped me. She kept me company."

Ah yes, the change room. Why didn't she think of that? All so simple, afterwards, once you knew what had happened. But what about the frantic beating of her heart? The desperation of not knowing. Could she really handle another child? Or was she doomed to failure, to desperate acts of uncertainty? She could handle a cut on Erin's finger. She could see it, measure it, deal with it. But a child out of her sight? She had come to grips with Errin going to school, trusting the teachers, the aids, the system. But she hadn't realized how tight and desperate the bond to her youngest really was.

Her phone rang. It was a cheery musical chime, and it lifted her spirits. Carla had been found, all was well, and now Jack had called. Her world was back to normality, in control.

"Jill, we are moving crews to the new site today and tomorrow. Some of the drills will be parked in the yard tonight, and most of the men will be taking the weekend off. I'm not sure yet if I will be home tonight, or what time. Probably be home, but not for supper. Just so you know."

"Okay Jack. I will leave some supper in the fridge, so if I have gone to bed and you are hungry, you can just put it in the microwave."

"Where are you right now? I hear lots of voices."

"I'm at the school remember? With Erin, a parent child day. Afternoon, really. She did well at her gymnastics. It's nice talking to the other parents. I talked to Eugene too. He's handling it well, single fatherhood. But, it must be hard without Betsy around anymore. Tomorrow is two years since the accident."

"I should go to see him. I need to upgrade the insurance anyway, with our additional equipment. I wonder if he will be working tomorrow."

"I didn't know you needed to see him, but he did say his parents were looking after his son tomorrow. Probably he is working in the morning for awhile."

"I'll give him a call later." after a brief pause, "Jill, with everyone taking the weekend off, I'm thinking of going with you to church on Sunday, just so you know."

"Really? Oh Jack. Two Sundays in a row!? Jack! What can I say? That's great! You sure?"

"Well, don't hang your hat on it, but that's my plan for now. I don't see any reason why I can't fit it in. I know it makes you happy. All appearances to the contrary, I like to see a smile on your face. So that's my plan."

"Me? Smiling? Whatever gave you that idea? Not a chance!"

"Okay then. No smiles. I don't know why I would think that. Sorry."

Both of them hung up, smiling.

Chapter Fifty-One

SO NOW JACK KNEW what McMorton's plan was. Here it was in black and white. On his cellphone. On his news feed. Both Edmonton newspapers. A huge heroin bust discovered in an east end home the night before, with more than a million dollars of heroin found. Seventeen packages of heroin. One package was half empty, likely sold. Only one man arrested. The rest were not there or had escaped the net. Police were very disappointed they did not catch more perpetrators.

Jack knew it was a lie. He wondered where it would lead. Would it flush them out?

He continued with his plans for moving his crews from one site to the other. So far, five drills were in his yard, along with the Cat dozer. They would be brought to Grande Cache on Monday, and then the rest of the equipment would also be picked up and brought down there from the site north of Peace River. The men had taken the weekend off. Only Richard was still hanging around, with apparently not much to do. But he was puttering around in the shop.

"Nothing to do, Richard? You got the weekend off."

"Thought I'd stick around, if its okay. I got no vehicle anyway. I could just stay in the bunk room."

"If you need a vehicle, just take a pickup truck."

"Thanks. Maybe I will. But right now I can't think of a reason to go to town."

"Up to you. If you want to stay in the bunk room, its okay with me."

Richard seemed a bit lost. The other men either had families, or were younger, and wanted to hit the town for entertainment or shopping. He decided to watch TV. As he was going up the stairs to the bunk room, Erin bounced into the shop. "Daddy, are you home today? Could you play with me? Could you pull me around in the sled? Please, please??" she tugged on his arm.

Richard turned around to look at her. She was a bundle of energy. What he wouldn't do to enjoy life like that. Forget about some of the poor decisions he had made in his past. Forget about the serious thing he and Kole had done a few days ago. Just enjoy life, enjoy everything that was there.

"Erin, I'd like to do that, but I have a few other things to do first. Can you find something else to do for awhile? Where is Carla by the way?"

"She is coming too. Mommy is dressing her up. Can't you pull us?"

His men could take the weekend off, but it seemed a manager/owner always had loose ends to tie up. Extra little essential jobs and tasks that needed to be done to make the whole operation run smoothly. Richard looked at Jack talking to his daughter and wondered maybe if he could help out. "Would it be okay if I pulled your girls around on the sled for awhile? I wouldn't mind doing it."

Jack looked up quickly, looked back at Erin, thought for a second, and then said, "that would be great, Richard! They would love it. You could use the quad in the side shed, that's the one I normally use. I think it needs some fuel. And maybe check the oil. That would be great!" So now Richard did have something to do after all. And, Richard thought, he would keep an eye on the kids, no one knew if more threats from the drug guys were coming.

o o o

Jack's phone rang in his pocket. He ignored it for the moment. It kept on ringing, then stopped. Jack kept on with his paperwork, organizing his crews for next week. He wanted to make them as efficient as possible. The drills all had to be moved to the new site, and some equipment still had to be picked up. The dozer needed some repairs, and some more drill stem had to be resurfaced. Who was going to do what, and when they would start on their lines, where they would stay at night, when would they be paid, what would they eat, who would work with who, it all had to be planned out. Somethings had been planned two weeks ago, such as booking the motel and the packed lunches.

Jack's phone rang again. Insistently. He pulled it out and looked at the number. It looked familiar. Not again! It looked like the caller from down south. He ignored it. It kept ringing. Finally he pushed the talk button. He said nothing for a moment, and the caller must have heard him breathing.

"I saw the news. On-line. News from Edmonton. They found the junk. Why did you give them the junk? I will send my friends back to your place. To ask you some questions."

Jack realized that the caller had no idea that he had given the drugs to the police. If he had inside information, he would not have waited to get the news from a newspaper. The man was just guessing. Just fishing for a response. Jack wondered how he should respond. Finally, he responded in a low vicious tone.

"Mister. I don't know you. Don't know your name. Don't know who you are. But you don't know me either. I don't know what you are talking about. Don't know where the junk in Edmonton came from. Your men took it there. To sell it. Got caught. Your problem. Not my problem. Don't send your men to my place. I have no answers. They saw the drill, the machine. They looked."

Jack paused, but the man on the other end seemed to be waiting. Waiting for some sign of something. Of some knowledge, some inside information.

Almost involuntarity, Jack blurted, "I don't want you making any threats. No more. If you hurt anyone here, we will come after you. I will go to the police. Police from Canada, from the USA. I will come with my men too. I am staying out of this. But if you hurt anyone, it will be a war. You don't want that. Keep your men at home. Keep them away from here."

Jack continued, "I don't like you. I don't allow drugs at my work or on my yard. You are selling drugs. Making men useless, and dangerous on the job. And women become useless. They don't look after their men. They don't look after their kids. They become terrible. So, I hate the junk. So I don't like the men who sell it. I don't like you. So don't call me. Don't ask me any more questions. If you have questions, call the police in Edmonton!" Jack pushed the off button. He wished he could slam down the phone, like in the good old days.

Chapter Fifty-Two

AS THEY LEFT THE church, Jill was positively beaming. Twice now Jack had come with her. The girls were bouncing in their seats in the back as if nothing was unusual, as if daddy had always come. It was a sunny day, only -10C, calm. The girls had a great day on Saturday, being pulled in the sled by Richard. He had pulled them as fast as he dared, but not too fast, then swung them from side to side on the driveway, with the sled swooping over the drifts of high piled snow on the sides. Only once had the sled tipped, with the girls spilling out. But they were game for more, and they had spent more than an hour zooming around.

It was too cold to make snowmen or snow balls. The snow would not stick together. With rosy cheeks, they spent another half hour throwing chunks of snow at Richard, and he tossed some back. Richard surprised himself with how he acted... pretending to be a kid again, falling down in the snow, running from the girls, and them just breaking down in laughter, unable to even throw the chunks of snow.

The hot chocolate in the kitchen afterwards had never tasted so good. Richard thought about his own life, maybe it was time he thought about a family for himself. Some kids. Some girls, maybe boys. He would need a wife first. A good wife.

Today, Richard had not gone to church with them, although they had asked him. He remained in his bunkroom. Church was too much for him. He didn't know what he thought about God. He believed there was a creator. Must have been a creator. But church? No. Better to worship the creator out doors, to see the sky, the snow, the sun. The creator would not be closed up in a building, locked up and hidden.

"You like the singing, don't you?" Jack thought he would ask Jill that.

"Yes. I love it. People singing together. The piano. The guitar. The harmony. It makes me feel special. It makes me happy. It makes me cry. I love it, yes."

"I can see that. Didn't you play the piano when you were younger? How come you don't play anymore?"

"I don't know why. Just got busy with other things. I wasn't that good anyway."

"Maybe because you don't have a piano in the house?" Jack chuckled. "Its hard to play without a piano."

"Yes, but we have a keyboard, and I don't play that either. So I don't know. The girls play with the keyboard sometimes. I would like them to learn to play."

"I was listening to him talk about forgiveness. He carried on from last week. And forgiveness sounds good and all. But somethings are hard to forgive. These drug dealers. They just completely mess up people's lives. And they don't care. They get people addicted, keep pumping the drugs, force them to steal, and lie and prostitute themselves. How can you forgive that?"

"Some of them are addicts themselves." Jill pointed out. "Some have been wrapped up in the vicious cycle. How can they get themselves out?"

"So you would forgive them? Even if they are beating or torturing people. Or murdering them?"

"I don't know for sure. But Jesus forgave everyone."

"Even if they are murdering innocent people? Bystanders? People who just happened to be in the way?"

"What are you worried about, Jack? You don't know any of these drug dealers?"

"If I did, I couldn't forgive them. Even God destroyed Sodom and Gomorrah. When people are wicked, they don't get forgiveness. They get destroyed." There was a finality to Jack's tone, that did not encourage debate. But that had never stopped Jill before, and it didn't slow her down now.

"If my kids were in danger, I would fight tooth and nail for them." she said. "But still somehow I know that I need God's forgiveness too. And somehow, that means that I have to find forgiveness in my heart for others, no matter how bad they are. No matter the evil they have done. I just don't know any other way."

Jack was silent a minute. He could almost smell dinner, even though they were not in the yard yet. Wondered how Richard was doing.

"Forgiveness is hard to understand. If a guy stops using drugs, I give him a second chance. If a guy has a DUI, I will still hire him, as long as he doesn't drink on the job. But if a guy hurts my girls, any of them, its not so simple. But lets change the subject. I think I will pull my girls around on the sled for awhile after lunch. I could use the fresh air."

"You remember your Mom and Dad are coming for a visit?" asked Jill.

"Yes, yes. I remember. Dad will want to go outside too. He could drive another quad."

Jack's parents lived an hour and a half south on a farm. Jack's father had farmed all his life, and probably would farm till he died, or at least for another twenty years. He had a grain farm, and they liked to go traveling in winter. They liked to visit their children before they left, and Jack and Jill and the grandchildren were next on their list. They usually visited their daughter Marie and her husband Rob on their way to the airport in Edmonton.

"Look, here they are. They beat us home." Their wine colored Chevy Duramax was parked near the house, and Jack's parents were nowhere to be seen. "Probably in the house already." As Jack parked the minivan next to the house, the shop door opened, and Richard popped out. Jack's father was right behind him.

"Hey son! About time you got home. Since when did you start going to church?"

"Hello! What are you doing in the shop?"

"I met Richard in the shop, and he was just going to show me your new truck! Sounds like you are moving all your stuff down to Grande Cache. You could stop by our place sometime on your way down there, maybe?"

"I might be able to do that. Why don't you come on in for dinner? You too Richard, come on in!" They waved and nodded at Jack.

Richard pointed out Jack's Kenworth, and they had a quick walk around, then walked to the house. Jill had found her mother-in-law already making coffee, and soon they had the table set and steaming soup, coffee, juice, buns ready to eat. The soup was a stew, really, and would fill the belly.

Before they ate, Jack looked at Jill. "Everybody, Jill is going to say grace." Jill thanked God for the day, for the beautiful weather, for the singing at church, for the message, and for Jack's parents, and for Richard. Then they filled their bowls and began to eat.

"Where are you going this winter, dad?" Jack asked his father David. David and Nell had been married since they were 21 years old, and they were very comfortable with each other. It was a marriage that Jack hoped he could imitate. David and Nell helped each other on the farm, doing their own roles, but picking up where the other person left off, and helping each other even in the less preferred tasks. Jack could remember serious arguments they had when he was younger, but somehow he remembered them as part of the experience of life, not as traumatic life threatening situations.

Once, his mother had been milking a cow, they never had more than one, and she became frustrated. She had been hearing Jack's younger sister crying in the yard, and the cow was not cooperative. Nell had grabbed the pail, thrown it across the yard, and picked up Marie and stalked off to the house, yelling at David, who was just about to climb into the tractor and start field work. David had stopped, climbed back down, picked up the pail and then milked the cow. After bringing the milk to the house and putting the cow back in the pasture, he had passed Jack on the way to the tractor. Although Jack was quite young at the time, David had said to him, "be nice to your mother. She's having a bad day. It'll be better later." Little Jack didn't know why his mother was having a bad day, but found out later that his grandmother was very sick at the time from cancer, but was too far away in the hospital to visit easily.

That was a long time ago, and today, Nell was cheerful. She wanted to spend time with Jill, and together they reminded the men they had promised to spend time outdoors with the young girls.

"Yes! Yes! Pull us in the sled! Behind the quad!" Carla and Erin were excited. Soon they were putting on their outdoor clothes, and Jack started one quad, while Richard started another.

"Maybe I'll just ride in the sled," said David. "Haven't done that in about fifty years."

"I think we could use two sleds. I've got another one around here someplace." Sure enough Jack found a second sled behind the old woodshed. The girls argued about who would get to ride with Grandpa, and soon the quads and girls were making hilarious noise, disturbing the peaceful Sunday quiet. The women watched from the dining room window.

"How is the pregnancy going?" was Nell's first question to her daughter-in-law.

"Good. No problems so far. Surprisingly no nausea. I barely notice it, actually."

"That's good to hear. Marie's last pregnancy was hard on her." Nell referred to her daughter by Spruce Grove. They continued on sharing stories of pregnancies, and children, and the weather, as they watched their men and the girls enjoy the beautiful day.

It was a Sunday to remember.

Chapter Fifty-Three

"THE BLOCK-HEATER ELECTRICAL CORD on the Peterbuilt truck was not connected. So it won't start because the block heater wasn't on." Tom was pointing this out to Kole, who had just started the Kenworth. They were getting everything started to bring equipment to the Grande Cache location. It was bitterly cold, -35C, and everything was stiff and resistant. Fortunately it was not windy, but the danger of frostbite, or of machinery parts cracking, especially brittle rubber hoses, or electrical cables was ever present. They would send seven track drills to Grande Cache, but the two rubber tire drills would not handle the rough terrain at this time of year, and they would be left home in the yard.

"Well, better plug it in. We'll have to use the torch to warm it up." Kole said this on the way to the Mack truck, which he now got into. It started fine. These trucks also had preheaters, but even those took some time to warm up the engines in this weather. The Peterbuilt would take some time to get going.

Tom went into the shop and grabbed a tarp. Jake helped him put it over the front of the truck and tied it down lightly. Then they put a propane heater at the front, directed under the engine, and turned it on, making sure it would not be too close to anything to start a fire or melt any truck parts underneath.

Kole and Tom had arrived a bit earlier than the rest of the crew to get the trucks running. Soon the entire yard was filled with trucks and men milling about, but as soon as possible, the men went into the shop. They were grouping into drillers and helpers as they waited for Jack to show up. The more experienced men bantered back and forth with each other.

"All right guys! Beautiful warm morning today! Only -35. Sun shining! Good to see you all!" Jack exuded his energy as a tonic to everyone. "Two out of three trucks running... not bad! Only three hours of driving before you can get to doing what you really like doing, breathing fresh mountain air in the snow and sun. Freezing your fingers off. Checking your toes to see if they are still attached! Making money!"

The men grinned. To themselves, or at each other. They were tougher than the weather. And if this was the coldest week of the year, so be it. It would get better later. Or not. Either way, they were into this. For some it was just work. Others, it was a challenge. For a few, it was a bigger picture, part of the entire stream of work that provided fuel and energy for vehicles, homes and industry, keeping the province and the country going. For Jack, it was all of these things.

Jack liked equipment and machinery. Period. The way it ran. The way it made noise. The smell of the fuel. The smell of the exhaust or tires spinning. The power it had to do work, whether plowing snow, or moving bales, or knocking down trees, or drilling holes. The power of a race car or a quad to produce speed and acceleration. Jack had a race car half built in another shed, lying in wait for more attention in the summertime, when work was slow. He loved the TV show Tool-time.... more power!! Arghh!!

But today, it was all about the men. Personal relations. Or rather, personnel relations. "Okay guys, we better get some of those forms filled out. The safety info sheets. I'm going to give you a brief safety session, which you have heard before, and then Eldon will give a more detailed safety on the drilling while the trucks leave with the equipment. Bill did it last time, so we'll see how Eldon does it this time. Bill will make sure you have all the equipment you need.... oil, hydraulic fluid, fuel, extra drill stem, toolboxes, and safety equipment."

"The brushing crews also took off the weekend but they will be back today. You will start where they left off, because they packed down the snow, and it didn't snow on the weekend. But the dozer will have to clear some lines that were brushed earlier. The dozer is on the Peterbuilt, so it won't get there till later today. The Mack and the Kenworth will be hauling three drills and one water truck, so you can get a start today. They will come back for the other drills. I want a helper on each truck to go with the driver. There are four guys already in Grande Prairie, and they are taking an extra day off, but will be there tomorrow."

"Okay, Eldon, it's all yours."

"Well guys, you know about wearing steel-toed boots and helmets. And mitts. If you lose a mitt, or it gets wet, we have lots of spares. In this weather, don't play tough guy with wet gloves. Its not worth it.... you won't be able to do your job. You all know about the safe way of handling the dynamite and caps, and for the drillers, there are no new guys here, so keep following the steps about handling the drill stem. You don't want to lose any fingers, and don't want a drill going through your foot." Eldon was handling the speech like a pro.

"Way to go, Eldon!" Bill took over. "I put the forms on the workbench over there, and some more on the lunch table. Just read them and check them off and sign them, and drop them off here on this bench right beside the door. Then go to your trucks, do the check list, put everything on it you think you will need. If you are due for an oil change, let Jake know, and he'll make a spot for you in the shop. Before you go, I will have a look at your truck and double check your equipment and supplies. I know Skyler's truck will need a new first aid kit, and a new helmet. Hey Skyler? Those helmets are tough, but driving over one? Really? Okay guys, you can get going."

"Jack, did you see this?" Tom was holding his cell phone for Jack to see. "A prisoner escaped from the Grande Cache prison. It says he escaped yesterday... he's going to have a fun day in this cold."

"What was he in for?"

"Ah... let me check. It says here he was in for manslaughter. But it was associated with drugs, with drug dealing somehow. Heroin. Details are poor."

"Another drug thing. Crap. Well, we are twenty miles out of town. This prisoner is probably headed south. Dollars to doughnuts he wants to get to Edmonton. So it shouldn't affect us."

"Yeh. Well, I guess I will get started? I've got the location on my gps, along with the printed map you gave me. I've got Eldon's helper with me."

"Sounds good. Keep your cellphone charged up. Don't want to be without in this weather. You're on the Mack?"

"Yep. Kole is taking the Kenworth. Who is taking the Peterbuilt when it gets started?"

"Probably Bill and Freddy. Richard will be going with Kole."

"All right, see you later then."

Jack went to his office to go over his check list to see if he had forgotten anything. Everyone had their maps. The brushers had left him a message that they had arrived at their work site. The two trucks were on the road.

He needed to order fuel for the fuel tank, which was being pulled on a fifth wheel flat deck behind Skyler's one tonne dually. And the machines at the previous site would need to be warmed up... or maybe not. Maybe they could just be winched on the trailers. But the dozer on the Peterbuilt trailer would need warming up before it could be driven off the deck when it got to the Grande Cache site. Actually, the dozer could use an inspection... maybe Jake could do that.

"Jake, could you check out the dozer? Apparently one of the idlers is a problem."

"Sure, Jack. Too bad Richard is gone; he could give me a hand. Maybe I'll grab one of the other guys from the truck needing the oil change."

As much as Jack liked having all his men come in, and talking to them, now that they were getting to their tasks, and he had a plan for almost everything, Jack was ready for a bit of a retreat. Time for a morning coffee with Jill. He didn't get a chance for that everyday. But hey, he was the boss. What was the point of being the boss if he couldn't take advantage of a few perks? Like coffee with Jill? Yeah.

"Coffee on?" He asked as he stepped into the porch, stomping his feet. "You didn't go back to bed?" He ducked as he avoided a dish towel thrown at him. Then he ducked further as he unlaced his boots. He could smell the coffee, and some fresh cookies.

"How about a kiss?... No? No kiss? Just one? A little one?" Then he grabbed her and turned her and planted a kiss on her lips. A big one.

"Thought you said a little one."

"I lied. We got a payment for our first job this fall. It's earlier than I expected."

"You get a payment, and it gets you a kiss? Is that how your brain works?"

"Yeah, my brain works weird sometimes."

"Not just your brain."

"Uh huh. Not just my brain, oh my delicate one. Not just my brain works." Large smile on his face. Small smirk on her face.

As he sat down, he noticed the coffee already poured. He added some cream and sugar and grabbed a cookie out of the center bowl. "Where is Carla?"

"Same as usual. Playing downstairs with her toys and her dolls. You got all your guys going already?"

"Yah they all know what they have to do. It's a cold morning out. I heard a prisoner escaped from the Grande Cache jail. Wouldn't even think about it if we weren't headed in that direction today."

"I saw it on the news this morning after Erin left for the bus. He was a drug dealer, in for manslaughter."

"The bus still ran, I guess. It came on time?"

"Yes, Rosie is pretty dependable that way. It takes awhile to get those buses warmed up though in this weather. And some of those teenagers, the way they dress. If that bus breaks down, they will freeze to death in there." Rosie the bus driver often berated the teenagers and their skimpy clothes, but it was a timeless problem. In fact, Rosie could remember when she herself was a child, her brother had worn cap and scarf out of the house, and hidden them in the snow before getting on the bus. Appearances were everything; survival and safety took second place. "At least Erin doesn't mind dressing warm.... not too worried about appearances so far."

"Carla will probably stay in today? And I forgot to ask: did my parents make it home okay last night? Have you heard?"

"Yes, your mother phoned me briefly this morning. It's cold there too. Carla might go out later if it warms up some. I can't help but wonder how that escaped prisoner is going to survive this cold. Wonder what he is dressed in. He will be looking for a building, a store or office. And maybe some warmer clothes. Unless he had someone waiting for him. I guess he could be nice and toasty by now. "

Chapter Fifty-Four

"WE NEED MORE BENTONITE. We already used up half of what we took. The holes are caving in too much because of gravel." Eldon had called Jack.

"We could put some more on Kole's truck when he comes past here with the last two drills. I'll call him to get him to stop by here." Jack was pleased with how things were going in spite of the cold weather. The cold slowed things down, but there were no major problems. The Peterbuilt would not make a second trip and had stayed down at the new site. The Mack and Kenworth had made it back last night, and this morning had left for the old location picking up the last of the machines, three drills and one water truck.

"With all those rocks, the drill rod must be taking a beating?" asked Jack.

"Yep. Wearing out about twice as fast. A few times we had to hammer our way through with the hammer drill. And we've had to abandon more holes than usual, and start over. But we are making progress."

"Other than that, going okay?"

"Yep, but one of the helpers said he wants to quit. He had a call from a friend, with a job offer. It didn't pay as good, but its all year round. Warmer too." Eldon laughed. "He's a good worker. But I don't blame him. He is smart enough to do different things. Warmer things."

"Yeah, it happens. Some guys can't handle it." Jack was used to staff turnover. It was a seasonal business to start with, and he did not really hire career-oriented people. He lost a few guys every season, sometimes after they had only worked for a week or two. It was too hard for some men.

"I'll have to hire another one. Maybe I can pick one up in Grande Cache. How is the dozer working?"

"It's working good. Jake must have fixed the track idler."

Jack called Kole first. After confirming his stop to pick up bentonite, he told Jake that Kole would stop by. Then he looked for the number for the employment office in Grande Cache. "You have anybody there who would be interested in working outdoors for the winter?"

"We had one guy who did, but he got another job yesterday. I can let you know if anyone shows up."

"That would be great! Here is my number."

o o o

The rumble of the engine in the Kenworth was soothing to the men in the warm comfortable cab of the truck. Richard was nodding off in the passenger seat when Kole's phone started ringing.

"You want to grab my phone? On the console there?" Kole asked Richard. Richard groggily sat up straight and reached for the phone.

"That you Kole?"

"No, its Richard. Kole is driving."

"Just wanted to ask you to stop by here and pick up some bentonite on your way down. You could pack it between the drills on your deck."

"How much we need?"

"Jake has the number of bags. At least it won't get wet in this weather."

As Richard terminated the call, Kole asked, "Have a nice nap? What did Jack want?"

"Wants us to stop by and pick up bentonite. I guess they are going through it quicker than we thought."

"We can do that." after a pause, Kole asked, "You ever rethink what we did?"

Richard knew right away what Kole was talking about. The night with Manny and Maurice. "Yeah, I've rethought it. But it don't do any good. It's done. Can't be undone. Only question now is whether anybody will ever find out."

"Seems like nobody will. If we don't talk. It's almost like Jack doesn't want to know?"

"You think he suspects?"

"Why would those guys leave the drugs behind? What reason could they have?"

"I think Jack suspects something." Richard was thoughtful.

"Maybe he is thinking, how close he would have come to the same thing."

"Maybe."

"Jack's going to church now. Twice in a row."

"Yep."

Kole didn't actually want to use the word. Killing someone. It was not like he could actually deny it, but not saying it somehow made it less real. Less significant. Less impactful. "Getting rid of those guys was a benefit to society."

"Yep."

"And it keeps other people from getting killed."

"Yep."

"Maybe less drugs peddled, less people hurt by drugs."

"Yep."

"That all you can say, Richard? Just yep? Life and death, and all you got is yep?"

"Yep."

"Well, I don't want Jack to know. Hope he doesn't ask anything."

"He will. Eventually." Richard was certain.

"Ten years from now. Twenty years from now."

"Maybe."

"Would you tell him the truth?"

"Maybe."

"Not me. Not right now. Those guys took the drugs and are selling them in Edmonton." If he said it often enough, maybe it would be true. If they had lived, it could have been true. Kole was not a softy, not an innocent. But he didn't want to convict himself of murder either.

Chapter Fifty-Five

"WE LOST THEM. CAN'T find them anywhere." Jack took this news from McMorton calmly as he sat in his kitchen having a late breakfast. He had come back late the night before from the Grande Cache job site. "We had them in Edmonton for awhile, had their hotel, but then they lost them."

"Didn't put a tracker on their car?" asked Jack.

"Yes, we did, but it must have fallen off. We found it on the street near the curb, about a mile from their hotel."

"Better get better equipment." Jack, ever mechanical, thinking like an engineer, came to the operational objectives before he absorbed the implications. "What's your best guess as to where they went?"

"Don't know. Maybe stayed in town. Maybe went to Calgary. Or Vancouver. Or back to the USA. Just a guess at this point." McMorton shuffled in his chair. Unspoken was the thought of both men as to whether they had decided to go back north. Would they do some more checking? More checking would mean asking questions. Maybe interrogations.

"I think we scared them off some." offered Jack as he got up from the table. "We had about twenty guys around them, most with rifles when they were checking the drill. Even shot a coyote while they were watching."

"Really?" McMorton chuckled. "Well maybe you scared them off. But they don't scare easily. And it goes two ways. They could also be afraid of their boss in Mexico."

"I should tell you. I got a call from him again. And I got mad. So I told him to leave me alone. I told him I would come after him. It would be big trouble for him. If he didn't leave me alone, I would go to the police."

McMorton said nothing for a moment. "Well, I promised to keep you informed. Thanks for telling me, too. We'll just have to wait and see what happens. We'll keep looking. If they haven't changed vehicles we should turn them up again if they are in the province. I think I will alert British Columbia, and the border officers as well."

"Okay. I've got another call, but we'll stay in touch."

Jack answered his phone again while he put his boots on with his other hand. "What's up Jake?"

"You know we ordered those rims for this new rig. They came today, but they are the wrong size."

"Oh, really? What's wrong with them?"

"They are too wide. They could work for the front singles, but not for the back duals. Not enough room. Should I send them back and re-order?"

"I think I ordered wrong.... I had been thinking both front tires and back tires, and they are good for the front, but I forgot about rethinking the back tires. So yes, just send them back and order the right ones. We'll have to pay the freight, and maybe service charge, but now that I think about it, it is definitely my mistake. Good thing we have time to fix it."

"Okay boss. See ya later."

"I'll be in the shop in a couple minutes."

Jack always like to keep a good eye on the job site so he had gone yesterday afternoon for a look, a couple hours after Kole and Richard had gone down. Things were running smoothly. By the time he got there most of the day was done so he had a chance to look at the topography, the depth of snow, and the soil and gravel coming to the surface from the holes. His men would have enough bentonite for a week but would need more again at the pace they were using it. They had found a good water source in a stream leading to the river, where the ice was not too thick, so they could break through and fill the water trucks. They were using more water than usual as well.

This job would not be as profitable as the last contract. Too many extra costs. But the men were happy. They were working and equipment breakdowns were not holding them up. When they were hauling or repairing equipment, they were paid an hourly rate. But when they were drilling, they were paid by the holes they drilled, which usually was a much higher rate of pay.

Jack had signed off the worker who was quitting, yesterday, and had supper with some of the men before he headed back for home. Bill had stressed the need for another man, possibly two so they didn't have to interrupt the drilling in order to fill the water trucks or keep the dozer working.

This morning, the need for another worker or two was pressing on Jack's mind as he entered the shop. Perhaps he needed to send Tom or Kole down to drive a water truck until a replacement was found. He checked his list of contacts, previous workers, and those who had asked for work, but he had hired all of the good ones, and was reluctant to hire the problem cases. Earlier this morning he had called one fellow, but the man already had a job elsewhere.

"Did you order the new rims, Jake?"

"Not yet," replied Jake without turning around. He was cutting a hole in a piece of metal with a two-inch hole saw on the drill press.

"I'll do it. I'll see if I can get it right this time." Jack went to the machine under construction in the back corner of the shop and used a tape measure to compare the space available to the size of the rims which didn't fit, according to Jake. He might as well order the tires now too, while he was at it. The rear tires would be a different size than the front ones.

His phone rang. As he answered it, he wrote down the numbers he wanted for the tires on a scrap of paper. "Yep, Jack here."

"This is the employment office at Grande Cache. I have a couple of men who might interest you for your job needs."

Jack stood up straight, interested. "Where they from? What can you tell me about them?"

"Both in their early twenties, looking reasonably fit. Not much experience though. Seem to have been unemployed quite frequently. One recently worked as night guard at a manufacturing business in Hinton. The other has done odd jobs in Grande Cache, working for a construction company."

"Do they know what the job entails?"

"Yes, I told them it was outdoors, hard work, hand work, with some driving. They were not discouraged by it, perhaps because of the pay rate you had mentioned."

Jack scratched his chin. He had just been down there yesterday, and didn't really want to drive back again today, another three hour trip. But what choice did he have? "Do they have vehicles?"

"One has a car, the other does not. But they also seem to know each other; perhaps they could drive together, if you need both of them."

"I'll have to come and talk to them. I never hire anyone blind, and my crew chiefs are too busy drilling right now to interview them. But I won't get there till noon. Can I talk to them?"

After some muffled conversation in the background, Jack heard a new voice on the phone. "Yah. Hello."

"Hello. I am Jack. Looking to hire someone to walk outside for eight hours a day in this really cold weather and help a driller. You up to it?"

"I think so. Do you supply some clothes? Like boots and mitts?"

Well at least the man was thinking ahead. "Yes, I supply some steel-toed boots, a hard hat, mitts, and insulated coveralls. Is the pay rate okay for you?"

"Pay sounds good. Its really good, more than I ever made before. When do I start?"

"Hold on a minute. I will have to come and meet you first. You know I don't allow alcohol or any drugs on the job. First infraction means you're fired, right?"

"Yeah, couldn't do that on the job. That would be bad."

"Good, good. You know you might be handling dynamite? Can you live with that?"

"Yep. Never did before, but I think so. I can learn."

"What about your buddy there? Can he handle the schedule? Ten days on, and two days off?"

"Yeah he is good with it too. He really needs the money. He wants to buy a truck."

"Okay. I will be coming to Grande Cache. I will meet you at the Grande Cache employment office at noon. Make sure you are there. If I don't change my mind when I see you, then I will get you to fill out some papers, and go through some basic safety training, and general job training with you. All right?"

"We will be here."

"You know, I didn't get your names?"

"I'm Roger, and he is Enrico."

"Okay, Roger, I will see you and Enrico at noon."

Well, that was a load off his mind. If these two guys were suitable then he would be good for awhile. Might not even need to supply hotel rooms for them. But now he would have to leave right away back to Grande Cache. He hoped he could avoid another speeding ticket.

As he looked at his phone again, he checked the weather forecast. Remaining cold, but no snowfall coming. And then a news blurb on the escaped prisoner popped up. This time it mentioned that he was a murder conviction, not manslaughter, but on circumstantial evidence, since the body of the victim had never been found. Jack put his phone away and grabbed the keys to his truck.

○ ○ ○

Kole listened to the radio as he helped Jake in the shop. Tom was busy resurfacing some more drill stem, while Kole was welding several pieces of metal together. The radio had a news announcement.

"Local politician decides to run again this fall for city council in Grande Prairie. It will be his second term if he wins, and he says he enjoyed it more than he thought he would. In other news, people are warned to be on the lookout for an escaped prisoner from the Grande Cache penitentiary. This prisoner has not yet been located and could be anywhere in northern Alberta. He is known to be familiar with the north and has had contacts in Grande Prairie and Peace River." After the announcement and warning, a few more details on the prisoner were given. "Research on the case of this prisoner reveals that he was convicted of second-degree murder in the Edmonton area. The conviction relied on circumstantial evidence and corroborating testimony, since the body was never found. Consider this prisoner to be dangerous, possibly armed."

After that, Kole did not hear the rest of the news broadcast, since his mind was churning around the circumstances of this prisoner. The body had not been found. Yet, he was convicted. Kole had this overwhelming desire to talk to Richard right now but knew that was an impossibility.

As he had so many times before, he went over the scene again with Manny and Maurice. Was there anything that could lead back to him? Nothing to see at the sight. But he and Richard had been the last ones to see the two men. That was obvious and undeniable. Something like that usually became suspicious. Very suspicious, after awhile. If not suspicious to the police, then suspicious to Maurice's boss. The underworld had its own investigative techniques and its own sense of justice, distorted as it might be.

Well, nothing he could do about that. What was done was done. Couldn't be undone. He would have to live with it.

Chapter Fifty-Six

ROGER FOLLOWED HIS DRILLER to their truck. He had worked all day outside after training, putting dynamite in the holes, attaching wires and caps. He had not fallen behind, because the driller was going slower than usual, having to deal with rocks and gravel in the holes, and putting bentonite in to keep the holes from caving in. It had been the hardest work he had ever done.

They drove a quarter mile to the next drill, where his buddy Enrico and his driller were just finishing their last hole. Enrico did not say a word of greeting. He was exhausted and sore. Probably blisters on his feet, although he hadn't checked.

They all got in the same truck, a quad cab diesel, as all of Jack's trucks were. Skyler the driller was driving, and Roger and Enrico were in the back. After ten minutes of driving on the snow packed trail, they arrived at the highway. Finally Enrico found some words.

"Well, that was a piece of cake." Enrico was lying through his teeth. They both knew it was not easy, no piece of cake. But they had made the day. They had not quit, not been defeated in disgrace. Bravado. They would maintain their bravado, false front or not.

"Looking forward to supper."

"And a drink."

"And a cookie." Roger raised his left eyebrow.

"And a movie."

"I'd advise you guys to take it easy tonight if you want to survive tomorrow.," said Skyler with the voice of experience. "Second day is usually worse than the first."

Enrico and Roger looked at each other wordlessly.

"Just one drink?" asked Roger.

"One is okay. I'd advise early to bed. Once your body gets used to this, it will be different, but not yet." Skyler spoke rather gently. When he himself had been a rookie, he had been ribbed mercilessly by his driller for being slow, for his sore feet, and his frozen fingers. Skyler did not follow that pattern of education.

Enrico called with his cell phone to a friend of his, who also knew Roger. They would meet in Grande Cache after supper. They would not get paid for two weeks but they would find something to do. Roger and Enrico lived in the same house, a small two-bedroom. The friend lived elsewhere but agreed to meet them.

"Supper is on the boss," said Skyler. "Then I can drop you off at your home. I will pick you up at 7, we'll have breakfast and then go to the jobsite." Jack had so many young guys working for him he made it a policy to feed them on the job and feed them well. It was a small price to pay to keep them healthy and content so they could do their jobs. Besides, the expenses were charged back to the contract.

After a delicious and filling supper at the hotel restaurant, the hotel where most of the crew were staying, Skyler brought Roger and Enrico to their home, an older house with no basement, in the poorer part of town. What Skyler did not know was that the friend they were going to meet was well aquainted with the darker side of life, and had recently escaped from the Grande Cache jail only a few nights before.

o o o

Next morning, before the sun was up, Enrico appeared at the door rubbing his eyes when Skyler rang the doorbell. "We're coming." he said, as Skyler, irritated but trying not to show it, stepped in to wait for them. Neither

Enrico nor Roger were ready, but were struggling to put on their clothes and boots. Skyler had initially waited, gave a brief honk of the horn, but didn't want to disturb the neighbors, so he had gone to the house, leaving the truck running.

Eventually, they got themselves out of the house, into the truck, and to the restaurant. Skyler thought they looked rather out of it, disconnected, and sometimes incoherent. He put it down to early morning blues, and the hard day yesterday. They did eat their food and grabbed a coffee thermos to take along with their bagged lunches.

Well, at least they were willing to work another day. Skyler had seen cases, where a new worker had disappeared after the first day, finding it just too hard to continue. When they arrived at the jobsite, they all went back to work.

Everything was good for awhile, but by 10:30 in the morning, it was obvious that something was not right. Roger was helping Skyler, and he was falling behind. He had two holes not yet done, which considering the slower pace that Skyler was forced to maintain due to the rough and rocky conditions, was unusual. Yesterday he had easily kept up.

After the distance between them widened some more, Skyler decided to check on Roger. He went back with his machine, and found Roger sitting on the ground. From a distance, he had thought Roger was busy working, but now he could see that Roger was just sitting there.

"What you doing, man? Taking a break? Muscles all sore from yesterday?"

Roger looked at him, eyes somewhat unfocused. "Yeah. Sore." Struggling to get up.

Skyler began to suspect something was wrong. In fact, he suspected Roger had been, or was still on the effects of some drug. It was a big change from the day before, and it was more than tired bones and muscles. The day was cold, and Roger was not wearing his mitts. Something was off.

"You on something, man? You're smoking something? Sniffing something?"

"Nah, nah, just tired. But I'm okay. I'm coming. I'll catch up in no time."

"It looks like you are on something. If you are, you might as well tell me. It won't work. I will have to check your work now. And if it looks wrong, we're going to have to fix it. This is not work you can fool around with. You were warned about no drugs."

"Yeah. No. I'm okay. I'm doing real good. Better than yesterday. Leave me alone." Roger was becoming aggressive and defensive.

Skyler could see that he was not okay. He cursed under his breath. Jack was back home at the shop again and couldn't solve this problem quickly. He called Bill.

"I've got a dud for a helper, Bill. Looks like he is on something."

"I just got a call from Eldon. He has the same story. Looks like those guys partied hard last night."

"Roger was slow this morning, but he is worse now. He seemed to be moving around lots, but it still took him longer than yesterday to get a hole done. I think he has some stuff with him; taking it right on the job now."

"Crap. That is going to slow us down. ..... well, you sure about it? Think he's sniffing on the job?"

"Yeah. I've seen it before. I don't trust his work. Going to have to check it all now." Skyler grimaced.

"Okay. Let me think... Eldon is going to try with Enrico for awhile, but if he is using on the job, then he is going to be shut down too. Check the holes back, and then come and look for me; you know where I am. Bring your helper along. I'll get you to drill with Freddy, and I'll bring Roger back to town. If they're using, then they are finished. Same for Enrico."

"All right. I'll get back to you in about an hour then."

Skyler took another look at Roger, who was moving, but in spurts and starts. He went back to check on Roger's work on the last hole, and then the one before that. Both were done sloppily, not up to standard at all. The hole before that seemed to be okay, and the one before that, also okay. It seemed perhaps that Roger had stopped to use something along the way. Skyler suspected cocaine. He had not smelled any cannibas at all, and Roger's response seemed to fit cocaine.

"You're sniffing coke." Skyler posed it as a statement, not a question.

"No way. I wouldn't do that on the job."

"I've seen it before. You're not fooling me. The last two holes you did were pathetic. And you are not keeping up."

"Think you are so smart? You are so good? Think you are better than me?"

"Quit lying. You don't fool me."

"It makes me work better. I feel better than yesterday." He shuffled his feet, almost like a dancer, except for the heavy boots and the snow.

"Yeah, what I thought."

"I can think better. And I don't get so cold."

"Sure." Skyler noticed his hands. Still bare. "Better put on your mitts. And hop in the cab. We are going to the truck."

"What? Why? Lunch time already?"

"Taking an early break. We have to meet with Bill."

"Okay then. Don't hurt my feelings to have a break." Roger walked to the machine and hopped in the cab. Few words were spoken as they arrived at the truck, climbed in, and drove to Bill's line.

Eldon's truck was already there with Enrico sitting in it. Leaning on the hood, Eldon was talking with Bill.

As they drove to town with Bill, Roger and Enrico realized the game was up. Enrico was silent, but Roger cursed most of the way to town. "We get a job, and you fire us on the second day? You no-good stupid, **&^#@ (*!! Wait till Jack hears about this. He'll fire you instead of us."

"I talked to Jack already. He doesn't keep guys who use drugs. And no tolerance for drugs on the job. It's too dangerous, and Jack hates drugs anyway."

At first, this response did not sink in with Roger, but eventually he realized the lay of the land. "Okay. What a stupid outfit. A little bit of coke or crack makes me work better. I can go faster, and I don't feel the pain. Don't know why you uptight little bigshots can't see that. You ought to try it. I'd even give you a bit for free."

"You got some on you?" Bill was fishing. Roger was silent. Which was answer enough.

"You got some from that friend you called last night?" Some more fishing. Enrico in the backseat stared at Roger, at the back of his head. Then he stared at Bill.

"So he gave you some. Did you pay for it, or do you owe him?" No response from the passengers. They hunched their shoulders, and Roger glanced back at Enrico. Enrico raised his eyebrow, and his fist, in a question.

"Don't get any ideas," warned Bill. " believe me, if you try to get rough with me, you will be sorry. I know all about tough guys on coke. I've been through it before, and I am alive to tell the tale. Don't even think about doing anything stupid."

"The thing is," he continued, "If you had left the stuff at home, you would have been okay. You'd have gotten away with it. And if you told me, or Jack, that you had a problem with it, he might even have given you a chance to work, as long as you promised to leave it alone. He hates drugs, but he gives guys a chance to fix their problem. But he can't have it on the job. And you knew that. You blew it."

Roger and Enrico's brains were not working the way they should. But they believed Bill. They estimated that attacking Bill might not work, that he had some kind of advantage over them, even though there were two of them. Although they were not the brightest cookies in the tray, they also realized that if they overpowered Bill, they would be the first suspects anyway. Unless they killed Bill, he would finger them, and Skyler and Eldon and Freddy already knew about the situation. Better to leave things alone, to lie low.

As if at a silent signal, both Enrico and Roger rolled down their windows and tossed something outside. Bill took note of the location, but said nothing. They continued to town.

Bill dropped the two at their home and gave them each a paycheck for a day and a half of work. Then he drove back the way he came. Once out of site of the house, he took a detour to the police station.

Chapter Fifty-Seven

"MCMORTON SPEAKING."

"Hey. How are you? Learn anything new about Maurice and Manny?" Jack was anxious for information. More anxious than he thought he would be.

"Nothing about them, but yes, about Emile and Pedro. They turned up in Calgary, and we found them just as they were heading back to Edmonton. We tailed them back to Edmonton, and I think we got a pretty good lock on their vehicle and their location now."

"Good, good. Anything else? Are they carrying any drugs now? They making any contacts?"

"We did lose them for awhile, so we don't know if they made contact in Calgary. We don't have access to their phone, we don't know their number. But we can listen in to some conversations, and we now have a mic in their room. They don't give much away. They are smarter than a lot of these dealers, and know when not to talk."

"Thanks for letting me know. I appreciate it. Do you know anything about the guy who escaped in Grande Cache?"

"Not sure its connected. He had been a dealer before prison. Was caught once in prison, dealing some junk. Just a small amount. Had six months added to his sentence."

"I've got crews working in Grande Cache now. So I'm thinking about this guy. I sometimes have guys hired who used to be on drugs. Those connections and temptations are always there. In fact, I had to let a couple guys go yesterday. Not heroin but coke. Local cops are aware. They found some stuff on the highway back to town. My foreman said it would be there because they tossed it out the window."

"Uh huh."

"The sergeant there told me this morning that they found the prisoner last night but didn't pick him up. They want to see if they can find a supplier to this guy."

"I was aware of that." replied McMorton. "In fact, I suggested it, and am sending a couple of detectives to check it out. I wouldn't be surprised that he is the friend your two former employees met with two nights ago. Maybe again last night."

"You are okay with a murderer on the streets? I mean, yes, get the drug suppliers, but a murderer?"

"Yes. The victim was a drug dealer, not some innocent. He took out one of his own. But we need to find the source."

"Makes sense."

"I should also point out to you, that the packages they found on the highway might be hard to use as evidence against your two former employees. No direct chain of evidence. So we are not arresting them, right now. Perhaps the sergeant didn't tell you, but I will tell you that one of the packages contained only cocaine. The other package had coke, two marijuana smokes, and a small packet of heroin. The heroin is interesting because it takes it to another level."

"And our guys, I mean Emile and Pedro, are into the heroin. Wonder if there is a connection?"

"We'll find out, one way or another."

"Have you contacted the FBI yet?"

"Yes, but just on information basis. They are always tracking drug smuggling, so this is not really new. But it helps them to know of all the verified methods being used. And the source locations. They will step in on our case when we can give them something solid. We don't have that yet."

"So far, no more phone calls from Mr. Big. So that's good. It's my main concern."

"Yes. I hope you are keeping all this to yourself. We can't have them suspecting what we are doing."

" They might suspect. But not because of me. If they check, or if they have a connection with Grande Cache, then they will know we have, well, my man Bill has gone to the cops about these drugs here. But there is no obvious connection to them. No reason for them to get concerned."

"Yes. I have another call to make, and we will stay in touch."

"Absolutely." Jack disconnected the call, and then dialed another number. "Bill, how is it going?"

"Between us, we decided that Skyler and Eldon would have to work together and leave one drill standing." Bill then chuckled. "They are neither one used to working as a helper."

"Exactly right. Just what I was going to suggest. It will take me a while to find replacements. I am going to check with Grande Prairie; that might be a better option than Grande Cache right now. Who is going to work as helper?" Jack chuckled at this also.

"They flipped a coin, and Eldon is helper this morning. At noon they will switch and Skyler will be helper."

"Let them know they will both get driller's wages, regardless. Its not their fault the helpers didn't work out. Maybe I'll have some guys there tomorrow. Otherwise, the next day."

"They are counting on it. Meanwhile, Freddy and me will see if they can keep up to us." Bill grinned. Might as well make a challenge out of it.

Chapter Fifty-Eight

"THIS FOOD IS GOOD tonight," Bill said to Freddy as they ate their supper at the hotel restaurant. It was about half full, mostly filled with Jack's men who had finished another day on the job. As the men were winding down and enjoying their supper, they wondered if Jack had found any replacements for Roger and Enrico. Bill finished his food and left for the washroom.

"You partying tonight?" The question was unexpected, and caused Freddy to raise his eyes from his dinner to meet those of Roger, who was standing at his table. He did not answer immediately, wondering what would give Roger the idea that they were on a friendly basis.

"Partying?" he replied, stalling for time.

"Yeah. You need any supplies for a party?"

"Supplies?"

"You know. Junk. Smoke. Whatever."

Now Freddy began to understand. Roger was trying to sell some kind of drugs. He must be desperate to just approach someone without ensuring he had a real convert. His carelessness could get him reported and arrested. He probably figured Freddy as a helper, and obviously native, would likely

SEISMIC TRAIL

be a user and likely not inform on him. What a jerk. But Freddy kept those thoughts to himself.

"What you got?" Freddy thought he would entertain himself by asking questions, getting some more information.

"Whatever you need." Freddy saw Bill returning, and then when he saw Freddy had company, Bill decided to go to his room upstairs, waved at Freddy and got on the elevator.

"Don't know if I need anything. How much you got?"

"Mind if I sit down a minute?"

"Its a free country."

"What's your preference?"

On a wild stab in the dark, Freddy asked, "You handle any junk, heroin?"

"I got a little." Roger was relaxing, apparently thinking he was speaking to a comrade of sorts. "Would have had more, but supplies are a bit tight right now. Did you hear about the cops found a million dollars of junk in Edmonton? Some of that was supposed to end up here."

"Really? How do you know that?"

"My supplier told me. Hah, hah, he just got out of jail and he is already tied in."

"Oh yeah?"

"Got me fired yesterday, using his stuff. But its a stupid job anyway. You still working?"

"Yeah, still working, plugging along. Where is Enrico?"

"Back at home, zonked out. He's smokin the weed."

"Okay. No party for me tonight."

"If you ever need anything, let me know. I'm here in town. I can get it for you." Roger got up, glanced around for other prospects, saw a possible candidate in a far corner and headed over to him. Skyler saw him coming, where he was going, and stepped up and between.

"Leave our guys alone, Roger. They don't want the drugs, and I don't want you chasing them. If any of them get into trouble, we will be coming after you. Understand? Leave em alone. Get out of here."

Roger hesitated, tempted to defy Skyler, but realized that would be a losing game. He turned sideways and headed for the door, leaving the hotel for the time being.

Skyler walked to Freddy's table and sat down without being asked. "He try to sell you something?"

"How d'you know?"

"I can tell. A long time ago, I used to try some of that stuff. No more. But I can see it coming. Besides, he was using stuff on the job, so its a natural guess. I ran him off."

"I don't touch the stuff. But I played him a bit. He said the big heroin bust in Edmonton a few days back interfered with his supply. Some was supposed to come here. To his supplier I guess."

"No surprise there, I guess."

"He was talking about a guy out of jail. His supplier, I think." Freddy turned to the waitress who was approaching. "Yeah, just one more cup of coffee would be good. Thanks."

Waiting for the waitress to leave, Skyler continued, "So this guy from prison, just out, was selling him heroin?"

"Sounded like it."

"Did he say what he was in for? There was a guy who just escaped a few days ago, what, last week, I think. Could it be him?"

"Good question. Didn't think to ask that."

"I'll tell Bill about this. Or Jack, if I see him. I know Jack will be interested. I wonder if Jack has found some new guys yet or not. Bill said he was going to check the Grande Prairie employment office." Skyler got up to go to his room. Freddy sipped his coffee, contemplating, and then set down his cup, and signed his meal ticket. It would be billed to his room. Freddy got on the elevator to his room.

o o o

Next morning, at 10 am, Bill got a call from Jack. "Found a couple more guys in Grande Prairie. Picked one up in Spirit River yesterday. So I'll be coming with three more guys in a couple hours. One of them has some drilling experience, so if I can get one more man, we will get the spare drill out your way."

"Sounds good. Eldon and Skyler are getting tired of each other's company. By the way, Skyler told me that Roger had been trying to sell

Freddy some drugs last night. At the hotel. Freddy did not bite. But he also told me that a guy who just got out of prison was his supplier."

Jack mulled this over. "Seems a bit of a coincidence that a guy just escaped from prison. Wonder if it was him."

"Don't know. Could be. Skyler ran Roger out of the hotel. But Roger will be looking for likely customers. He is selling heroin and other stuff. Oh, Roger had told Freddy that the drug bust in Edmonton had interfered with their supply. Some of it was supposed to come to Grande Cache."

"Thanks for keeping me informed. You hear anymore, please let me know. I'll be there in a couple hours. Round noon."

"See ya later."

o o o

As Roger and Enrico lay around in the living of their old house, in teashirt and jeans, watching TV, dazed from some fresh weed, chewing on corn chips and sipping on a beer, they heard a knock on the door. Then they heard someone rattling the door knob. But one thing they did as habit, was to lock their door. They did not need anyone walking in unexpectedly. They might need time to hide some stuff before opening the door.

"You gonna get the door?" Roger asked Enrico.

"Nah. You get it. You're closer." Enrico took another sip from his bottle. "What time is it anyway?"

"It's dark out. Must be 5 o'clock or something, at least. Wonder who it is." Roger made no move to get up.

More knocking on the door. Louder and persistent. "Open up!! Open up!"

"It's not cops, right?" Enrico suddenly sat up, wondering. "Couldn't be cops." He got up to take a look through the window. He saw no flashing lights, nothing that looked like a cop car. It was hard to see the man on the step at the door, but certainly he looked nothing like a cop. Wait a minute! It looked the supplier they had seen two days ago. Better open up.

"Bout time you opened the door. It's cold out there."

"What you want? We got enough stuff for now. I couldn't sell any last night." Roger made his comments from his slumped seat on the sofa. He made no move to get up, and no move to ask their visitor to sit down.

"Can I stay here with you guys for a couple days? I think someone is watching me over where I am. I need to get away."

"And if they find you here? An escaped prisoner? Where will that put us? You shouldn't even be here. We can find you if we need you."

"Look. I need a place to stay. Can't let them find me. But can't leave Grande Cache either. This is my territory. I got more stuff coming. I gotta stay here." It sounded like he wasn't asking anymore. They had heard about him being convicted of murder. They hadn't found the body. They didn't want to be another disappearing body. Roger made a show of protesting.

"We got no room. You gotta find another place."

The man looked into the bedrooms. Looked at the sofa. The kitchen. The bathroom. It was a small house. Only two bedrooms. He walked back to the larger room. "Who sleeps here?"

"That's my room" responded Roger. "And its full."

"It'll be fuller now. I'm sleeping in there. I'll be on the floor. Only a couple days."

Roger swore. "Only two days then. That's it."

"Two days and I'll be out of this dump."

Chapter Fifty-Nine

THIRD SUNDAY IN A row. Jack shook his head as he drove to his in-laws' home after church. Jill was quiet. Content. Happy. The girls in the back seat were singing a song together, "The more we get together, together, together. The more we get together the happier we'll be." Poking each other. Giggling. Bouncing.

It had been a busy week. He had found the workers he needed. The weather had cooperated. Equipment had not broken down, at least nothing serious, just minor on-site repairs. He had been home on the weekend. Progress being made on the drill in the shop. Suzy, they called it.

He had asked Kole if he wanted to come with them to church. Kole had laughed. "No. I understand staying away from drugs and drinking. I stay away from church too. Just another drug. Another addiction. Not for me. You better be careful; it will mess you up."

Richard was working with the rest at Grande Cache. Jake had never gone to church. So, Jack went to make Jill happy. And the girls. He was becoming intrigued himself. This morning the message had been about forgiveness. Again. Was it always about forgiveness? The pastor had told a story about the Amish, one story in particular, where a man had shot a bunch of Amish school kids, and then shot himself. The Amish men had gone to the man's widow and made peace. They had told her that they forgave her husband, even though he was dead. They brought her food, and sat with her, in her confusion, grief, frustration and loneliness.

Jack was pondering these things. He wondered what he would be like if someone had shot his girls at a school. If the guy was deranged? Or if he was sane? Would the motivation matter? Would he bring food while his daughter's body lay in the morgue?

"Hey! Come on in!!" Jill's father Bernie called from the step. The day was calm. Blue skies, and cold. Frosty breath poured from their mouths as they responded to Bernie's welcome.

"Shut the door, Errin." Jill's reminder brought Errin to an abrupt stop as she was running to the house. She turned back and pushed the door of the van closed, and then ran to the house again. Jill said no more, as she went back to close the door more securely, since Errin had not closed it completely. At least Errin was trying.

"What did you think of that message this morning, Jack?" Jill's parents went to the same church they had attended. "I'm not sure I would be as forgiving. At least not so quickly." said Bernie, as they hung up their coats and shucked off their boots in the porch of the house.

"I'd be inclined to shoot someone." Jack put his gloves in his boots. "But the guy was already dead, so couldn't go after him."

"God forgave us for everything bad we did, right Daddy?" Jack didn't realize that Carla was listening. "So we should forgive others, right Daddy?"

"You are right Carla," said Jill, over-riding Jack's speechlessness. "Forgiveness is really important."

Glancing at Jill, Jack decided to keep quiet. "I've got the soup ready!" yelled Susanne, Jill's mother, from the kitchen. "Come on and get in here!" The smell of the soup convinced everyone to make their way to the table. Soup was steaming, buns and sandwiches, cold meat, cheese, coffee and juice filled the center of the table. Bernie said grace and they all began to satisfy the hunger pangs that had started during the ride home from church.

As they finished the soup, and chewed on a sandwich, Bernie and Jack relaxed a little. Jill and her mother were discussing one of Erin's latest adventures, while the girls had gone to another room where Jill's parents kept some toys for their grandchildren. "The Amish are peaceful people. Anti-war." mentioned Jack. "Letting other people do their dirty work."

"Hold on a minute," Susanne had overheard the remark and interrupted her own comments to Jill. "They believe in turning the other cheek, like Jesus asked us to do. Are you arguing with Jesus?" Then she turned back to Jill, continuing with her comment about another grandchild about Erin's age, and how the two girls did similar things.

"The Amish help their neighbors, instead of fighting them." Bernie's response seemed to agree with Susanne. "They are conscientious objectors. But some of them do help in the wars by being medics, or working in supplies, etc. They just do not want to fire a gun at people."

"Do they not even defend themselves? If someone came to shoot their wife, or let's say, rape their wife, would they not stop them?"

"I suppose they would try to stop them. But not with violence. At least not with a gun. They would not want to kill the criminal. As far as I know."

"Not just Amish. Some Mennonites are the same. Won't serve in the military. At least not shooting people." Jack had a couple Mennonites working for him. "They will have a gun for hunting but not for self-defense."

"How do you prevent evil people from taking over, being like that?" Bernie was sympathetic. "but I can understand that killing people is not the answer for everything either. They believe forgiveness will win over hearts for Jesus. They believe that if you do not forgive others, God will not forgive you. It's in the Bible somewhere."

"Looking after women and children, isn't that in the Bible somewhere too? Letting them be hurt, injured, or killed, wouldn't Jesus be unhappy about that too?" Jack leaned towards protecting them.

"Yeah, I'm sure looking after widows and orphans is mentioned in the bible as one of the most important things for God's people to do. Protecting the weaker ones, especially women and children, makes sense." Bernie also leaned towards protection. He felt himself rising like a bear from his chair, as he thought about someone hurting his grandchildren. "No way anyone is hurting my grandgirls. Let's go outside for awhile and run the snowmobiles. Wonder if the girls would like that."

Sure enough, the girls didn't mind getting dressed and sitting on the back of the sleds as they roared around the yard and fields nearby. Erin rode behind grandpa Bernie, while Carla sat in front of Jack. Speeds were moderate as the men considered their passengers. The girls loved the outdoors, and their grandpa. The cold drove them back in the house, their red cheeks and frosty eyelashes proof of their adventure as they ran to their mother and grandmother in the living room.

"Had fun? Better get your coats off and then you can come back and tell us all about it."

"We saw three deer by the creek. Just standing there!" Carla started her tale.

"And a moose!" Erin wanted to get her two-bits in. "A big moose! A really big moose!"

"That was by the beaver dam," added Carla. Jack and Bernie grinned. They enjoyed the bracing air, and the sights. Jack especially was often too busy to enjoy the nature around him, the scenery, the animals, and the extremes of winter and summer which he loved. Today was a good day.

His phone rang. "hey Jack, we're almost done for the day. Those two new guys from Grande Prairie are working out pretty good. We will need some more bentonite again by Tuesday, the way it is going." It was Bill, updating Jack during a quick break.

"Okay. I'll get some to you tomorrow. Me or maybe Tom will bring it."

"Yesterday Roger tried to sell some dope to one of the new guys, but he didn't find a customer. He is still at it."

"Did you get rid of him?"

"Yeah, I told him to buzz off. Skyler had told him the same earlier, but he doesn't seem to take it seriously."

"Well don't rough him up. Call the cops if he tries it once more. I don't know if any of the new guys are tempted, but we don't need someone like Roger bothering them. I don't need to lose anymore workers."

"Will do, boss. No problem."

Chapter Sixty

"HELLO JACK."

"Hello. Thought I would give you a call. That guy Roger in Grande Cache, is still selling dope and junk. Thought you should know. You hear anything about Pedro and Emile?" Jack leaned back in his chair in the kitchen, watching Jill leave to call the girls for breakfast. He kept his voice down.

"Interesting you should ask," said McMorton. "We had been following them and it looks like they are now headed south to the border. We alerted the FBI. They must have been contacting people, and checking the drug bust we announced in the papers, but we have not gotten any leads in the meantime. These are a couple of their smarter guys. Know how to hide their trail."

"Well, not so smart. You found them."

"Yes, but we don't know who they are talking to. We saw them talk to a couple street peddlers in Edmonton, but when we followed up, it seems they were just asking general questions. Street news. Not hardcore questions. Not any indication they knew what happened. Street peddlers so far have not caught on either. Our ruse is still working."

"Maybe the street peddlers were giving you a line. Leading you on. Not giving you the whole story."

"I don't think so. But Emile and Pedro may have caught on. If the street doesn't know what happened, and if no one knows, they may begin to suspect it is a set up. No one arrested. No one complaining directly about getting shorted their supply. Seems suspicious. But we'll stick with the story. It protects you better."

"The news item did say you had arrested someone."

"True, the story did say that. But there is no one in jail. No trial planned."

"Okay, thanks for that." Jack was relieved, some. But was beginning to wonder about the future. How long could they keep this up? And where were those first two guys? How long could they hide? Especially without a job, or without drugs to sell? "Have you seen or heard anything about Manny and Maurice, the first two guys that came to me?"

"Haven't heard a thing. Seems like they disappeared off the face of the earth. Wonder if they did. If they died. Or seriously changed identities."

Jack had suspicions, but nothing really to base it on. And he wasn't going to press the issue. In this case, ignorance was bliss. Although ignorance was also stressful. What if they came back again? What if they hooked up with Pedro and Emile?

"How far are they from the border?" Jack wondered aloud.

"Between Fort Macleod and Lethbridge, more or less." McMorton paused. "They are not stopping along the way so far, other than gas, so that's why we think they are going to the border and heading back. We'll know for sure by tonight. This afternoon, actually. We'll stay in touch."

"Oh, and don't worry about Roger." added McMorton. "We have an eye on him too. I have a feeling his supplier will lead us to some contacts in Edmonton."

"Yeah, it seemed like he was counting on that heroin from the bust."

"He is the only lead we have on that right now. Waiting for him to make a move. Maybe he will go to Edmonton to locate some more supply. If he does we are on him."

"Sounds like a tough guy." Jack noticed the girls coming to the kitchen, with Carla following. Usually they could get themselves up, but today apparently they needed Jill's encouragement.

"Yes. He won't be shy. He'll call it as he sees it. Which probably won't be the way he likes it, so there will be a ruckus. Just what we want."

"All right. As long as it doesn't come back to me."

"Can't guarantee that. But we'll stay on top of it."

"Okay, see you later. I've got some work to do."

○ ○ ○

"You noticing that car behind us, two cars back?" Emile, driving, asked Pedro.

"What car? Which one? I didn't notice." Pedro turned to look.

"That blue one, the Impala. It never passes. And we never lose it. It never gets close, and never too far. Hard to see, but I think two guys in it."

"Oh, yes. I see it now."

"We know we been followed in Edmonton. But they got nothing on us. Nothing to get anyway. We never found nothing. I think they follow us."

"What we going to do?"

"Nothing. We keep going. Maybe later we do something. Not now. Maybe I make a call."

"You will call Cortes? You want me to call him?"

"No. I call him later."

Chapter Sixty-One

BEFORE ERIN LEFT TO catch the bus to school, she ran back from the porch where she had just put on her boots. She gave Jill a hug, and then gave Jack a hug, and a kiss on the cheek. And a smile. Then with a wave, a loud drawn out "Goodbye!", and a slamming of the door, she was gone. Jill could see the bus lights in the distance through the bare branches of the trees. Carla stood staring out the window, with her hands on the window ledge. Jack sipped his coffee, his feet stretched out on the chair next to his, and his elbow resting on the table.

"Busy day planned today, Jack?" Jill had both elbows on the table, both hands holding her cup an inch from her lips, as she paused in sipping her own coffee. Used dishes were still on the table, along with cereal boxes and milk jug and juice bottle.

"Just normal. Things are going decently well."

"What was the phone call about?"

"Nothing much. Just some work stuff. We are making good progress on the new drill. The men call it Suzy. They like names for their machines."

"How is Tom getting along with Jake?"

"Same as usual."

"Here comes a vehicle down the driveway. Looks like Jake's truck. I better get this table cleared off. And you better get to work." Jill finished the last of her coffee and stood up, piling dishes, and bringing them to the counter just above the dishwasher.

Jack leisurely finished his own coffee, refilled his cup, and then started to dress for the outdoors. He hadn't checked his cows for a couple days; they would need some more feed today. But first he would go to the shop, check the email, and call Bill to see how things were down at Grande Cache. His phone rang.

"You called the cops." The gravelly voice was familiar. Jack thought he was finished with this guy after their last conversation, which had not ended on a friendly note.

"I called the cops?" he asked rhetorically. "What cops?"

"Someone is following my men. Around Calgary, Edmonton, and other places."

"What men?" Jack was giving nothing away.

"Emile and Pedro. They gave you a visit."

"I told you to stay away. I have nothing to do with Emile and Pedro."

"No one tells me to stay away. No one. You do not tell me what to do. I tell you. I said, don't go to the cops. Now the cops are on them."

"Yeah, well the cops found those drugs. So now they are checking Emile and Pedro. Probably they have drugs on them. Or asked too many questions about the drug bust." Jack was thinking on his feet now. He had not expected another phone call. He was reluctant to just hang up, since more information was always better than less. Even if he didn't like what he was learning.

"Emile and Pedro are good men. They had no drugs on them. They are clean." Jack assumed that by "good men", Cortes meant they were not stupid, and knew how to avoid trouble. Not that they were inherently good, with good motivations, and guiltless activities.

"Look, I told you to leave me alone. Now you are calling again. Are you threatening me again? Because if you are, I will have to go to the police."

"No. I am not threaten you again. Not yet. Maybe the police found out some other way about Emile and Pedro. So this is not threat. Just warning. Be careful."

"Did you find Manny and Maurice yet?"

"No. Not yet. Maybe never. Maybe tomorrow. I will find something."

"Don't call me again." and Jack slammed down the phone. He would have slammed down the phone, but it didn't work so well with a cellphone, so he just ended the call abruptly, not giving Cortes the last word. He continued his walk to his shop.

During the rest of the morning, Jack realized that Cortes did not respond well to threats. He wondered if he had made a mistake, threatening Cortes, even though done in frustration and anger. Protecting his family was about the most important thing to him, he was discovering. He realized that sometimes one didn't know what was most important, until it was threatened. Until you thought you could lose it. He wondered if that was also why he had attended church three Sundays in a row. Not looking for God, so much as being with his family.

Now he wondered what would happen next. Should he have a back up plan in case the drug lords ever came back? Back in Mexico they seemed to have little problem killing and hanging weaker men and women to make their point. A couple of little girls would not slow them down in getting what they wanted.

Jack remembered the message from last Sunday. Forgiveness was easy if it didn't involve life and death. If it didn't involve the weaker smaller members of your family. Or any members of your family. Should he just trust that God would look after them? That God would prevent them from getting hurt?

The Amish school children had still been killed. They were still shot, injured, dead. But that guy was crazy. Mixed up in the head. What Jack was dealing with was deliberate evil, deliberate planned malevolence, wickedness, perversion of people, constant harm, manipulation and domination for money and power. They never stopped hurting people. They didn't commit suicide afterwards.

Maybe it wouldn't come to that anyway. Cortes thought it was possible that there really was a genuine drug bust. That Manny and Maurice had betrayed him and gotten away. That he had not informed the police. So, he would have to let it play out. But, a backup plan would also be useful.

Chapter Sixty-Two

A LITTLE AFTER LUNCH, as Jack was looking over the work that Jake had been doing, he felt his phone buzz in his pocket. It was from Bill.

"Jack, we had an accident. Richard was driving the water bombi and trying to fill up next to the creek, but it was too steep, and he rolled his machine."

"Oh yeah? How bad is it?"

"It rolled twice and ended up in the water. It broke through the ice. The water was only a couple feet deep, but we have to bring the dozer here with the winch to pull it back upright. The tank is dented, the cab is bent, windshield destroyed. Probably will have to drain the engine because it is upside down now, so oil will get into the cylinders before we can get it righted."

"Do I have to ask how Richard is?"

"He is out of the machine. But hurt. Freddy is checking him over. He is not unconscious, but he is in pain."

"Did he call you? Was he good enough for that?"

"No. We happened to see his machine when we were between holes. Don't know how long he was there, but he couldn't get at his cellphone. He was partially under water, so he likely has some hypothermia. But he is still conscious, so it couldn't have been too long."

"You called 911?"

"Yes, but it will take them a while to get here. If his back and neck are okay, we will put him the truck and start bringing him to town. Otherwise we'll have to warm him up somehow."

"Good thing Freddy has his First Aid. Tell Richard I'm coming to see him tonight. Kole will come down too. Tomorrow with the Kenworth. He needs to come to haul the water bombi back to our shop."

"Will do. I'll let you know... wait a minute.... it seems Richard likely has a broken arm, and maybe a broken foot. According to Freddy, his back and neck are okay. He's lucid now and responding to questions. He's moving around now."

"Good to hear. Really good." Jack sighed in relief. He had dealt with injuries before. It was a dangerous business in many ways, and fingers, toes and arms were often injured. But a rollover came with different potential. The men never wore a seatbelt in these machines. They travelled slow of course, and that reduced the potential danger, but rocks, hills, slopes could cause serious problems. In wintertime snow provided a cushion, but ice was frozen hard, and rocks hidden under the snow were still unyielding.

"He is cold though. He's shivering, shaking. Can't hold his hand still. Stuttering."

"Warm him up then. Get him in the truck, and to the hospital as soon as possible. Do whatever you have to, to get him a private room." Some oilfield crews had permanent medical trucks on standby, with a guerney and bed inside, along with other emergency medical equipment handy. Jack generally didn't hire one. He did have one truck with a canopy on the back, and a cot in the back, but it was unheated, and usually used for hauling other supplies. He made a note to himself to put an auxilary heater in that truck, in the back. He had not expected someone to end up in the icy water, at least not more than a single foot perhaps, which could be warmed up in the cab of a truck.

Jack turned to Jake and Kole and explained the situation to them. Jake would have to change his work schedule once the machine arrived at the shop. Kole would get the Kenworth ready for the trip down the next day.

That would give Bill and Freddy time to get the dozer running and down to the water bombi, and flip it up, and pull it to the road where it could be loaded on the Kenworth trailer.

At the job site, Freddy and Bill loaded Richard into the back seat of the truck. The truck was already warm. Richard groaned every time they moved him, and it was obvious the pain was in his arm, just below his left shoulder. Freddy found a large rag, and turned it into a sling, which he used to tie around Richard's arm and his neck to support the sore arm which they suspected was broken.

"Should we lay him down on the seat?" Bill wondered. "Probably not a good idea. He will be okay sitting up." They sat him up and strapped him into the seat belt. Then they loosened the seat belt again and put a heavy parka around him for more warmth and padding, and put the seat belt back on. Bill turned up the heater and directed it to the back of the cab. Freddy pulled out his thermos of coffee and gave him a few sips. Then some more sips, and then put the thermos away.

Freddy got into the back seat with Richard, and Bill drove. He turned the truck around and headed down the trail to the road. Every bump was agony for Richard. Every bump was agony for Bill too, because he was doing his best to avoid them, but branches on the trail that normally wouldn't be noticed, and frozen lumps, dips in the ground were plenty. Eventually they made it to the gravel road, which was much smoother, and covered in snow.

Bill decided to drive slower than usual, even though Richard was in pain. A slower drive would be smoother and easier on his injuries. After ten miles of gravel, they arrived at the highway. Bill turned south, and increased his speed. The highway was smooth, having been repaved two years before. He turned on his flashers. Five minutes later they saw the ambulance.

The emergency medical technicians examined Richard and put an electric warming blanket around him as they laid him on the guerney. They quickly put him into the ambulance where they could work on him out of the weather. After improving on the arm sling, and examining Richard from top to bottom, one of the medics came out to talk to Bill briefly.

"He is suffering some hypothermia. And has a broken left arm. And a broken ankle. But he is not cut or bleeding seriously anywhere. Has a scrape on left hand, and on his cheek. He doesn't need an airlift to Edmonton. We will take him to Grande Cache to the hospital. Will you be coming there to see him?"

"Yes." replied Bill. "We will come there tonight if he is okay for now. We have a few things to tidy up here before we go to town. Thanks for your help. You guys are great!"

The ambulance headed south to town, while Bill and Freddy hopped back into the truck and back to their job site. They had left their machine running. And they had not checked the water bombi for Richard's things. He must have his ID and wallet on him, though they had not checked. They would get his other things, his thermos and whatever else he might have, if it was not buried in the water.

When they got back to the water bombi, they noticed ice was already forming around the machine. One track sticking up in the air was damaged, and partially off the rollers. Looking everything over, they saw Richard's cellphone, half in the ice, and his thermos floating on the water inside the cab. They broke the ice and grabbed both items seeing nothing else other than a pair of gloves, which they left there.

Arriving at their own machine soon after, they looked at the sun and their watches. "Think we have time for another couple holes?" Bill asked Freddy.

"Sure we do."

"We'll see Richard tonight."

"Yeah, I know. No problem. Can't do much there anyway. They will look after him and we would just be standing around like a sore thumb. Let's do some work." Soon Bill had the drill roaring again. But then a thought came to him. He shut off the machine.

"Freddy, we have to get the dozer. If we can get it started, I think we have time to drive it down to the creek to turn over the water bomby. It's only a mile and a half from here."

Bill and Freddy got back in the truck and drove to the dozer. After almost an hour of warming it up, they got it running and Freddy drove it to the creek and the downed bomby. Bill followed behind in the truck.

Freddy backed up the dozer, and they unwound the winch line. Hooking the cable to the roll bars on the cab of the water bomby, they slowly pulled the bomby upright. The one track of the bomby was partially off the idlers, but maybe it would work.

They had to reattach the cable to the rear frame of the bomby, and then pulled with the dozer. The track stayed on about half-way up the creek bank, a slope about a hundred fifty feet long, but then it crumpled off to the side. "Keep going!" Bill yelled, motioning with his arms. It skidded along on the frozen ground behind the dozer, and then stopped. Freddy hopped off the dozer.

"We should attach a cable or chain to the tracks so we don't have to come back to get them." Bill agreed. He yanked a chain off the bomby and hooked it up. Freddy got back in the dozer and drove it to a spot on the trail where a truck could load it the next day. They unhooked the bomby and then drove the dozer into a spot just off the road and parked it there for the night. By this time, it was getting dark so they headed to town.

Chapter Sixty-Three

"HOW IS HE DOING?" Jack was standing just outside of Richard's hospital room. He had made the long drive from home, and he went straight to the hospital to see Richard. It was not a private room, but the second bed was empty. Bill and Freddy were in the hall, having just come out. They had finished their work, had cleaned up, and then gone to see Richard. Now they were headed for some supper.

"He is good. They put a cast on his arm and shoulder, and a plastic adjustable cast on his foot. The foot needs more work, not sure what. They did some x-rays on the foot but haven't told Richard what they saw." They went back into the room, following Jack as he opened the door.

Richard was in a semi-reclined position, with his eyes closed, but opened them when he sensed them coming in. He looked groggy.

"They got you drugged up?" asked Jack.

"Yeah, some Demerol. I don't feel much pain, but I sure feel like sleeping. I was hoping to get something to eat first."

"Ah hah. Look at that. Here she comes!" Freddy pointed his face towards the nurse entering with a tray of food. "Hospital food is getting better all the time. And served with a smile!"

The nurse did indeed smile, and she put the tray on Richard's side table which rolled over his bed. "Anything else I can get you?"

"Nope. Looks good. After I eat this, I'm taking a nap. Maybe a long nap."

"Okay then. Enjoy." She started to walk out of the room. Freddy looked after her. Appreciatively.

"You have any spare beds?" asked Freddy. "I think I might have a kidney stone or something. Maybe appendicitis. Any spare beds on your ward?"

The nurse turned and brushed her hair from her face. She paused for a moment. Then, "Would you like me to check your tummy? Or your back? I could do it right now?"

"Sure! Absolutely!"

"Okay, just bend over right here... now. And I will check your back and see if you need a bed." Freddy leaned his hands on the bed, and bent his head and shoulders down, wondering what the nurse would do next. Bill had a huge grin on his face. Richard paused in his eating, also smiling.

She came up behind Freddy, put her hands on his back, and then swiftly kneed him in the behind, sending him flying face down on the bed, right on top of Richard's ankle cast. Richard winced, slightly, but then grinned at Freddy's position. She walked back to the door, turned, and asked, with a smile, "Does it still hurt? Or is it better now?"

Freddy groaned, but straightened himself up. "Good thing you didn't check my appendix. I think I'm okay now. Thanks for your help." Bill and Jack roared with laughter as the nurse left the room.

"Don't see that too often", said Jack, wiping his eyes. "Freddy, I think she likes you."

"If she likes me, then I'm in trouble. I think I like her too."

"She could be in big trouble if you reported her. Could use that to your advantage." Bill grinned at Freddy.

"A risk taker. Wouldn't be boring, that's for sure." Freddy nodded. "I'm getting hungry, Bill. We were on our way, maybe we should get going."

Bill agreed, and the two left the room to find a restaurant. Freddy was hoping for another glimpse of the lively nurse.

Jack turned back to Richard, who was about half done his supper. He had been hungry. "I'm curious how the accident happened. But if you are not up to it, we can talk about it later." He sat down in the chair at the foot of the bed and loosened the zipper on his coat.

Richard stuffed a bun in his mouth, and chewed, and swallowed. "I'm trying to remember exactly. I was going down the slope to the creek. I got down close, and then turned. I think there must have been a rock or fallen tree on the ground under the snow on the high side. Being on a slope already I guess it was enough to flip me. I was close to the water, and I ended up right in the creek. I must have broke the ice and banged my head on the frame. It knocked me out for awhile. By the time I woke up and started to move, Bill and Freddy were there. Don't know how long I was unconscious."

"You couldn't get yourself out?"

"Hard to say. My arm and shoulder really hurt and I couldn't use them. I couldn't push with my left leg either."

"So they saved your life then. You are going to owe them now." Jack grinned at Richard.

"Don't tell them that. I would have got myself out. Somehow. Tell them that." Richard grinned back at Jack, although a bit restrained, a bit drowsy, and still finishing the fruit in his dessert cup. "Sorry about your machine."

"It happens. I just want to know the details so I can put it in a safety report. And so I can see if we need to change any procedures or training in the future. Kole will come tomorrow to pick it up, and we'll take it to the shop and Jake will fix it up again, good as new." Which was ironic, since it never had been new to start with.

Richard sipped on the coffee that had come with his meal. "I'm sorry. I should have been more careful. Now I won't be much good to you for awhile."

"Don't you worry about it. You'll be on workmen's compensation for awhile. It could have been worse. You could be in a morgue, instead of a hospital. 'Course, you wouldn't be getting any workman's comp then..." Jack ended with a grin. "And it would be worse, because we would have to waste time at your funeral."

With a half smile Richard acknowledged his attempt to cheer him up. "I haven't had too much time to think, but maybe I will go visit my brothers, since I can't do much else."

"Good idea!" Jack responded. "Why don't you call them to see if they can pick you up. Or maybe I can take you back to my place when they let you go, and they can pick you up from there."

"I lost my phone. It fell in the water, and its no good now."

"Here, use mine!" Jack handed him his own phone. Richard paused. "I don't know his number."

"Hey, give me his name. And his town... I think you said Jean D'or Prairie, right? I will find his number for you. If not tonight, then tomorrow. I know people up there."

After Richard gave the names of his brothers, with his preference of who to call first, Jack indicated he would leave and let Richard get some rest, some sleep if possible. He left the hospital for the hotel restaurant, hoping to meet some of his men there.

Richard finished his coffee, laid down his head, and soon fell asleep. Caffeine had never bothered him, and with the effects of the demerol, sleep came quickly and solidly.

Two hours later, Richard felt a bump on his elbow. His right arm. He opened his eyes slowly, seeing a man through the blur of his eyelashes and mucous covered eyes. Then he recognized the man. It was Roger, who had worked with them for a couple days before being fired. It had been Roger and Enrico, buddies, both fired, but just Roger was here in his room.

"I heard you got hurt."

Richard did not care for Roger, but he did not let on. "News travels fast."

"You rolled. Did you get fired?"

"Nope. But I'm laid off for awhile."

"I see you have a broken arm. And a cast on your leg. You in pain?"

"A little, not much." Richard did not like the conversation. He wished he could go back to sleep. "Why are you here? I need to sleep."

"I got something for you if you need to kill your pain. Some real good stuff. I will give you the first shot for free.

"No thanks. They been looking after me good. Got no pain."

"Okay. But if you need anything, if you need me, just come and find me." He left a piece of paper with a phone number on it. No name, no other indication, just a number.

"Don't think I'll need anything. You can leave now."

Roger left, taking one last glance at Richard, who was watching him, and who closed his eyes the minute the door closed behind him. Before he fell asleep again, he wondered exactly what Roger had available, and whether it could be useful or not in the future. Would the pain come later, after the demerol wore off? Would they give him some more pain meds? What about when he was discharged? Then Richard was dead to the world again, snoring lightly in the semi-dark room in the quiet hospital ward.

o o o

Jack sat with Bill and Freddy, who had just received their meal when Jack entered the restaurant. Skyler and Eldon sat at a table across the aisle. Skyler and Eldon had finished their meals and were enjoying a cup of coffee as they relaxed with full stomachs. Their helpers had decided to eat in the hotel lounge, with a drink or two.

"How's Richard?" asked Eldon.

"Broken arm. Broken foot. Both on the left side. A few scrapes. Not bad."

"You gonna fire him?" Skyler asked, knowing full well he wouldn't. Jack had a great loyalty to his employees. Mistakes and accidents were not causes for dismissal. Unless drugs were involved. Everyone knew that Richard was not using drugs.

"No. I'm going to fire you for asking." Jack glared at Skyler, but both knew he was not really angry. Just playin'. "Actually, he will be off for awhile to recover. Probably going to visit his brothers up north. When he gets better, he will come back."

"You are short a water tank now. That'll slow us down."

"Haven't figured out what to do about that yet. I'll think of something." The waitress came to take Jack's order, poured him a coffee, and then left. "You guys seen anything more of Roger and Enrico?"

No one had seen anything since the last time Skyler had kicked Roger out of the restaurant. "One of the helpers said he had seen Roger walking around town with another man, at night in the dark. Didn't know this other guy, but he looked like a tough, apparently. He was smoking weed." Bill offered this information to all.

"I wonder if they found that prisoner yet, the one who escaped." Eldon asked this curiously. He had found it strange that there was no news on this, neither good nor bad. Jack did not enlighten his men. For the time being, they would have to be kept in the dark.

Jack turned to the plate which had just been set down before him and began eating. Eldon and Skyler stood up with their goodbyes, indicating they would turn in early. Bill and Freddy stayed to keep Jack company. When done, they all stood up and left for their own rooms, except for Jack who still had to get a room for the night, as he had not expected to be there. Kole was coming in the morning, and Jack wanted to be around for that.

Chapter Sixty-Four

AFTER BREAKFAST, EVERYONE HEADED to the work site. Soon, machines were running and men working. Jack inspected the water bomby and decided not to get it running for now. By ten o'clock, Kole showed up with the Kenworth and lowboy trailer. He backed it up to the water bomby, hooked his winch cable to the rear frame, and pulled it onto the ramps and the deck of the trailer. Jack's phone buzzed. He pulled it out of his pocket.

"Hello?"

"Hey Jack. We are finished brushing the lines here, or will be in a few hours. What you got for us?" The call was from the brushing crew foreman.

"Hey, good for you! I didn't expect you to be done for another couple days." Jack had forgotten about those guys, with all the additonal stress of the drug runners, broken machines, Richard's injury. "Let me think a minute... well our next job is not too far from here, back up the road north, south of Grande Prairie. You know what? Kole is here right now with the Kenworth. He has one machine on his deck. It might be big enough for the brushers to go on behind it. Hold on a minute."

Turning back to Kole, who was tying down chains and boomers, he asked, "Think you could put two brushers on behind?" Kole looked at his trailer. How big were those brushers...?

"I could try. I would have to move this machine up closer to the front. Maybe I could squeeze them all on."

"Why don't you give it a try. They are four miles from here... let me draw it out." Jack kneeled down in the snow and made a map for Kole. The machines were four miles away, but Kole could not go there directly since their trails were not wide enough for the big truck. He would have to go around about ten miles to get there. He fixed the directions in his head and nodded.

"I've got their number, and I've got your number. If I run into problems I'll call."

"Sounds good."

"I was going to visit Richard. How's he doing?"

Jack explained Richard's condition. Then he paused. "You know? You have to go around to get the brushers. You'll only be two miles from the highway. Why don't you go to see Richard first, then come back and get the other two machines."

Kole nodded. Then Jack rethought his plan. "Why don't I take you to town. I'd like to see Richard again anyway. You can leave your truck here and I'll bring you back."

Kole nodded again. Amazed at how Jack considered his men. Jack loved making money, loved work. But he would take time off for his men.

As they travelled to town, Jack let Kole drive. He described where he wanted Kole to bring the brushers. He gave the brushers another call, then called Jill. "Jill, can you email a map of the next job, job #3, to me? I will download it and print it at the hotel. I need it because they are ready to go to the next job; they finished this one. I'm on my way to Grande Cache with Kole. We are going to visit Richard there."

"Sure, darlin'." drawled Jill in a southern imitation. "Whuteva yu want."

"Thanks." Jack raised his eyebrow. What was up with her? Some mood, he guessed. Quirky. He grinned.

Kole dropped off at the hospital, while Jack took the truck to the hotel. He downloaded and printed the map in the hotel lobby, then returned to the hospital. Richard was sitting up, and Kole sat in the chair at the foot of the bed. They looked almost guilty, but Richard(reeshard) responded quickly when Jack asked how he was. "Doing okay. They keep me doped up so I don't feel much."

"Any news on the x-rays?"

"Not yet. But soon." and, speaking of news, a doctor walked in with some mylar photos, black and white. He asked Richard if he was ready for news on the x-rays.

"Sure. Don't worry about these guys. They can hear it too."

The doctor explained that the arm was a clean break, and it would heal in time. The foot was a different problem. The break was just above the ankle, but some tendons had also stretched in the ankle itself. The break was set well, but the adjustable plastic cast would have to be worn for six weeks. In the meantime, crutches would have to be used for the first two weeks, with lots of wheelchair time to reduce pressure on the ankle.

When the doctor left, Richard raised his eyebrow at Jack as a question. "Going to be out for awhile."

"Yeah, for awhile. At least two weeks, maybe six weeks. Unless I can find something for you that you can still do."

"I could probably still drive. I still have my right hand and right foot."

"True, but getting in and out of vehicles will be impossible for a bit. I'll see what I can come up with. In the meantime, go visit your brothers."

"They said they would let me go tomorrow."

"I found your brother's number. I know a county councilor up there, and he knows people in Jean D'or. Here it is. Call him. On my phone."

Richard dialed, and waited for the ring tone. After four rings, someone picked it up. It was his brother, Jacques. "Richard? Is that you? Where you bin? I haven't heard from you for a long time."

"I had a job. In Grande Cache. But had an accident."

"Hurt bad?"

"I'm in the hospital. But not too bad. Just a broken arm and a broken foot."

"Oh." he did not say he was sorry to hear that. But Richard could tell he was surprised. Sympathy would have to be assumed from this particularly stoic brother. Richard liked him because he didn't make a fuss. He was dependable.

"Wondering if I could come and see you. Stay there for a couple weeks until my arm and leg get better." Richard hated to ask, but what else could he do. A brother would help.

"Sure. You need a ride?"

"I get out tomorrow. Might have a ride to Grande Prairie or Peace River. I'll let you know."

"Okay. Let me know." Richard's brother hung up. Richard turned to Jack. "Did you hear that? He will get me when I get out."

"Okay. So far I don't have anyone going back tomorrow. Kole is going back today. Brushers naybe… I'm not sure. Two with machines will go up today. The other two tomorrow. We'll figure something out."

Jack's phone buzzed. He walked into the hall to take the call. It was Edmonton. McMorton. "They crossed the border south. The FBI are on them, but not touching them. Just thought you should know."

"Are we done with them then?" Jack kept walking down the hall to a sitting room. One elderly white-haired lady was sitting in a chair, a patient in hospital gown, with a ten year old boy, slightly overweight, who was sitting beside her and playing on his I-Pod. Probably her grandson, lost in his own world.

"For now. Who knows what'll happen later, but maybe they gave up. They could be lining up more junk, more heroin. Or going back home to disappear for awhile. I think they suspected they were being followed. They didn't leave a single suspicious trace of anything. Or they could be taking a different approach. Those guys don't give up easily when they think someone has turned on them. Manny and Maurice are in big, big trouble when they find them."

"Thanks for letting me know." Jack put them out of his mind. They were gone. He had other things to deal with. He decided to spend some time checking the work of the drillers and helpers, and then take Richard back up north himself tomorrow. He would stay another night. He called Jill and let her know. He would see her and the girls tomorrow.

Jack walked back to Richard's room and gave him the news. They would call Richard's brother Jacques, when they knew their schedule tomorrow. It would take him about 4 hours to get to Jack's home place, and he would take Richard from there back up north to his mother and brothers. Hopefully that much traveling would not bother Richard's injured arm and leg too badly.

Chapter Sixty-Five

JACK DROVE HIS TRUCK back to the worksite, to the Kenworth, where he dropped off Kole. Kole had the map with him now and headed to where the two brushing machines were sitting. The two drivers were sitting in their truck, waiting for him, and they all got out when they saw the Kenworth approaching. Looking at the deck of the trailer, they measured it with their eyes.

"It'll be close." said one.

"Real close." said the other. "We'll need every inch we can get."

Kole agreed. He began to loosen the chains and boomers, and then winched the water- bomby up tighter to the front of the deck, as close as it could go. One brusher was driven up the ramps and against the water-bomby. Then the second brusher. Its tracks were mostly on the deck, with about a foot sticking out the back. Between them, they tied down the three machines with chains and boomers which normally hung on the back of the Kenworth cab. Kole went around and checked all the chains, and when satisfied he turned to the other two.

"We'll make it. Here is your copy of the map of the lines that we need at job #3. Can you follow it?"

They looked at it for awhile. A page for directions to get there, and then four pages diagramming the lines that needed to be cleared. "Yeah, I think we can get there. We will need the lines put on the GPS so we can keep them straight. But this will get us started."

"Let's talk to Jack a minute. He should get the GPS set up."

Jack was sitting in his truck with some diagrams, some maps of the lines for job #2. But he wasn't looking at those; he was looking at his laptop and punching in various keys. Kole approached him.

"Jack, these guys need their GPS set up for the next job." Jack looked up and nodded.

"I have the map on here with the coordinates. I just need to download it on a stick, and then they can put it in their GPS, and it should work." Jack punched in some more keys, looked at the screen, and nodded. Then he pulled out the stick from his laptop. "I've only got job #3 on this stick. Try it out and see."

They inserted the stick and looked at their screen. "It's working. At least we can see the map. We are off the site, so we won't know how well the coordinates work in real time until we get there later, but so far it looks good."

"I will follow you down there. Don't go too fast; I don't want to lose you." Kole was anxious to get going.

They climbed into their truck, and Kole turned in behind them as they drove down the road to the highway.

Jack drove down to the first line on job #2. He dressed warmer, putting on hat and mitts, and then started checking the workmanship on foot. It gave him an excuse to walk, to exercise, to brace the cold air, and check his own legs and lungs. All was working fine. And the workmanship of his crew was also fine.

That night, Jack went to see Richard for awhile after supper. After some ordinary conversation, Richard informed Jack that they would let him out tomorrow afternoon, as long as all his vital signs were okay. They wanted to make sure that the hypothermia did not have lingering effects. They had given him some pain killers that morning. Richard wondered if he would get any more, since he was beginning to feel his injuries.

Jack told him that he had inspected the workmanship, and so far it looked good. He told him that Kole and the brushers had left. He himself would inspect more lines tomorrow morning on a random basis, until it was time to pick up Richard and head north to home. That sounded good to Richard, and Jack left for his hotel room.

o o o

Later that evening, Richard had a visitor again. Roger. The guy was thick-headed. Didn't he ever give up? "What you doing here now? I'm going to sleep. I need my sleep." Richard did not hide his irritation this time.

"I just wanted to check. Make sure you are okay. I have some stuff for you. Some junk. I'll just leave it here, in this drawer next to your bed, where you can reach it. See you later." And just like that, Richard was guilty, and Roger was gone. It was hidden, but Richard could still see it right through the top of the cabinet. What if someone found it? They would assume the worst. Should he report it? What should he do? Soon he was snoring softly, head on his pillow, dead to the world.

About two hours later, Richard woke up. He looked around and wondered what had awoken him. He saw no one in the shadows of the dim lights of the hospital corridor. He realized he was sweating, and then it hit him. The pain, he felt the pain! Richard could handle pain, even a lot of pain, but the weight of the sheets on his foot was huge. No matter which way he turned his foot with the cast, it hurt. His arm hurt too. He did not dare to move it. Then he moved it anyway when he turned his leg to change positions. Everything hurt.

Of course! It would be that! He had to use the washroom. It was close, but he would have to work hard to get there. Where were his crutches? Just out of reach, but one step away, if he could hang on to the edge of the bed, he could get them. He grunted in pain, grabbed his crutches, snugged them under his arms and caught his breath. After a moment, he cautiously worked with right leg and crutches in the direction of the washroom. It was working! He made it!

After he did his business, he washed his hand, grabbed his crutches and edged out of the washroom. As he did so, his right crutch slipped on a little patch of water on the floor, and he went down with a crash and clatter of crutches. Oh boy. That did not feel good. He was sore in more places than he realized. He waited for someone to respond to the noise, but no one came. Struggling up, he felt every movement. By the time he got back in bed, he was panting with exertion. Should he call for some pain meds? Richard was in no mood to talk to anyone. No mood for it.

Richard remembered what Roger had left him. You got to be kidding! He wouldn't touch that stuff! But it weighed on him. It brought back distant memories of murky times. He knew it could relieve the pain. At least he could check and see what it was. Roger had said junk, heroin. But how strong was it?

He opened the drawer. Then he opened the paper bag. A note inside lay on top of the small packet. "This stuff is pure. Use only a little." But how much was a little? How the brain worked. Amazing, he could now remember the size of a dose of pure stuff. He would cut it in half. He had no intention of getting high, just wanted to relieve the pain. And get some sleep.

Chapter Sixty-Six

RICHARD STUMBLED AROUND ON the sidewalk, on his crutches, outside the hospital. He started walking towards the hotel, only a couple blocks away. He had left the hospital early. He had the rest of his junk packet in his pocket, and he didn't want to be caught with it on him. The small amount he had used brought back all kinds of memories, including why he had quit drugs in the first place. The desire to use more had arisen like a phoenix out of the ashes.

He had revisited all his decisions, his choices in life. Wrestled with them. He had stomped on the foolish ones. Now he had to get rid of the packet before Jack came back to get him.

As he walked, he heard footsteps behind him, two sets. They easily caught up to him, one on each side. Thinking they were merely some other pedestrians, he did not look up. It was Roger on one side, an unfamiliar person on the other.

"Sleep well last night?" Roger smirked. "Slept like a log, I bet."

Richard did not reply but kept walking. Hobbling along, actually. Felt a hand on his right arm. "I'm talking to you. Don't ignore me." Roger seemed to be putting on a show for the other man.

Richard shrugged him off, but he barely managed to keep his balance. He kept walking.

Then a hand on his injured left arm. "You heard the man. Don't ignore him." This time Richard could not shake him off.

"Don't Blaine. I can handle it. Leave it to me." Roger was definitely intent on proving himself. Asserting his own authority. But it was obvious to Richard that the other man, Blaine, was one step up on the ladder. "You owe me for the junk I gave you yesterday."

Richard stopped moving, stopped struggling, turned and looked at Roger straight in the eye. "I never asked for the stuff. Never wanted it. I owe you nothing."

"But you used some, right?" Richard's silence was an admission.

"You can have it back." Richard grabbed the packet out of his coat pocket and threw it on the ground in front of Roger. Roger looked at it, bent over and picked it up. Suddenly he slapped Richard's head with his hand.

"Smart guy, huh?" he slapped him again. Blaine held him still, and every slap reached through his body into his left arm, causing renewed pain. But Richard maintained an expressionless face. Roger kicked him in the leg. The left leg. It was not good. Pain was coming back. Richard did not know how this would end.

"Tell me about those two guys you saw up north. The ones checking one of your machines, the machine that came from Venezuela." This growled command came from Blaine, with a shake of Richard's arm.

This time Richard was knocked off balance, mentally. "What? What do you want to know?"

"Did they find the stuff in the machine? The junk they were looking for?"

"Don't know if they found anything. They must have found it. They took enough time looking for it." Richard hoped his answer would prevent any more pain. It didn't work. Blaine shook his arm again.

"That's all you know? Were they happy or mad when they left?"

"Don't know. We were too far away to see. They seemed happy enough from what we could tell. They didn't stop and talk."

Blaine kicked Richard's right leg out from under him, and Richard sprawled on the ground. Roger gave him a kick in the left shoulder, just above the cast. Blaine knelt down, grabbed his cast and twisted it. Richard groaned. Roger slapped him a couple more times, then grabbed his hair and banged his head on the sidewalk. Blaine left the cast, and then stepped on his right hand and ground his boot into it.

"You telling us everything? You better not be leaving anything out. This is just a small taste of what you'll get if you are leaving something out."

Richard tasted blood on his lips. He grunted from the overall pain. "You guys are making a big mistake," he squeezed out hoarsely. "You got the whole story."

Roger lifted his head and motioned to Blaine. "Cops. Better get going." he gave Richard one last kick in the mid-section, and walked off briskly, quickly disappearing down the alley. Blaine followed him, peering back from behind a building to see the policemen stop by Richard.

"He knows my face. Wonder if he knows who I am... course, you were stupid enough to use my name. I'm screwed now." Blaine and Roger left the area.

"You wanted to talk to him," was Roger's rejoinder, defensively. "It was your idea. Not mine. What's all this about a machine from Venezuela?"

"He knows what its about. You don't need to know. I had to ask him questions. I was told. And you do not need to know by who. But I was told to get rough with him. So I did. Did what I was told. Remember that. I did my job."

Back on the sidewalk, Richard was sitting up. The policeman in the car had come out to check on Richard. When he saw the crutches and the bruises, he became concerned. Should he call the ambulance? "Are you okay?" he asked Richard. "You need an ambulance? What was going on there?"

"Two guys knocked me down. I'm okay." Richard wasn't ready for more confrontation, in his condition. He tried to get up, and then realized his arm wouldn't hold on to the crutch, while his right hand was too sore and injured. This was bad. He didn't relish being so helpless.

"Looks like you need help. An ambulance." The policeman got out his radio and called for assistance.

"Do you know who did this to you?" Richard shook his head. "What did they look like? Did they steal anything?" Richard described the two men in detail but provided no names and no other indication of who they were. The policeman wrote it down along with Richard's name and contact information and put his note pad in his pocket. In less than a minute, an ambulance showed up and the medics were all over Richard.

"Again? You need us again?" one medic asked with a degree of humor in his voice once he realized that Richard's injuries, though serious, were not critical.

Richard half-smiled through swollen lips. "Sorry about that. Sorry about the trouble I'm giving you."

"It's why we are here, buddy. I'm glad you are a lot closer this time. We are bringing you back to the hospital."

Richard resigned himself to his fate.

Jack drove up to the hospital, the community health complex, just behind an ambulance which had just arrived. He parked in the lot, and walked towards the welcome desk. "I'm here to pick up Richard. Is he coming down here, or should I go to his room to get him?"

"Richard? Oh, yes. Richard left an hour ago. He was walking towards downtown."

This made Jack wonder. What in the world was going on? Why would Richard not just wait for him, with his crutches and broken arm?

As he left the building, he noticed the medics bringing a man on a guerney into the adjoining emergency door. He took a second look. Something familiar. Long hair, the man's coat sleeve. On a hunch, he took a few steps closer. It couldn't be … it was. It was Richard. What?! What was Richard doing on a guerney, being only an hour out of the hospital?

"Richard! What happened?" The medics continued to push him into the hospital, while one asked Jack if he knew the man on the stretcher. "Yeah I know him. He works for me."

"Well, come along then. He was mugged and injured and we are bringing him to emergency to get checked over."

"Mugged? By who?"

"Two guys. I'll tell you later."

Jack followed them in, and soon a doctor was examining Richard. Jack was present and noticed the additional injuries to the right hand and face. Apparently no bones were broken, but the hand was swelling enormously.

The arm and foot were still in place, protected by the casts, but even more sore than before.

"We'll give you a bed for the night and check on you in the morning. We should take an x-ray of the hand just to be sure of it." The doctor was solicitous. Richard looked like a mess, his hair disheveled, face swollen, coat dirty.

While they took an x-ray of the hand, Jack sat in a chair in the waiting room. What to do now? Leave Richard here? Phone Richard's brother? Could Richard still travel? Maybe take him to Grande Prairie, to a larger hospital with more facilities and equipment?

Jack called Richard's brother. "Jacques, Richard got mugged. Just an hour ago. He's in emergency again, and they're doing an x-ray on his hand."

"Is he coming out?"

"Don't know yet. They could keep him another night and keep an eye on him. I haven't talked to him much yet. Don't know who did this. If it was a random thing, or if they knew him."

"I'm halfway to your place now, I guess I'll keep coming."

"Yeah, for sure. If necessary, you can sleep in the bunkhouse. In fact, count on it. We're going to be delayed and even if we leave today, it'll be late."

"I took one of my other brothers along. One of us could take Richard's place if you need someone."

"You guys work as hard as Richard?"

"No. Richard is smarter, and works harder. But we can do alright."

"Let me think about it. I'm down one machine right now, and it has to get fixed before I can use someone else. But thanks for the offer. I'll get back to you when I find out more about Richard."

The doctor came to Jack. "We have a bed ready for Richard. Would you like to see him now before we bring him to his room?"

"I was wondering, doctor. Could Richard travel? I'm thinking what if I took him to Grande Prairie, to the hospital there? It would get him out of town, and to a bigger hospital, and his brother is coming to pick him up, so it would shorten his trip too."

The doctor paused. A two hour trip for Richard? "It could be okay, I suppose. He has no back or neck issues. He will have to keep his leg up for awhile once he gets to Grande Prairie, to avoid blood clots in his foot. It may bother his arm, but if he agrees, I don't see any immediate harm done by such a trip. We have already given him some pain killer that should last a couple hours."

Jack went into the emergency examining room. Richard was lying calmly on the raised bed. "Richard, your brother Jacques is partway down already. With another brother. How would you like to go with me to the hospital in Grande Prairie, instead of staying here?"

Richard nodded.

"Okay then, that's what we'll do. I'll let the doctor know, and you can sign the release papers, and we'll be on our way."

Richard nodded again.

As they drove north together towards Grande Prairie, in one of Jack's red trucks, Jack managed to pry the story out of Richard. He regretted the day he had hired Roger and Enrico. This other guy was also a problem now. What was his name?

"Blaine. Roger called him by his name, Blaine. Don't know his last name. He's the one stepped on my hand."

"So they both are involved in the drugs."

"Yeah, Roger wasn't hiding anything from him. Probably his supplier."

"Roger supplying this guy?"

"Other way around. Blaine supplies Roger. My guess, anyway." Richard was grunting with the effort of talking.

"Someone told these guys to rough you up. Wonder who."

"Don't know."

"Something to do with Manny and Maurice, though. Something to do with the drugs we found in the drill. I'll bet it was the same guy threatening me. On the phone, from Mexico. Trying to find out if we know more than we say."

"Could be." Richard was not interested in putting all the pieces together. He was interested in keeping his pain levels low, getting better, and then coming back to beat those guys into the dust. If he hadn't already been so injured, they would not have been able to mug him the way they did.

Jack stopped at the side of the road. He checked his phone list and punched in a quick dial number. "Jack here. Richard's boss. The guy who was mugged... the one you got to the hospital." A pause while someone on the other end was speaking. "Yeah, you got it. I want to tell you a bit more about the situation. The two guys who mugged my man, were Roger and Blaine. Roger worked for me for a day. Don't know who Blaine is, but he is also involved in drugs."

"Oh yeah?" Jack listened while the police explained they had Blaine under surveillance. They didn't want to arrest him yet, because they were hoping for bigger fish to fry. "You got about two days," said Jack. "When they attack my men, there are consequences. I can't have people assaulting my men. That's not in their job description. I don't tolerate drugs on the job, and I don't tolerate mugging of my men. I'm taking Richard to Grande Prairie, and when I come back, these guys better be arrested, or I'm talking to them myself." Pause again while Jack listened.

"Yeah, I understand. I know you got objectives. Good objectives. But I also have objectives. Once guys like this think they can beat up people, it doesn't end. I'm not putting up with it. It doesn't have to be tied to the drugs. It can be kept separate from that." Jack listened some more to the cop on the other end.

"Well, you know where I stand. I'll talk to you later." Jack terminated the call. Then he put the truck in gear and resumed traveling down the highway again.

Chapter Sixty-Seven

"WE ARE GOING TO the Grande Prairie hospital. They will check on Richard, maybe keep him overnight. Wanted to get him out of Grande Cache in case those guys tried something again. They were not random muggers. They were looking for him." Jack relayed this information to Richard's brother. "You can stay in my bunkhouse, or come down to Grande Prairie."

"How about you phone and let us know how he's doing first, when you are in Grande Prairie? You will probably be there about the same time."

"Yeah, I can do that."

Richard was now sleeping, head lolling against the window. Jack called Jake. "How's the water bomby now?"

"Not as bad as it looked at first. We drained the oil. We pressured the water tank and it popped back out, so its okay... has some small dents and creases, but its holding air, so it should hold water. The track will be fixed soon. The cab is not pretty, but we straightened it out enough to bolt on a new windshield. We could have it back tomorrow afternoon."

Jack pondered that, wondering if one of Jack's brothers could take on the job that Richard was doing. He punched in another number.

"Hi Jill. How are the girls?"

"They are fine. You coming home?"

Jack then updated Jill on Richard's adventure, and subsequent events.

"Hope Richard's okay." Concern seeped through Jill's response. "He's sleeping? I want to talk to you about Christmas. We could use a break. Are you planning a break for Christmas?"

"Usually do."

"How about Disney for a few days? The girls would like that."

"California or Florida?"

"So you're okay with it then. I'd have to check on flights, schedules. I'm thinking after Christmas, maybe leaving on boxing day." Jill knew the girls would be excited. The warmer weather would be nice too.

"Yeah, I'm okay with it. The crews will have Christmas off, work a few days and get New years Day off, a couple days. Or more if they want it. I'll just leave Bill in charge out in the field."

"Okay, see you soon."

As they arrived at the Grande Prairie hospital, Richard awoke. He peered around, and then grunted, in pain. Jack noticed, but he said nothing. He parked the truck near the emergency entrance, walked in and asked for a wheel chair. After some explaining, a medic brought one and wheeled it out to Jack's truck. They opened Richard's door, then helped Richard from the truck into the hospital, and into an examining room. They were expecting him.

Jack went back to the waiting room and started making calls. First to Jacques, who informed him that he and his brother would continue on their drive to Grande Prairie. Then to Kole, who would drive the repaired water bomby back to Grande Cache the next day. Jack asked him to stop near the hospital or at least to check with him before he went back.

Then Jack called Bill, just to stay in touch… everything was going smoothly there. Jack informed him that his inspections of the work had found nothing amiss.

Next was another call, to the police in Grande Cache. Nothing new had happened there.

A call to McMorton, informing him of incidents in Grande Cache. McMorton did not comment much, just noting the information for later use. Nothing new had transpired with Emile and Pedro. FBI were monitoring them.

Jack fidgeted. He was not good at waiting. He had run out of people to call. He went into the examining room and the doctor there was talking to Richard. After introductions, he talked to both Richard and Jack, explaining that the x-ray on the hand showed a broken knuckle. Nothing could be done except to take it easy, do no work with that hand, and wait for it to heal. More serious was the possibility of internal injuries from the kicks that Richard had received. He would like to keep Richard over night at least.

Jack agreed with that, and then gave Jacques a call. "they're keeping him overnight. How about I meet you somewhere and we talk? How about Rycroft, and we'll have dinner there." That was agreeable to Richard's brothers. They were headed south, and it would take them another half hour to drive to Rycroft from where they were.

When they met at Rycroft, which was a forty-five minutes drive north of Grande Prairie, Jack had everything planned. After introductions in the parking lot, he took his attache case with him into the restaurant and they sat down to talk. It was a bit early for supper, so they started with some coffee.

"I'm going to explain the work to you, and give you a quick safety course. One of you can do Richard's work... you can decide who it will be. Then we can sign some papers, get your social insurance number and contact info."

"It'll be me working," replied Jacques.

Jack went through what the job would entail. On site, Bill would do the training and explaining of the actual operation, and the mechanics of the machine, which would come back down to Grande Cache the next day. Jack's plan was that Kole would pick up Jacques when he brought the water bomby down, taking him to the job site, while the other brother would take Richard back home.

"Your expenses, including your cell-phone, will be covered by me now," he told Jacques. When you get to Richard, trade your boots with him, and make sure you have warm coats and mitts. We have extra mitts in the trucks. Get a hotel tonight on me, and wait for Kole tomorrow. Here is his phone number."

"I'm a little short on cash." Jacques apologized.

"I'll call and book your room. You can put your meals on the room tab. They will pack a lunch for you. Bill will get in touch with you to take you to the job site."

By this time, supper had arrived. Jack ate his in a hurry. He was happy with Richard's brothers, and felt he could depend on them. He was ready to get back home and see his family. In a short while, they all departed the restaurant, and went their separate ways.

o o o

It was well past dark by the time Jack got home. Tomorrow he would have to check his cows again. Tonight, time with Jill. The girls were probably in bed. Stars were shining in the sky, and the northern lights were in full display. Green and yellow shimmering waves of light were dancing across the skies in a slow pulsating rhythm of energy. It was never humdrum or boring, these northern lights. Jack felt like the hand of God was guiding a paintbrush in the night sky.

Then, as he got out of his truck to go to the house and check on the friendliness of his wife, Jill, on this cold winter night, it crossed his mind for no reason whatsoever, that at least this time of year he didn't have to deal with pesky mosquitoes which could badger a person mercilessly in the early wet summer days in the tall grass. He opened the door, stomped his feet, removed his gloves, and with head turned up to the ceiling, yelled, "Hi Jill! I'm home!"

Chapter Sixty-Eight

JILL AND JACK SAT in the third row. The auditorium was packed. Jill's parents sat beside them, with Carla bouncing in her seat between them. Jill's parents were thrilled. Their oldest grandchild. Their closest grandchildren were here. They had only one other grandchild. So this was very nice, to be able to see this, to be a part of it.

Christmas decorations, ribbons, tinsel, spruce branches covered the walls. A couple paper santas, and a dozen elves were taped to the walls. The nativity scene was painted/colored on the opposite wall. "Silver Bells" was playing in the background.

It was two weeks before Christmas, and the school Christmas program was in process. People were still filing in and finding seats. A buzz of noise filled the room as people shook hands with people as they passed down the rows to their seats. Others turned around to see who was there and waved at friends and acquaintances. Children ran up and down the aisle to talk to parents before they ran back to their seats in their class room groups in the side seating.

"Did you see the program, Daddy? We are almost at the beginning!" excitement surrounded every syllable of Erin's announcement as she stood in front of them, a hand on the knee of each parent.

"Yes, Erin. You will be great!" Jack couldn't help grinning from ear to ear at his daughter's enthusiasm. The general noise and cheer was infectious and filled the air like a warm sun on a cloudy day.

"Erin, did you remember your lines? And your song?" asked Jill, knowing she did remember, and hoping she would remember at the right time in the program.

"Of course, Mommy! Look! There goes Sally. I have to talk to her! Bye, bye."

Jill and Jack smiled at each other. A daughter they loved. A daughter they had produced together. Here she was, living and enjoying. Carla was also entranced by the whole thing. A new baby was on the way, maybe a boy. Life was good. Love was good.

The school band, junior high students, played "Silent Night" and "Joy to the World" from just below the stage. Then the kindergarten class came to the front of the stage. Twenty of the twenty-one students recited together the first six verses of the Christmas story. The twenty-first student, a little blond-haired boy, was staring at the audience, petrified. Maybe looking for someone, maybe his parents, but the lights had been dimmed. He turned his head to one side of the hall, then the other side. One of those children in a different world, thought Jack. He wanted to hug the boy. That was him when he was younger. Just a bit different, not following the crowd, not a total conformist. Seeing things differently.

Next up was Erin's class. Together, they recited the remainder of the Christmas story. They were clearer and louder. One brown-eyed boy could be heard above the whole class, his heart and soul poured into the recitation. These were the words that Erin had to know, and she did.

Now they sang a song. Erin sang the first verse of "Silent Night" and then the rest of the class joined in for the next two verses, with a lot of help from the teacher. Two children also played the triangles, metal ringing on metal in rhythmic accompaniment. Applause rained down on their completion, and the children left the stage with broad smiles on their faces.

A tiny boy with brown hair and oriental features, a grade two student, came up to the stage with a violin, bowed, and began to play "It came upon the Midnight Clear". It was clear he was a genius, an expert, a child prodigy. Jack hated him. How will my children keep up to that? He is going to make my children seem ordinary. Then he wanted to give him a hug. Imagine being hated in jealousy by other parents. What a sad place to be in. Let him be great. I hope he does great!

The program continued, but Jack's mind wandered. Today he had been working in the shop, helping Jake and Kole put the finishing touches on the repairs on the water bomby. Tom had been working on resurfacing more drill stem. The water bomby still looked rough, but it was functional. It would be re-finished in the spring, after the field work was done. Jack had been so happy he could stay home for this Christmas program in the evening. He didn't want to miss this one.

Richard and his brother had left the hospital in Grande Prairie this morning. They arrived at Jack's shop at noon and had some dinner in the house with Jack and Jill and Erin. Richard was suffering in every movement, and had been taking painkillers, although he tried to keep them to a minimum. Jack had taken some pictures of Richard and his various injuries, just for the record.

It would be a four-hour trip back home for Richard, which he was not looking forward to, but it couldn't be helped. Richard's brother teased him some about the injuries, but Richard was quiet, not responding in kind. Jill had given them some snacks to take along, filled their coffee cups, and sent them on their way.

"Make sure you call when you are ready. When you are better." said Jack as they left. "You got a job here when you need it."

Kole had eaten his lunch in the bunkhouse but was ready to leave with the Kenworth and the repaired water bomby. He had filled his cup, grabbed a few snacks from the fridge, and climbed in the cab. The machine had already been driven on deck and tied down, and he was off. He would have to pick up Jacques in Grande Prairie along the way.

As Jack was reminiscing about the day's events, he marvelled at the complexity and diversity and contrasts. Here he was, enjoying a concert, a Christmas program with his kids, his family. Some of his workers were recovering from a cold day out in the field. Other workers recovering from injuries. Muggers wandering out doing mischief. Drug lords evading the police and destroying people's lives. Good situations, bad situations. Good people, bad people.

The Christmas program... something he took for granted. So many people took it for granted. But what was it all about? Santa on one wall; Jesus on the other wall. Little children singing, reciting, performing.

Santa was the fairy tale. Just be good and you will get candy and presents. Was Jesus also a fairy tale? A nice story about a baby who became a man and performed miracles, made people well, and was very wise? How did Jesus fit in to this question of good people and bad people? Did Jesus have anything to do with good and evil? What exactly?

The school band was playing again. "Good King Wenceslas". They were actually quite good. The songs were old familiars, but the children jazzed them up a bit. Two more numbers and the program was over.

As Jack and Jill and the girls drove home, Jill sat contentedly in her seat, hands folded in her lap. "Mom and Dad enjoyed the program."

"Really nice they could make it," responded Jack. "It was a good program."

"Your mind was wandering. Yes?"

"Yeah, for awhile it was. But I was glad to be there. I was thinking about work, and the trouble Richard had, and the machine being fixed. Believe it or not, I was thinking about good and evil, and how Jesus fit into it all. I even wondered how Santa and Jesus fit together, or if they did."

"Christmas makes you think. Someone once told me that without Easter, there would be no Christmas. That made me think." Jill offered pensively.

"Really? You mean without Jesus dying, there would be no birth? That makes no sense. It should be the other way around." Jack stopped at the stop sign, then turned the corner and continued the drive home.

"It does make sense, though. We celebrate Jesus birth. But why? What makes Jesus great? What makes him worth celebrating? It's because he died. He was crucified unjustly. It's because he rose from the grave. So we celebrate that at Easter time. But that's why we celebrate Christmas too. Without an Easter to celebrate, we would have nothing to celebrate at Christmas!" It was like Jill had finally put into words something that had been lurking in the back of her mind for some time.

"I guess you're right. That makes sense after all.... The band was pretty good, wasn't it?"

"Yes, they played well. Mom and Dad really like them too.... I think the girls will enjoy getting the Christmas tree on Saturday."

"Or Sunday, if Saturday is too busy for me. But yeah, I saw a nice one in the field while I was feeding the cows. Maybe we can convince the girls that they saw it first?" They laughed together.

The rest of the trip home was in the comfortable silence of an evening which had truly been enjoyed by all.

○ ○ ○

Kole broke the silence as he and Jacques drove to the job site near Grand Cache, with the repaired water bomby on the back of the truck. It was a light load and the roads were good. Sun was going down in about an hour. He had picked up Jacques in Grande Prairie at the casino on the bypass. He had explained as much as he could about the water bomby on the back, how it operated, what to check for, hazards of driving through bush, importance of draining hoses and keeping the heat going. The heat was primarily generated by an exhaust pipe going through the middle of the tank, and this kept the water from freezing.

"What kind of work have you done before?" Kole was curious about his experience.

"Fire fighting, trapping, some highway roadwork. About the same as Richard."

"Uh huh. Any winter work?"

"Trapping is mostly winter. I had a six mile line."

"Driving? Any driving jobs?"

"Just ordinary vehicles. Not something like this on tracks. My license is clean."

Kole paused, pondering. "What do you know about Richard's mugging?"

"What he told me. Two guys jumped him. He couldn't fight back because of his injuries."

"Did he know the guys?"

"I have a feeling he knew them. He didn't say so. But I know Richard. He's hiding something."

"What's he hiding? Any idea?"

"He did say he had tried a small dose of heroin for pain, the night before. Didn't say where he got it from, but he said he wouldn't use anymore. It reminded him of too many bad experiences."

"Did you ask about his supplier?"

"Yeah, actually I did. But he changed the subject."

"Maybe the mugging is connected to that." Kole stroked his chin.

"How is it connected?"

"I don't know how, but it would not surprise me if it was connected. Drugs. Same town. Next day mugging. Just too coincidental. I got a question for you."

"Yeah?"

"Jacques, I gotta ask you. Are you happy that Richard was mugged?"

"What? Of course not."

"Neither am I. Richard became my friend. Someone mugging him really gets under my skin. Just beating on him. Him with two casts and crutches. A couple of low-life, miserable, worthless..." Kole continued under his breath words too vile for utterance. "You interested in doing something about it?"

Jacques turned in surprise. "Hadn't really thought about it. But yeah, could be possible."

"I say when we get to Grande Cache, I am not going back home. Going to stay in a room in town... you have to get a room anyway, and I'll share with you. Then we'll do some checking around. You up for that?"

Jacques sat up straighter. More alert now. "Yes. We should. I'm with you on that. Cops will probably do very little to solve the problem. I'm with you."

"Okay, here's what we'll do." They discussed various options and continued their planning until they reached the job site. They unloaded the water bomby and continued on to town.

Chapter Sixty-Nine

EDMONTON WAS CALLING AGAIN. McMorton sounded a little more excited than last time they had spoken. "What's up?" Jack wondered aloud as he put his boots on to go to the shop.

"Had a call from the FBI. Emile and Pedro have turned around and are heading back north. They were in Arizona at the time, near Tucson. Don't know exactly why they didn't cross the border to Mexico, but the FBI are keeping an eye out. They said they saw another vehicle close by, that seems to be following, but not obviously. They are not sure whether the two vehicles are connected or not."

"Heading north? Doesn't sound good. But could be one of a dozen things, right? Maybe going to Nevada. Or Utah. Not coming back here."

"Could be, but I wanted to let you know. These guys will continue their trade one way or another, so I'll bet you they are not going somewhere to set up a nursing home."

"Nope. Nor a soup kitchen neither. But who knows where. I guess we'll know better if and when they get close to the border?"

"Yes. In the meantime, the FBI are giving them lots of room. They wanted to find out about the whole chain, from one end to the other. We'll work on this end, and them on that end."

"You know that Richard got mugged, right? I been thinking about that, and I'm not happy letting that guy run around free."

"We have to for now. We can't give the game away. How is Richard doing?"

"He's patched up. Going back home, up north until he recovers. If you put that guy in jail again, you won't be giving any game away. It'll just be because of the mugging, not because of any drug dealing."

"It'll shut down our connection from his end. We won't be able to watch him make any contacts. I suspect he will be making a trip to Edmonton soon. Just a gut feeling."

Jack was doubtful. It was just as possible that the guy would disappear. Or that he would end up hurting someone else. He probably already had access to the drug supply and he had probably supplied Roger. So there was no need to go to Edmonton... the supplier could come to him instead. But he did not express all this to McMorton. For now they would have to wait and see. He terminated the call and opened the door to the shop. "Good morning, Jake! How's it going?"

What he didn't know was what had transpired earlier, the night before.

o o o

After supper, Kole and Jacques had gone to their room. After a quick trip to the hospital, and some other preparations, Jacques came down from the room by himself. Now he looked different. He was using a pair of crutches, and had "borrowed" a cast for his foot. A huge bandage on his left arm looked like a cast, and his hat was low on his head. Jacques had hair much the same as Richard, so now with Richard's boots and a coat similar to Richard's, he hobbled down the street towards the hospital, slowly. Kole watched from his hotel window on the second floor until Jacques was out of sight, and then quickly walked down the stairs to the street.

As Kole followed Jacques at a distance of almost two blocks, he saw nothing happen. Not at first. Then he saw a man flip his head in an abrupt stare at Jacques. Jacques was aware of the man but kept his head down. Then, in an apparent state of exhaustion and weakness, Jacques sat down on bench next to the sidewalk, which was designed for seniors in their walks down the street.

The man was Enrico, and he disappeared quickly. Not long after, two men came from the same direction, and about that time, Jacques got up slowly and laboriously from the bench, prepared to resume his walk to the hospital. Apparently, the two men, without doubt Roger and Blaine, had no idea that Richard had left town. Here was another chance to finish what they had started.

They soon gained pace with Jacques. They started shoving him back and forth in the dark. Jacques did not react and did not speak. "You're walking again, are you? I guess we can fix that for you." Roger had to start the game. But Blaine was not hesitant to jump in.

"Maybe we should take off that cast. It's making you slow and clumsy. Yeah, that should work." Blaine punched him in the shoulder. Jacques winced, but did not react.

Blaine kicked him in the right leg, while Roger shoved him from behind. Jacques went flying. Roger kicked him. Suddenly, Roger also went flying. Kole had arrived and was making his presence felt. After knocking Roger down, Kole turned around and gave a wicked right hook directly at Blaine's head, which snapped back and staggered Blaine.

By this time, Jacques was back on his feet, and he gave a mighty kick with the cast on his left leg at the back of Roger's leg. Roger tumbled to the ground, and Jacques jumped on him, using first his right arm, then his supposedly broken left arm to inflict serious damage on Roger's nose, his eyes, his ears, his mouth. With a couple of head bangs to the cement sidewalk, Roger was now comatose.

Meanwhile, Kole was working on Blaine. Blaine fought back like he probably had in prison, but he was no match for Kole. Kole was tasting blood as Blaine managed to get a punch landed. Kole hit him again and sent him staggering back. Blaine pulled a ten inch blade from somewhere and held it in front of him. Kole wondered if Blaine had a gun but suspected he did not or he would have pulled it already. Kole backed up until a light pole was just behind him. Taking a sideways glance, he saw that Jacques was making good progress with Roger.

As Blaine came at him with the knife, Kole stepped sideways and kicked Blaine's shin, barely avoiding the swinging knife arm. Then he grabbed the arm and pulled on it, completing the forward momentum and swinging

Blaine directly at the steel light standard. Blaine wrapped his arms around the pole, and banged his head on it, stunning himself. In the next motion, Kole grabbed his head and banged it against the pole, three times. Blaine dropped the knife. Blaine's nose was cracked and bleeding, and the tears in his eyes distorted his vision. He swung wildly at where he thought Kole was, but Kole easily avoided him and hit him twice in the jaw, the second time from underneath. Blaine crumpled to the ground.

Kole should have been done, but he wasn't. He got down on his knees. He examined Blaine's face carefully. Then he jabbed at each eye, just enough to cause the swelling he was aiming for. Two thumps to the mouth, and a couple broken teeth were the result. Then he stood up. By this time Blaine was almost unconscious. Kole jumped on his right hand with the heel of his boot. Then jumped on Blaine's left foot, right at the ankle.

That was enough. That would send a message. Don't start something you can't finish. Don't get in over your head. Don't ever attack an injured man and think that there won't be consequences.

By this time, Jacques was just watching. "You done?"

"Yeah, I'm done. Let's go." both men were still lying on the sidewalk, not moving. Kole put the knife back in Blaine's crushed right hand. His left hand moved slightly. Roger's right leg was curling up, and his breathing was steady. Kole searched Blaine's pocket for a phone.

He looked around in the dark and saw no one nearby. The altercation had been quiet and had not attracted any attention. Cold winter nights did not see many people on the streets after the stores were closed.

"Yes, emergency? I think I saw two guys fighting with each other on the street just down from the hospital. One is hurt pretty bad. You think the other could be that escaped criminal from prison? He kind of looks like the picture in the paper. No, I can't stay. Don't want to get involved. No, I can't give you my name. ...It's up to you. I thought I should call." Kole put the phone back in Blaine's pocket.

They stood at a vantage point two blocks away as the flashing lights of a police car parked beside the two men who had now sat up. One of the men was standing, while the other was not. Kole and Jacques did not wait to see anymore and went up to their room.

Chapter Seventy

IN THE MORNING, KOLE and Jacques went for breakfast. They met Bill at an empty table and sat down, while the waitress anticipated them with a coffee pot and menus.

"Just the regular for me," said Bill, who had been there everyday now for two weeks. The waitress was the same everyday, except for weekends, when a younger school aged teenager took over. She nodded and then looked at Kole.

"The big one. Bacon and eggs, three pancakes, hashbrowns. Orange juice."

"Okay. And you?" This time she looked at Jacques.

"I'll have the same." She whirled around, picking up some used cups along the way as she headed back to the kitchen.

"Bill," Kole spoke deliberately. "You know the guys who messed up Richard? We found them last night."

"You did?" Bill looked at him quizzically while he sipped his coffee.

"We gave them some medicine, straightened out their looks, and called the cops."

"Oh? How much medicine did you give them? No overdose, I hope."

"About what they gave to Richard. One of them pulled a knife on me."

"Think the cops will do anything?"

"The cops showed up. One guy had a knife, we think he was the escaped prisoner. Probably one or both had drugs on him. Maybe the cops will find it. They can't really trace it back to us. But they will suspect a friend of Richard, because Jacques set up to look like Richard... that's why they attacked him. Which is what we wanted."

"Good thinking. Maybe you should phone Jack and tell him."

"I'll call him right now."

Kole called Jack and got him up to date. Jack wondered out loud how this would affect the entire drug investigation. He told Kole that Emile and Pedro were headed back north but didn't know exactly how far north. Bill thought back to the incident in the field, where Emile and Pedro had been confronted with most of Jack's men. He asked a question.

"Do you think Emile and Pedro will come back with re-enforcements?"

"Could be. For now, we won't worry about it until I hear from Edmonton. Can you find out if Blaine is back in jail?"

"I could, but I don't want to be obvious, or they will have reason to suspect us. I'll have to think of something." Kole also wanted to know where Blaine and Roger were. He didn't want Jacques or anyone else to be always looking over their shoulder.

"Bill is about ready to leave, right after we eat. He will take Jacques, and I am ready to come back to the shop. That okay with you? You don't need me for anything else at the moment?"

"No, just come back. Nothing else to haul back yet."

"See you in a few hours then." As Kole terminated the call, the waitress brought their food, and they ate in silence.

o o o

"Who was that?" Jill was curious, as she added toast to the plates of Carla and Erin. Carla and Erin buttered their own toast, added some jam, took a sip of juice, and started chewing. Carla was still sleepy, but Erin was bright and chipper. She poked at Carla, who responded in a half-hearted fashion. "Eat your food, Erin." said Carla, as she took another bite of toast.

Jack was chewing his own toast, which was lined with some strips of bacon and an egg, over easy, soft but not runny. Just the way he liked it.

"That was Kole, just bringing me up to date. He will be back here probably around noon."

"So who is this guy in jail?"

"No one. Just an escaped prisoner. It's been in the news. He escaped from the Grande Cache prison and they haven't found him yet." Jack hated hiding things from Jill, but he couldn't give her the whole story. Not yet anyway. Not unless it was necessary.

"What did he do? Why was he in prison?"

"Murder apparently. Circumstantial evidence though, because they never found the body."

"I see. Would you like some more coffee?"

"How about my mug with the lid. I see Jake coming in and I should talk to him."

Jack scooped up the last slice of toast, this one with jam, stuffed it in his mouth, and began putting on his coat and gloves and boots. By the time he arrived at the shop, he had finished chewing, and Jake was inside. Jack updated Jake on the latest events in Grande Cache.

"Good for Kole. Those cops always need too much evidence and too much protocol. Those two guys got what they needed, and hopefully the cops put the guy back in jail."

Jack agreed, silently, but also wondered if there would be any repercussions. It couldn't be helped. Obviously Roger would continue to do what he was doing if he wasn't stopped, and Blaine was the same. Just barely out of prison and doing exactly the same illegal stuff again. Drugs and terror. Jack shrugged. It was good that his main men knew what was going on, just in case.

"How is the new drill coming along?"

"I lost some time doing the water bomby repairs, but this drill is coming along. Should be ready in about a week now. If there are no more interruptions." Jake sounded pleased. They walked to the unit, and Jack also was pleased with not only the progress of all the working parts, but also the sleek appearance of this machine. Some conveniences had been added in terms of blue-tooth, better heating, comfort seats, larger fuel tanks and water tank. As a rubber-tired unit, it would not be available for all locations, but would travel faster in open fields, wherever the line was wide enough and smooth enough.

Usually Kole assisted Jake, but this morning, Jake greeted Tom as he walked in. "Come and give me a hand, will you? Just until Kole gets back."

Jack walked into his office and looked at his incoming mail. Kole arrived just after lunch and greeted Jack in his office. "I'm back."

"Good. You can go back to helping Jake again. But hold it, I want to talk a minute." Of course, in this case, a minute could mean anything, including a half hour, or an hour. "I called the cops in Grande Cache. They put Blaine back in jail, but let Roger go. He will probably be looking for revenge. Did you think about that?"

"Yeah. But we had no choice. We didn't go looking for them. We just set them up and they fell for it. So we had no choice. If they are looking for revenge, too bad. They were going to do damage anyway." Kole knew he wasn't giving his boss much room to differ with him, but he was adamant.

"You have a point. But why not just notify the cops?"

"Cops let Roger go anyway, even when they were notified. So what's the point? And if the cops knew what we did, they'd probably arrest us."

Jack nodded. "But violence never ends. Everyone just has to one-up the other guy. Nothing but threats, and beatings. One guy pulls a punch. The other packs two punches and several kicks. One guy pulls a knife, the other pulls a gun. And then one day, someone will kill somebody. I don't like it."

"We are already there."

"What do you mean, we're already there?"

"Those guys, threatening your family, your wife, your girls. Think they didn't mean it?"

"Well..."

"They meant it alright. They had killed families in Mexico, and in Texas. Not just a gunshot, but an actual ritual murder, hanging and beheading. Now bringing it up here. Maybe it would have been better if we had just stopped to let them have the machine for a half day, but we didn't." This hung as an unspoken accusation to Jack's part in this. Kole was not letting him off the hook. "And besides if we had let them get the drugs from the drill, then they would just be ruining other people's lives and terrorizing other people. I know just enough of it, to know how that goes. It'd be like

Roger and his friend beating on a defenseless guy on crutches with a couple casts on his arm and leg. They just don't care."

Now Kole couldn't stop. He was getting pretty hot. "Manny and Maurice deserved what they got."

"What do you mean, what they got? What did they get? What do you know about it?" Although Jack didn't show it, he hated even to ask the question, but it was out before he could stop himself.

"We did it to them, we should know. Richard and I didn't actually want to tell you. But maybe its better if you know. We finished them off and buried them where no one will ever find them. With the way things went with Emile and Pedro, you might as well know about this."

Jack remembered how many of his men had come together, most of them armed, to intimidate Emile and Pedro, and to protect Jack and Kole and Richard at the previous job site. It easily could have ended up in bloodshed, but it didn't. But now? Some of his vague suspicions had been confirmed. Manny and Maurice had not left the drill voluntarily after all. That made sense with the drugs still in the machine. In spite of that, Jack swore out loud to show his frustration. He stood up from his desk and started pacing.

"Well, now what? Do I report you to the police? Do we forget about it? Continue to keep it secret?" Head down, pacing, frowning, banging his hand on his desk.

"Yeah, we keep it secret. I told you because I didn't want to keep it from you. Never asked Richard, so he might get mad at me for telling you. But I want you to know something. We asked those guys about those threats on your family, when we were at the drill. They had nothing to lose. They could speak whatever truth they wanted. And they repeated the threats and told how they had murdered other people. Innocent people, just for fun, some of them. We tied them up, told them to repent. We gave them about twenty minutes to repent, but then didn't listen to them anymore because they would probably lie to us. We couldn't take the chance. Cops had no evidence against them and couldn't hold them. They won't threaten anyone anymore, and they won't be hanging and beheading people."

"Crap. Crap! But we going to kill every guy that threatens us?"

"Your girls. You going to let someone hurt them? Kidnap them?"

"No. For sure not. No."

"You have deniability. You don't even have to lie. You had nothing to do with it. That's why we did it the way we did, because you would have been the first suspect. You didn't even ask us to do it."

"If it gets known that I didn't report, I'll be in big trouble. Maybe even jail time."

"I'm sorry about that. But if they had kidnapped one of your girls, that would be worse. You know that."

"Yes. It would have been worse."

"We good?" Kole was a bit anxious about this question. The future was always unpredictable, but he needed to know how Jack felt, how he was going to react.

"Look, its not what I would have advised. But you have a good point about the alternative not being great, and they deserved what they got. It's done. We'll leave it. I won't report it, ever. Unless maybe you are dead already, but otherwise not. Their disappearance will be a harder pill for Cortes to swallow than their death, because life doesn't mean much to Cortes. But betrayal means a lot. His pride means a lot. Being stopped in his plans, in his program, means a lot to him."

"So, we good?"

"Yes, we are good."

Jack and Kole went back to their work, not realizing that Jake had heard part of the conversation as he had maneuvered around the shop. Jake kept it to himself for future reference.

Chapter Seventy-One

FREDDY HAD A HARD day at work that day. Bill had been impatient, grumpy. One of those days. It was a cold day, with a stiff wind. Wind was not so bad in the trees, but the open spots had been miserable. By the time they came back to the hotel, Freddy was done in. Now, after a big, delicious supper and sparse conversation, Freddy just wanted to be by himself for a short while before turning in. Walking around the hotel, he soon began to question himself why he was outside, since he had been outside all day. Well, he was walking on solid sidewalks, not in deep snow on uneven ground over branches and fallen trees or through tall slough grass.

"Hey! You one of those seismic workers?" The question caused Freddy to raise and turn his head. Roger was standing there. Didn't Roger remember him? He stopped and turned to face Roger.

"Don't you remember me? You worked on our crew for a day."

"Yeah, yeah. I remember. I thought you were one of those guys. You guys think you can do what you like, huh?"

"What do you mean?" Freddy was confused. He thought Roger and Enrico were gone, not part of his life. Why was Roger accosting him now?

"The cops let me out. Blaine is back in prison, but they let me out. You guys got another thing coming."

"Really? They didn't find any drugs on you?" Freddy didn't really know what Roger was talking about. He had no idea what Kole and Jacques had been up to the day before. But he was playing it cool, wanting to hear what Roger had to say.

"No. Blaine had some, but not me. Somebody started a fight with us yesterday. Then called the cops... well someone called the cops, but the number was on Blaine's phone. Blaine sure didn't call any cops. One of the guys stepped on Blaine's hand, same as he did to Richard. So my bet is its someone who knew Richard. One of the guys looked just like Richard, even put on a phony cast and used crutches. So we got it figured. Blaine's supplier is not happy. He's got contacts, and somebody is going to get hurt. Might be you. If I find Richard, he's going to be wearing four casts instead of just two."

"Uh, huh." Freddy decided Roger was not going to take him on by himself. He decided to finish his walk around the block since he was more than halfway. He looked around nonchalantly to make sure he was not being ambushed. Then he gave his advice for Roger's benefit, "I wouldn't advise it, Roger. It won't go well with you. Better leave it alone."

Roger stood looking at Freddy's parting back side but didn't follow. Then he also turned and headed in the opposite direction.

o o o

Jack put down his wrench and pulled his buzzing phone out of his pants pocket. It was McMorton again. "Jack, they are in Montana now." Jack did not need to ask who they were talking about. "It looks more and more like they are headed back to Canada. The FBI have not stopped them, and they will inform customs to check them out a bit, but not to detain them or alert them that they are under watch."

"So if they are coming up here, they could be here tomorrow or the day after, if they don't wander or get delayed."

"Yes, true. The FBI is not certain, but based on passengers, no females, and travelling more or less at the same speed and direction, they suspect three other vehicles, with three or four guys in each. Probably have guns.

Maybe drugs. But we want to see the connections, and nail as many people as we can. So we won't be arresting them. If we stop them without evidence, we will just be tipping them off and they'll all get away."

"I understand. Just let me know what's going on so I don't get ambushed or blindsided."

"Exactly, Jack. That's why I'm calling."

As he hung up, Jack answered Jake's quizzical look. "Emile and Pedro have been spotted heading north again. Maybe three more vehicles with another twelve guys coming too, if they're guessing right."

Kole paused, looking carefully at Jake. Jake nodded, and asked Jack, "You going to let us know if they get closer? We might have to be ready. Like the last time, but better, more so."

Having heard Kole's tale, Jack was greatly conflicted. Putting on a show was one thing. But a full-scale battle would be something different, not all palatable to Jack. However, he nodded to Jake, and Kole was both relieved, and somewhat more tense than he had been.

o o o

Jake called Bill ostensibly to discuss how the water bomby was doing. "How is it holding up?"

"Okay so far, Jake. No problems. Richard's brother is managing with it."

"I wanted to let you know that Jack got a call from the Edmonton police. Emile and Pedro are back in Montana, heading north. Probably going to cross the border. Can't prove it but my bet is they are not finished with us here."

"I'll let the guys here know to be ready, with eyes wide open." Bill was calculating. "They could be here in a couple days then."

"If that is their plan. Jack has mixed feelings. He really wants to avoid violence and bloodshed. But these guys live to die. They live to kill. In my opinion. So we better be ready for anything. They are bringing more men, it sounds like. Maybe a dozen more."

"If they are coming, we should not wait for them to come all the way to us. Especially with that many guys. We'll have to pick the spot."

"Yeah, that makes sense. But out in the bush, isn't that the best? They come from a different place, a warm climate, probably city boys. They are going to have trouble in the cold, in the bush."

"I'll keep that in mind." It sounded like Bill was taking charge of things. "Jake. You should inform some more people around there. Maybe Jack's father and father-in-law. Anyone else you can think of. Hunters, especially. If we need them, we won't have to explain later."

"What about the police?" Jake wanted to be on the right side of the law.

"They already know. But they have their own agendas. They let people go so they can fry bigger fish. They need concrete evidence to press charges and make arrests. It sometimes gets them killed, like the four cops shot in Mayerthorpe. You remember that? We don't need that. When it comes to it, we'll let them know so we don't end up with them attacking us. As long as they don't get too tight on their jurisdiction, or stop us from defending Jack, and Kole and Richard. Which reminds me, I should call Richard and let him know too. We don't need any surprises." Bill terminated the call.

By this time, Freddy had caught up to him. "Having trouble with your machine?"

"No. I was on the phone, talking to Jake. He was telling me those guys might be coming back to Canada. If they do come this way, we have to be ready."

"Yeah, Roger was hinting at something yesterday. The cops can't handle them?"

Bill paused, "Cops are letting them come to see if they can nail some serious drug operations. FBI are trailing them too. But if they have a mind to come back after us, I don't think cops will be quick enough. I could be wrong. But in any case, it doesn't hurt to be ready for them."

"Like last time?"

"Yeah but sounds like this time they might have another dozen guys along. Who knows? Those guys play for keeps."

"You're kidding. It would be better if the cops took care of them." Freddy did not relish taking on gangsters.

"Too many laws in the way. Freedom of movement. Racial discrimination. Lack of concrete evidence. Can't arrest them until they actually do something. That sort of thing. Lots of laws in the way. Some are good laws, but sometimes people get hurt before the police can do anything." Bill spoke forcefully.

Freddy was quiet. It made him uncomfortable. Some kind of shooting war? In this day and age? Out in the bush? Nah, not possible. Not likely, anyway. "What's in it for them? Why would they come back? Didn't their guys betray them? What do we have to do with it?"

"I don't know, but they made a lot of threats against Jack's family. Against his two young girls. They were looking for drugs, never found them, over a million dollars worth. And they don't like being pushed around. Last time we stopped them, they were probably embarrassed. They want to be big men; we made them small. They will want to get back at us for that."

Freddy nodded.

"We just have to be ready. We'll let all the guys know tonight. We better get going and finish this row of holes." Bill climbed into the track machine, and drove to the next hole, while Freddy resumed his duties at the hole Bill had last drilled.

Chapter Seventy-Two

MCMORTON HAD COME IN early this morning. Sipping his coffee and looking at the papers scattered on his desk, he wondered about the girl who had gotten shot in Winnipeg the day before. It was not prominent on the news. Just a byline. "Teenage indigenous girl dies in crossfire between a street gang and local police." Just a byline on the third page. A gang member had also gotten shot, but not fatally. He could imagine the story behind it. The amount of time the police has spent tracking the young men of the street gang. The drugs they had been peddling and using. The girls they had been lining up and pimping out. The confrontation at a particular time and place when they thought they had the evidence they needed, and the possible immediate danger these thugs were posing to the public. It was a perennial tale, an often repeated scenario, with its many variations, new gangs or new members to take the place of those arrested. The battle against crime, against evil, had begun the day Cain murdered Abel, and it wouldn't end until the second coming of Christ. Not that McMorton was particularly religious.

McMorton wondered about his own case, particularly the drug runners from the USA, who were now in Montana. Would they come up here? And if they did, what would he do? How would he handle it? Hearing the stories from his friend Jack up north, he wondered too how they would react. Jack and his men were not pacifists, not laid back let the police do everything kind of people. Maybe it was a good thing. Police were often restricted and constrained by the laws of evidence, which were heavily skewed in favor of the defendants. But McMorton knew that he would still have to uphold the law, even if the good guys broke it. He did not relish the possibility of having to arrest Jack or any of his men, if they got carried away. He would deal with it when the time came. If it came.

As if responding to his thoughts, his desk phone rang. He checked his watch. Seven thirty. Still early. "Yes? McMorton speaking."

"They are ten miles from the border. I'm sure they are coming over, if they can. We could arrest them before they cross, but we don't have much to go with. We have no evidence of any crimes so far in America. If you can handle it, we suggest letting them through. We can send a couple men with them for extra surveillance if you want." It was the FBI. They had done their job.

"How many men are there? How many vehicles?" McMorton had given a previous preliminary alert to the detachment at Lethbridge, but they were stretched for the things they could do.

"Four vehicles altogether, we think. Two half ton trucks and two cars. The two cars are black, the two trucks are brown. We are sure of three at least. Emile and Pedro and one other are in one vehicle. They have been switching who is first from time to time, usually keeping about a half mile between vehicles. But in the cities sometimes they would get together, two vehicles at a time. The other three vehicles have 10 men."

"So that's thirteen altogether. If they are sticking together, their target will be Edmonton." McMorton was certain of this. They would return to the area the drugs had been found. "We'll tail them and add men at Calgary. But they can't know or it will make them harder to follow. Do you have license plate numbers? Hopefully they don't commit any traffic offenses or some cop will stop them, and the game might be up."

"Are you going to tail them right from the border?"

"No. If they are coming north, they will come through Lethbridge. From there its a couple of choices, but by then we should be on them."

McMorton was considering all the logistics. "I'd better go; I have to phone the border, and then Lethbridge. We'll stay in touch."

At the border, the two brown trucks and the two black cars were separated by several semi-trailer trucks and a number of other vehicles, mostly more pickup trucks. When they were asked if they were carrying firearms, the drivers all shook their heads. No firearms, no alcohol, no cigarettes, except a couple packs in their pocket for the smokers. No large amounts of cash. Passports were from the USA, two vehicles from Arizona, and one vehicle from Texas, except for the third vehicle, a car, where all the passports were from Mexico. They were only planning to stay for two weeks, they said. One truck indicated a three-week visit.

The customs agents examined one of the trucks, the second one, bringing a dog around to sniff for drugs, and looking under the seats, in the glove compartment, and under the hood. They held a mirror under the truck, checking for contraband, and then finding nothing obvious, they sent them through. The other vehicles were not searched. Pictures of the vehicles were immediately sent to McMorton and he forwarded them to Lethbridge. An hour later, an inconspicuous late model Impala with two non-uniformed officers, one male and one female, was accompanying the four supposedly unconnected vehicles.

McMorton gave Jack another call.

"Jack, they have crossed the border. Almost at Lethbridge now. We are on them."

"Thanks, McMorton. Good to know."

"Jack, why don't you call me Charles. I appreciate the formality, but in your case, I'd appreciate Charles. I feel like we are friends, not just agents, not just cop and citizen. And I want to say, I sure hope I never have to arrest you for anything." McMorton chuckled out loud, but he was sending a message; he was friendly, very friendly with Jack, but at the same time Jack needed to be careful not to back him into a corner by doing unlawful stuff. McMorton would give Jack all the leeway he could, but McMorton's duties and role as an officer of the law would take precedence in the end.

"Okay Charles. I'll try to remember that." Jack was hinting he would remember both Charles' name, and his role. "We all have to do what we have to do, and we have the same goals. You don't want to arrest me, and

I don't want to be arrested." At this they both laughed out loud, reducing the tension underlying their conversation. McMorton knew he would do everything he could to give Jack the benefit of the doubt. Sometimes however, people up above him forced his hand. He tried not to think about it.

o o o

Thinking through his previous conversation with McMorton, Jack calculated timelines. Coming through so early in the morning, if this was their destination, the gang from down south could be here by evening. On the other hand, if they stayed in Edmonton first, it would take longer. If they even came at all. Maybe Edmonton was their only destination. But they had quite a crew for such a job. Thirteen men. They were not just doing some reconnoitering; they were geared for business. Probably already had guns with them, and who knows what else. Jack was starting to sweat.

He punched in some numbers on his phone. "Bill, Emile and Pedro have crossed the border. Thirteen men in four vehicles. Two brown pickup trucks and two black cars. Cops are keeping an eye on them. In my gut I feel they are headed up for us. Hope I'm wrong."

"All the guys down here know about them since last night. I'll let them know today again. You have a plan?"

"Depends which way they go. I don't want them coming to the farm or my shop. Especially not to the house. We need to head them off. The cops can't do anything until they do something illegal. By then it could be too late."

"Those crooks have all the advantages." Bill sounded resentful. "The cops have to abide by the law. People like us also tend to abide by the law. The crooks use the illegal automatic rifles, and we are stuck with the five-clip rule and the semi automatic, or maybe a seven clip shotgun with pellets or buckshot. That gives them a big psychological advantage. In a pitched battle, it gives them a physical advantage." Bill was thinking out loud again.

Jack had to agree with Bill. "The government keeps adding on regulations and restrictions for law abiding gun owners in Canada, but does next to nothing about the illegal trade, and the guns for criminals."

"Makes it hard on the hunters and turns innocent law-abiding people into lawbreakers by changing laws. By trying to steal their property. The government turns allies into enemies, for no good reason." Bill was on his rant, one he had been on many times before. Bill was convinced that laws making it hard on ordinary gun owners, hunters, collectors, sports shooters, would make it easier on criminals who thought they had nothing to fear from ordinary citizens who had been deprived of their own guns. Bill had never expressed these thoughts on the internet. He left that to others. But he held these beliefs strongly.

Jack was sympathetic to Bill's concerns, but usually did not give it much time. He had no reason to, up to now. The idea of a pistol pressed to the head of one of his loved ones, or a gang surrounding some citizens and hanging them all from a bridge, made him realize how primitive and visceral his feelings were. He would give his life in the attempt to save the lives of his loved ones. Every advantage he could get, he would take. Hopefully he could get enough advantage to stop the shedding of blood.

"We don't know what they are thinking." Bill paused in his response. "They already know the drugs are not in the track drill, so they won't follow the machine. They will be headed for you, or for Kole and Richard. My guess is Kole and Richard. That's why Blaine went after Richard."

"Yeah, Bill, you're right. Richard is way up north, which they might know, if Roger gave them an indication. Kole is here at the shop. Their contact now might be Roger, and maybe we can use that to draw them in. I'll send Kole to Grande Cache with Tom. Jake will stay here with Jill's dad as backup, with an indirect warning to the police here as backup. But if we can get them headed to Grande Cache, we'll be better off."

Bill agreed with that. Soon he was calling the other drillers, Eldon, Skyler and Jared, as well as letting Freddy and Jacques know what was the state of affairs. They kept on working but worked in a state of high alert. Jacques called his brother to let Richard know. Back at the shop, Jack called Jill's father, and then his own father, and his sister in Spruce Grove. He called two of his hunting buddies, one of whom was actually in the bush, hunting moose. It seemed silly to call some hunting buddies who knew nothing of what had gone on. They did not mind being called and seemed to understand immediately what was at stake after Jack gave them a brief update. "If you need me, give me a call right away. Don't even think twice about it. Just call me. I'll be there, where you need me."

Jack was surprised at first at the response, but then realized that he himself would probably respond the same way. He wasn't the only one who detested those drug runners, pimps and murderers. Jill sometimes had tried to tell him another side to the story. How lost and desperate these criminals really were. How they probably had no fathers to care for them, or maybe had gangster fathers. How they had no one to teach them about love and caring for others. How they likely had known nothing but power and violence and brutality all their lives.

Jack wondered how Jill would respond if she knew the kind of threats they had made against her and the girls. If the situation came home, instead of being a million miles away, would she be empathetic for the men who shot others, beheaded them and hung them from bridges? Jack had no intention of letting her know these men were in Alberta, but he knew if things got out of hand, she would likely find out anyway.

Jack wondered at the fact that he had not received another call from Cortes lately. What was he doing? Where was he?

Chapter Seventy-Three

BY THE TIME EMILE and his gang arrived in Edmonton, they had soon been supplied with extra firepower. The surveillance team had noticed the pizza delivered to their hotel rooms, but had not seen the contents of the boxes, which were filled with parts for automatic rifles, delivered not by a pizza delivery man, but by a good impersonation of one. Some of their pistols had been brought across the border in their cursorily checked vehicles, as well as a few short-barreled rifles and shotguns. Plenty of shells were available, although Emile didn't think they would need that many.

Emile told the men to stay away from drugs and alcohol. He wanted them alert and sharp, and he wanted no incidents that might cause the police to get involved. Any celebration would happen after everything was finished. Most of the men were agreeable to that.

Two of his men had a different idea. One was a black man originally from Louisiana, who had moved to Arizona and become part of the organization. A young single man, he was big, and strong, full of testosterone and bravado. He was like a young stallion, only semi-broke to the halter, and constantly testing the limits. Emile hoped he would not have to kill him.

The other man was a Caucasian from California, half Latino, who had also migrated to Arizona, running away from legal problems and from police investigations. He had gotten together with the black man before they joined the organization, and today these two wanted to play the tourist in a city where they had never been before. We'll just go for a walk, they said, and did indeed go for a walk for about two blocks before they felt they were out of sight of their friends, and into a bar around the corner. No drugs maybe, but a few drinks would be okay, and soon they were betting on a game of pool with two other men who looked like they lived in the bar.

It wasn't long before an argument ensued, claiming that rules were being made up on the fly, that the other guys didn't know how to play, and that the money bet on the game would not be paid. A punch landed squarely, followed by another. A pool cue, broken over a hairy head, and a broken nose, caused by a cue ball in the hand used as a sledgehammer. Testosterone thick in the smoky air, lights were broken, and several glasses broke into a thousand pieces as they landed on the floor. Spectators all around, eager to get involved, but not yet having the proper justification for adding their own fists to the fray.

A blue uniform entered the hive of activity, putting a stop to the entertainment by grabbing the left arm of the assailant from California originally, now from Arizona, and twisting it viciously behind the back. The two regulars scattered, while the black man appeared to be gathering his resolve to assist his partner and free him from the clutches of this insolent police officer. He scattered quickly as he noticed a second blue uniform entering the place of business from the street side. The bouncer also finally stepped up to the plate, a bouncer in name only, since he had bounced no one, and although of large and intimidating size, did not have a heart to match, and thus failed to insert himself between the four busy pugilists. The two uniforms left with their victim, after having failed to detain any of the others, hauling him off to the local holding cell.

When Emile heard what had happened to two of his men, he told the black man to sit in a chair. Then he told two others to hold him, one by each arm, while a third hit him in the body twice, and in the head twice, hard. That would be his lesson this time. Next time it would not go so easy. The man, almost unconscious, was left on the floor in his room, while the others went to theirs.

Charles McMorton heard about this not long after. One of his men had followed the two to the bar and had surreptitiously been nursing a beer at a corner table when the altercation had broken out. He had almost intervened himself, thinking the first officer was in danger, when the second officer had entered, rendering it unnecessary to offer assistance. McMorton realized that the local altercation would not concern Emile and Pedro overly much, as long as there was no connection made to the larger group, or to the mission of the organization as a whole. McMorton decided to let the local police handle it, and not interfere. It would put one bad guy out of commission for a day or two, maybe long enough to reduce the manpower by one. Apparently, this man had assaulted a police officer in the aftermath, while being installed in the squad car. He would endure a longer stay behind bars.

Meanwhile, Kole had driven to Grande Cache with some more bentonite. The drillers were using more of it than they had expected, and drilling was going slow. Tom had not come with him, and he had hauled it on a triple axle trailer attached to a dually one tonne quad cab pickup truck. After bringing it to the job site, he had not returned back home, but had gone to Grande Cache itself, to the hotel, and booked a room. Then he had begun to wander around town, first to this bar, then to that one. To the grocery store, the liquor store, the hardware store, to the gas station up on the hill. Back again to the hotel. Then to the hospital. Through the residential district nearby. Back to the hotel. Finally when it got dark, he made a couple stops at the local bars, and then for supper not at the hotel, but the restaurant on main street. And back to the hotel.

By this time, Roger had seen him. This was Kole's purpose. Roger was not likely to attack Kole physically, the way he had attacked Richard in his injured state. Roger had experienced the wrath of Kole, and stayed well out of his way, especially now since Blaine was back in prison, and unable to help him. Enrico could potentially be an accomplice for Roger, but Enrico was small, not aggressive. Roger would stay low. Roger made a phone call however, to a man named Emile.

Chapter Seventy-Four

CHARLES MCMORTON, CHIEF DETECTIVE, inspector at the RCMP division in Edmonton, received a call from his surveillance team at the Quality Motel where two of the teams from Emile's gang were staying. "They are leaving. Heading west. We have followed them past the highway 43 turnoff, so they are not going to Peace River. Three of the vehicles are going west. One did turn north. One of the brown trucks. I have no idea why they split, but we have the other team following them up north."

"Interesting. I wonder if they found out where Jack and his crew are, especially Kole, and are heading that way. Stay on them. I am sending reenforcements, although they will be an hour or two behind. I will alert the boys in Hinton, but they don't have enough men if there is trouble."

"Better wear body armor. These guys mean business."

Road conditions were fair. It was getting cloudy in the west, although the sun was shining clearly in the east. Forecast was for flurries, which could mean anything. It would be a four and a half hour drive to Grande Cache, and another half hour to the job site north of town. The plain clothes officers settled in for the drive. They had food and drink with them, prepared for any eventuality. The team heading north was similarly prepared.

○ ○ ○

"Mommy, look, grandpa is here!" Carla was all excited. "Maybe he'll pull me on the sled!"

"It's too cold this morning, Carla. This afternoon would be better. I wonder why he is here?"

"Can I go to meet him? Can I?" Carla loved company and loved her grandpa. Living in the country, every visitor was a treat, but especially her grandpa. He was much better entertainment than the workers and drivers who often came into the yard but were preoccupied with their work. As much as she loved her dad, grandpa certainly seemed to have more time for her.

"Just wait a minute, Carla. He will be here in a minute. Unless he's going to the shop. ... no, he's coming here." Carla ran to the door to open it for grandpa Bernie. "Where's grandma? Where is she?"

Bernie grinned at his young granddaughter. "Grandma didn't come, but she will come here in a couple hours.... she has some things to do. I can't stay, because I have business in Grande Prairie. But I wanted to come and see you before I left." He sat down at the table but didn't settle in too comfortably. Jill poured him a cup of coffee anyway, and he started drinking it.

"You staying home today?" he asked Jill.

"Yes, staying home. Will check on the cows in a bit, after you leave. Me and Carla have an inside day all planned. Right Carla?"

"Yes mommy." Carla replied in a half excited manner. She like spending time with mom, but on the other hand, it would have been fun to have grandpa around longer. He gave his full attention to her.

Bernie hesitated about saying why he was going to Grande Prairie. Mainly he hesitated because he was going to go through Grande Prairie, all the way to Grande Cache. It was about three and a half hours to the job site. Some of Jack's hunting buddies had already left, and Bernie would pick up David, Erin's other grandfather, along the way. Jake and Tom were going to stay and work in the shop. They would keep an eye on Jill and daughter. Suzanne would keep informed and let Jill know to pick up Erin if necessary. If not necessary, Jill would not find out at all, about the reason for everyone's movements.

"Thanks for the coffee, Jill. I've got to get going." he hugged both of them, put his boots back on, and went outside. Soon his truck was gone. Jill and Carla were on their own again.

o o o

The third vehicle, a black Impala, fell behind the rest. It pulled off the road and stopped at a turnout. The two officers following in the unmarked car decided to pass it and stick with the other two that they were following. Stopping behind it would look suspicious, as if they were tailing it. Eventually the third vehicle would get back on the highway again, they were certain.

Sure enough, the third vehicle resumed travelling before they were out of sight. It picked up speed quickly, and soon was only a few car lengths behind. Traffic was light. The officers concentrated on the vehicles ahead. Tinted windows hid the activity in the Impala as it drew nearer. The muzzle of a gun peeked out through the slightly opened window, and the officers did not hear the sound of the gun as it fired at them twice. Their vehicle started to wobble erratically, as their left rear tire was punctured by the bullet. As they slowed down to inspect the problem, the third car which had slowed behind them, turned off on a side road, taking a one mile detour around the unmarked police car. The officers had no idea where the third car was. They were concentrating on the tire problem.

The officers saw a shredded tire, but did not suspect bullet damage, having heard nothing other than the pop of the tire. They called back to headquarters to let them know what had happened, as they busily changed their tire, but now would be twenty minutes behind. McMorton called ahead to the Edson police to keep them informed and asked for a change of vehicles when the two plainclothesmen arrived in Edson.

When Emile, Pedro and their three vehicles passed through Edson, they were being observed surreptitiously by two officers sitting in an unmarked white Ford pickup truck. Shortly afterwards, the officers from Edmonton parked behind the truck, they all got out and changed vehicles, and the pursuit continued. An hour later, two officers from Edson headed in the same direction in a marked truck, flashers off.

○ ○ ○

The lone pickup truck that headed north on hwy 43 had no idea it was being tailed by two plainclothes officers, a male and a female. The occupants had seen the more obvious tail following the other three vehicles west-bound. They had not realized there was a second tail. When they stopped at the Whitecourt Esso for a cup of coffee, they did look around for anything suspicious, but the officers did a good job of being inconspicuous, and did not stop at the same place, instead waiting near the end of town for them to pass by, before following them again.

Chapter Seventy-Five

AT HINTON, EMILE AND Pedro stopped their vehicle to fill up with fuel. The other two vehicles in their caravan stopped also, but at different filling stations. No police were in sight. As they left the logging town, with its unique smell of pulp mill and sawmill bio-cogeneration, they saw no one following. Two minutes later, they were followed by the Ford truck with the two Edmonton officers. Five minutes later, two vehicles from the Hinton detachment followed with two more officers. Ten minutes later another vehicle marked with a light bar, from the Edson detachment, continued with another two officers. As expected, the caravan turned north on Hwy 40, towards Grande Cache.

Emile and Pedro were checking behind them for vehicles but did not see anything suspicious. This Hwy showed as a single highway on the map. No significant turnoffs for 100 miles, so anyone on it, was most likely headed all the way to Grande Cache. The only way to discover someone tailing was to stop, and then see if they also stopped or kept on going. Emile decided no one was following. It was possibly true.

Meanwhile, the gang's truck on Hwy 43 had passed Valleyview and continued north. Its occupants, feeling they had not been followed, were rather relaxed as they picked up a coffee at the Shell station, along with a fuel fillup. The weather was still cold, but sunny. Their sunglasses kept the glare of the sun on the snow from hurting their eyes. From Whitecourt to Valleyview, radio stations had been sparse, and not to their liking. They now found a channel on the radio with music they liked and were drumming their fingers on the dash.

o o o

Back in the bush near Grande Cache, Bill took off the glove of his right hand, laid it on the deck of his track drill, and answered his phone. It was Jack.

"Bill, I just got a call from McMorton in Edmonton. He said three vehicles from the gang are turning north. They filled with fuel in Hinton. One unmarked truck is following them."

"Just one truck? That's it?" Bill leaned against his track drill, blowing softly on his right hand to keep it warm while holding the phone.

"No, they have more. Two vehicles, four men from Hinton. Another vehicle, with two men from Edson. So that's eight policemen. They are a bit behind, half an hour, or three quarters an hour, behind the others. Their vehicles are marked, with uniforms."

"Okay, that's better. But the three vehicles... how many gang members?" Bill wondered if he should get in his machine to warm up.

"Nine men, it seems. Nine or ten."

"Will the police be able to handle them?"

"Depends on what they have for weapons, and whether they can have the advantage of location and surprise. I'm reminded of the four police who were shot at Mayerthorpe. Four trained officers ambushed by one man with a rifle. Simple numbers, and even firepower are only half the story. We have to find a way to give the police an advantage."

Bill decided to get in his machine. Freddy was finishing up the last hole, and would be trudging toward him soon, but he could not drill and talk at the same time. His hand was getting cold. It was either get in the machine, or put his mitt back on, but it was dirty with frozen mud, so that was a poor idea.

"What's the plan?"

"I've been thinking. We need to surprise them. Get them off balance. If all the men were in the same place, and this gang came into the bush, they would be surrounded. You would have to entice them somehow, or they would have to think you didn't know about them, so they would be overconfident." Jack sounded a bit uncertain. Hunting one moose was a lot different than capturing a herd of elk. He wanted a solution that didn't involve shooting all of these men.

"Jack, I've been thinking too. How much time do we have?"

"They just turned off the Yellowhead highway and headed north. About an hour and a half before they hit Grande Cache."

"That's not much time. But I've got a different plan. How about this?" Bill outlined his plan to Jack. Jack was sorry he could not be there. "Look Jack, we don't want you here for this. If it all goes bad, we need you to pick up the pieces. We can afford to lose a man here or there, maybe if injured, but we can't lose you. You are the one who keeps the operation going and gives us our work. Watch your family. Stay in touch with Edmonton, with the police, and let them know our plan, at least part of it, and let us know what is going on. We've always done your work, and we'll look after this too."

Jack grated his teeth at the situation, which he felt he was ultimately responsible for causing. He didn't want his children threatened, and he didn't want Kole and Richard hurt. He hated, really hated the drug trade and all the violence, sickness and desperation that went along with it. He recognized Bill's common sense on this. "Bill, you are a good man. Best man I got. Wish I could be there. Keep an eye on Kole... he can lose it sometimes." If only Bill knew how.

Freddy had now arrived at the track drill, and Bill told him his plan. They started packing up the drill and equipment as quickly as possible, and Bill started phoning the other crews while Freddy drove the machine back to their truck.

o o o

Up at Fort Vermilion, Richard walked with his two brothers to their truck. Jack had called to warn him about the vehicle from the states, which was headed north. "Don't know yet, if this vehicle is coming to us, or to you.

But I wanted you to know." Richard was concerned also about his brother Jacques at Grande Cache. He was concerned about Jack, back at the shop, and he had talked to his other two brothers about it. They had decided not to wait, but to head south. With their indigenous rights and rifles. Men who dared attack their brother when he was already injured, deserved a response, and they were there to provide it. They had a description of the vehicle, didn't know exactly what they were doing, but were not going to sit still and wait for things to happen.

"I'll call you when I know something. Don't get yourself all shot up."

His brothers grinned back at him. "We'll try not to roll this truck. Just because we're brothers, doesn't mean we roll vehicles."

"I could whack you on the head with my cast. Save those guys the trouble of getting rid of you." Richard grinned at them. He would hate to lose either one of them. "Put some gas in that truck. You'd look stupid trying to hitch a ride from those guys."

"We could put some gas in. It probably wouldn't run out from rolling over, like someone we know."

Richard thought the fun at his expense was going a bit too far. "I'll call up those gang members and let them know you're coming. Then I won't have to listen to your crap all the time, after they finish you off."

"Uh huh. Sure. You do that. You got some magic powers, you got their number? We're off. Stay in touch. We are keeping the phone plugged in for charging. See you later. When you get off those crutches, we'll beat you up. Do everyone a favor. See ya later."

It was minus 40C when they left. Minus 40 was the same in Celsius as in Fahrenheit. Cold. Bitterly cold. Not too much wind, but still cold. Two hours south, the temperature was fifteen degrees warmer. Fifteen Celsius degrees warmer. Twenty-seven Fahrenheit degrees warmer. Still cold, and a bit breezy. The truck was warm. Coffee cups full. Radio on.

o o o

The two officers who had followed Emile's men north on highway 43, shared stories about their kids. The younger female had two children not yet attending school. The adventures and sometimes the misadventures of the young children were amusing. She had been kept awake the night before, because the youngest one was teething, and couldn't sleep. She and her husband took turns tending the infant. The toddler was a little boy, always getting into things. "If he keeps it up, I'll be arresting him when he gets older."

"You'll have a chance to straighten him out before then. He is just being a boy. Lots of energy. Lots of zip. Good for him. Get used to it." Her older companion grinned. "Wait till they get older. The girls are the worst. Well sometimes they're the best, but the drama! Wow! It makes no sense to me. When they get that way, I just want to go back to work." He had a seventeen year old boy, and a fifteen year old girl.

"What you are saying, is that it is bad now, and just going to get worse later?"

"Yep. Love them both, but I hope when they grow up, they really do grow up."

"That bad, huh?" she asked.

"They have their good days. The boy is really smart. Good grades. But he also likes to build stuff, and fix things. Loves his motorcycle. Spends more time tinkering with it than driving it."

"I remember doing that with my first car a few years back. So many things to learn. Put bigger tires on it, and straight piped the exhaust."

"That's illegal, you know."

"I discovered that later. It sounded cool though. I didn't drive loud through town, only in the country or on the highway. But later I had to change it. Kept the car though... I still have it. Hey look, they turned off to that rest stop." The rest stop was near Peace River, and was a large one, half hidden behind some trees.

They looked at the vehicle they were following, which turned and parked next to the washrooms and the confectionary. "Think we can turn here? Or will they notice us?"

The senior officer did not comment right away. Arriving at the turnout, he slowed down and turned into it. It was a large pad, with room for twenty vehicles, and some large washrooms. Drinks and snacks were being sold, as well as tourist brochures, but it was rather quiet, since it was wintertime. "If we keep our heads down, they probably won't notice us. I need to use the can. I could use a coffee."

They parked at the other end of the lot, and then used the facilities. With a cup of coffee in one hand, a chocolate bar and cinnamon roll in the other, they walked back to their vehicle. The older officer suddenly growled at the younger. "Your gun is showing. Your jacket is hooked behind it. Better cover it, you idiot."

The younger woman turned red, and awkwardly shifted her jacket with her left hand, which held the bag containing chocolate bar and muffin. "I hope those two didn't see your gun. Boy I hope they didn't see it. They will suspect something right away."

However, the two gangsters did not appear to have been affected. They simply got in their vehicle with their own snacks and drove out of the rest area. The officers followed them at a distance. When the officers came around the corner, they saw that the gangsters' vehicle had stopped and the the driver was signalling to them to stop. Not knowing the reason for this, the officers decided to play it cool, and play the helpful businessmen routine. They brought their vehicle to a stop. They would have a conversation with their fugitives.

o o o

Bernie and David stopped at the Petro Canada station in Grande Cache for fuel, a coffee and some muffins. They had an enjoyable trip together, talking about their children and grand children. They were waiting for a call from Bill as to the next step in his plan.

"A bit warmer here than back home." David made the off-hand comment to maintain a sense of normalcy, as he put a lid on his coffee cup. This whole business was strange. He would never have dreamed of getting involved in something like this. Yet, here he was, with Jill's father, both of them not young men, taking things in their own hands, doing things they should not be doing.

"Yeah, a bit warmer. But wind is picking up. Might snow too." Bernie was rubbing his hands after pumping his own gas. "We're here. But where is everyone else?" Just then he noticed Jack's hunting buddies drive up to the pumps. "There they are. At the pumps." His phone rang in his pocket.

"Bernie, this is Bill. Here is what I want you to do."

SEISMIC TRAIL

○ ○ ○

Emile and Pedro with their companions passed the turnoffs to Switzer Provincial Park, Grey's Lakes, Muskeg River, Forestry Trunk Road, and Foothills Forestry Products. The winter scenery with the spruce covered hills to the west, and white snow-covered mountains in the distance, was beautiful, but scarcely noticed, certainly not appreciated by this gang of men who were more accustomed to arid southern temperatures. A herd of elk had crossed the road a half mile ahead of them at one point and they slowed to watch it. Frost and snow were rare in their experience. Some of them had actually not seen snow until this very trip. They were focused on the task at hand, trying not to let the fear of the winter conditions become obvious to their companions. A few had no fear, which was foolish.

○ ○ ○

Roger and Enrico drove to the job site with anticipation. Emile had contacted them, telling them to meet them on the way there. Emile would provide guns, and they would have a party, especially with Kole as entertainment. Roger looked forward to paying Kole back for the damage to his hand, and other parts of his aching body.

Roger and Enrico pulled up their car at the spot in the bush where the track drills were parked. Why were they parked? Why were the men not working? Checking from line to line, they saw no one. Not a man. Where had they gone? Disappointed, Roger waited, wondering what had happened.

○ ○ ○

Emile's group applied the brakes when they saw the barricade up ahead. It was a lonely stretch of highway, and shadows were lengthening. A reason for the barricade was not obvious, but four workmen dressed in bright yellow reflective vests, were putting up orange pylons, directing traffic to a narrow side road. What was this? Hopefully the detour was not long. Emile turned right on to the side road, looking for directional signs. The gravel road was a single winding road with no turn offs, and it made a few bends before another barricade appeared a mile later. He came to a full stop with four vehicles behind him.

Nothing happened for awhile. He noticed men dressed in camouflage, walking in the trees next to the road, trudging through the knee-deep snow. One man cradled a rifle in his arm, another had one slung on his back. They disappeared behind the trees.

Another vehicle pulled up behind theirs. Two vehicles now, both red pickup trucks, blocking their return down the road. Two vehicles could barely pass each other on this snow-covered road, with large banks of snow on each side. Another red truck came from the other side of the barricade towards them, parking itself in the middle of the road. Then one more truck, another red one, just behind it. A single driver in each. What municipality was this?

Emile looked closely. It was not a municipality. It was... an environmental company? Seismic environmental? Alarm bells started to go off in his head. Seismic. That was the machine, the track machine. A seismic driller. Why would a seismic company direct vehicles off a highway, and then block them in here? "Pedro, something is not right. These red trucks are not highway trucks. They are not from a municipality. They are company trucks from a seismic company."

Pedro looked closely and saw that Emile was right. "Emile", he sputtered, "you think we must do something?" He put his phone on the dash.

Emile did not reply. He was watching two men walk towards his vehicle. One man he recognized... it was the man who had fired his rifle while they were at the previous work site up north. The other one had also been there, the first one to confront them. The boss, the one in charge, was not here, at least not yet. Emile did not remember any of the other men who had been at the previous confrontation. He remembered most of them had rifles. He still bristled at the arrogance of these men, thinking that they could tell him what to do. Pushing him around as if they were some boss men, bigger men than he.

He was Emile. Not as big as Cortes. Emile feared Cortes. But he, Emile was also a big man. He had hunted men, killed them. Hung them. Used their women. Beheaded them. Mexicans. Texans. They did what he wanted, or they died. But these Canadians? They thought they could push him around? He saw only four. He wondered about the two men in the trees, so maybe two more. With rifles only. These two didn't even carry rifles. How foolish.

Kole approached on Emile's side. He knocked on the window and signaled for it to be opened. Emile decided to wait a bit before he killed him. He pushed the button for the window to roll down. He was silent.

"I want you to tell your men to throw their guns outside. All of them."

"Yes. We will do that. Just right away." Emile paused. Then he grinned. "Are you crazy? We will shoot you like dogs. You will do what we want. You will move your trucks, and you will answer my questions. What happened to Manny and Maurice? If you tell, we let you live. If you do not tell, you die. If you do not know, you also die. Simple."

"I will tell you," said Kole. "But first you will throw your guns outside, then step out with your hands on your heads."

A window opened in the back door, and a pistol pointed out at Kole. "So you want to tell us? No, we tell you."

"First, I give you fair warning. We have fourteen men in the trees. Every man with a rifle. Every man a hunter, with a scope, a good shot. If there is one shot..." Kole left the conclusion unspoken. Bill rapped on the window on the other side. When Pedro opened that window, suddenly there was a pistol in his face. Bill spoke directly to Pedro.

"Your tires will be shot out first. You cannot get our vehicles, because the keys are gone. In the trees with the men. So you will get shot, or you will escape and freeze to death. We will let you go and let you freeze. It will not take long. You are not dressed for cold weather. You are not used to cold weather. It will soon be dark and you will not know where you are, or where you are going. Every man in the trees is a hunter. Every man has shot a deer, or a moose, or an elk. Some have shot bears. Every man is used to this cold. This is not a place for you. It is a place for us. Throw out your guns. Tell the other ones to throw out their guns."

Pedro hesitated. Emile was his boss, but he did not want to die. He did not want to freeze to death. These two men were fearless. One with a pistol, the other with nothing. How could it be? In the face of ten men with automatic pistols and rifles?

"You see, there is a rifle aimed at every head. You can maybe shoot the first bullet, but not the second. You cannot see a single man, so what will you shoot at? They can see you, but you don't see them. They are hunters. One bullet, because they do not miss." Bill knew these men were good shots. Maybe not as good as he was saying, but maybe not too far off. These men were like sitting ducks. Intimidation was a good weapon to use, and Bill was milking it for all it was worth. Would it work?

Pedro grabbed his phone. He called the vehicle behind them. "Throw out your guns or we are dead!" He threw his own out the window. The vehicle behind him lowered their windows and guns slowly were dropped outside. Three of them. Pedro pushed buttons on his phone again to call the third vehicle. Suddenly, a shot rang out. Pedro dropped his phone, shaking his hand. Emile's gun was pointed directly at him. Emile had hit him in the hand, destroying his phone and several fingers on his right hand. The bullet had embedded in the door, and Bill had ducked down outside, towards the front of the vehicle.

With the shot, Kole had grabbed the pistol from the backseat passenger, twisted, almost breaking the man's wrist in the process, and then also ducked down. Shots whistled from the trees, and two tires on each vehicle immediately went flat. One bullet entered the driver's window opening and hit Emile in the left shoulder. He grunted in pain, and swung around, trying to get his right arm with his pistol through the window, aiming at Kole. Kole did not make an easy target, by now hunched over beside the left front fender, with pistol in hand.

Emile fired several bullets and Kole went down. Another shot came from the trees, hitting Emile in the chest on his right side. He dropped his pistol, and his face turned white. He slumped in his seat.

The four occupants of the third vehicle had seen the guns thrown out but had not known why. They also knew that when the second vehicle threw out three guns, that was only half of their armament. Another five or six guns were still in the second vehicle. Was it a ruse? The shooting of one of their men however, made them realize that all was not as it appeared. Their tires had been shot. And now a man shot. From somewhere in the trees, although they could not see anyone. The shubbery was thick, and shadows were lengthening. Would they all die?

Kole continued to lie there, unmoving. Bill opened the door and yanked Pedro out, pointing his gun at the backseat passenger who had lost his pistol, and was trying to grab a rifle. He gestured at the man to leave the rifle and get out of the vehicle. Emile was in no shape to move, Pedro still holding his wounded hand.

When the two men from the first vehicle stepped out, the others kept still. Their leaders already out of commission, would someone else take up the cause? Apparently not. Three men in the second vehicle, seeing their cause was hopeless, opened their doors, slowly. As they did, six men in the trees stepped from behind their cover, and kept their rifles trained on them. The men stepped out, hands up, and away from the vehicle.

The third vehicle occupants, having heard no command, and unable to see the first vehicle clearly, was more uncertain. Bullets spat from a gun in the third car for a brief moment, before being silenced by return fire from the trees. The driver of the third vehicle, a pickup truck, suddenly gunned the engine, reversing into the red truck behind him, trying to push it out of the way. He banged it once, went forward, tires spinning, stopped and then tried to squeeze around it, backwards. He got about halfway past, his rear end sliding into the snowbank on the side. Although it was a four-wheel drive, the snow was too much for it, especially with two flat tires. Soon it was imbedded in the snow, tilting sideways about 30 degrees spinning tires uselessly in the snow. No one fired a shot at the vehicle. Jack's men had enough experience to know that this truck was going exactly nowhere. They waited for them to get tired.

Knowing the three men had left the second vehicle, they doubted their ability to change the tide, particularly as one of their four-some had already been shot, and was not moving. They gave up. They too then tossed their guns out the windows, slowly opening their doors, leaving empty hands well exposed. It seemed possible death if they surrendered, but certain death and defeat if they did not cooperate.

Kole's body was not visible to the occupants of the second and third vehicles, due to the angle of the first. The other gangsters had no idea that he had been hit, so it gave them no reason to think that these men in the red trucks and in the trees were vulnerable. As three of the four occupants of the third vehicle stood up away from the vehicle, another six men in the trees also stood up, out of their cover. The gangsters realized that these were no fearful farmers, but men with purpose and capability. This game was up. They might be in trouble, but maybe they would live to see another day. Maybe these men would not execute them or hang them. Maybe.

As the men came down from the trees around the vehicles, Bill told them to take these gangsters in hand. Freddy began searching the vehicles for guns, and with help from Jared, took all the visible guns out, bringing them to a red truck on the other side of the barricade. Eldon and Skyler took zip ties out of their pockets and handcuffed every man behind his back. For three of the men they tied up their legs together as well.

Bernie and David finally stepped out from behind the trees, along with the hunting buddies. They grinned at each other. This had gone well. No one mentioned who had fired the shots that mattered. No one knew. No one would know. Perhaps bullets could be matched, but perhaps not.

When Freddy came back from the red truck after unloading his armload of guns in the back, he saw Kole's body. He ran to Kole and checked his pulse. Was there a pulse? "Get your hand off me." Yes, there was a pulse. Must have been a pulse, else why was Kole moving and rolling over?

"I thought you were hit? Where did you get hit?" Freddy was concerned, looking for blood, for the wound.

"Leave me alone. I'm okay. Wearing Kevlar, but I'm not taking off my coat to show you. It's too cold." Kole grimaced a half grin. The bullet had knocked him down, but he and Bill had been wearing vests, obtained from Jack's friends at the Grande Cache police department. A couple of old vests, since it was against department policy to participate in this way. The police had not known all the details, just enough to find these old unused vests, not yet recycled in favor of the newer ones recently received.

Two bullets had hit him in the back, and Kole's kidney was mighty sore. He was alive, and all in all, it was a small price to pay for the trouble he had caused. He struggled to stand up, and grabbed the door of the vehicle, looking at Emile. Emile opened his eyes to see Kole looking at him.

"You wanted to know what happened to Manny and Maurice," grunted Kole. "I will tell you. We did not torture them. We gave them a chance to repent. But they threatened children, and women. They murdered others. Badly. In very bad ways. You probably know. They threatened children again. So they are buried. Somewhere. They will never be found. They can never harm children again. Never hurt women again. Never shoot farmers again. Now you know." Emile opened his mouth, but no words came. To Kole it looked like he might survive.

Pedro did not turn his head. He was leaning against the car door which still had an open window. The news that Kole had given to Emile registered with him. It made sense. No one had been able to find these two men, not even heard anything about him. The drug bust had been a plant, a set-up, a lure to get them to focus on Edmonton. Pedro kept quiet.

Flashing lights lightened the grayness as the police from Edmonton, Edson and Hinton arrived at the scene. Two medivacs from Grande Cache also pulled up. Emile was loaded into one, the injured passenger from the third vehicle into the other. They were headed to Grande Cache, the closest medical center. If necessary they would be medivacked to a more capable hospital, either by ground or by air.

The police were not prepared for eight other criminals, and barely had enough room for them in their vehicles. Adding metal handcuffs to the zip ties, tying up the remaining ankles, they stuffed the men into their vehicles. The two plainclothes detectives took Pedro with them, along with another prisoner. He had been treated by the medi-techs and would suffer until they got to Hinton, and then get some more treatment there.

"Am I too late? Is it all over?" Rob, Jack's brother-in-law from Spruce Grove had also arrived. He was indeed, too late.

"You can follow the cops back to Hinton, and to Edmonton, in case they need any help. Just shoot anyone who escapes." Bill said this loudly, so the prisoners could hear. They had no doubt that Rob would be able to do this. The police pretended they had not heard Bill.

When the medivacs had left, the barricades removed and put back into the red trucks, and the red trucks had left, a tow truck came to remove the criminals' vehicles. Bill got into his own truck, which Freddy had already warmed up. He called Jack.

"It's over, Jack. Nobody killed, although maybe two of them won't make it. Emile being one. He was shot twice. They are all tied up, and headed back to Edmonton."

"Great! Great, Bill! I'm impressed. You had a good plan."

"Rob came down but he was too late." Bill chuckled.

Jack was relieved, and he chuckled at the large effort that Rob had made to miss out on the whole thing. "He'll have his own story, I guess."

"I gave him a job. To shoot any escapees on the way back. He seemed pleased with the idea."

"So that's done. For now. As long as they don't need witnesses for trials, that kind of thing. But it's not over completely. Two of the guys are still headed up north. Richard's brothers are planning to meet them along the way, if they can, but it is getting dark, and hard to see. They could easily miss them."

"Ah, if they have eyes like Richard and Jacques, they can see in the dark. Besides two cops are still trailing them, right?"

"That is the sad part. The two cops were shot. One is still alive."

"Oh crap. Crap! Too far away for us to get to."

"The brothers could do something maybe. And a couple cops from High Level are looking for them too. But nighttime is coming soon."

"Any idea how they figured the tail on them? I thought they were undercover, in a plain car."

"It was a truck, unmarked. Somehow they figured it out at a rest stop. McMorton knew something was wrong when the gps locator didn't move anymore. The live cop had been knocked unconscious, and when he came to, he still had his phone to call Edmonton. The female cop is dead. A medivac is on the way. I called Richard, who gave me his brother's number, and then I talked to them. They have the location, so are looking for the vehicle, which we know... we even have the license number. Maybe these guys are not too bright. There's no other road they can go off on, for awhile at least. Richard's brothers are fairly close, within fifteen minutes."

Bill digested that, realizing it was out of his hands. "I'll stay here in Grande Cache. I want to keep an eye on the two in hospital until they are gone. I don't think they are much good healthwise, and they can't do anything, but you never know. Maybe they are playing possum, making it look worse than it is. The rest of the guys will get back to work tomorrow, but maybe a special treat tonight."

"A bonus, Bill. A bonus of some type. You can tell them the bonus is just recognition and appreciation. It doesn't come close to what they deserve. I know they didn't do this for a bonus."

"Sure boss. Maybe I'll let you tell them. I'm not so good at that stuff."

"I'll be down tomorrow, if the other two guys get tied up. We'll know by morning."

"Okay, see you later."

o o o

Richard's brothers peered into the gloom, trying to see vehicles past the glare of their headlights. Several vehicles had looked similar but were not the one. "I think that's it! The one that just passed us. It's the right size, right color. Right timing too."

They turned their vehicle around and pushed the accelerator to the floor. Soon they were up behind the other vehicle and checking the license plate. It matched! Flashing their headlights, they inched closer to the other vehicle. It accelerated quickly, and soon both vehicles were doing 180 km/hr.

Richard's brother let up a bit, creating some distance between the two. The other brother was already calling the police. They looked at each other, and then decided to get serious. The second brother grabbed his rifle from the back seat, loaded it with a five clip, and opened his window. Being right-handed, it was perfect. The question in his mind was, what kind of shot should he take? Warning shot? Tire? These guys had killed one cop, and almost killed another. Nor was it in a misunderstanding, or a fight. The cops had been pretending no interest, with no confrontation. No, it was an assassination by these guys. His decision was made.

With the wind whistling through his hair, blurring his eyes as he sighted the scope on his rifle, he had to work hard to hold on to the rifle. He squinted, only a pinhole of sight left in his right eye which cleared briefly, but the vehicle was not steady. It smoothed out, the crosshairs lined up on the driver's head for a brief instant, when he pulled the trigger, once.

The bullet went through the back window and went through the side of the driver's neck. The truck veered sideways, hitting the left shoulder and then rolling twice before coming to a stop in the deep snow in the bush beyond the ditch. No vehicles were nearby at the time, although lights were approaching from the north, perhaps a couple miles away. The brothers, headed north, had passed the rolled vehicle already, and slowed down for a u-turn to check on their quarry.

As they approached the vehicle, which was upside down and now facing the opposite direction from which it had come, they saw that the rear of the truck cab was packed with snow through the broken rear window. Wheels were still spinning as they parked, got out, and waded through the snow to the vehicle. The two men in it were suspended in their seatbelts, with the passenger moving slightly, and groaning. The driver, surprisingly, was also moving his arms, although blood was pouring from his neck.

They found a rag and pressed it to the neck to stop the bleeding, not being too careful or considerate. "He might make it, he might not."

"Did 911 send an ambulance?"

"I asked for cops. I'll call them again."

As it turned out, they had sent an ambulance which was only ten minutes away. The lights they had seen in the distance, not the first set, but the second set, had been the police, who were on their way. As the police stopped, the brothers wondered about their action, and how it would be taken. "They were after my brother. Their friends beat up my brother already, when he was on crutches, with two casts on. We heard these two killed a cop."

When the police saw two rifle barrels sticking out of the snow on the back seat of the upside-down truck, along with several boxes of ammunition, and examined their wallets and identification, they told the brothers to leave. "We'll call you if we need you. These two are part of a larger gang, and Edmonton police are after them. They killed a cop, and the other cop isn't doing so well. Thanks for stopping them. Now get going. Leave! Before the medivac gets here."

Richard's brothers left, one making a call to Jack, letting him know what had happened.

Chapter Seventy-Six

JACK PUT DOWN THE phone after talking with Richard's brothers. Jill was sitting at the supper table, wondering, having heard only half the conversation. "What was that all about?" she asked, partly off-handedly, but also a bit concerned at the apparent serious nature of the call.

"Nothing much. Just some work stuff." Jack was disinclined to give her all the details.

"What do you mean just work stuff? Since when have you kept work stuff to yourself?" Jill was irritated. Jack did not seem to be himself, keeping secrets from her. Treating her like she couldn't understand what happened with his work, when she was a partner, even doing payroll and safety paperwork from time to time. What was going on?

Jack sensed her irritation. He realized that the time had come to tell all. He told her the whole story. Everything except for what Kole and Richard had done. He told her about the threats to her, to their children. Jill's face alternated between white fear, and absolute red rage.

Jack told her about the drugs in the machine, the set up by the Edmonton police, the trailing of Emile and Pedro, and all the men that had come back up to Canada. He told her of the capture of the men, the cooperation of his men, her father and his father. That Rob had come up to help. His hunting buddies. Then he told her about the two cops that had been shot near Peace River, and about Richard's brothers. Other than Kole's and Richard's dramatic action earlier with Manny and Maurice, he left nothing out.

"But you are not a witness. You can't tell other people about this. It's probably better not to even talk to your dad or my dad about it. Too many loose lips can cause serious problems if the wrong person gets excited about it. We did the right thing, but that doesn't always stop problems and prosecutions. Even cops get prosecuted for not following procedure. I doubt we followed procedure. Promise me, please keep it quiet. I just wanted you to know how serious it was, and that you are everything to me. You and the girls."

Jill was silent. Shocked actually. Pleased that Jack had not been doing something he was ashamed of, and pleased that he was protecting her.

"Couldn't you have just let them get those drugs from the machine back in Texas?" As she said this, Jill already regretted her question. "Forget it Jack, don't answer that. Nothing makes me more upset than these people peddling drugs. The hurts, the addictions, the sickness, the complete mess. My sister...."

She left the statement unfinished. Not often spoken about anymore, both Jack and Jill remembered all too well the impact of drug addiction on Jill's younger sister. She had started off with the lighter stuff, smoking weed, and a bit of cocaine, then some morphine, and heroin. Heroin had hooked her. She couldn't unattach. She had moved to Vancouver, where reports were scarce. A cousin had seen her a few times. Bernie had gone down to look for her without success. Finally, a year later, a news item had appeared about the death of a young heroin addict, a prostitute who had overdosed on a fentanyl mixture. The description of the deceased was familiar enough that Bernie had phoned to check on the details. Identification was minimal, but pictures were sent. Jill's parents agreed it was their daughter. The body was shipped to Alberta, and a quiet sad memorial and burial was held with only the immediate family. It was a year ago; it seemed so long ago, yet just yesterday.

"Jill, it's hard for me to decide whether protecting my young girls, and you, is more important now, than fighting the very thing that could be the death of them later. I never would have expected your sister to be a victim of it, but it has sometimes clouded my thinking. I hate to be so angry, so absolutely crazy mad at these monsters who mess up the lives of pretty young girls." he paused to clear his head, but his head was not clearing. "I suspected drugs from the beginning, and I hated the arrogance of two guys trying to stop me from moving my machine. Then, later, I decided that maybe it was better to let them have it, instead of putting my girls at risk. That was not an easy decision. I mean, I just felt like I was giving in, defeated. That I was part of the whole problem of the drug trade, refusing to fight it." At this point, Jack wanted so bad to tell her what Kole and Richard had done. But he did not want to make Jill an accomplice in anyway. "They looked, didn't find the drugs, and disappeared. And we found the drugs later in the machine, and then set up the rest of the gang. I did the best I could. And Bill. Wow! He really looked after us. And kept me out of the front line, protecting you and all of us so we could do our jobs. Kole too. And the police."

"You know what confuses me the most?" Jill responded. "It's hard. Those drug dealers make me so mad. They mess up so many lives. But still I can forgive those gang members if it comes to that. They probably have their own terrible history and bad experiences which made them what they are. But they haven't really done anything to me. Could I have forgiven them if they had hurt my girls, or raped me, or killed you? I don't have a good answer for that."

"They need to be stopped." Jack was emphatic. "They need all the hard times we can give them. But yes, they are still human beings too. I don't have a good answer either. Crime and evil need opposition, not tolerance. If a drug dealer says to me, 'I'm sorry, I won't do it again, ever.' and he turns from his wicked ways, throws all the drugs in the toilet... or pours gasoline on them to burn them, then I think if he proves his word, I could forgive him. But if he pulls out a gun, and shoots a customer who can't pay, or forces a girl into prostitution to support a drug habit, then he must be stopped. Even if he dies as a result."

Jill wiped a tear from her eye. With blurred eyes she looked at Jack. "I guess the men are happy, Jack. They beat a bunch of crooks from the USA and Mexico. They outsmarted them, and they were tougher. They had a victory of justice over evil. And I should be happy. I am happy, in a way. But sad too. So many lives ruined. So much blackness in their thinking. So much hate. When will it ever end?"

"Jill, you keep telling me it will end. Someday. That's what you believe, right? I am starting to believe it too. I have to believe it, because you are right, otherwise, it is nothing but sadness and blackness."

"Oh Jack. Thanks Jack, for reminding me. All this evil. The drugs, the killings. And it will end, when Jesus comes again. When we are in heaven with God. There will be no more sorrow, no more tears. Yes, thanks for reminding me."

"There are many good things in this life too, Jill. You know that. Sledding with the kids. Meals with your folks and mine. Hard work and vacations and a warm house. Freedoms to say what we think, to go to church, to read a newspaper."

"Yes, praise the Lord for the good things!" She smiled again, getting up to get a coffee and some sugar cookies for her and Jack.

o o o

Roger entered the hospital quietly, stopping at the registration desk. He came alone, leaving Enrico back at home.

"Can I help you?" the receptionist was cool, but friendly. She had been at her desk for seven hours already and was looking forward to going home.

"Yeah. A friend of mine had an accident, and I wondered if he is still in the hospital?" Roger and Enrico had waited at the job site for almost an hour, before deciding that plans must have changed dramatically. He was not getting a response on the phone. They returned to town and had some supper. Then Roger decided to hunt for information at the local bar. Interesting stories about a confrontation were being circulated. It made him wonder who had gotten the worst of it, but his suspicions were confirmed by the appearance of several of Jack's workers, who were laughing, joking and congratulating each other. He had not approached them.

"What's his name?"

"He had a gun accident." Roger did not know details of the injuries. All he knew was that the whole thing had gone wrong, that some men had been shot. Maybe one or two had been brought to Grande Cache.

"We had two gun-accident victims here, but they are both in an ambulance going to Hinton." The protocol had been to identify them as gun accidents, not

crime related shootings. No need in this case to alarm the locals. The local newspaper reporter had not frequented the bars to get the rumors. "If you give me the name of your friend, maybe I can give you more information."

However, Roger was not inclined to give any more clues to the desk clerk. He wanted information, not trouble. Emile's gang was gone in any case, and he was out of the loop. Maybe he would find out later what had happened. In the meantime, where was he going to get more junk, more crack? He would have to make some calls.

"My friend was not hurt bad enough to go in an ambulance. These must be different guys that you are mentioning. My friend maybe didn't go to the hospital after all." Roger nodded his head in dismissal, then turned and left the hospital.

Chapter Seventy-Seven

MCMORTON WAS RELIEVED. NONE of his men had died or been injured at the Grande Cache capture. He hated to admit it, but Jack's men had done a superlative job of capturing the entire gang. Other than the bruises to Kole's kidneys, all the injuries were to the gang members. A couple were serious; Emile was on the critical list. He had lost consciousness, due to loss of blood and internal injuries. The passenger in the third vehicle who had been shot, was conscious, but also critical. No injuries to Jack's men were mentioned, except for Kole being knocked down. McMorton shook his head. Kevlar... these guys had thought of everything. Where did they get it, he wondered. He decided he didn't want to know.

He called his FBI counterpart. "We have captured the gang members. Tried to let them play out their action, but they were going in the wrong direction; some citizens blocked them from going further. It ended our fishing expedition."

"You got all of them?"

"Yes. Well no. There's still two going further north. They shot some cops and killed one. They are still on the loose. It just happened a few minutes ago. We don't have any cops there within a half hour; its pretty remote on that highway."

Mc Morton continued, "Emile is seriously injured. Critically. Don't know if he will survive. Pedro has an injured hand. Emile actually shot him. But he's okay, just really hurting. One other man was shot, also critical now."

"What's the plan now?"

"We'll follow what we discussed earlier, ... hold on, I have another call, and its urgent. I'll call you back. It's probably involving the other two guys who killed the officer on the highway, given the number that is calling me. I'll get back to you."

"Yes? Mc Morton here."

There was a pause on the other end, and McMorton wondered what had happened. "Did you catch the shooters?"

"We have them, but they had an accident. Rolled their vehicle in the ditch, and the driver is dead. The passenger is seriously injured, but not critical. Whiplash we think, and the medivacs are taking both to High Level."

"Single vehicle accident? Any idea what caused it?"

"Yeah, we have an idea. But we would rather not say. These guys shot two cops. They deserved what they got. Someone did our job for us. But we found them in the ditch, upside down in their truck. We would have liked to leave them there. Someone had tried to stop the bleeding with a rag, but it didn't work. The driver lost too much blood. The medics watched him die but couldn't do anything about it."

McMorton was intrigued. Jack's men had been in Grande Cache. Someone else was stopping these two guys? Were they connected? How had they known? He wasn't sure he wanted to pursue this train of thought too far. The older cop who had been shot was a friend of his. Had been to his place several times for birthday parties, and their kids had played together. Now his partner's kids would be without a mother. Her husband without a wife. He ground his teeth together. It meant nothing to these drug gangs, but it meant a lot to him. As far as he was concerned, every time a cop died, ten drug dealers deserved to die. It didn't actually work that way, but if he could tilt the odds, he was happy to do so.

"Okay then. It was an accident. How long before we get them to Edmonton?"

"The body doesn't matter, right? But how soon do you need the other guy?"

"We have a bunch of guys from the same gang coming here today. As soon as we can, we are shipping them off back to the States. It would be good to move them all at the same time. See if they can get him stabilized, and then maybe we can get Stars Ambulance to bring him here by helicopter."

"What do you want us to do with the body of the dead guy?"

"Send it to the morgue in Edmonton. We will have to examine it, identify him, and make sure paperwork is in order. Do you know if he is an American citizen?"

"His driver's license says he is American. But he also has a Mexican driver's license, and a credit card from Mexico. We found an American passport and a Mexican passport."

"Okay, we'll have to do some digging to find out what he is. Send everything down. Drive it down in the back of a truck. You have a truck with a canopy?"

"Not ready, sir. But we do have a large SUV, a Suburban."

"Not a good idea. Body will get too warm. Better put a canopy on a truck. Since this is significant evidence, we need one of your men on it personally. Can't hire someone else to do it."

"Yes sir. We will follow up and expedite. Thank you sir. We will keep you informed."

McMorton hung up the phone and called his FBI friend again. "We got the other two gang bangers. The two that shot the two cops. They were in an accident. One is dead. Someone shot him, I think. We don't know who, but anyway they are in medivacs and going to hospital. Then they will come to Edmonton, probably tomorrow. It's an eight-hour drive, so we'll probably use a chopper. The body is coming in a truck. Not sure if he is American or Mexican."

"Okay. You want me to send some men up?"

"Not necessary. No use alarming anyone. We'll bring them down and meet you near the border when we are ready. Then they are all yours."

"No intentions to lay any charges?"

"Not at the moment. All of them are guilty of possessing firearms without a Canadian permit. Most of the guns were illegal anyway; we don't allow fully automatics. They were carrying without permits, without hunting licenses. That's the straight up goods on them. Besides that, what were their intentions and motivations. Where were they headed? Killing police officers? Shooting at unarmed men? That many men altogether? It would look bad for them in any case."

"What about all your laws of innocent until proven guilty? Of rights to legal defense?"

"They are proven guilty already. And they will have legal defense, if they ask for it. We will convince them they are more guilty here, than they are in your country. It will be up to you to do the rest."

"We will do our best. Especially with the non-citizens. Some may get off."

"Have you talked to your DA?"

"Yeah I have. It's too bad you didn't get more on these guys. Like actually shipping drugs or kidnapping someone."

"You're kidding right? About the kidnapping I mean. They were not carrying any drugs that we could see. One guy did have some weed, but that's not worth pursuing; it was a small amount for personal use."

"All the same, we have skimpy grounds for holding on to them."

"My civilian friends couldn't take any more chances. I don't blame them. They were looking to hurt someone, no doubt about that. Emile and Pedro had threatened women and children. A fellow named Cortes had done the same. I told you about him. They had already beat up one of my friend's men... although it was a couple locals that did it. One had escaped from prison. He is now back in there."

"When do you think you will have them at the border?"

"Tomorrow or the next day. Two guys in critical condition and we'll have to see what they need. Or if they survive. Otherwise, you might get them in two batches, with the injured coming later."

"All right. Two batches are okay. Tomorrow then?"

"I'll let you know."

"Sounds good. Goodbye."

Mc Morton pondered the conversation. He hoped he was not part of an elaborate revolving door. Maybe this was exactly why Jack's men had taken things into their own hands. He still wondered what had happened to Manny and Maurice. He would not investigate any of Jack's men on that account. He would limit his search to Edmonton and Calgary and surrounding areas. If they were there, he would find them. If he didn't find them, he would assume they had headed back to the USA.

He shook his head in admiration, which was not something he would ever do for the press. Jack's men had managed to round up the whole gang without losing a single man. Only shooting two of the gangbangers. Getting the police involved at just the right time. Collecting a pile of weapons. Then the other two guys in an accident. Was it just an accident? It was interesting they had been going up to Richard's home territory. In any case, those two gang members were incapacitated as well. It didn't get him much closer to finding the head and the many tails of the drug running and dealing. But it did get some dangerous men off the street. It would send a message to Cortes as well. Especially if he heard all the details.

McMorton wondered what he would tell his superiors. What would he tell his wife. Would the stories be the same? The story was not over yet.

Chapter Seventy-Eight

WHEN HIS OFFICERS RETURNED from Grande Cache and Hinton, along with the Hinton and Edson police who escorted the prisoners, Inspector Chief Detective Charles McMorton had an opportunity to hear some of the finer details of the adventure. It was an adventure to some of his officers, who were conflicted as to whether they should have laid charges against some of Jack's men. After all, they, or someone, had shot two of the men they were looking for. Possibly they did not all have legal permits and maybe all the guns in their truck had not all belonged to the crooks. Or possibly some of the guns belonging to the crooks had been kept and stashed away by Jack's men. If the inspector sent them back, they would have to investigate all these possibilities.

It was a story to remember. Twenty or more ordinary citizens, workers and friends, had ambushed this drug dealing gang, taken their weapons, captured them and had them ready for the police when they arrived. None of them injured, two of the gang shot, well three if you count the injured hand. It would be interesting to see how the press handled this story.

Meanwhile, the three who had gunshot wounds were being attended to at the Royal Alexandra Hospital. Emile was in a bad way. His heart was still beating, but internal bleeding from the two bullets had rendered him unconscious an hour before arriving in Edmonton. The doctors were giving blood transfusions now but were not hopeful. He had not regained consciousness. Quite possibly he had sustained brain injury due to insufficient oxygen.

Pedro was complaining about the pain in his hand. His middle finger had been severed by the bullet, and it did not look like he would keep it. Or it would be considerably shorter if attached. The complaining would soon stop, as serious pain killers were beginning to take effect. He would live to see another day.

The man in the third car had been shot in the right shoulder, the bullet having gone through his arm, and entered his chest under his arm. It had punctured the lung, causing bleeding, but had stopped just as it entered the lung. Surgery was now removing the bullet and stopping the internal bleeding. The man had been conscious, though quiet. Pain killers undoubtedly were helping him, but he seemed to have a high pain tolerance. Possibly he was already on some type of drug which dulled his pain from the beginning. They had not done a toxicology analysis of his blood, yet, but it would be done for him as well as for Pedro and Emile.

The surviving gang member from High Level, had just arrived by Stars Ambulance helicopter. He was being examined at the University Hospital. His head had banged against the side window as the vehicle had rolled. Glass splinters were imbedded in his neck and his face. He was suffering from whiplash and had regained consciousness at the hospital in High Level. Ribs were bruised from the seatbelt. It was likely that he could be released with a neckbrace. Blood samples had been collected in High Level, to determine any levels of drugs in his system.

McMorton made arrangements to move the entire gang, except for Emile and the dead man. He phoned the local prison to ask about a prison bus. He wanted to send the Edson and Hinton men back to their detachments but needed to ensure a secure form of transport. The bus was available, and all the men would fit on it, handcuffed to the seats, with two guards watching them. When it arrived at his headquarters he sent it to the Royal Alex to pick up Pedro, after which it returned to pick up the rest of the gang from his holding cells.

The bus with two guards and a driver, followed by a squad car with one officer, headed to the University hospital to pick up the man with the neck brace. Guarding him was another officer, who brought him down to the prison bus. Soon he was handcuffed and ankle cuffed to the seat, and the bus was rolling towards the southern end of the city.

McMorton called Jack. Jack was busy in the shop with Bill and Tom.

"Just want to let you know that the prisoners are headed south in a prison bus, Jack. Except for Emile and the fellow from High Level. The body of the dead guy is still coming. Four of them are Mexicans, and the rest Americans, most likely."

"Thanks, Charles. Anything to tie them to the drugs?"

"No more than we had before. One guy had a little pot on him, but not significant, really. They're going to the border, and the FBI will get them. They also have a special plan for Cortes. Can't say anymore than that."

Jack didn't want to ask about the legal details. Like did they ask for an attorney, or plead asylum, or anything like that. Extradition was hard, and could cause long-term problems, but on the other hand, they were short term visitors, with no work permits, no immigrant status, no resident status. Jack was glad to hear they were headed back.

"Too bad we couldn't have let them lead you to more evidence, to a drug dealing connection. Sorry about that."

"I understand. I truly do. It's not your fault. Another time maybe we'll get them, or someone from their organization."

"Anything else, Charles? I have another call coming on my phone."

"That's it Jack. Have a good day."

Jack walked into his office and punched his phone, and the new call came on. "So you think you got us, hey?" It was Cortes. Jack had not heard from him for a while. "My men are in jail. Emile is shot. I am angry."

"Yeah, you are angry. I am not surprised you are angry. So. You now you know how I feel. You should have kept your men at home. Away from me. The police have them now. We let them off easy. Only one man dead."

"It's over for now, Mr. Jack. But I do not forget. I have hundreds of men. I have a long memory. You know Emile's missing finger? I cut it off myself. I want you to remember that. Someday, when you do not expect it, something will happen that you do not like. Something very bad. Something very sad. But something very amusing to me."

"You are already sad, Cortes. Very sad. You have lost this round. And it will get worse for you. Goodbye." Jack ended the call. Maybe he shouldn't have warned Cortes. Hopefully Cortes just regarded it as a bluff. Other wise it could put him on his guard.

Jack returned to his work.

That evening, after the girls were in bed and they were relaxing in the living room, Jack turned to Jill from his seat in the recliner. "Jill, I am going to tell you about some things that were happening lately. Things that made you wonder about me." Jill sat expectantly on the couch, holding a cup of hot tea in her hands, as she sipped expectantly.

"Okay Jack. What is it?"

"Those guys, Manny and Maurice, and later Emile and Pedro who were in your kitchen, actually threatened you and the girls with horrible things. Including murder. I didn't want to tell you at the time because I didn't want you to worry."

"Well now I'm worried. You already told me about this. Why are you bringing it up again?"

"Because now they are all captured and headed back to the states. They were going to come after Kole, and two of their gang were headed to Richard at his home. All got captured, three were shot, and one died. One more might still die. There is no reason to worry anymore."

Jill looked at Jack long and hard. "I can worry if I decide to worry. It's a mother's privilege. But I will worry as a mother always does. Not as a frightened flighty rabbit. I have a lot of confidence in you Jack, to protect us and do the best you can. I have a lot of confidence in the police too. And in our friends and in your workers. You do a good job of selecting workers who can be trusted. Who are capable. I don't worry more than I should."

"Besides that," she continued, "I trust in God. He takes care of us whether we realize it or not. He used Bill and the rest of the men to be there, to do the right thing, even when you couldn't do it yourself. So why should I live in fear? Why should I worry too much?"

"You shouldn't worry too much. But be cautious. These guys have egos bigger than the Eiffel tower. They want to have the last word. The big display of power. Eventually its not just about money. It's about revenge. About being bigger than everyone else. About not letting anyone dominate them or show them up. Until he dies, this leader, this Cortes will not forget. When conditions are right, he will rise up again."

"Now I'm worried. Really?"

"Just be cautious. It's not likely he will try anything in the near future. He may have other bigger problems soon. Just be cautious. Not paranoid."

Jill sat there. Immobile. Holding her cup of tea.

"Jack, you have been going to church lately. Not last Sunday, but before that. You know about forgiveness, about Jesus even dying for us. Now we are killing people to defend ourselves? Is that being like Jesus? Will it never end, these struggles against drugs, against evil things?"

"I don't have a good answer for that, Jill. In the movies, in the books, it seems easy to come up with a solution where victims forgive the murderer, the murderer comes clean, and then comes to Jesus. He becomes a new person. That would be the best. That's what I would like."

"Well? How do we do that?"

"I don't know, Jill. I am ready to forgive. But I am not ready to lose my wife or my children. I am not ready to let my workers get abused or hurt or murdered. I am not ready to let people get addicted to drugs and lose their life, because some drug dealers want to make lots of money."

"We have to pray more Jack, to ask God for solutions, instead of trying to fix everything ourselves."

"Yes, pray more. I don't do enough of that. For sure. God does things for us, that we just can't do. But I believe that we have to do somethings ourselves too. God gave us brains and ability to do some things. Not to use our brains and ability for good things is like denying God, don't you think?"

Jill was silent. Thinking. Took another sip of tea.

"Enough of that," said Jack, rising from his chair. "Can I get you some cookies? Some sugar cookies? I need some myself." As Jack walked to the kitchen to get the cookies, Jill did not respond. When he came back, he put the cookies on the table in front of her, put his hands on her shoulders, and kissed her on her forehead. Then on her cheek, then her neck, then her lips. She put the cup of tea down and wrapped her arms around his neck. No one ate any cookies for a long time.

Chapter Seventy-Nine

TEN DAYS LATER, IN the early evening after dark, two men walked into the Royal Alex hospital and walked up to the fourth floor where Emile was recovering from his gunshot wounds. Emile was sitting up, watching television, with a guard just outside his room. The word from the doctors was that he could be released in two days, and he would be taken to the border to be given to FBI agents waiting for him.

One of the men asked the guard if Emile had received any visitors that day, while the other man slid into the room. Continuing to make conversation with the guard, it was not long before the man who had gone into the room, came back out of the room, walking down the hall away from the guard. The second man asked a few more questions, made a few more comments and then followed the other down the hall. The guard adjusted his pants, clasped his hands together and stood beside the door, as before.

Out in the parking lot, the second man to leave was now ahead of the first, opening the back door of an SUV for the the other. Then he closed the door, hopped into the driver's seat, and drove the vehicle into the street. In fifteen minutes, they were on the freeway on the edge of town, headed south.

"How are you doing, Emile?" asked the driver.

"Fine. Keep driving. Don't talk." grunted Emile. Then contradicting himself, he asked his driver, "Where am I supposed to go?" He was still very sore; having put on clothes similar to his look-alike visitor so that he could leave the hospital had made him realize how weak he still was. The walk down the stairs and into the vehicle had not helped.

"Going to Calgary. Have a house there for you."

"Big house?"

"Big house. Nice house. A good customer owns it."

He was stable. He would recover. At least he was free for the moment. Until he recovered fully, he would get lost in Calgary and stay low.

Chapter Eighty

TWO MONTHS LATER, DEEP in Mexico, in Cuernevaca, south of Mexico City, in the dark early morning on a cloudy night with a gentle pittering rain, a man all dressed in black with a black mask covering the bottom of his face, entered a hotel room quietly. He had dispatched the hotel security guards standing with rifles on their shoulders at the entrance to the hotel, rendering them unconscious and trussed up, hidden in a black windowed vehicle. The two private guards in the hallway protecting this room were lying in their own blood, in a room down the hall.

Soundlessly he made his way to the side of the bed, using his black-gloved hand to point a pistol with a silencer at the head of the man lying on the bed, sleeping, snoring softly the sleep of the dead. The woman in the bed had long black hair, being young and pretty. She lay beside Cortes, facing away from him, and did not wake up until it was too late. Warning her not to scream, he tied her up. By eight am, the man was on a commercial flight back to Houston.

o o o

Jack and Jill looked at the clock on the wall as they sat on the sofa in the dim quiet evening. Soundlessly, they looked at each other and then got up, holding hands as they walked down the hall to their bedroom. On the way, Jack opened the door to their daughters' bedroom, and they paused, standing for a full minute, watching the quiet breathing of their girls in the dark with the sheets rising and falling with each breath. Jill had her other hand resting softly on her swelling belly as they listened to the soft sighing of air passing out of restful open mouths, with hair straggled over the side of their faces, and one of Carla's arms flung up over her head. When they had drunk their fill of the sight, they gently closed the door, then continued on their way to their bedroom, still holding hands, tightly.

CPSIA information can be obtained
at www.ICGtesting.com
Printed in the USA
BVHW030741060521
R12201900001B/R122019PG606337BVX00006B/6